LEARNING R
SANTA FE CO

FORGOTTEN REALMS

FANTASY ADVENTURE

Realms of Magic

Edited by Brian Thomsen and J. Robert King

LEARNING RESOURCES CENTER
SANTA FE COMMUNITY COLLEGE

REALMS OF MAGIC

Copyright © 1995 TSR, Inc.
All Rights Reserved.

All characters in this book are fictitious. Any resemblance to actual persons, living or dead, is purely coincidental.

All TSR characters, character names, and the distinct likenesses thereof are trademarks owned by TSR, Inc.

This book is protected under the copyright laws of the United States of America. Any reproduction or other unauthorized use of the material or artwork herein is prohibited without the express written permission of TSR, Inc.

Random House and its affiliate companies have worldwide distribution rights in the book trade for English language products of TSR, Inc.

Distributed to the book and hobby trade in the United Kingdom by TSR Ltd.

Distributed to the toy and hobby trade by regional distributors.

FORGOTTEN REALMS is a registered trademark owned by TSR, Inc. The TSR logo is a trademark owned by TSR, Inc.

Cover art by Blas Gallego

First Printing: December 1995
Printed in the United States of America
Library of Congress Catalog Card Number: 94-61634

9 8 7 6 5 4 3 2 1

ISBN: 0-7869-0303-1

TSR, Inc.
201 Sheridan Springs Road
Lake Geneva, WI 53147
United States of America

TSR Ltd.
120 Church End, Cherry Hinton
Cambridge CB1 3LB
United Kingdom

CONTENTS

PROLOGUE

Tym Waterdeep Limited had been the publisher of Volothamp Geddarm ever since the day that the wandering rogue and the savvy entrepreneur had first struck a deal, each side convinced he had taken advantage of the other. Many volumes later, Volo was justifiably known as the most famous traveler in all the Realms, and Justin Tym as Faerûn's most successful publisher.

In the intervening years, Volo had been handed off to numerous editors, each a bit more willing to take partial credit for the gazetteer's success, and it had been more than a few seasons since the great publisher and the noble rogue had had a "face-to-face." The recent dismissal of his last editor, coinciding with the master traveler's scheduled stopover in the City of Splendors, afforded an ample reason for a meeting between the two gentlemen.

As Volo remembered it, Justin had always been a late sleeper—no doubt a habit borne out of many nights of routinely wining and dining authors, agents, and booksellers (a practice the gazetteer wholeheartedly endorsed). So, needless to say, Volo was more than a little surprised to find a message at his accommodations moving their meeting up from the civilized hour of "noonish" (with the tacit promise of a gratis lunch) to the ungodly hour of market opening, thus necessitating an early morning call that proved most inconvenient for both himself and his hostess, Trixie. Still, Justin's advances did indeed finance his extravagant accommodations, and so, slightly bleary-eyed, and not entirely rested, Volo set off for his publisher's office.

The streets were brimming with eager merchants en route to trade, peddlers hawking their wares from makeshift mobile markets, and laborers trotting off to their common jobs. Volo did not envy any of his fellow commuters, and quietly resented Justin's subjecting him to Waterdeep's legendary early-morning rush hour. Still, bills had to be paid. By this time tomorrow, with any luck, he would once again be flush with gelt and ready to enjoy the freedoms of the open road, where appointments were scheduled as "when you get there," and deadlines were set as "when the manuscript is done."

All told, Justin's advances were more than worth this temporary inconvenience.

The crowded storefronts along the thoroughfare soon gave way to extravagant office space for consulting wizards, high-priced solicitors, and even more high-priced tavern clubs. Volo was entering the district where Tym Waterdeep Limited had been situated since its origin as a print shop of "exotic pamphlets and titillating tomes" years ago. As business had prospered, so had the neighborhood, and the shadowy warehouse district had become the new "in" place for professionals to set up shop.

Despite many buy-out offers from Kara-Turian interests and Cormyrian holding companies, Justin had steadfastly maintained his independence, and prosperity had followed him.

In Tym's words, "he hadn't traded up; everyone else had traded down," and that was the way he liked it.

A new floor had been added to the storefront offices, overhanging yet another section of the already narrow street. The road here was shadowy, not unlike some underworld back alley rather than a main Waterdeep thoroughfare.

Business must be good, Volo thought. I wonder when

Justin will buy out his across-the-lane neighbor? Another
expansion out and up, and he would undoubtedly overhang their property.

As he had expected, the door was open, and Volo proceeded upstairs without impediment. Knowing Justin, he
thought, his office has to be on the top floor.

Four floors up, just beyond an unmanned reception
desk with an office overlooking the busy thoroughfare
below, sat a tall, bespectacled, and almost entirely bald
rogue. The publisher was nattily dressed in the most fashionable attire gelt could acquire for his unathletic form.
He took to his feet immediately to greet his star author.

"Volo, my boy, how long has it been?" he enthusiastically hailed.

"Longer than either of us would like to remember," the
gazetteer responded, adding, "and since when have you
become an early bird? I almost doubted that the message
was really from you."

The publisher hesitated for a moment and then jibed,
" 'Tis the early bird that catches the wyrm, in business as
well as in dungeon crawling, I'm afraid."

Volo chuckled at the fellow's response, thinking to himself, Justin has never seen the inside of a dungeon in his
life, let alone crawled around in one. Still the old coot is a
queer bird, if not an early bird at that.

Justin motioned to a chair for the house's star author
and quickly returned to his place behind the desk.

Volo took a seat, kicked it back on its rear legs, set
booted feet against Justin's expensive desk, made himself
at home, and asked absently, "So, how's business?"

"Couldn't be better," the publisher replied.

"Any new hot titles coming up?"

"Sure," Justin replied, pausing for just a moment till he
had located a mock-up cover from the top of his desk.
"We've got a really hot new book on Cormyr coming out.
Here's the proposed cover."

Volo looked at the handsome illustration of a purple
dragon against a mountainous landscape, framed at the
top by the title and below by the author's name.

"*Cormyr: A Novel,*" Volo read aloud, "by Greenwood

Grubb. Don't you think the title is a little dull?"

"Not at all, my boy," Justin replied with a smile that bespoke all of the sincerity of an orcish grifter. "Besides, the editor-in-chief and the author picked the title. I picked the art."

"I see," said Volo, surprised at the hands-off manner the controlling rogue seemed to have adopted.

"Still," the publisher added, "I did just fire the editor-in-chief. Maybe I should reconsider. . . ."

"Why did you fire him?"

"You mean her," Justin corrected. "She was a ninny and a bit of a flake, even for a gnome, if you know what I mean."

"In what way?" the author asked, realizing that editors, good or otherwise, might truly be the most endangered species in all Toril.

"She kept changing the spelling of her name. I was going to go broke if I had to keep printing new letterhead and business cards for her."

"I see," the gazetteer replied.

"She also kept trying to take credit for books she had nothing to do with. Once she even claimed to have discovered you, and signed you up for your first book. Of course, I knew she was lying, but everyone else didn't. When I pressed her to clear the matter up in public, she claimed she had meant that she landed Marcus Wands, also known as Marco Volo. Ever hear of him?"

"On occasion," Volo replied, wishing that the scurrilous scoundrel would change his name and avoid this ongoing confusion, which had already caused him much inconvenience.

"Needless to say, Marco Volo is no substitute for the real Volo, Volothamp Geddarm."

"Of course," the gazetteer replied, glad his publisher was taking the time to butter him up.

"But enough of this chitchat," Justin said. "What wonderful new volume do you have for us today? I want a good strong title to follow up on our expected success with *Volo's Guide to the Dalelands* . . . like, maybe, *Volo's Guide to the Moonsea*. Ever since that big blowup at Zhentil Keep, the market has just been clamoring for information."

"*Moonsea* is already in the works," Volo replied confidently, "in fact, I'm on my way to Mulmaster after I finish my business here in Waterdeep. I figure a few more months of research, tops, and it will be done."

Justin furrowed his brow. "That's fine, I guess," he replied hesitantly, "but I was sort of hoping for something we could publish a little sooner."

"But, of course," Volo replied, adding seductively, "that's why I've brought along another project."

"Good," the publisher agreed, " a little something to tide us over between guide books."

"No," the author contradicted adamantly. "Something that will outsell all the guides, combined. *Volo's Guide to All Things Magical, the Revised, Authorized, & Expanded Edition.*"

Before the author had even gotten out the word "magical", Justin was already shaking his head no.

"Sorry, old boy," the publisher insisted. "There's just no way. *The Guide to All Things Magical* almost put this company six feet under, for good. When Khelben and company ban a book, they ban a book. Every copy—*poof!*—disappeared without ever a mention of refund for production costs or lost sales revenues. I have no desire to play that game again."

"Neither do I," the author replied confidently. "That's why it's revised."

"How?"

"This time it is all based on interviews, stories, and legends that I have gathered from the far corners of Faerûn. Nothing pilfered or stolen, which is not to say that there was anything improperly obtained the last time."

"But, of course," the publisher conceded absently, while trying to concentrate on coming up with a diplomatic reason why refusing this volume would not constitute the breaking of an option, thus allowing his star author to go elsewhere. He concluded that there wasn't a diplomatic alternative.

"Volo," the publisher said firmly, "I can't do it. Even a revised tome of secret spells and such would get us in trouble. The text would once again be suppressed, and who knows what Khelben would do to a repeat offender."

"I'm not scared of old Blackstaff," the cocky gazetteer replied. "He owes me one for saving his butt and all of Faerûn during that doppleganger conspiracy[1]."

"I wasn't thinking of you," Justin replied. "I was referring to me."

"Afraid he still remembers that hatchet-job unauthorized biography by Kaeti Blye you published?"

"It was supposed to be a solid piece of investigative journalism," he justified. "How was I to know that that dwarf was more adept at turning out fiction than turning up facts?"

A wide smile crossed Volo's face.

"Well you don't have any such worries this time, I assure you," he stated in his still-cocky tone. "This time, *Volo's Guide to All Things Magical, the Revised, Authorized,* etc., is no notorious exposé of the arcane and dangerous, but a well-researched compilation of documented second-hand accounts of various magic subjects in all the Realms. After all if people told me these tales, they would have told anyone. Ergo, they're all accessible to the public, depending on one's travels, and contacts . . . and as you well know, no one travels better or has better contacts than Volothamp Geddarm."

Justin leaned back in his chair and scratched his ear as if it had been tickled by the almost nonexistent fringe that remained of his once-full head of hair.

"Go on," the publisher pressed. "What type of accounts would be in it?"

"Basically anything magical from *A* to *Z*. Magic items, places, and spells, both the famous and the obscure. Enchanted artifacts from the past, spectral creatures, and famous feats. Personalities like Elminster and Khelben . . . nothing to offend, mind you . . . notorious mages and lowly apprentices . . . you know, stories about student wizards . . ."

"I see, " interrupted the publisher, "but . . ."

"I even have a few stories about 'smoke powder', the latest

---

[1] See *Once Around the Realms.*

forbidden substance, which everyone is talking about."

The publisher was perplexed. Obviously a collection of stories on "all things magical" was a poor substitute for the wonderfully desirable tome that had been suppressed . . . but since no one had ever gotten to read the original, no one would have a basis for comparison. Who's to say it wasn't just another collection of stories?

"You'd be willing to call it *Volo's Guide to All Things Magical,* etc., etc.," the publisher pressed.

"Of course," Volo replied, glad to see that he had hooked his publisher and would be dining high that evening on the advance that was sure to be handed over. "So we have a deal?"

"Not so fast," Justin replied shrewdly. "You don't expect me to buy a pegasus in the clouds do you?"

"Of course not," Volo replied, feigning indignation at the inference that he might try something less than aboveboard. "Would you like to see the manuscript?" he added, removing a sheaf of pages from his pack.

"Hand it over," the publisher replied, leaning forward, his arm reaching across the desk to accept the pile of pages.

"Careful," Volo instructed, handing over the manuscript. "It's my only copy."

Justin began to rifle through the pages.

"What are you doing?" asked the impatient author.

"Looking for the good parts," the publisher replied.

Volo fingered his beard in contemplation. He didn't want to be here all day waiting for Justin to peruse until he was satisfied. Suddenly a solution occurred to him.

"Justin," Volo offered, "I know you are a busy man. Why don't I just *tell* you some of the good parts."

Justin set the manuscript in front of him on the desk and leaned back in his chair. "You always were a good storyteller, Geddarm," he replied, "so *do* tell."

Volo rubbed his hands together, took a deep breath, and began to tell the tales.

GUENHWYVAR

R. A. Salvatore

Josidiah Starym skipped wistfully down the streets of
Cormanthor, the usually stern and somber elf a bit giddy
this day, both for the beautiful weather and the recent
developments in his most precious and enchanted city.
Josidiah was a bladesinger, a joining of sword and magic,
protector of the elvish ways and the elvish folk. And in Cormanthor, in this year 253, many elves were in need of protecting. Goblinkin were abundant, and even worse, the
emotional turmoil within the city, the strife among the noble
families—the Starym included—threatened to tear apart all
that Coronal Eltargrim had put together, all that the elves
had built in Cormanthor, greatest city in all the world.

Those were not troubles for this day, though, not in the
spring sunshine, with a light north breeze blowing. Even
Josidiah's kin were in good spirits this day; Taleisin, his
uncle, had promised the bladesinger that he would venture to Eltargrim's court to see if some of their disputes
might perhaps be worked out.

Josidiah prayed that the elven court would come back
together, for he, perhaps above all others in the city, had
the most to lose. He was a bladesinger, the epitome of
what it meant to be elven, and yet, in this curious age,

those definitions seemed not so clear. This was an age of change, of great magics, of monumental decisions. This was an age when the humans, the gnomes, the halflings, even the bearded dwarves, ventured down the winding ways of Cormanthor, past the needle-pointed spires of the free-flowing elvish structures. For all of Josidiah's previous one hundred and fifty years, the precepts of elvenkind seemed fairly defined and rigid; but now, because of their Coronal, wise and gentle Eltargrim, there was much dispute about what it meant to be elvish, and, more importantly, what relationships elves should foster with the other goodly races.

"Merry morn, Josidiah," came the call of an elven female, the young and beautiful maiden niece of Eltargrim himself. She stood on a balcony overlooking a high garden whose buds were not yet in bloom, with the avenue beyond that.

Josidiah stopped in midstride, leapt high into the air in a complete spin, and landed perfectly on bended knee, his long golden hair whipping across his face and then flying out wide again so that his eyes, the brightest of blue, flashed. "And the merriest of morns to you, good Felicity," the bladesinger responded. "Would that I held at my sides flowers befitting your beauty instead of these blades made for war."

"Blades as beautiful as any flower ever I have seen," Felicity replied teasingly, "especially when wielded by Josidiah Starym at dawn's break, on the flat rock atop Berenguil's Peak."

The bladesinger felt the hot blood rushing to his face. He had suspected that someone had been spying on him at his morning rituals—a dance with his magnificent swords, performed nude—and now he had his confirmation. "Perhaps Felicity should join me on the morrow's dawn," he replied, catching his breath and his dignity, "that I might properly reward her for her spying."

The young female laughed heartily and spun back into her house, and Josidiah shook his head and skipped along. He entertained thoughts of how he might properly "reward" the mischievous female, though he feared that, given Felicity's beauty and station, any such attempts might lead to something much more, something Josidiah could not become involved in—not now, not after Eltargrim's proclamation and the drastic changes.

The bladesinger shook away all such notions; it was too fine a day for any dark musing, and other thoughts of Felicity were too distracting for the meeting at hand. Josidiah went out of Cormanthor's west gate, the guards posted there offering no more than a respectful bow as he passed, and into the open air. Truly Josidiah loved this city, but he loved the land outside of it even more. Out here he was truly free of all the worries and all the petty squabbles, and out here there was ever a sense of danger—might a goblin be watching him even now, its crude spear ready to take him down?—that kept the formidable elf on his highest guard.

Out here, too, was a friend, a human friend, a ranger-turned-wizard by the name of Anders Beltgarden, whom Josidiah had known for the better part of four decades. Anders did not venture into Cormanthor, even given Eltargrim's proclamation to open the gates to nonelves. He lived far from the normal, oft-traveled paths, in a squat tower of excellent construction, guarded by magical wards and deceptions of his own making. Even the forest about his home was full of misdirections, spells of illusion and confusion. So secretive was Beltgarden Home that few elves of nearby Cormanthor even knew of it, and even fewer had ever seen it. And of those, none save Josidiah could find his way back to it without Anders's help.

And Josidiah held no illusions about it—if Anders wanted to hide the paths to the tower even from him, the cagey old wizard would have little trouble doing so.

This wonderful day, however, it seemed to Josidiah that the winding paths to Beltgarden Home were easier to follow than usual, and when he arrived at the structure, he found the door unlocked.

"Anders," he called, peering into the darkened hallway beyond the portal, which always smelled as if a dozen candles had just been extinguished within it. "Old fool, are you about?"

A feral growl put the bladesinger on his guard; his swords were in his hands in a movement too swift for an observer to follow.

"Anders?" he called again, quietly, as he picked his way along the corridor, his feet moving in perfect balance, soft boots gently touching the stone, quiet as a hunting cat.

The growl came again, and that is exactly when Josidiah knew what he was up against: a hunting cat. A big one, the bladesinger recognized, for the deep growl resonated along the stone of the hallway.

He passed by the first doors, opposite each other in the hall, and then passed the second on his left.

The third—he knew—the sound came from within the third. That knowledge gave the bladesinger some hope that this situation was under control, for that particular door led to Anders's alchemy shop, a place well guarded by the old wizard.

Josidiah cursed himself for not being better prepared magically. He had studied few spells that day, thinking it too fine and not wanting to waste a moment of it with his face buried in spellbooks.

If only he had some spell that might get him into the room more quickly, through a magical gate, or even a spell that would send his probing vision through the stone wall, into the room before him.

He had his swords, at least, and with them, Josidiah Starym was far from helpless. He put his back against the wall near to the door and took a deep steadying breath. Then, without delay—old Anders might be in serious trouble—the bladesinger spun about and crashed into the room.

He felt the arcs of electricity surging into him as he crossed the warded portal, and then he was flying, hurled through the air, to land crashing at the base of a huge oaken table. Anders Beltgarden stood calmly at the side of the table, working with something atop it, hardly bothering to look down at the stunned bladesinger.

"You might have knocked," the old mage said dryly.

Josidiah pulled himself up unceremoniously from the floor, his muscles not quite working correctly just yet.

Convinced that there was no danger near, Josidiah let his gaze linger on the human, as he often did. The bladesinger hadn't seen many humans in his life—humans were a recent addition on the north side of the Sea of Fallen Stars, and were not present in great numbers in or about Cormanthor.

This one was the most curious human of all, with his leathery, wrinkled face and his wild gray beard. One of Anders's eyes had been ruined in a fight, and it appeared quite dead now, a gray film over the lustrous green it had once held. Yes, Josidiah could stare at old Anders for hours on end, seeing the tales of a lifetime in his scars and wrinkles. Most of the elves, Josidiah's own kinfolk included, would have thought the old man an ugly thing; elves did not wrinkle and weather so, but aged beautifully, appearing at the end of several centuries as they had when they had seen but twenty or fifty winters.

Josidiah did not think Anders an ugly sight, not at all. Even those few crooked teeth remaining in the man's mouth complemented this creature he had become, this aged and wise creature, this sculptured monument to years under the sun and in the face of storms, to seasons battling goblinkin and giantkind. Truly it seemed ridiculous to Josidiah that he was twice this man's age; he wished he might carry a few wrinkles as testament to his experiences.

"You had to know it would be warded," Anders laughed. "Of course you did! Ha ha, just putting on a show, then. Giving an old man one good laugh before he dies!"

"You will outlive me, I fear, old man," said the bladesinger.

"Indeed, that is a distinct possibility if you keep crossing my doors unannounced."

"I feared for you," Josidiah explained, looking around the huge room—too huge, it seemed, to fit inside the tower, even if it had consumed an entire level. The bladesinger suspected some extradimensional magic to be at work here, but he had never been able to detect it, and the frustrating Anders certainly wasn't letting on.

As large as it was, Anders's alchemy shop was still a

cluttered place, with boxes piled high and tables and cabinets strewn about in a hodgepodge.

"I heard a growl," the elf continued. "A hunting cat."

Without looking up from some vials he was handling, Anders nodded his head in the direction of a large, blanket-covered container. "See that you do not get too close," the old mage said with a wicked cackle. "Old Whiskers will grab you by the arm and tug you in, don't you doubt!

"And then you'll need more than your shiny swords," Anders cackled on.

Josidiah wasn't even listening, pacing quietly toward the blanket, moving silently so as not to disturb the cat within. He grabbed the edge of the blanket and, moving safely back, tugged it away. And then the bladesinger's jaw surely drooped.

It was a cat, as he had suspected, a great black panther, twice—no thrice—the size of the largest cat Josidiah had ever seen or heard of. And the cat was female, and females were usually much smaller than males. She paced the cage slowly, methodically, as if searching for some weakness, some escape, her rippling muscles guiding her along with unmatched grace.

"How did you come by such a magnificent beast?" the bladesinger asked. His voice apparently startled the panther, stopping her in her tracks. She stared at Josidiah with an intensity that stole any further words right from the bladesinger's mouth.

"Oh, I have my ways, elf," the old mage said. "I've been looking for just the right cat for a long, long time, searching all the known world—and bits of it that are not yet known to any but me!"

"But why?" Josidiah asked, his voice no more than a whisper. His question was aimed as much at the magnificent panther as at the old mage, and truly, the bladesinger could think of no reason to justify putting such a creature into a cage.

"You remember my tale of the box canyon," Anders replied, "of how my mentor and I flew owl-back out of the clutches of a thousand goblins?"

Josidiah nodded and smiled, remembering well that

amusing story. A moment later, though, when the implications of Anders's words hit him fully, the elf turned back to the mage, a scowl clouding his fair face. "The figurine," Josidiah muttered, for the owl had been but a statuette, enchanted to bring forth a great bird in times of its master's need. There were many such objects in the world, many in Cormanthor, and Josidiah was not unacquainted with the methods of constructing them (though his own magics were not strong enough along the lines of enchanting). He looked back to the great panther, saw a distinct sadness there, then turned back sharply to Anders.

"The cat must be killed at the moment of preparation," the bladesinger protested. "Thus her life energies will be drawn into the statuette you will have created."

"Working on that even now," Anders said lightly. "I have hired a most excellent dwarven craftsman to fashion a panther statuette. The finest craftsman . . . er, craftsdwarf, in all the area. Fear not, the statuette will do the cat justice."

"Justice?" the bladesinger echoed skeptically, looking once more into the intense, intelligent yellow-green eyes of the huge panther. "You will kill the cat?"

"I offer the cat immortality," Anders said indignantly.

"You offer death to her will, and slavery to her body," snapped Josidiah, more angry than he had ever been with old Anders. The bladesinger had seen figurines and thought them marvelous artifacts, despite the sacrifice of the animal in question. Even Josidiah killed deer and wild pig for his table, after all. So why should a wizard not create some useful item from an animal?

But this time it was different, Josidiah sensed in his heart. This animal, this great and free cat, must not be so enslaved.

"You will make the panther . . ." Josidiah began.

"Whiskers," explained Anders.

"The panther . . ." the bladesinger reiterated forcefully, unable to come to terms with such a foolish name being tagged on this animal. "You will make the panther a tool, an animation that will function to the will of her master."

"What would one expect?" the old mage argued. "What else would one want?"

Josidiah shrugged and sighed helplessly. "Independence," he muttered.

"Then what would be the point of my troubles?"

Josidiah's expression clearly showed his thinking. An independent magical companion might not be of much use to an adventurer in a dangerous predicament, but it would surely be preferable from the sacrificed animal's point of view.

"You chose wrong, bladesinger," Anders teased. "You should have studied as a ranger. Surely your sympathies lie in that direction!"

"A ranger," the bladesinger asked, "as Anders Beltgarden once was?"

The old mage blew a long and helpless sigh.

"Have you so given up the precepts of your former trade in exchange for the often ill-chosen allure of magical mysteries?"

"Oh, and a fine ranger you would have been," Anders replied dryly.

Josidiah shrugged. "My chosen profession is not so different," he reasoned.

Anders silently agreed. Indeed, the man did see much of his own youthful and idealistic self in the eyes of Josidiah Starym. That was the curious thing about elves, he noted, that this one, who was twice Anders's present age, reminded him so much of himself when he had but a third his present years.

"When will you begin?" Josidiah asked.

"Begin?" scoffed Anders. "Why, I have been at work over the beast for nearly three weeks, and spent six months before that in preparing the scrolls and powders, the oils, the herbs. Not an easy process, this. And not inexpensive, I might add! Do you know what price a gnome places on the simplest of metal filings, pieces so fine that they might be safely added to the cat's food?"

Josidiah found that he really did not want to continue along this line of discussion. He did not want to know about the poisoning—and that was indeed what he considered it to be—of the magnificent panther. He looked back to the cat, looked deep into her intense eyes, intelligent so far beyond what he would normally expect.

"Fine day outside," the bladesinger muttered, not that he believed that Anders would take a moment away from his work to enjoy the weather. "Even my stubborn Uncle Taleisin, Lord Protector of House Starym, wears a face touched by sunshine."

Anders snorted. "Then he will be smiling this day when he lays low Coronal Eltargrim with a right hook?"

That caught Josidiah off his guard, and he took up Anders's infectious laughter. Indeed was Taleisin a stubborn and crusty elf, and if Josidiah returned to House Starym this day to learn that his uncle had punched the elf Coronal, he would not be surprised.

"It is a momentous decision that Eltargrim has made," Anders said suddenly, seriously. "And a brave one. By including the other goodly races, your Coronal has begun the turning of the great wheel of fate, a spin that will not easily be stopped."

"For good or for ill?"

"That is for a seer to know," Anders replied with a shrug. "But his choice was the right one, I am sure, though not without its risks." The old mage snorted again. "A pity," he said, "even were I a young man, I doubt I would see the outcome of Eltargrim's decision, given the way elves measure the passage of time. How many centuries will pass before the Starym even decide if they will accept Eltargrim's decree?"

That brought another chuckle from Josidiah, but not a long-lived one. Anders had spoken of risks, and certainly there were many. Several prominent families, and not just the Starym, were outraged by the immigration of peoples that many haughty elves considered to be of inferior races. There were even a few mixed marriages, elf and human, within Cormanthor, but any offspring of such unions were surely ostracized.

"My people will come to accept Eltargrim's wise council," the elf said at length, determinedly.

"I pray you are right," said Anders, "for surely Cormanthor will face greater perils than the squabbling of stubborn elves."

Josidiah looked at him curiously.

"Humans and halflings, gnomes and, most importantly, dwarves, walking among the elves, living in Cormanthor," Anders muttered. "Why, I would guess that the goblinkin savor the thought of such an occurrence, that all their hated enemies be mixed together into one delicious stew!"

"Together we are many times more powerful," the bladesinger argued. "Human wizards oft exceed even our own. Dwarves forge mighty weapons, and gnomes create wondrous and useful items, and halflings, yes, even halflings, are cunning allies, and dangerous adversaries."

"I do not disagree with you," Anders said, waving his tanned and leathery right hand, three-fingered from a goblin bite, in the air to calm the elf. "And as I have said, Eltargrim chose correctly. But pray you that the internal disputes are settled, else the troubles of Cormanthor will come tenfold from without."

Josidiah calmed and nodded; he really couldn't disagree with old Anders's reasoning, and had, in fact, harbored those same fears for many days. With all the goodly races coming together under one roof, the chaotic goblinkin would have cause to band together in numbers greater than ever before. If the varied folk of Cormanthor stood together, gaining strength in their diversity, those goblinkin, whatever their numbers, would surely be pushed away. But if the folk of Cormanthor could not see their way to such a day of unity . . .

Josidiah let the thought hang outside consciousness, put it aside for another day, a day of rain and fog, perhaps. He looked back to the panther and sighed even more sadly, feeling helpless indeed. "Treat the cat well, Anders Beltgarden," he said, and he knew that the old man, once a ranger, would indeed do so.

Josidiah left then, making his way more slowly as he returned to the elven city. He saw Felicity again on the balcony, wearing a slight silken shift and a mischievous, inviting smile, but he passed her by with a wave. The bladesinger suddenly did not feel so much in the mood for play.

Many times in the next few weeks, Josidiah returned to Anders's tower and sat quietly before the cage, silently communing with the panther while the mage went about his work.

"She will be yours when I am done," Anders announced unexpectedly, one day when spring had turned to summer.

Josidiah stared blankly at the old man.

"The cat, I mean," said Anders. "Whiskers will be yours when my work is done."

Josidiah's blue eyes opened wide in horror, though Anders interpreted the look as one of supreme elation.

"She'll do me little use," explained the mage. "I rarely venture out of doors these days, and in truth, have little faith that I will live much more than a few winters longer. Who better to have my most prized creation, I say, than Josidiah Starym, my friend and he who should have been a ranger?"

"I shall not accept," Josidiah said abruptly, sternly.

Anders's eyes widened in surprise.

"I would be forever reminded of what the cat once was," said the elf, "and what she should be. Whenever I called the slave body to my side, whenever this magnificent creature sat on her haunches, awaiting my command to bring life to her limbs, I would feel that I had overstepped my bounds as a mortal, that I had played as a god with one undeserving my foolish intervention."

"It's just an animal!" Anders protested.

Josidiah was glad to see that he had gotten through to the old mage, a man the elf knew to be too sensitive for this present undertaking.

"No," said the elf, turning to stare deeply into the panther's knowing eyes. "Not this one." He fell silent, then, and Anders, with a huff of protest, went back to his work, leaving the elf to sit and stare, to silently share his thoughts with the panther.

* * * * *

It was for Josidiah Starym a night of absolute torment, for Anders would complete his work before the moon had set and the great panther would be slain for the sake of a magical item, a mere magical tool. The bladesinger left

Cormanthor, heedless of the warnings that had been posted concerning venturing out of the city at night: goblinkin, and enemies even greater, were rumored to be stalking the forest.

Josidiah hardly cared, hardly gave any thoughts to his personal safety. His fate was not in the balance, so it seemed, not like that of the panther.

He thought of going to see Anders, to try one last time to talk the old human out of his designs, but the bladesinger dismissed that notion. He didn't understand humans, he realized, and had indeed lost a bit of faith in the race (and, subsequently, in Eltargrim's decision) because of what he perceived as Anders's failure. The mage, once a ranger and more attuned to the elven ideals than so very many of his rough-edged race, should have known better, should not have sacrificed such a wondrous and intelligent animal as that particular panther, for the sake of magic.

Josidiah moved through the forest, then out of the canopy and under a million stars, shining despite the westering full moon. He reached a treeless hillock. He effortlessly climbed the steep slope through the carpet-thick grass and came to the top of the hill, a private and special place he often used for contemplation.

Then he simply stood and stared upward at the stars, letting his thoughts fly to the greater mysteries, the unknown and never-known, the heavens themselves. He felt mortal suddenly, as though his last remaining centuries were but a passing sigh in the eternal life of the universe.

A sigh that was so much longer, so it seemed, than the remaining life of the panther, if the cat was even still alive.

A subtle rustle at the base of the hillock alerted the elf, brought him from his contemplations. He went into a crouch immediately and stared down at the spot, letting his vision slip into the infrared spectrum.

Heat sources moved about the trees, all along the base of the hill. Josidiah knew them, and thus was not surprised when the forest erupted suddenly and a host of orcs came screaming out of the underbrush, waving weapons, charging the hill and the lone elf, this apparently easy kill.

The lead orcs were right before the crest of the hillock, close enough for Josidiah to see the glistening lines of drool about their tusky faces, when the elf released his fireball. The gouts of flame engulfed that entire side of the hill, shriveling orcs. It was a desperate spell, one Josidiah hated casting in the midst of grasslands, but few options presented themselves. Even as those orcs on the side of the hill fell away into the flames, charred and dying, they were replaced by a second group, charging wildly, and then came a third, from the back side of the hill.

Out came the elf's twin swords, snapping up to the ready. "Cleansing flames!" the elf cried, commanding the powers within his swords. Greenish fires licked at the metal, blurred the distinct lines of the razor-sharp blades.

The closest two orcs, those two who had been right before the elf and had thus escaped the fury of the fireball, skidded in surprise at the sudden appearance of the flaming blades and, for just an instant, let their guards drop.

Too long; Josidiah's left sword slashed across the throat of one, while his right plunged deep into the chest of the second.

The elf spun about, deflecting wide a hurled spear, dodging a second, then picking off a third with a furious down-cut. He dived into a roll and came up charging fast for the back side of the hill, meeting the rush of three monsters, cutting at them wildly before they could get their defenses coordinated.

One fell away, mortally wounded; another lost half of its arm to the searing sweep of the elf's deadly blade. But almost immediately Josidiah was pressed from all sides, orcs stabbing in at him with long spears or rushing forward suddenly to slash with their short, cruel swords.

He could not match weapons with this many, so he moved his flaming blades in purely defensive motions, beginning the chant to let loose another spell.

He took a spear thrust on the side and nearly lost his concentration and his spell. His finely meshed elven chain armor deflected the blow, however, and the elf finished with a twirl, tapping the hilts of his swords together, crying out a word to release the spell. His swords went back up straight, his thumbs came out to touch together, and a burst of flame fanned out from the elf in a half-circle arc.

Without even stopping to witness the effects of his spell, Josidiah spun about, swords slashing across and behind. Ahead charged the bladesinger, a sudden rush of overwhelming fury that broke apart the orcish line and gave Josidiah several openings in the defensive posture of his enemies.

A surge of adrenalin kept the bladesinger moving, dancing and cutting down orcs with a fury. He thought of the panther again, and her undeserved fate, and focused his blame for that act upon these very orcs.

Another fell dead, another atop that one, and many went scrambling down the hill, wanting no part of this mighty warrior.

Soon Josidiah stood quiet, at the ready, a handful of orcs about him, staying out of his reach. But there was something else, the elf sensed, something more evil, more powerful. Something calmed these orcs, lending them confidence, though more than a score of their kin lay dead and another dozen wounded.

The elf sucked in his breath as the newest foes came out onto the open grass. Josidiah realized then his folly. He could defeat a score of orcs, two-score, if he got his spells away first, but these three were not orcs.

These were giants.

* * * * *

The cat was restless, pacing and growling; Anders wondered if she knew what was to come, knew that this was her last night as a mortal creature. The thought that she might indeed understand shook the old mage profoundly, made all of Josidiah's arguments against this magical transformation echo again in his mind.

The panther roared, and threw herself against the cage door, bouncing back and pacing, growling.

"What are you about?" the old mage asked, but the cat

only roared again, angrily, desperately. Anders looked around; what did the cat know? What was going on?

The panther leapt again for the cage door, slamming hard and bouncing away. Anders shook his head, thoroughly confused, for he had never seen the panther like this before—not at all.

"To the Nine Hells with you, elf," the wizard grumbled, wishing he had not revealed Whiskers to Josidiah until the transformation had been completed. He took a deep breath, yelled at the cat to calm down, and drew out a slender wand.

"It will not hurt," Anders promised apologetically. He spoke a word of command, and a greenish ray shot forth from the wand, striking the panther squarely. The cat stopped her pacing, stopped everything, just stood perfectly still, immobilized by the magic of the wand.

Anders took up the figurine and the specially prepared knife, and opened the cage door. He had known from the very start that this was not going to be easy.

He was at the cat's side, the figurine in hand, the knife moving slowly for the creature's throat.

Anders hesitated. "Am I presuming to play the role of a god?" he asked aloud. He looked into those marvelous, intelligent eyes; he thought of Josidiah, who was indeed much like a ranger, much like Anders had been before devoting his life to ways magical.

Then he looked to the knife, the knife that his hand, his ranger hand, was about to plunge into the neck of this most magnificent creature.

"Oh, damn you, elf!" the mage cried out, and threw the knife across the cage. He began a spell then, one that came to his lips without conscious thought. He hadn't used this incantation in months, and how he recalled it then, Anders would never know. He cast it forth, powerfully, and all the cabinet doors in his shop, and the door to the hallway, and all the doors in the lower section of the tower, sprang open and wide.

The mage moved to the side of the cage and slumped to a sitting position. Already the great cat was stirring— even the powerful magic of his wand could not hold such a creature as this for long. Anders clutched that wand now, wondering if he might need it again, for his own defense.

The cat shook her head vigorously and took an ambling step, the sensation at last returning to her limbs. She gave Anders a sidelong glance.

The old mage put the wand away. "I played god with you, Whiskers," he said softly. "Now it is your turn."

But the panther was preoccupied and hardly gave the wizard a thought as she launched herself from the cage, darting across the room and out into the hallway. She was long gone before Anders ever got to his tower door, and he stood there in the night, lamenting not at all his wasted weeks of effort, his wasted gold.

"Not wasted," Anders said sincerely, considering the lesson he had just learned. He managed a smile and turned to go back into his tower, then saw the burst of flame, a fireball, mushrooming into the air from the top of a hillock to the north, a place that Anders knew well.

"Josidiah," he gasped, a reasonable guess indeed. That hillock was Josidiah's favorite place, a place Anders would expect the elf to go on a night such as this.

Cursing that he had few spells prepared for a confrontation, the old man hustled back into his tower and gathered together a few items.

* * * * *

His only chance lay in speed, in darting about, never letting his enemies close on him. Even that tactic would only delay the inevitable.

He rushed to the left but had to stop and spin, sensing the pursuit coming from close behind. Backing them off with a sweeping cross of his blades, Josidiah turned and darted left again and, predictably, had to pull up short. This time, though, the elf not only stopped but backtracked, flipping one sword in his hand and stabbing it out behind him, deep into the belly of the closest pursuing orc.

His grim satisfaction at the deft maneuver couldn't hold, however, for even as the dead creature slid from his blade, even as the other few orcs scrambled away down the side of the hill, Josidiah noted the approach of the three giants, fifteen-foot-tall behemoths calmly swinging spiked clubs the size of the elf's entire body.

Josidiah considered the spells remaining to him, tried to find some way to turn them to his advantage.

Nothing; he would have to fight this battle with swords only. And with three giants moving toward him in coordinated fashion, he did not like the odds.

He skittered right, out of the range of a club swipe, then went straight back, away from a second giant, trying to get at the first attacker before it could bring its heavy weapon to bear once more. He would indeed have had the strike, but the third giant cut him off and forced him into a diving roll to avoid a heavy smash.

I must get them to work against each other, the elf thought. To tangle their long limbs with each other.

He put his sword up high and screamed, charging straight for the closest brute, then dipped low, under the parrying club and dived into a forward roll. He came to his feet and ran on, right between the giant's widespread legs. Up thrust one sword, out to the side slashed the second, and Josidiah ran out from under the giant, meeting the attack of one of its companions with a double-bladed deflection, his swords accepting the hit of the club and turning it, barely, to the side and down.

Josidiah's arms were numbed from the sheer weight of the hit; he could not begin to counterattack. Out of the corner of his eye, he noted the sudden rush of the third giant and knew his daring attack on the first had put him in a precarious position indeed. He scrambled out to the side, threw himself into yet another roll as he saw the club come up high.

But this giant was a smart one, and it held the strike as it closed another long, loping stride. Josidiah rolled right over a second time and a third, but he could not get out of range, not this time.

The giant roared. Up went the club, high and back over its head, and Josidiah started a sidelong scramble, but stopped, startled, as a huge black spear—a spear?—flew over him.

No, it was not a spear, the bladesinger realized, but a panther, the old mage's cat! She landed heavily on the giant's chest, claws grabbing a firm hold, maw snapping for the stunned monster's face. Back the behemoth stumbled, overbalanced, and down the giant went, the panther riding it all the way to the ground.

The cat was in too close for any strike, so the giant let go of its club and tried to grab at the thing. The panther's front claws held fast, though, while her back legs began a running rake, tearing through the giant's bearskin tunic and then through the giant's own skin.

Josidiah had no time to stop and ask how, or why, or anything else. He was back on his feet, another giant closing fast. The one he had hit shuffled to join in as well. Out to the side rushed the bladesinger, trying to keep one giant in front of the other, trying to fight them one at a time.

He ducked a lumbering swing, ducked again as the club rushed past from a vicious backhand, then hopped high, tucking his legs as the giant came swiping across a third time, this time predictably low. And getting the club so low meant that the giant was bending near to the ground. Josidiah landed in a run, charging forward, getting inside the range of the coming backhand, and sticking the monster, once, twice, right in the face.

It howled and fell away, and its companion shuffled in, one hand swinging the club, the other clutching its torn loins.

A sudden blast, a lightning stroke, off to the side of the hill, temporarily blinded both elf and giant, but Josidiah did not need his eyes to fight. He waded right in, striking hard.

* * * * *

The giant's hand closed on the cat, but the agile panther twisted about suddenly, biting hard, taking off three fingers, and the behemoth fostered no further thoughts of squeezing its foe. It merely shoved hard with its other hand, pushing the cat from its chest. The giant rolled about, grabbing for its club, knowing it must get to its feet before the cat came back in.

No chance of that; the panther hit the ground solidly, all four claws digging a firm hold, every muscle snapping taut to steal, to reverse the cat's momentum. Turf went flying as the panther pivoted and leapt, hitting the rising giant on the head, latching on, biting, and raking.

The behemoth wailed in agony and dropped its club again. It flailed at the cat with both arms and scored several heavy blows. But the panther would not let go, great fangs tearing deep holes in the behemoth's flesh, mighty claws erasing the features from the giant's face.

* * * * *

Josidiah came up square against his one opponent, the giant bleeding from several wounds, but far from finished. Its companion moved in beside it, shoulder to shoulder.

Then another form crested the hill, a hunched, human form, and the second giant turned to meet this newest enemy.

"It took you long enough to get here," the elf remarked sarcastically.

"Orcs in the woods," Anders explained. "Pesky little rats."

The human had no apparent defenses in place, and so the giant waded right in, taking up its club in both hands. Anders paid it little heed, beginning a chant for another spell.

The club swished across, and Josidiah nearly cried out, thinking Anders was about to be batted a mile from the hilltop.

The giant might as well have hit the side of a stone mountain. The club slammed hard against Anders's shoulder and simply bounced off. Anders didn't even blink, never stopped his chanting.

"Oh, I do love that spell," the old mage remarked between syllables of his present casting.

"Stoneskin," Josidiah said dryly. "Do teach it to me."

"And this one, too," Anders added, laughing. He finished his present casting, throwing his arms down toward the ground at the giant's feet. Immediately, earth began flying wildly, as though a dozen giants with huge spades were digging furiously at the spot. When it ended, the giant was standing in a hole, its eyes even with those of the wizard.

"That's more fair," Anders remarked.

The giant howled and moved to raise its club, but found the hole too constricting for it to properly get the weapon up high. The wizard began yet another chant, holding his hand out toward the monster, pointing one finger right between the giant's eyes and bending the digit to show the giant a bejeweled ring.

With its weapon tangled in the tight quarters of the hole, the monster improvised, snapping its head forward and biting hard the wizard's extended hand.

Again, Anders hardly finished, and the giant groaned loudly, one tooth shattered by the impact.

Anders thrust his hand forward, putting the ring barely an inch from the monster's open mouth and loosing the magic of his ring. Balls of lightning popped forth, into the open mouth, lighting up the behemoth's head.

"Ta da!" said the old mage, bending his legs, more of a curtsy than a bow, and throwing his arms out wide, palms up, as the giant slumped down into the hole.

"And the grave is already dug," Anders boasted.

The second giant had seen enough, and started for the side of the hill, but Josidiah would not let it get away so easily. The bladesinger sprinted right behind, sheathing one sword. He let the giant get far enough down the hillside so that when he leapt for it, he came in even with the monster's bulbous nose. He held fast and brought his swordarm in hard around the other side, slashing deep into the monster's throat. The giant tried to reach up and grab the elf, but suddenly it was gasping, stumbling, skidding to its knees, and sliding down the hill.

Josidiah's sword arm pumped furiously, widening the wound, tearing at the brute's arteries and windpipe. He pushed away as the giant tumbled facedown, coming to a standing position atop the monster's back. It was still alive, still gasping, but the wound was mortal, Josidiah knew, and so he turned back for the hilltop.

Anders's self-congratulatory smile was short-lived, dissipating as soon as the mage looked to the battered panther. The cat had done her work well—the giant lay dead on the ground—but she had been battered in the process and lay awkwardly, breath coming in forced gasps, backbone obviously shattered.

Anders ran to the panther's side; Josidiah joined him there a moment later.

"Do something!" the elf pleaded.

"There is nothing I can do," Anders protested.

"Send the cat back into the figurine," Josidiah said. "She should be whole again when she returns."

Anders turned on the elf, grabbed him by the front of his tunic. "I have not completed the spell," he cried, and only then did it hit the mage. What had brought the panther out here? Why would a panther, a wild panther, run to the aid of an elf?

"I never got close to finishing," the mage said more calmly, letting go of the elf. "I just let her go."

Josidiah turned his wide-eyed stare from Anders to the panther. The questions were obvious then; neither the elf nor the mage bothered to speak them aloud.

"We must get her back to my tower," Anders said.

Josidiah's expression remained incredulous. How were they to carry six hundred pounds of limp cat all the way back to the tower?

But Anders had an answer for that. He took out a swatch of black velvet and unfolded it several times, until he had a patch of blackness several feet in diameter on the hilltop. Then the mage lifted one side of the cloth and gently eased it against the rear of the panther.

Josidiah blinked, realizing that the cat's tail had disappeared into the cloth!

"Lift her as I pass this over her," Anders begged. Josidiah did just that, lifting the cat inch by inch as the mage moved the cloth along. The panther was swallowed up by the blackness.

"Extradimensional hole," the mage explained, slipping

it forward to engulf the cat's head. Then he laid the cloth flat once more and carefully folded it back to a size that would fit in his pocket. "She is quite fine," he said. "Well, except for the giant's wounds."

"Wondrous toys, wizard," Josidiah congratulated.

"Spoils of adventuring," Anders replied with a wink. "You should get out more."

The mirth could not hold as the pair ran off, back for Beltgarden Home. What might they do there but make the dying cat comfortable, after all?

Anders did just that, opening his portable hole and gently easing the panther part of the way out of it. He stopped short, though, and Josidiah winced, understanding that the cat was drawing her last breaths.

"Perhaps I can finish the figurine enchantment," Anders reasoned. He looked sympathetically to Josidiah. "Be gone," he said, "for I must slay the cat quickly, mercifully."

Josidiah shook his head, determined to bear witness to the transformation, to the mortal end of this most wondrous cat, to this intelligent panther that had come, unbidden, to his rescue. How might the elf explain the bond that had grown between him and the cat? Had Anders's magical preparation imparted a sense of loyalty to the panther, given her the beginnings of that mindless slavery she would have known as a magical tool?

Josidiah looked once more into the cat's eyes and knew that was not the case. Something else had happened here, something of a higher order, though perhaps in part facilitated by the magic of Anders's preparation.

Anders moved quickly to retrieve the figurine and placed it beside the dying panther. "You will take the figurine," he said to Josidiah.

"I cannot," the bladesinger replied, for he could not bear to see the panther in the subsequent lessened form, could not bear to take the cat as his slave.

Anders did not argue—there was no time for that. He poured some enchanted oil over the cat's head, weaving his magic, and placed his hand over the panther's eyes.

"I name you Whiskers," he began, putting his dagger against the animal's throat.

"No!" Josidiah shouted, rushing beside the mage, grabbing the man's hand and pulling the dagger away. "Not Whiskers, never that!"

Josidiah looked to the cat, into the marvelous yellow-green eyes, shining intently still, though the moment of death was upon her. He studied the animal, the beautiful, silent friend. "Shadow," he declared.

"No, not shadow," said Josidiah, and he held back the dagger once more. "The high elvish word for shadow." He looked right into the cat's eyes, searching for some confirmation. He had not chosen this name, he suddenly understood; this had been the panther's name all along.

"Guenhwyvar."

As soon as he uttered the name, there came a black flash, like the negative image of one of Anders's lightning bolts. Gray mist filled the room; the cloth swatch contracted and disappeared altogether, and then the panther, too, was gone, dissipating into nothingness.

Anders and Josidiah fell back, sitting side by side. It seemed for a moment that there was a profound line of emptiness in the room, a rift in the universe, as though the fabric of the planes of existence had been torn asunder. But then it was gone, everything—panther, hole, and rift, and all that remained was the figurine.

"What did you do?" Josidiah asked the mage.

"I?" balked Anders. "What did *you* do?"

Josidiah moved cautiously to retrieve the figurine. With it in hand, he looked back to Anders, who nodded slowly in agreement.

"Guenhwyvar," the elf called nervously.

A moment later, the area beside the elf filled with the gray mist, swirling and gradually taking the shape of the panther. She was breathing more easily, as though her wounds were fast on the mend. She looked up at Josidiah, and the elf's breath fell away, lost in the intensity, the intelligence, of that gaze.

This was no slave, no magical tool; this was the panther, the same wondrous panther!

"How did you do this?" the elf asked.

"I know not," Anders replied. "And I do not even know

what I, what we, have done, with the figurine. It is the statuette that transforms into the living beast, and yet, the cat is here, and so is the statuette!" The old mage chuckled, locking gazes with the elf. "Send her away to heal," he bade.

Josidiah looked to the cat. "Go, Guenhwyvar, but I shall summon you forth again, I promise."

The panther growled, but it was not an angry sound, and she began a slow, limping pace, melting away into gray mist.

"That is the joy of magic," Anders said. "The mystery of it all. Why, even the greatest wizards could not explain this, I should guess. Perhaps all of my preparation, perhaps the magic of the hole—ah, yes, my dear, lost hole!—perhaps the combination of all these things.

"The joy of the mysteries," he finished. "Very well, then, give it to me." And he held out his hand for the figurine, but Josidiah clutched it all the tighter.

"Never," the elf said with a smile, and Anders smiled, as well.

"Indeed," said the mage, hardly surprised. "But you will pay for my lost hole, and for my time and effort."

"Gladly," said the elf, and he knew, holding that statuette, holding the key to the wondrous black panther, to Guenhwyvar, whom Josidiah realized would be his most loyal companion and friend for all the rest of his days, that it would be the most worthwhile gold he ever spent.

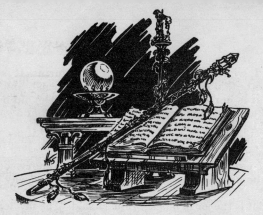

SMOKE POWDER AND MIRRORS

Jeff Grubb

On reflection, Jehan Wands realized why most adventures begin in taverns. It takes a combination of noise, bustle, the late hour, wrong-headed opinions, and ale, all in specific amounts, to convince otherwise rational people to do stupid things like go on quests and slay dragons. And only a tavern could bring all this together in one spot.

The tavern in question was the Grinning Lion, located in the northern, well-monied reaches of Waterdeep, gem of the north, City of Splendors, and great jewel of the Shining Sea. The Lion was no wharf-side dock or adventurer's dive in the lower quarters of the city, but a clean, softly lit watering hole frequented by locals and the most recent generation of the city's noble families. Here, individuals who would flee in terror from the common room of the Bloody Fist or Selune's Smile farther down the city could quaff a few with others of similar social station and disposition.

There were no dusty Dalesmen here, no Red Wizards in mufti, and no axe-wielding dwarves. Most of the crowd were local, young, and in varying degrees of inebriation, their numbers mixed with a smattering of the wealthy merchants who catered to the wealthier families. A boisterous game of darts dominated one corner, a high-stakes Talis game another, and a third had been commandeered by a wag of middling years telling "Volo stories" to a crowd of younger sports.

The fourth corner held a quiet table of three young apprentice wizards. These were new mages, just trained in their first cantrips, whose lives were still filled with the inglorious grunt work of wizards' assistants—cleaning kettles, running errands, fetching spell components, sweeping the summoning room floor, and other odious tasks their mentors assigned. Like employees of every stripe, regardless of profession, they were taking this opportunity of temporary freedom to complain about the masters they had just left behind.

"Familiars get treated better than we do," said Jehan Wands. He was the tallest of the three, a youth with dark hair gathered in a ponytail behind a golden earring (the latter worn only when he was away from his magical master—his granduncle, Maskar Wands).

His friend Anton, a russet-headed youth, grunted an agreement. "I've seen spell components that were better handled than apprentice wizards. Don't these old husks remember when they were young?"

"They probably do," said Gerald, a gangly blond boy with short hair and a scowling demeanor, "and they want to treat their apprentices just as badly as they themselves were treated." Gerald was supposedly Anton's friend, but Jehan had drunk with him only a handful of times in the past few months.

"And I have it doubly bad," said Jehan, "for I'm working for the family patriarch himself. He's so old we call him Maskar the Mummy. Practically embalmed, and as stiff-necked as they come. If I make the slightest mistake, he pays a 'social call' on my father, and I get one of the 'Your mother and I are very disappointed in you' talks. I hear he used to change his apprentices into frogs and newts. It would be an improvement over listening to my folks complain."

"Huh. I can triple that misfortune" challenged Anton. "My master claims to have studied under Elminster himself. Everything is 'Elminster this' and 'Elminster that' and 'When I was your age and worked for Elminster.' I don't think he's been farther west than the Rat Hills, but don't let him hear me say that. He *would* turn me into a frog."

Gerald shook his head. "I beat your ill curses fourfold. I serve the great and powerful Khelben Blackstaff Arunsun, who's just plain crazy. He's been involved in so many plots, he's stone-cold paranoid, and borderline violent to boot. If he thinks you're a danger to Waterdeep in any way, shape, or form, *poof!*" The blond youth grabbed his forehead with his hand, fingers splayed. "He throws a feeblemind spell on you and burns out your brain cells."

Anton put in, "Ah, but at least you have Laeral, Khelben's prize student, hanging around. I hear she's most easy on the eyes."

Gerald sniffed. "You think she'll give an apprentice the time of day? No, she worships the ground Blackstaff levitates over." He took a pull on his mug for effect and, realizing it was empty, signaled for another round.

"I bet he doesn't tell your parents on you," said Jehan. "And you don't have to live up to your family name. Just once I'd like to have old Maskar treat me like a rational, thinking being instead of his nephew's youngest whelp. Maskar thinks everyone else in this city is a lower form of life, especially his students."

Gerald nodded. "And rival mages are barely worth their notice. Khelben calls your master 'the Old Relic.'"

Jehan sniffed in turn. "And yours reminds me of a skunk, what with that white stripe in his beard. I've heard my master call him 'the Old Spider.'"

The blond youth flashed a sly, toothy grin, his first of the evening. "Everyone calls him that, and he likes it that way, I think. Blackstaff and the other big-name wizards revel in the illusion of their power and wear it like a fur-trimmed cloak. Threatening the help is part of the deal. One of the perks, I suppose."

"It wouldn't be such a problem," said Anton, "if they were at least listening to new ideas."

"Don't get me started on that," said Jehan, getting starting on *precisely* that. The subject was a favorite of the young mage, particularly since it showed the shortcomings of the elder wizards. "They're paranoid enough about their powers getting into the hands of inexperienced pups like us. New magic is beyond their aged brains, and it scares them."

"New magic?" asked Gerald.

"You've heard about Maztica, right? The land across the Shining Sea?" said Jehan. Gerald nodded. "They have a completely different flavor of magic out there, based on feathers and fangs. These Mazticans use it to move water through pipes, like a well-pump. Think about what such interior plumbing would do for Waterdeep. I tried to ask old Maskar about it and got a lecture about learning the basics first before getting involved in 'speculative' spell-casting. Speculative! There's another culture that can transform our world, and he's turning his back on it."

"Aye, and you're seeing more wood-block printing around," said Anton. "But we're still writing spells out longhand."

Gerald nodded. "And weapons technology is at the same level it was when the elves abandoned Myth Drannor, as if we haven't improved anything in the past thousand years."

Jehan said, "You're talking about smoke powder, right?"

Anton shifted uneasily in his chair, but Gerald nodded readily. "There are a number of things, but yes, smoke powder is Blackstaff's pet peeve."

Jehan laughed. "Peeve? I hear the Old Spider is flat-out paranoid about the stuff, blowing it up wherever he finds it, and a good chunk of the city along with it. The way I hear it, the powder comes from other planets, other planes."

Anton harrumphed into his mug. "I have to confess, I'm not comfortable talking about this. I hear smoke powder is dangerous."

Jehan shook his head. Anton was so cautious sometimes, he thought. "Don't worry. It's not like the Old Spider is listening to us, waiting for us to speak treason about smoke powder. I mean, what is it? A magical mixture that explodes on contact with fire. They're already making arquebuses down south to use that explosive force to fire sling bullets, and cannons that fire iron-banded stones."

Anton tried to shrug nonchalantly. "So it makes a big bang. Don't we have enough spells we can learn that create a big bang?"

Gerald leapt in, "Yes, but those spells are only for wizards. Smoke powder, like printing, can bring that ability to the masses, eh?"

"Exactly," said Jehan, warming to the subject as the most recent round of ale warmed his belly. "But the Old Hounds in the city, Maskar the Mummy and that skunk-maned Spider among them, don't see it, *won't* see it until it's too late. Keeping us from knowing too much about the stuff won't keep others from learning. But no, they're caught in the 'Fireballs and Lightning Bolts' mind-set, and nothing can dissuade them."

Anton muttered something about the beer running through him, and he staggered off. Jehan and Gerald barely noticed his disappearance.

Gerald said, "So you don't think we mages would be replaced if there were smoke powder freely lying around?"

Jehan laughed. "No more than we'd be replaced when more people learn how to read. You still need mages to make the stuff. And not to mention that wizards would still be needed to make smoke powder safer, and improve the weapons that use it. The big problem for most arquebuses is that they sometimes explode. A wizard can strengthen the barrel, as well as improve the accuracy and distance. It's a whole new world, but the Old Hounds with all the power don't realize it, and they're keeping us, the next generation, in the dark about it."

By the time Anton returned, Gerald and Jehan had moved onto other ideas, like golem-driven boats and clock-work familiars, which the Old Guard were either ignoring or blatantly quashing. The three apprentices agreed that the problem was that since the old wizards controlled what knowledge was being passed on, they controlled the advance (or lack of advance) of spellcasting.

Gerald excused himself at this point, saying he had to get back to Blackstaff Tower or the Old Spider would send hell hounds out after him. Anton bought one last round, and the conversation switched to other matters, such as the purported easiness of the Fibinochi sisters. Then Anton had to leave as well, since his master mage was cooking up something noxious at dawn and expected the kettles to be spotless.

Jehan swirled the last of his ale in his mug, thinking about how entrenched the old wizards had gotten. And the problem was, since they were all older than the Cold Spine Mountains, they kept anyone else from learning new things. Supposedly, they were fonts of information, but in reality they stood in the way of progress. Jehan resolved that when he attained the ancient and august title of wizard, he would never stand in the way of new ideas like Granduncle Maskar, Khelben, and the rest of the Old Hounds. In the meantime, he would have to sweep the floors, learn what he could, and keep his eyes out for new ideas. After all, there was nothing that kept him from a little independent study.

A merchant intercepted Jehan as the young man was making for the door. "Excuse me?" the merchant said in an odd accent, touching Jehan softly on the shoulder. "Do I understand you are a wizard?"

Jehan blinked back the mild, ale-induced fog around him and looked at the merchant. He couldn't place the accent, and the cut of the man's clothing was strange—the tunic a touch too long to be fashionable, and the seams stitched across the back instead of along the shoulders. "I am a wizard's student," Jehan said. "An apprentice."

"But you know magic?" pressed the man. His inflection rose at the end of every phase, making each sentence sound like a question.

"Some," said Jehan. "A few small spells. If you need magical aid, there are a number of name-level wizards in Waterdeep who can help. . . ."

"I'm sorry," said the merchant, "but I overheard you talking and thought you were knowledgeable? You see, I have a small problem that requires an extremely discreet touch? And I'm not comfortable talking to the older mages in this city?"—here he dropped his voice to a whisper—"about smoke powder."

That last was a statement, not a question. Jehan raised his eyebrows and looked at the strange little man, then nodded for him to follow.

Once on the street, Jehan said, "What about the . . . material you mentioned?"

"I understand that it is not . . . proper to have this material in this city?" He said, flexing his voice on the last word.

"It is illegal," said Jehan. "Extremely illegal. And there are a few mages in town who would destroy any of this material they find. And anyone standing near it."

A pained look crossed the merchant's face. "I was afraid of that. You see, I have come into possession of some of this material without realizing it was illegal? And I want to move it out of the city as quickly as possible?"

"A sound idea," nodded Jehan, trying to sound as sage and puissant as he could.

"But I have a problem?" continued the odd-speaking merchant. "I was doubly cheated, for I did not know the material was illegal? And further was unaware that someone had mixed it with sand? If I am to get it out of the city, I need to pull the sand out?"

"I . . ." Jehan's voice died as he thought about it. The merchant had to have overheard their conversation about the paranoid and powerful Khelben Blackstaff, and now was trying to get his stuff out of town as soon as possible. The right and proper thing was to go to the sage and aged authorities and have them destroy it.

Of course, getting it out of town was as good as destroying it, and if Jehan could get some for his own experiments, so much the better. Just a bit for independent study. The idea warmed him, and the ale strengthened his resolve.

"I'll be glad to do what I can," said Jehan, "for a small sample of the material. Where do you have it?"

The merchant led him past the City of the Dead, toward the Trades Ward. The well-tended walls of the various noble families gave way to town houses, then to irregular row houses built by diverse hands in diverse centuries, and finally to the gloomy back alleys of the warehouses, off the beaten track and home only to teamsters carrying goods and merchants selling them.

It was as if they had entered a different, alien, city, far from magical instruction and friendly taprooms. Jehan might have worried, but the ale and his own resolve eliminated doubt from his mind. Besides, he was a mage, and even with his simple cantrips, he'd be a match for any ordinary citizen, common merchant, or rogue of Waterdeep.

The merchant went to a heavy oak door and thumped hard with his fist, three times. A bolt clicked audibly behind the oak, and the merchant slid the entire door aside on ancient, rusty runners. Without looking back, he entered and motioned for Jehan to follow.

The warehouse was a middling-sized member of its breed, one of those that would have six or seven tenants, who would either quickly rotate goods or store them forever and forget them. From the dust and debris accumulated on most of the supplies, it looked like the majority of the tenants were in the latter category.

Great iron-banded crates marched in neat rows across the central space of the warehouse, and the deep, gray-boxed shelves reached from floor to ceiling. The only odd piece stood at the far end of the space—a large, badly corroded statue of a winged deva, cast in bronze. Possibly a wedding present, thought Jehan derisively, gratefully accepted, then quickly hidden. The entire area was given the slight glow of moonlight through a frosted skylight in the ceiling.

In the center of the room were about a half-dozen small quarter barrels, their lids popped open, next to an empty full-sized tonne keg. In the center of the room was also a large humanoid creature of a type Jehan had never seen before. It was half again as tall as he was, with a broad, ogre-sized body and a huge-mouthed head that reminded Jehan of a hippopotamus. The massive creature was dressed in black leggings and a crimson coat, the latter decorated with metallic awards. In its broad belt it had a pair of small crossbows. No, corrected Jehan, they were miniature arquebuses, long, pistol-like weapons. The huge creature recognized the mage's presence with a curt nod of its massive head.

The merchant, locking the sliding door behind them, caught Jehan gawking at the creature. He said. "His name is Ladislau? He's a giff, one of the star-faring races? He's normally not this cranky, but the present situation has made him bitter?"

Jehan could not tell if the giff was bitter, cranky, or in blissful ecstasy. All he knew was that the creature could swallow him to the waist in a single bite.

The young apprentice put on his most serious face, the one he used when Maskar was lecturing him. "Is this your . . . material?"

Ladislau the giff made a loud, derisive snort that sounded like an air bubble escaping a tar pit. "Is this the best you can do, Khanos. Are there no better groundling mages on this dirt speck." The hippo-headed creature's voice was level and flat, and his questions sounded like statements.

"I think he will do, Laddy?" rejoined Khanos. "You don't need a large gun to shoot down a small bird, do you now?"

Ladislau grumbled something Jehan did not catch and motioned to the barrels. Jehan stepped up to the containers and pulled the loosened lid from the closest.

The smoke powder itself was hard and granular, a grayish-black shade shot with small pips of silver. Jehan had never heard of these pips, and inwardly congratulated himself on the discovery. Here was some other fact about the powder that the Old Hounds kept to themselves.

Jehan picked up a nodule of the powder between two fingers. It was heavier than it looked, as if it had been cast around lead. He tried to break it between his nails, but he might as well have been squeezing a pebble.

Jehan looked into the container. The small nodules were mixed with a grit of a soft, lighter gray. The largest particle of the grit was slightly larger than the smallest bit of smoke powder. Doubtless, the merchant had already considered sifting it through a screen. Jehan rubbed the grit between his fingers; it broke apart easily and drifted slowly downward in the still air of the warehouse.

The young mage licked his dust-covered skin. It tasted

like the floor of old Maskar's summoning chamber, and the grit clotted into a ball that Jehan rubbed between his fingers.

No sieve then, and no water to separate the two, Jehan thought. He said aloud, "You could do this without magic, and in a city safer than this. Perhaps it would be smarter merely to remove the smaller barrels now and separate it later.

The giff made a noise that sounded like a human stomach growling, and Khanos put in, "We felt it would be easier to move one barrel than six, especially through this city? We don't want these to fall into the wrong hands? Can you separate the two?"

Jehan scooped up the mixture with one hand and sifted it between his fingers. Some of the larger nodules stayed in his palm, but most of the silver-shot grains fell back into the barrel with some of the grit. The grit drifted more slowly, like dandelions on the wind.

At length he nodded. "It can be done. You want to have the powder in the large keg at the end of this?" Khanos nodded enthusiastically. "Then if Mr. Ladislau here would be so kind as to pour the smaller barrels *slowly* into the larger, I can come up with something to remove most of the debris."

The giff grunted and hoisted the first barrel. Jehan recalled the basics of the cantrip, the small semispell that Maskar had taught him to aid in his sweepings. It was a simple spell—"half an intention and a bit of wind" as Maskar described it when he first taught it. Of course, Maskar the Mummy would never think to use a floor-sweeping cantrip in this way.

Jehan cast the minor spell and nodded at the great creature. The giff began to pour the mixture into the larger barrel. Jehan directed the sweeping wind across the entrance of the larger container. The breeze caught most of the grit and dust, blowing them away from the container's mouth. The heavier nodules of smoke powder fell into the barrel, forming a dark great pile mixed with silver sparkles. Without the dust, the sparkles glowed brighter in the moonlight.

Ladislau the giff finished the first small barrel and picked up the second and, finishing that, the third. Jehan wondered if he could make the spell last long enough for all six barrels, and redoubled his concentration as Ladislau started on the fourth barrel. By the fifth barrel, perspiration dripped from the young mage's brow, and by the sixth, small stars were dancing at the edge of his vision.

The giff poured the last of the barrel into the container, and Jehan tied off the end of the incantation. He took a deep breath and blinked back the dizziness he felt. The back of his head ached, and Jehan realized he had sweated off the effects of the ale, spellcasting himself into a mild hangover.

He looked at the others. The dust in the air had yet to fully settle, giving the entire warehouse a fog-enshrouded look in the moonlight. The great giff's nostrils twitched, and he scratched his snout with a heavy hand. The merchant was positively radiant, and pulled up a handful of the smoke powder, letting the rough nodules slip between his fingers. Then he grabbed the barrel's lid and slipped it into place.

Jehan cleared his throat softly. Then, afraid his interruption might be merely interpreted as a reaction to the dust, cleared it again. The merchant scowled at the young mage.

"Before you close the barrel," said Jehan levelly, "about my fee."

"Your fee?" said Khanos. The smile returned to his face. "I had quite forgotten. Ladislau, can you give the young man his fee?"

The giff pulled the arquebuses from his belt-sash and leveled them on Jehan.

The last of the little stars plaguing Jehan's vision evaporated, and the mage's attention was fully riveted on the ends of the gun barrels.

"Good-bye, groundling," said the giff. "We couldn't leave you alive to tell your superiors." His inhuman face was illuminated by the twin fires of the exploding smoke powder as he pulled the triggers.

Jehan dropped an instant before the guns fired, tum-

bling forward. Even so, he felt something hot plow a graz-
ing path along his left shoulder.

The pain roused him to action. When he struck the hard,
cool floor, Jehan immediately scrambled on his hands and
feet, trying to put as much distance between himself and
the giff's weapons. He half ran and half crawled away from
the pair, deeper into the dusty darkness of the warehouse.
Behind him he heard Khanos cursing at his companion.

Jehan's shoulder burned as if someone had dripped acid
on it. Now scared, wounded, and sober, the young mage
cursed himself for being so stupid, so trusting. He should
have left a message at the tavern, or contacted Gerald or
Anton at the very least. But no, he was so sure he could
handle this little bit of magic, this little bit of free-staff
spellcasting, this independent study. He was so sure that
his little magics could handle anything a mere merchant
could throw at him.

But could he handle enemies armed with smoke powder, bringing them to the level of wizards themselves?

Jehan leaned against a stack of boxes and tried to contain his breathing. His wounded shoulder held a coldness
that was beginning to spread down his arm, and his shirt
clung to him stickily there. He would have to escape this
place and be pretty quick about it. His opponents were
somewhere in the dusty darkness between him and the
only door.

Jehan mentally cursed Maskar the Mummy as well, for
not teaching him any *useful* spells for such a situation.
One more example of the Old Hounds keeping their
knowledge to themselves.

Jehan was suddenly aware of a tall humanoid near him
and started, almost crying out. It was only the ugly deva
statue he had noted before. Beneath spread wings, its
angelic face was impassive to Jehan's plight, its features
practically glittering in the moon's radiance through the
skylight.

The statue reached halfway to the skylight above, and
there were shelves above it. Most skylights had an interior
latch, easily sprung. Even lacking that, Jehan could probably smash the skylight and get away before they could

fire on him.

And they would not expect a groundling mage to take to the skies.

Slowly, painfully, Jehan pulled himself up around the base of the deva statue. His shoulder was getting worse now, and the young mage wondered if he could make it all the way up. Still, it would be better to hole up in the spaces above rather than being found passed out on the ground.

The statue stood on a pedestal, with about two feet of clearance between its back and the wall. Jehan set his back against the wall and his feet against the deva and slid upward. He slowly pulled himself up, leaving a wet, dark slick against the wall as he moved.

He had almost reached the wings when he heard the heavy clump of feet below. Wedging himself tightly in place, Jehan held his breath.

The giff warrior trudged slowly up beneath his hiding place, swinging only one hand arquebus. Jehan realized Khanos would have the other one, using it either in searching some other part of the warehouse or in standing guard by the entrance. Jehan simultaneously offered prayers to Azuth for favor and curses to himself for inexperience. Were he a full-fledged mage, he thought, he would be able to handle the pair with ease. The increasing pain in his shoulder gave lie to that last thought.

The giff stopped at the base of the statue, and Jehan's heart stopped as well. The great creature's nostrils flared and snorted, and the warrior peered about, surveying the surroundings. Then he looked upward, along the shelves and at the statue.

Jehan panicked. The statue offered only minimal protection for an immobile target wedged between it and the wall. Jehan's legs stiffened to push him back into the wall itself.

The wall did not move. The statue did. It tipped forward on its loose mounting.

Jehan's panic that he would be shot was suddenly replaced with a similar concern that he would fall from his perch. With a shout, he leapt forward to grab the statue behind the wings and rode it down as it tipped forward.

The giff had time to look up at the plummeting statue, open his huge maw in a shout, and raise his gun. The pistol detonated as the great bronze deva, Jehan on its back, slammed into him.

On impact, Jehan rolled free and felt something give in his right leg. He rose slowly to survey the damage. The giff had been pinned beneath the heavy statue, a large pond of blackish blood pooling beneath him. The creature was still struggling, and as Jehan watched, he started to shift the heavy statue off himself. Of the gun there was no sign, and Jehan had no time to search for it.

Jehan looked up at the skylight, now as unapproachable as the moon beyond it. The only way out would be past the merchant, who likely had the other gun.

Jehan dodged over three rows of crates before heading for the door, hoping Khanos would search out his companion at the sound of his cry. Indeed, Azuth and Mystra were smiling on him, for the area in front of the great oak door was clear. Jehan tugged on it with his good arm, then realized it was still locked. He reached over and, grunting, unlocked the door.

"Stand away from the door, would you, boy?" said a voice behind him, raising the last word in an odd inflection.

Jehan cursed softly and turned slowly to face Khanos. He wished he had some lightning bolt or other spell to slay the merchant on the spot, but he was a novice mage, and the wind-sweep cantrip had emptied his mind.

Khanos was there, and had the other arquebus in his hand. There was no sign of the giff. The merchant had a lopsided smile on his face.

"I really wish we could let you live?" he said, emphasizing the last word. "But it just wouldn't do, would it? I mean, your magical brothers might want to hunt you down when they themselves start dropping from assassin's bullets? Oh yes, the powder isn't leaving the city, not when it can be put to much better use here? A few well-placed shots against the more powerful mages, and the rest will retreat into their towers? Wizards are cowards like that, aren't they? And by the time they emerge, we'll

have a ready supply of powder from Ladislau's friends? So
unwittingly, you helped bring a new thing to Waterdeep—
and greater independence from mages?"

Jehan was not thinking of the advancements to Waterdeep, but rather the distance between the two of them.
Four steps. More than enough distance for the merchant
to get off a shot before Jehan could get the gun. And from
the easy way he held the weapon, Khanos seemed a better
marksman than the giff had been. Still, it was move and
die, or stay and perish just as surely.

Jehan started to move forward when the door behind
him rolled aside on its squeaking runners. A fresh breeze
blew aside the dust still hanging in the air. Khanos
pointed his gun at the doorway as a new figure entered
the warehouse.

Jehan gasped. The new arrival was himself, or rather
an unwounded, unbloodied Jehan, dressed as he had been
when he left the tavern, unblemished and unarmed. No,
this Jehan was a little taller, perhaps a little fiercer, but
otherwise it was he.

"Another wizard?" spat Khanos. "You'll come no closer?"

"I don't think so," said the other Jehan, using Jehan's
voice and mannerisms. "I think it's time to wrap this little
play up, eh?"

"I'll shoot?" said the merchant.

"Be my guest," said the other Jehan, striding forward
and in front of the young wounded mage. Jehan saw that
magical energy was already dancing at the ends of his
duplicate's fingertips.

The other Jehan took two steps forward, and Khanos
fired, the thunder of the gun echoing through the warehouse. The other Jehan did not flinch or fall. The bullet
struck him with a metallic *splang,* then rebounded in the
darkness.

The other Jehan took another two steps and reached
up, grasping the merchant by the forehead. Yellow lances
of energy raced across Khanos's face, and the foreign merchant screamed, his skull shuddering under the other
Jehan's grip. After a few moments, the merchant toppled
forward, his ears and mouth streaming with thin wisps of

white smoke.

The other Jehan turned to the young mage and scowled, that serious scowl that Jehan used when listening to his master. "Now that this is all taken care of, you'd best get home. I'll see to the disposal of the powder."

The original Jehan shook his head. His voice cracked as he spoke: "There is another one here, a giff. He has a pistol, as well."

"That is true," said Ladislau, standing by the barrel of smoke powder. The giff's face and topcoat were slick with black blood, and he had lost an eye to the bronzework deva. He aimed the gun at Jehan's duplicate.

"You saw what happened to your ally," said the other Jehan. "Do you think you can hurt me with mere bullets?"

The giff gave a bloody-mouthed smile and said, "No, not with bullets." He aimed the gun at the barrel of purified smoke powder. "Not with bullets," he repeated. "But a single shot will blow us all to our respective afterlives."

The other Jehan took a step forward and snapped his fingers. A single flame appeared and danced at the tip of his index finger. "Run, boy," he said to the battered, original version.

Jehan ran, making long, limping strides. As he cleared the door, he heard the giff shout, "I'm not bluffing."

The other Jehan replied coolly, "Neither am I."

Jehan made it ten, maybe eleven steps past the door when a huge hand grabbed him and pressed him flat against the ground. Then the thunder, this time like a thousand arquebuses firing at once, swept over him and pressed him farther against the cobblestones. Then the heat washed over him in a single blast, pushing past in its rush to escape the alley.

Jehan rose slowly and saw that the warehouse was in flames, the fire already licking up through the broken skylight and setting the roof ablaze. The single entrance was an inferno, and while the walls seemed to have resisted the blast, nothing could live within it.

The other Jehan stepped out through the doorway, unblemished by the explosion, and unsinged by the flames. He looked around, spotting the unsteady youth, and walked toward him.

As he walked, the duplicate's features changed. He became taller, almost gangly, and his hair changed from Jehan's dark ponytail to an icy blond tint, worn short. Gerald, Anton's friend.

Then he changed again, the blond darkening to a night-black shade, worn free over the shoulders, the face aging and gaining a full beard, black with a white stripe in its center. The shoulders widened, and the wizard's stride became long and measured. Khelben Arunsun, the Black-staff of Waterdeep. The Old Spider.

"Are you all right, child?" asked the elder mage.

Jehan, propped against a wall, managed a weak nod. He noticed that no mind-killing lights danced at the older man's fingertips.

"Good," said the wizard. "Maskar takes a dim view when I get his apprentices damaged, and doubly so when they are his relatives. Of course, he's dismissed apprentices for much less serious crimes than this."

Jehan's mouth finally found purchase. "What . . . ?" he said. "What happened?"

Khelben's mouth formed a thin line. "For what it's worth, you can tell your master that my original plan did not involve you. I had found this little bit of smoke powder, and put the sand in it, hoping to turn up the conspirators. Then as Gerald, I would hang out at the better taverns loudly declaring my anti-elder, pro-powder thoughts, waiting for someone to contact me to solve the little problem I had given them. I did not count on another young whelp making a better case than myself on the use of smoke powder. I did not even know you had been contacted until an abjuration I had placed here warned me that the powder had been purified. At that point, it seemed to make more sense to imitate your appearance, and throw the conspirators off-balance, should they have killed you. My 'Gerald' identity failed to impress them earlier, and I would set them to immediate flight in my natural form, the one you so aptly titled 'skunk-maned.' "

The elder mage paused in his lecture, as if just remembering Jehan was still there, leaking his blood into the wall. He looked at his battered companion and added, "So, child, you still think everyone in Waterdeep should have smoke powder?"

Jehan looked at the flaming wreckage of the warehouse. Already the locals had responded and were forming bucket brigades from nearby cisterns. Everyone was ignoring the two mages—more magic of the Old Spider, no doubt.

"I think," Jehan started, too tired and battered to be properly respectful or afraid, "I think you just can't blow up the future and hide in the past. Somewhere, someone is going to get past you, and you need to be ready for the day. You can't stop progress."

That was when Khelben surprised the young mage. He laughed—a sharp, staccato chuckle. "Ah, so at least we agree on something. You are right: we can't stop progress. Smoke powder, the printed word, new forms of magic—it's all coming. But we can slow it down from a run to a walk, so at least we can be ready for it. So we can be its master, instead of it being ours."

Jehan groaned. "You think the Old Rel . . . Maskar will dismiss me for this?"

Khelben nodded at the wreckage. "Well, he no longer changes apprentices into newts for forgetting the lemon in his morning tea . . . but yes, this is pretty serious. I could put a good word in for you. Or perhaps . . ."

Jehan looked at Khelben, but his eyes refused to focus properly. "Perhaps?" was the best the youth could manage.

"I *could* use another youth to scrub the pots, sweep the conjuring floor, and learn what snippets of magic I deign to teach. And an adventurous youth would be suitable, since I think my Gerald persona should leave town for a while." The Old Spider chuckled again. "And Maskar *would* be relieved of having to face your parents with your latest escapade."

Jehan tried to smile, but the effort broke his last bit of willpower. He fell into soft, warm darkness.

The young mage awoke at home, the healer speaking to his parents in the next room in quiet, relaxed tones—the tones of one confident the patient will recover without further interference. Jehan's shoulder and leg were still sore, but it was the soreness of strained muscles and bruises as opposed to ripped and bloodied flesh.

His parents wavered between anger at him risking his life in some damned-fool adventure and pride in the impression he had apparently made on the great Blackstaff, who had brought him home and spoken of his heroism. Even now, they said, Khelben was talking with Uncle Maskar about taking Jehan under his wing. Imagine, one of the Wands family learning from the Old Spider himself. But of course, regardless of the outcome, he should not have taken up with that sinister merchant in the first place.

His parents were still trying to determine if they were angry at Jehan or proud of him as he drifted back to sleep.

He awoke much later, having slept through the entire day. Beyond his open window, Waterdeep lay spread out before him with a thousand flickering lights, marching southward toward the sea.

Suddenly there was a series of bright flashes, down by the wharves. A moment passed, then another, then at last the staccato of small explosions reached his ears. Khelben probably had found the rest of the smoke powder stashes, Jehan thought. The ripple of thunder sounded like Khelben's chuckle.

Jehan sat there for a long time, looking out over the darkened city, but the effect did not repeat itself. The young mage wondered, Is Khelben rewarding me by making me his apprentice, or punishing me?

Or is he up to something else entirely?

Jehan was still trying to figure this out, the first of many puzzles Blackstaff would pose to him, when sleep finally reclaimed him.

THE MAGIC THIEF

Mark Anthony

I am penning this story as a warning, so that it will not
happen to another as it happened to me. My first mistake
upon meeting the thief was that I pitied him. But then I
have always pitied his kind: those who have longed all
their lives to become wizards but—by some cruel trick of
birth or accident—are incapable of touching or shaping
the ethereal substance of magic. How easy it was for me,
so comfortable in my wizard's mantle of power, to feel pity
for such a man. Yet pity can be a weakness. And as I have
learned, it is not my only one. Here then is my tale.

It was just after sunset when I received the curious
invitation.

Outside the window of my study, the last day of autumn
had died its golden death, and twilight wove its gray fabric
around the countless spires of the Old City. I sighed and
set down my quill pen next to the sheaf of parchment I had
been filling with musings of magic. As it had with growing
frequency of late, a peculiar restlessness had fallen upon
me. Absently, I gazed about my sanctuary. Thick Sembian
carpets covered the floor. A fire burned brightly in a copper
brazier. The walls were lined with shelves of rich wood,
laden with books, scrolls, and crystal vials. Everything

about my study bespoke learning, and comfort, and quiet dignity. I decorated it myself, if I do say so.

I took a sip of wine from a silver goblet, wondering at the source of my unease. Certainly nothing could harm me here in the haven of my tower. Over the years I had bound walls, doors, and windows with protective magics and charms of warding. No one could enter the tower without my leave. I was utterly and perfectly safe.

I set down the goblet and caught a reflection of a man in its silver surface. He was tall and regal, clad in garb of pearl gray. His handsome face was unlined, and his eyes gleamed like blue ice. A long mane of golden hair tumbled about his shoulders. The man looked far younger than his true years. Yet magic can have a preservative effect on those who wield it.

This I knew, for the man was me. Morhion Gen'dahar. The greatest wizard in the city of Iriaebor.

I shook my head, for I had not chosen this title. True, years ago I had traveled on perilous adventures. I had helped defeat beings of ancient and terrible evil. Perhaps, in those days, I had known something of greatness. Yet what had I done since then? Nothing, save keep to the peaceful fastness of my tower. I was secure, and comfortable, and safe. Yes, *safe*. That was the word, and suddenly it was like a curse to me. I clenched a fist in anger.

After a moment I blinked. Bitter laughter escaped my lips. If this tower was a prison, I had wrought it for myself. Drawing in a resigned breath, I reached for my quill pen once more.

I halted at the magical chiming of a small bronze bell. Someone stood upon the front steps of my tower. Curious, for I had few visitors these days, I hurried from my study and descended a spiral staircase to the tower's entry chamber. Belatedly I waved a hand, dismissing the spells that bound the door—which otherwise would have given me a nasty shock—and flung open the portal.

There was no one there.

The path that led from the Street of Runes to my tower was empty in the gloaming. Oddly disappointed, I started to shut the door. I paused as something caught my eye. It was a piece of paper resting on the stone steps. I bent down to retrieve the paper. A message was written upon it in a spidery hand:

I wish to meet you. Come to the Crow's Nest at moonrise. I believe there is much we can gain from one another.

—Zeth

I gazed at the words in mild interest. It was hardly the first such invitation I had received. Usually they came from would-be apprentices, wandering mages seeking knowledge, or—on occasion—brash young wizards wishing to challenge me to a duel of magic. I studied the paper, wondering to which category this Zeth belonged. That last line was unusual. Most wanted something of me. Yet this man seemed to believe I had something to gain from him.

Intriguing as it was, I knew I should discard the invitation. Yet I was suddenly loath to return to the safe confines of my tower. I had heard of the Crow's Nest. It was a rough tavern on the riverfront, a dangerous place. Yet was I not the greatest wizard in Iriaebor? I thought with a sharp smile. What did I have to fear? Before I knew what I was doing, I grabbed my dusk-gray cloak from a hook in the entry chamber. I shut the door of my tower, rebinding the enchantments with a wave of my hand, and headed into the deepening night.

I moved quickly down the twisting Street of Runes. The numberless towers of the Old City loomed above, plunging the winding ways below into thick shadow. Soon I came to the edge of the labyrinth and, following a steep road cut into the face of the Tor, made my way down into the sprawling New City below. Here the streets were broader and more open than in the Old City, lined by bright torches.

I was just on the edge of a shabby, less savory section of the city when I was accosted by the girl.

"Would you like to buy some magic, milord?" she asked in a pert voice. A grin lit up her grimy face as she pulled something from her tattered clothes.

"So this is magic, is it?" I asked solemnly, accepting the

proffered object. It was a small tube woven of straw.

The urchin nodded enthusiastically. "If someone puts his fingers in each end, he won't be able to pull them out. And the harder he pulls, the more stuck his fingers will be. That's the enchantment."

A low laugh escaped my lips. "And a powerful one it is." No doubt this girl was an orphan, and under the power of some petty thief. If she failed to sell her wares, it was likely she would be beaten. I drew out a silver coin and flipped it to the girl.

"Thank you, milord!" she cried as she snatched up the coin and vanished into the gloom. I tucked the cheap finger-trick into a pocket and, wearing a faint smile, continued on my way.

I reached the Crow's Nest just as the pale orb of Selune lifted itself above the city's sentinel towers. Moonrise. The ramshackle tavern stood on an old quay thrust out into the turgid waters of the Chionthar River. The scents of fish and garbage hung on the air. I opened the tavern's door and stepped into the murky space beyond.

A dozen eyes fell upon me, then just as quickly looked away. This was a violent place. Its clientele were murderers, pirates, and thieves. But all knew a wizard when they saw one. Drunk as most were, none were fools enough to think their fists or knives a match for true magic. They hunkered over their ale pots and returned to their talk. The palm of my left hand tingled, and I rubbed it absently. My fingers traced the familiar pattern of an old, puckered scar: the Rune of Magic, which had branded me a wizard long ago.

I scanned the smoky interior. In one corner sat a man, pale and nervous, fidgeting with—but not drinking from—a dented flagon. It could be no other. Zeth. He was older than I had guessed. His thin face was sharply lined though not unhandsome, and gray flecked his dark hair. Drab clothes hung loosely upon his lean frame. At once I knew he was no mage. I wended my way through the tavern and sat opposite him. He glanced up, his expression one of surprise. Yet it seemed a strange smugness shone in his dark eyes.

"I didn't think you'd come," he said in a hoarse voice.

"Yet, here I am," I countered smoothly.

He fumbled with the flagon. "Would you like a drink?"

"No," I replied.

Silence settled between us. The first move was up to him. He shifted uncomfortably in his chair. "I can feel it radiating from you, you know." A hunger filled his voice. "Magic, I mean. It's . . . it must be . . . intoxicating."

With these words, I knew him. Without doubt, Zeth was one of those few who are utterly dead to the touch of magic—what some mages cruelly called *geldings*. Their kind was rare, but had been known for centuries. Occasionally, masters encountered students who, no matter their intelligence or effort, could not learn even the simplest of spells. For reason unknown, they could neither sense nor channel the forces of magic. Most geldings gave up their arcane studies and turned to other pursuits, leading normal lives. Yet I had heard tales of geldings who had been driven mad by their ill-fated desire to wield magic.

"I'm sorry," I said, speaking the first words that came to my mind.

Anger flared in his eyes. "Save your apologies, Morhion Gen'dahar," he hissed. He clenched his hand into a trembling fist. "I want your power, not your pity."

I gazed at him unflinchingly. "I cannot give it to you, Zeth."

He slowly unclenched his hand. His thin shoulders slumped. "No, I suppose you can't," he whispered. He stared despondently at the table. "I had hoped that maybe you would know a way to help me. I should have known better."

This must be torture for him, I realized. He must be drawn to mages even as he loathed and resented them. It was a cruel illness, but one of which I could not cure him, one which I would only inflame with my presence. "I believe I will go now, Zeth," I said quietly.

He nodded jerkily, still staring at the table, then looked up as I started to rise. "Please," he choked. "Let me at least shake your hand before you go—so that I can say I have indeed met the great wizard Morhion Gen'dahar."

I hesitated. It seemed wrong to aid his delusions in any

way. Yet such was the haunted look in his dark eyes that I could not resist. "Very well," I replied finally.

He stood and held out his hand—his left, rather than his right. This was odd, but I thought little of it. I reached my left hand toward him.

"May Mystra guide you—" I started to speak. The words faltered on my lips.

An intricate symbol was tattooed on the back of his left hand. The glyph filled me with a sudden inexplicable dread. I tried to snatch my hand back, but it was too late. Zeth's fingers closed around mine. Agony raced up my arm like white fire. I arched my spine, throwing my head back as a scream ripped itself from my lungs. There was a brilliant flash, and the reek of lightning filled the air. At last, Zeth released my hand. I reeled backward, stumbling weakly against a wall. I stared at him in pain-clouded confusion. Strangely, he was laughing.

"You cannot give it to me," he said mockingly, "but I can take it from you." He held up his left hand. On the palm was a puckered scar, as if from a hot brand. It was a symbol I knew well: the Rune of Magic. His laughter rose to a maddening din in my ears. I clutched at the wall, trying to keep my feet. Then the room spun around me, and I fell down into darkness.

By the time I regained consciousness, Zeth was gone.

I blinked, trying to make out the blurred faces that hovered over me. Crimson light pulsed behind them, in time to the sharp throbbing inside my skull. A wave of nausea crashed through me. I retched into the sour straw that covered the tavern floor, coughed, then managed to draw in a gasping breath. At last, the faces came into focus. A half-dozen thugs loomed over me, leering expressions on their coarse faces.

"I guess he ain't dead after all," one of them grunted.

"Well, he ain't much alive, either," another replied, baring yellowed teeth. "That other fellow did something to him before he skipped out of here. Something nasty. I say we see what he's got."

Alarm cut through the haze of pain. No longer were the ruffians looking at me with fear and awe in their eyes. I tried to pull myself off the floor, but my limbs were as heavy as stone. I slumped back against the wall. I felt weak, hollow—as if part of me had been torn away. What had Zeth done to me?

"Hold him down, lads," the second thug growled. "I'll see what he has in that fat purse of his."

The others hesitated, exchanging nervous glances. They were wary to lay hands upon a wizard, even one who seemed incapacitated. That gave me a moment. I shut my eyes and opened my mind to recall the words of a spell.

Blankness.

My eyes flew open in shock. I had performed this action a thousand times. Words of magic should have flowed into my mind like water into an empty vessel. Instead, there had been nothing. Hastily I tried again. I willed the words to come. Again there was only blankness. I searched with my thoughts, then found it, as a man who has had a tooth pulled by a barber probes the empty socket with his tongue. It was a ragged hole in my mind, a darkness where all the spells I had mastered should have been.

Seeing my confusion, the ruffians grinned. A sawtooth knife flashed in the bloody torchlight. In desperation, I fumbled for the purse at my belt and, with what remained of my strength, flung it away from me. Thick gold coins spilled out, rolling across the floor. For a moment, my assailants stared at each other; then as one, they turned and dived, scrabbling for the coins lost amid the rotted straw. Their leader snarled at me, brandishing his knife. He hesitated, then swore, leaping to join the others in the search for gold.

I did not waste the chance. Forcing my trembling limbs to work, I crawled away, following the corner of the wall until I reached the tavern door. Somehow I managed to lurch to my feet. I stumbled outside and wove my way drunkenly down the quay to the street. Just then shouts went up from the Crow's Nest. My absence had been noticed. I tried to quicken my pace. As I did, my foot slipped in a slimy gutter. I fell hard to the filthy cobblestones and slid wildly down a steep alley, landing amid a heap of rotting fish and other foul refuse. I froze. Above me, dim shapes ran past the mouth of the alley. Angry shouts vanished into the night.

Gagging from the reek, I pulled myself out of the garbage heap and stood, trying to understand what had happened. I reached out with my will, trying to feel the ether of magic, which flowed between all things. Yet I was a blind man searching with numb fingers. Nothing, and nothing again. I could remember casting spells of power, could recall crackling magic flowing from my fingertips. But the words, the intonations, the intricate gestures were all gone. I pressed my burning forehead against the cool, dirty wall. Was I going mad?

A strange quietness descended upon me. No, I was not mad. It was something else. Something far worse than mere insanity. *You cannot give it to me, but I can take it from you,* he had said. Zeth. Somehow he had stolen my magic and had taken it for himself. Again nausea washed through me. This was what it felt like to be a gelding.

As if of its own volition, my left hand rose before my face. The palm, which had been branded by the Rune of Magic upon my initiation into the arcane arts, was now smooth. On the back was the tattoo that I had glimpsed on Zeth's hand: an intricate knot formed of angular lines. Certainly it was a sigil of power, and I sensed that I had seen its like before. But where? I searched my mind. My magic was gone, but all my mundane knowledge—philosophy, mathematics, history—remained. Then it came to me.

Netheril. It was a name few knew, for the ancient empire had vanished a millennium ago beneath the sands of the vast desert Anauroch. The reticulated knot had been a common motif in the art and magic of Netheril. Now I recalled reading of the ones called the *gor-kethal,* the thieves of magic. They had been the scourge of Netheril. In that empire, the nobility had ruled by right of magic, and all feared the *gor-kethal,* who could usurp a sorcerer's power—and rule—with a touch.

At last the pieces of the puzzle fell into place. In his tortured quest for magic, Zeth had somehow stumbled upon the secret of the *gor-kethal.* And I had been his unwitting victim. Like the magic thieves of long ago, he had stolen my power. Rage flared hotly in my brain, but I willed it away, forcing my mind to cool. It was an unalterable law that for every magic there was a countermagic. There had to be a way to reverse the transference. I had to remain calm if I was to find it.

Weird laughter tumbled from my lips. Of course! Here was the answer before me. The sigil of the *gor-kethal* was on my own hand. I was the magic thief now. All I need do to reverse the transference was to find Zeth and touch him. Not that this would be so easily done. Zeth would be wary, expecting pursuit. And he was the wizard now. Still, it was a hope, and that was all I needed.

I glanced again at the sky. The orb of Selune shone directly overhead. A new dread chilled my blood. Besides the reticulated knot, the moon was another integral motif of Netherese magic. With sudden certainty I knew that, once Selune vanished behind the horizon, it would be too late. If I did not find Zeth before moonset, the transference would be permanent. I would be without magic forever.

With no time to waste, I hurried up the slope of the alley and through the shadowed streets. Though still weak and ill, I was already growing used to the emptiness inside me. Before, I had hardly noticed the dilapidated buildings and filthy ways of this part of the New City. Always in the past I had walked such streets without fear, oblivious within the protective aura of my magic. Now I felt the danger that lurked behind every turn. Remembering the ruffians in the tavern, who had meant to rob me and slit my throat, I moved as quickly as I could. As I did, I wondered how I would discover where Zeth had gone.

This was not so difficult a matter.

Not far away, a pillar of green fire shot into the night sky. It could be but one thing. Magic. Following the telltale beacon, I came to a broad plaza. In the center was a tall bronze statue, a monument to some long-forgotten ruler of the city. Now magical emerald flames engulfed the statue. Hard bronze sagged, melted, and dripped down the statue to flow in molten rivulets across the cobbles. Zeth had been playing with his newfound power.

Disgusted at this irresponsible waste of magic, I hurried on. Zeth seemed to be moving toward the Tor. I could not let him get too far ahead of me.

I passed the open door of an inn, from which spilled golden light and the sounds of merriment. But the music was eerily frantic, and the laughter had a manic note to it. I peered through the doorway. Inside, men and women whirled around in a chaotic dance, jerking like marionettes under the control of a mad puppeteer. Garish smiles were plastered across their faces, yet terror shone in their eyes.

A young woman spun wildly past the doorway and saw me standing outside. "Please, help us!" she gasped, her face gray with exhaustion.

I shook my head in sorrow. There was nothing I could do. They would dance, consumed by the enchantment, until they dropped dead from exertion. Even as I watched, the woman whirled on and careened into a wall. A crimson blossom appeared on her brow. Pain racked her eyes, but her smile only broadened as she danced on.

"Damn you, Zeth," I hissed, forcing myself to turn away from the ghoulish scene. He was drunk with magic, wielding it with no regard for the consequences. He had the power but none of the discipline usually required to gain it. Urgency renewed, I ran onward.

The trail of mayhem left in Zeth's wake continued to trace a direct line toward the Tor. For some reason he was making for the Old City. Glancing up, I saw that the moon had passed its zenith. Time was slipping away. At last the dark bulk of the Tor loomed above me. I turned onto the road that wound up the crag. Abruptly I lurched to a halt.

Iron bars blocked the way. The gate was closed.

I cursed my stupidity. No doubt Zeth knew what I had forgotten. The wealthy citizens who lived high on the Tor preferred to keep the rabble down in the New City at night. By law the gate to the Old City was shut at midnight and would not open again until dawn. No doubt Zeth had passed to the other side by means of magic. How was I to follow?

Torches lined the stone wall that surrounded the Old City. The wall was high and smooth, crowned by a sharp overhang. A master thief would have been hard pressed to scale it, let alone an out-of-shape wizard. I turned my attention to the gate that covered the arched opening in the wall. The bars were thick and closely spaced. A heavy iron lock held the gate securely shut. I pulled on the bars, but half-heartedly. No human strength would be enough to bend them.

I turned away from the gate. The moon was steadily descending in the jet dome of the sky, and my hopes sank with it. In the past, I would have waved a hand and strode through like a proud lord. Yet what was I now? Weary, bedraggled, powerless. I was nothing without my magic.

Or was I? I still had my mundane knowledge. How would a scholar confront the problem of the locked gate?

My mind raced. I found my eyes lingering upon a torch that had burned down to a black stub. Then it struck me. I dug into the pocket of my doublet and came out with a handful of soft, yellow rocks. Brimstone. I often had some about me, for it was useful in the casting of many spells— none of which I knew anymore. However, the brimstone might serve me yet. I moved to the wall and pulled down the burned torch. That would provide the necessary charcoal. Now all I needed was one more ingredient. My gaze moved down the street. Then, in the fading moonlight, I saw what I was looking for: a mortar and pestle hanging above a doorway. An apothecary's shop.

I did not like resorting to thievery, but such moral regrets are better suited to less desperate moments. With a stray rock, I broke through the shop's window. By the time a wavering light appeared in an upper story and angry shouts rose on the night air, I was gone with what I needed. Hiding in a shadow near the gate, I examined my prize: a clay pot filled with small white crystals. Niter. It was commonly used by physicians to treat seizures. I had another use in mind.

I spread a handkerchief on the ground before me and emptied the clay pot onto it. I crumbled the charcoal and soft brimstone with my fingers and added these to the niter. With great care, I mixed the three ingredients until they formed a dark gray powder. Gathering the corners of the handkerchief, I tied them tightly, forming a bundle with the powder inside. I found a stray bit of frayed rope and tucked one end inside the handkerchief. Then I wedged the bundle between the bars of the gate next to the lock. I reached up and took one of the burning torches from its sconce, touching it to the free end of the rope. A flame curled up the length of cord. I turned and ran for cover.

The dry rope burned faster than I had thought. I had gone less then ten paces when a brilliant flash and a clap of thunder burst the night asunder. A great force struck my back, like the invisible hand of a giant, throwing me to the ground. After a stunned moment I pulled myself to my feet. Acrid smoke clouded the air.

While the Red Wizards of Thay claimed that smoke powder—which they were infamous for making and using—was a powerful enchantment, this was a lie. Smoke powder was not the result of magic, but of alchemy. It was no more magical in nature than a fire burning on a goodwife's hearth, though it was infinitely more powerful.

As the smoke cleared, I approached the gate. It was still shut, and for a moment I thought my plan had failed. I reached out to push on the iron bars. As my fingers brushed the still-warm metal, there was a dull *clink*. The weakened lock broke. The gate swung open. At the same moment, a hue and cry went up somewhere along the wall. It seemed my little trick had not gone unnoticed by the city watch. I hurried through the gate and, keeping to the murk and shadows, made my way unaccosted up the Tor, to the many-spired Old City above.

At first, I despaired of finding Zeth's trail amid the mazelike streets. I need not have feared. After a few moments, I stumbled upon a smoking pit that had been torn open in the middle of a lane. Not far ahead, a majestic old ash tree was twisted into contorted knots. Anger and dread filled me at these sights. The more powerful the magic Zeth tried to wield, the less he was able to control it. Ignoring my weariness, I pressed on, following the trail of destruction left by the magic thief. Then, at last, I knew where he was going.

The moon hovered just above the western horizon when I stopped before my tower on the Street of Runes.

I gazed up at the dark spire that had been my dwelling

for many long years. A light glowed in the window of the topmost chamber. Finally I understood. Zeth did not simply covet my magic. He coveted my *life*. He had come to my tower to claim it for his own. I almost laughed at the irony. Over the years I had woven my tower with myriad wards and protections. Now I was the one they would prevent from entering. Yet enter I must. Somehow.

Stealthily, I circled the tower. "Think, Morhion," I whispered to myself. "There must be some chink in the armor you conjured to protect yourself. Certainly you could not have been so perfectly safe as you believed."

Yet, even knowing where and what they were, I could see no way to get past my own defenses. The door was bound with enough arcane energy to roast an elephant. The thick walls were made smooth and slick by magic. A dusky vine wound up the western face of the tower, passing near the study window, and might be climbed. Yet even from here I could see the faint blue sheen that covered the window. Anyone trying to pass would be instantly struck dead. The only way to enter the tower was to be invited by the wizard within.

Excitement flared in my chest as an idea struck me. It would not exactly be an invitation, but it might work. That is, if I could count on Zeth's curiosity and lack of magical control. I glanced up at the rapidly sinking moon. There was no time to think of a better plan. Hastily, I began searching in the bushes near the base of the tower. I needed something that had once been alive. Then I came upon the dry carcass of a small bird. That would do.

Standing in a patch of gloom, I tossed the dead bird onto the stone doorstep of the tower. Above, I heard a faint chiming. There—the bell had been rung. Now I could only hope Zeth would take the bait. I might have simply waited in the shadows in hopes of ambushing him. But he would be expecting someone outside the door, and I had something more surprising in mind.

Running to the west side of the tower, I grabbed the thick tendrils of the vine that clung to the wall and began pulling myself up. In moments, my arms burned fiercely, but I clenched my teeth and kept climbing. At last I reached the study window. I could see the firelit room beyond. No one was within. The deadly blue aura still gleamed across the open window.

For several tense moments, I clung to the vines with white-knuckled hands. Then I heard the sound of a door opening below. At the same moment the blue magic barring the window flickered and vanished. Despite my exhaustion, I grinned fiercely in victory. Just as I had suspected, Zeth did not possess the fine control required to dismiss only one of the tower's protective magics. To open the door, he had been forced to lower all the wards. Before he could rebind the tower's protections, I pulled myself through the window and into the study beyond.

I was sitting in a comfortable chair, sipping a glass of ruby wine, when the study's door opened.

"Good evening, Zeth," I said smoothly.

He had clad himself in my best gray robe trimmed with silver thread. For a moment, his gaunt face paled in shock, then grew crimson with anger.

"Good evening, gelding," he spat. "I should have known you would find a way to follow me. But you have come too late." He gestured to the window. "Look. Even as we speak, the moon sets."

As I turned my head to gaze at the window, he thrust an outstretched finger in my direction. That was exactly what I had expected. I dived to the floor and rolled away as a bolt of green magic struck the chair, blasting a smoking hole in its back. I lunged forward, reaching out with my left hand—the hand that bore the sigil of the *gorkethal*.

However, before I could touch him, he shouted a fearful word of magic and rose into the air. Floating swiftly across the room, he landed and turned to me. I tried to scramble to my feet, slipped, and fell back to the floor. He splayed his fingers in my direction. My plan had failed.

"You didn't have to come here, you know," he said, his voice almost sad. "You could have lived your life."

"As a gelding?" I said quietly. "No, Zeth. It would have driven me mad. Just as it has you."

His sadness gave way to renewed rage. "I need you no

longer, Morhion Gen'dahar. There is no magic you possessed that I cannot now wield." Crimson sparks crackled around his outstretched fingers.

I gazed at Zeth in dread, knowing that this time there was no escaping his magic. Framed by the window behind him, the pale orb of the moon began to slip beneath the distant horizon. Instinctively I reached into the pocket of my doublet, as if to find the catalyst needed to cast a spell. But I knew no spells. All my hand found was a small, crumpled tube of straw. . . .

"You're wrong, Zeth," I said suddenly. "There is one magic of mine you have not mastered." From my pocket I pulled the woven straw tube I had bought from the street urchin. I tossed it at his feet. "Unlock the riddle of this magic, wizard!"

Zeth's eyes narrowed in suspicion, but it was clear my words had pricked his arrogance. Like a starving man presented with a banquet, this onetime gelding could not resist even the smallest morsel of magic. Banishing the deadly crimson sparks with a careless wave, he bent to pick up the straw tube. Frowning, he studied it. He inserted a finger in one end, probing within, then stuck a second finger into the other end of the tube. He snorted in disgust. "There is nothing to master in this."

I nodded solemnly. "If that is what you believe, Zeth, then it is indeed time to kill me."

A cruel sneer crossed his face. "As you wish."

Zeth lifted a hand to cast a spell. Caught as it was in the straw tube, the other hand followed. With a puzzled look, he tried to pull his fingers free. They did not budge. With a look of growing panic, he tugged harder. It was no use. He could not free his fingers from the trap. Staring at me in sudden terror, he tried to cast a spell. However, without the use of his fingers to trace the arcane patterns necessary, working magic was impossible.

Now was my chance. I leapt to my feet. Zeth tried to lunge away but stumbled, crashing into a bookcase. I grabbed his collar. Before he could squirm away, I pressed my left palm against his sweating forehead.

Again came a flash, and this time a vast rushing sound as

bright energy flowed into me. I stumbled backward, gasping. Every fiber of my body tingled with power. My magic had returned. Groaning, Zeth slumped to the floor. Branded now across his forehead was the sigil of the *gor-kethal*.

He raised his hands weakly, fingers still caught in the cheap finger trick. "There is no magic in this, is there?"

I shook my head. "No, Zeth. No magic at all." Now that I had defeated him, I found I could not hate the magic thief. His was a tortured soul. "Let me help you, Zeth," I said solemnly. "Maybe, working together, we can find you some peace with your fate."

For a moment, hope shone in his dark eyes. Then it was replaced by loathing, a hatred not directed toward me. "I said I don't want your pity," he snarled. "You think you've defeated me, but I still have won a victory. Now you will forever know that your power is flawed. I possessed all your magic, and yet you bested me with a mundane trick. It could happen to you just as easily. Let that knowledge gnaw at you for the rest of your wretched life, Morhion Gen'dahar!"

Too late, I saw what he intended. With a last, desperate cry, Zeth lunged to his feet and hurled his body through the window. He was dead before he struck the ground, slain by the magical aura that guarded the opening.

So passed Zeth, the *gor-kethal,* last of the magic thieves.

As I end this tale, I find myself gazing once more at the invitation Zeth left upon my doorstep. *I believe there is much we can gain from one another*, he had written.

Strangely, I know now that Zeth did give me something. He was right. My magic *is* flawed. I am not all-powerful. Yet he was wrong about one thing. That knowledge does not eat at my soul. For, as I learned in our final confrontation, sometimes there is weakness in power, and power in weakness. No longer am I so perfectly safe here in the fastness of my tower.

And by that I know that I am truly alive.

THE QUIET PLACE

Christie Golden

They were murderers, thieves, rapists; villains all. They
deserved to die at least three times over for their crimes.
But they were also men, and because the being who
watched them prepare for their slumber was not human,
he felt he could not pass proper judgment.

He waited patiently in the shadows, listening to their
stories of mayhem and cruelty. His blood, had it still
flowed warm in his veins, would have run cold at the tales
and the bragging tones in which they were told. At last,
with only one to watch—and he sitting a distance away
from the firelight—they fell asleep.

The vampire waited until his exquisitely sharp sense of
hearing picked up the sound of steady breathing; waited
for the telltale rise and fall of barrel chests. Then he came,
more silent than the shadows in which he had lurked.

In life, he had been a gold elf, a native of the fair, magical realm of Evermeet. His name was Jander Sunstar, and
unlike most of those who had been turned into undead, he
remembered compassion and fairness. He came, as
always, only to feed, to slake the unbearable thirst that
raged through his cold flesh. He did not come to kill. He
never did.

Jander's nose wrinkled at the scent of unwashed bodies, but beneath that sour stench came the sweet fragrance of hot blood pumping through living flesh. Jander's fangs started to emerge, and his mouth ached. He loathed his body's cry for the red fluid, hated that he could smell it, that he was incapable of resisting its hellish call. At least, he thought, I am kinder to my victims than these men were to theirs.

Jander bent over the first man, turned him gently with a soft touch of cold fingers, knelt, and bared his fangs. A slight nick, and the flesh of the neck yielded up its honey to the famished vampire. He was repelled by the sweaty taste of the man's skin, yet captivated by the sweet flavor of his blood. A few more swallows, and he was done.

He rose, moved softly to the next man. A few mouthfuls from each of the six who slept, and Jander would be sated while his victims suffered no lasting harm. Kneeling quietly, he again manipulated the man's head so that the neck was easily accessible.

But this one had drunk less than his fellow and awoke, disturbed even by the butterfly-soft touch of the elven vampire. He screamed, and the night's peace shattered.

Instantly the other men woke, alert and dangerous. Startled, Jander hesitated only an instant, but it was time enough for them to see the golden, tunic-clad shape, time enough to glimpse his face. He turned and fled, the cries of fear and anger from the six marauders echoing behind him.

He would have to slake his thirst elsewhere tonight, and the thought gave him no pleasure.

* * * * *

The third night after this misadventure, Jander gazed up at the moon. It was nearly full, its soft light caressing the trees and silvering the grass. Though he loved beautiful things, the moon's splendor did not cheer him. He knew that for the rest of his unnatural existence, he would see only the moon, never the sun; drink only blood, never wine.

A tear, bloody and crimson, escaped his eyes. "It was not my choice," he said softly, though there was no one to hear him as he stood alone in the moon-gilded meadow near Mistledale. "Is there no forgiveness, no mercy, anywhere?"

Only the soft sounds of a summer night greeted him, and they gave him no peace. He wanted quietness. He did not wish to have his heightened senses; they only reminded him of what he was.

His mouth ached, and he scented blood. Hare, deer, it didn't matter. They would all go to quench his abominable thirst. He wiped at his golden, angular face, erasing the mark of pain that had sat upon his cheek.

He walked as an elf. Not for Jander Sunstar the speed of the wolf or bat, not when it could be helped. So soft was his tread that his booted feet did not even disturb the dew on the grass as he followed the scent. He was not particularly hungry, so there was no hurry. The forest was dense, riddled with caves in which to sleep when the sun rose its beautiful, deadly, golden head.

Then, abruptly, the forest thinned. There came to the vampire's unnaturally sharp ears the sound of running water. Other than the normal threat posed to an undead creature by running water, there was no danger Jander could scent. Drawn by the water's laughter, a reminder of happier times, he stepped cautiously out of the wood's protection.

Ahead was a ring of huge, ancient oaks. There was no evidence of pruning or tilling, so the elf assumed the trees had naturally grown in such a circle. Though such things were rare, they were not unheard of. The clean smell of water reached his nostrils. The elf moved forward, thinking only to pause a moment by the stream that flowed through this peaceful place, to rest briefly before moving on. But then he heard the singing, and he froze where he was.

Elf? he thought to himself with a sudden deep ache. No, this voice was sweeter, purer even than any that issued from the throats of the Fair Folk. A nymph or naiad? He dismissed that thought as well, for such a creature would have sensed him as surely as he sensed her. She would have fled, he thought miserably, fled from the monstrously unnatural thing he had become.

The sweet, feminine voice continued singing, as pure as if the water itself had been given tongue. The loveliness of the song that graced his pointed ears drew Jander like a bee to a flower. He entered the circle formed by the mighty oaks, and saw her.

The spring bubbled up in the center of the circle, and the woman sitting on a boulder in the midst of the water was lovely beyond words. She was the singer, and as Jander watched, enraptured, she lifted her head, dark as the oaks themselves, and fixed him with a luminous gaze.

"Come forward, Jander Sunstar," she invited. "The sacred grove knows of your pain and your trials, and makes you welcome. The water waits to cleanse and revive you."

The vampire found words, he did not know how. "If the grove welcomes one such as myself, Lady, then the world has gone mad."

She smiled, and it made his heart ache. "Nay, vampire, the rules are being bent, that is all. A great heart may sometimes triumph over a great hurt."

She rose, and he saw she was clad in flowing green garb. It was almost like leaves, almost like water . . . "Come. Bathe, and accept the quietude of Eldath."

Eldath, the Quiet One, Goddess of Singing Waters! Jander's thoughts tumbled through his head. Running water over his dead flesh would kill him. Jander knew it. Yet what sweeter way to finally die, to know peace, than to bathe in the pool of Eldath! Surely the only way a holy place would permit him to enter would be in order to grant him his death. It was a death worth embracing, and Jander choked back a sob as he broke into a run, slowing as he approached the Quiet One.

"This," and she spread her arms, "is an oak grove sacred to Silvanus. The spring is sacred to me. The trees listen well and remember what they have heard. All across the Dalelands, they speak well of you, of he who fights his curse, who helps the hurt, who will not kill. The forest itself has guided you here."

Her large, soft eyes grew sorrowful as she continued. "I cannot take away your curse. I cannot bring you the sun again, for that is not within my domain. Yet within the confines of this grove, I can temper your grief and sorrow—quiet the call that haunts you. Will you accept my gift?"

Jander felt tears trickling down his cheek. He made no move to wipe away the telltale streaks of red; she knew who—what—he was. Knew, and forgave.

"Aye, Lady, with deep gratitude."

"Kneel first, and lave your face," she said. He obeyed. The water was cool and refreshing. He splashed some on his eyes and cheeks, washing the blood away but unable to stop the tears. Jander wiped at his face—and stared, stunned, at his gold palm that glistened with only water.

"They are salty still, but no longer of blood," Eldath murmured, suddenly sitting beside him. "Will you enter the spring?"

Not daring to believe, he did so, careless of what the water did to his boots and clothes and tools. Jander waited for the pain of death as the running water enveloped him. None came. What did come, softly and sweetly like a gentle dream, was a sense of deep peace. With soft fingers, Eldath, luminous in the moonlight, reached and touched his ears, nose, mouth, and shoulders.

"These ears are sharp, but they shall no longer hear with the ears of the bat. This nose is keen, but it shall no longer scent with the nose of the wolf. This mouth is hungry, but it shall no longer crave the taste of life. These shoulders are broad, but they shall no longer move with the strength of the *nosferatu*."

Suddenly, unexpectedly, she reached out both hands and pushed him under. Fear replaced joy as the waters closed over his wheat-gold head, and Jander struggled. If he had doubted her divinity before, he did so no longer, for her strength and her will were far beyond his power to resist.

With equal unexpectedness, the pressure keeping him under was gone. Jander shot to the surface. Eldath had vanished, leaving Jander desperately gasping for air. It took a few seconds before he realized the import of that simple fact.

He needed air. Dear gods, for the first time in nearly a hundred years, *he needed air!*

He laughed as he gasped, and struggled to the bank. He clambered out, wet and cold—*cold!*—and shivering. Jander continued to laugh between coughs, remembering the goddess's words. When he had caught his breath, he inhaled deeply through his nose. The fresh scent of a forest at night came to his ears; that was all. No scent of deer or squirrel; no smell or sound of living blood pumping through veins and arteries.

On an impulse, he reentered the spring, splashed his way to the boulder upon which the goddess had sat, and put his arms around it. Grunting, he tried to pick it up. He had lifted heavier things in days past, but now, his uncanny vampiric strength had gone. Shaking, he sank down into the water, making a slow way toward the bank.

She had done it. The blessed Eldath the Quiet, with the approval of Silvanus, the Lord of the Oaks, had taken away most of what it meant to be a vampire. Jander understood that he would never be able to leave the relatively small circle of protection provided by the grove. That was no hardship, not in exchange for what they had given him.

But the night was fading fast, and Eldath had warned him that she could not protect him from the ravaging rays of the sun. Dripping and shivering, the elf followed the circumference of the grove. He found the protection he needed; a cairn of boulders over a deep ditch in the earth. It would effectively shield him from that beautiful but deadly light.

The magical night began to grow lighter, and the vampire that had been, his heart light for the first time in decades, sought his rest.

* * * * *

Jander emerged at twilight, eager to begin his first full night without the dreadful thirst. He breathed deeply of the cool evening air, closing his eyes and enjoying it.

"Good even to you, friend!"

Startled, Jander whipped around. "Who calls me?" he asked, his customary defensiveness aroused.

But it was only a young man, clad in robes of earth-tones and forest green. His hair was as red as that of Sune Firehair, and freckles dotted his open, friendly face. Jander could not smell his blood at all.

"Oakbrother Endris, of Oakengrove Abbey." He indicated the two wooden buckets he carried. "I've come to get some water from the spring. And who might you be, friend?"

Sudden fear clutched at Jander's heart. "Don't send me away," he pleaded.

A shadow of puzzlement fell across Brother Endris's face. "Why would we do that?" He strode forward and began to draw water from the spring.

"I . . . I . . . " Jander floundered for words. "Oakbrother Endris, do you believe in miracles?"

Endris shot him an incredulous look. His blue eyes were wide. "And what kind of a priest would I be if I didn't?"

Jander felt suddenly embarrassed. "I meant no insult," he apologized. "But until last night, I had certainly ceased to hope for a miracle."

Jander relayed an edited version of what had transpired to him, leaving out the shame of his condition. He said he had been "absolved of a great evil," that he was "charged to remain within the circle as a symbol of his repentance." He expected to see disbelief or possibly even anger on Endris's countenance. Instead, the brother listened quietly. At last he spoke.

"Such is not unheard of here," he said quietly. "It would seem that Silvanus and Eldath must have work for you to do."

"But . . . I cannot leave the grove," said Jander. "What work could I do to earn my keep?"

"If the gods have taken you under their wing thus far, they'll make their wishes known soon enough. In the meantime," and he grinned like halfling, "you can help me draw the water."

Jander laughed, and gladly did so. He escorted Endris to the ring of the grove. "Thank you again for permitting me to stay here," he said.

"None of my doing," replied Endris cheerfully. "But it's good to see an elven face. Far too few folk come visit us these days. I look forward to speaking with you further, Jander Sunstar."

Silently, Jander was grateful that few folk visited the abbey. No doubt his name was being passed along rapidly among the Mistledale folk, ever since that incident a few months ago. . . . No. That was part of the past. This, he thought to himself, looking around the peaceful grove, was the future.

When Jander turned to walk back to the spring, he stumbled. He glanced down and found the discarded antlers of a deer that had passed through the grove, along with a few limbs that had fallen from the old trees.

And then he knew their meaning. "I understand," he said softly to the hush that filled the sacred place. Reverently, Jander picked up the items, seated himself on the boulder next to the spring, pulled out his knife and began to carve.

By dawn, when Endris returned for more water, Jander had accumulated three completed carvings. Smiling, he presented them to the astonished young oakbrother.

"They're . . . they're exquisite," Endris said softly, examining the two carved wooden likenesses of Eldath and the cluster of oak leaves and acorns Jander had created from the antlers.

"Have your oakfather bless them, and you can sell them as talismans," said Jander. "You can raise money for the abbey."

Endris lifted shining eyes to the vampire. "I told you the gods would let you know what they wanted from you. Thank you, Jander. Oakfather Raylen will be most appreciative. Oh, I almost forgot. I've got something for you, too."

He'd been carrying a large, bulky pack. Now he rummaged through it, humming in an off-key voice. "Ah, here we are." From the pack emerged a brown and green robe with a simple rope belt, some fruit, and a bottle of wine. "Anybody who has the favor of the gods like you do gets treated very well by the abbey." He grinned.

Jander's throat worked. "I . . . thank you, Oakbrother. Thank you." The words were inadequate, but they would have to do. They were all the surprised elf could manage.

The nights fell into a pattern for the next few weeks. Jander would talk with Endris at the beginning and the end of night, and carve during the rest of the time. He had been an adventurer for most of his days, and at first he feared that the quiet, the peace, and his inability to leave the confined space would wear upon him. But it did not. He had lived a long time as a breathing being, had existed for nearly a century as one of the undead. Now, he simply *was,* and that was more than enough. For long hours, as Jander carved in silence, he would meditate on the stillness that surrounded him, would think of events long past, of people long since crumbled to dust. And he would think with subdued joy to himself, *I do not need to feed upon blood!* And that thought made what some might call a strange exile into a paradise.

Endris, too, helped pass the time. He was a jovial fellow, and it seemed every other day he had a new joke to tell his friend. From him, Jander learned about the day-to-day events that occurred in Oakengrove Abbey, only a short walk away over a small green hill. Jander could even glimpse its stone walls when the branches moved in the wind. But as far as the vampire was concerned, the abbey might as well be as distant as Evermeet, for he would never move a single step closer to it.

One twilight, Jander waited longer than usual for the customary arrival of Endris. But the oakbrother did not come. The night wore on, and Jander became concerned.

It was then that he heard the bell tolling and saw the night sky lit up with an evil, orange hue.

Fire!

Jander's first impulse was to run and help. He almost reached the edge of the circle when he skidded to a halt. If he left, he would never be able to return. He hesitated, torn between his concern for his friend and his blessed peace. At last, angry with himself but seeing no alternative, Jander turned and went back to the spring, hoping miserably that his aid was not needed.

Shrieks pierced the night. Jander tensed. A fire was frightening, of course, but self-assured monks wouldn't panic and cry out in terror—would they?

"Please, Silvanus, protect your own," he murmured. His golden hands clenched and unclenched, reflecting the war that raged within him.

Abruptly, joining the shrieks of terror and pain, came the sound of raucous laughter. The vampire leapt up and raced to the limits of his sacred space, pacing like a caged panther. Unable to help himself, he cried aloud, "Endris? Anybody?"

"Jander!" The voice was weak but recognizable. It was Endris, and after a few seconds that seemed agonizingly long to the agitated elf, the oakbrother stumbled into view.

His face was covered with blood, and he cradled his left arm awkwardly. Jander, who had seen a hundred fights in his day, realized at once that it was broken.

Jander cringed, thinking he knew what Endris was about to say. The oakbrother had no idea—*could* have no idea—of the real depth of the evil that had haunted Jander Sunstar. He couldn't know that if Jander set one foot outside of the grove, the maddening bloodlust would return, that he would be driven to hunt and harm; that he would again become one of the undead. And Jander knew Endris was about to ask for aid. What would he say? What *could* he say?

He braced himself for the plea, but Endris's words shocked him—and moved him.

"Jander," gasped the young monk, "hide yourself! Marauders have come to the abbey. They posed as pilgrims, and once they were inside . . . they will surely slay you if they find you!"

"But," said Jander, "my help . . ."

"You are only one elf, with no weapon," Endris replied, wincing as pain racked him. "You cannot stand against six such as they!"

Jander began to feel a dreadful, sick feeling in the pit of his stomach. "Six?" he repeated. No, surely it could not be—there were many ruffians out in the woods. . . .

But he had no time to question further. From the direction of the burning abbey came a chorus of laughter and whooping. Endris turned horrified eyes on the four men who emerged from the shadows, cried once more, "Hide yourself!" and charged, weaponless, at his enemies.

It was perhaps the single bravest gesture Jander had ever witnessed in several centuries. For a moment he stared, dumbfounded. He recognized these men. They were the band of six killers upon whom he had attempted to feed a few weeks ago. He realized, with a dreadful shudder, that they had followed him. In all ignorance, he, Jander Sunstar, had led them to this place, had caused them to butcher the innocent priests, had given them the opportunity to defile the grove that succored him.

They were busy beating Endris. They did not bother using weapons; they could draw out the pleasure longer if they slew Endris with bare hands and skilful blows. The men, their faces burned into Jander's brain, had not seen him. Not yet. He could do as Endris had wished him to—hide in his protective cairn, wait out the storm, and emerge whole, sane, his soul still reprieved.

But that would mean letting Endris, and all the other good men who had shown him only kindness, die senseless, brutal deaths.

Tears stung Jander's eyes as his heart broke.

With a cry of mingled outrage and deepest grief, Jander charged the group of thieves and murderers. He transformed into a gold wolf as he left the protective circle, the quiet place, and felt the full weight of his curse resettle upon him. The red thirst raged, more powerful than he had ever known it. Strength flooded his limbs, and his rage knew satisfaction when the eyes of the nearest man fastened upon him and widened in horror.

The wolf's jaws crunched down, severing the throat. Blood flowed down Jander's chin, and he almost forgot his true purpose in the overwhelming desire to lap up the crimson fluid. By sheer strength of will, he turned away from the dead man, found another victim, and again launched himself at the man's throat.

Now it was the interlopers who screamed in fear. To terrify them further, Jander permitted himself to change back into his elven form. But no elf who breathed air looked like this; golden face covered with blood, long fangs extended, gray eyes snapping with fury.

Two were dead. The other two fled, but Jander outran them with ease. One he slew with his dagger; the other's neck was snapped with a single twist of one powerful, sharp-nailed hand.

Four were dead. That left two more, raiding and defiling and destroying inside the abbey. Jander tensed himself and prepared to run in that direction. A hoarse call from Endris brought him up sharply.

"Jander!"

The anger ebbed, to be replaced by fear. Others, knowing his true nature, had rejected him. What would Endris do? Slowly, the elven vampire turned around.

Endris had been badly beaten. Jander tasted a sudden fear that perhaps his intervention—his sacrifice—had not been in time. But the young man struggled to prop himself up on his good elbow, a bloody, broken hand reaching out for the vampire. Jander went to him. If Endris wished to spit in his face, he had the right to do so.

Endris coughed, struggled for breath. "You spoke . . . of evil . . . I did not know. Go back, Jander. You left . . . sanctuary for good cause . . . Go back in."

Hope flared suddenly in Jander's heart. Would Eldath and Silvanus indeed understand why he had rejected their greatest of gifts? Would they give him another chance? Endris's words gave him new resolve. As gently as he could, Jander slipped his arms beneath his friend's body.

"You need help," he said quietly when Endris protested. The young man, though strong and muscular, weighed next to nothing in Jander's grip, thanks to the return of his vampiric strength. Quickly, keeping his pace as rhythmic and steady as possible so as not to jar his friend, Jander ran toward the abbey. At the first few steps, Endris moaned and went limp in his arms. He was still breathing; he had merely fainted from the pain. Jander thought to himself that this was probably for the best.

He was met halfway by a crowd of angry brethren, brandishing powerful-looking canes. One or two of them were clad in the beautiful, oakleaf-shaped armor that was traditional among priests of Silvanus. When they saw the bloodied elf and the precious burden he bore, they at first thought him another marauder. One of them charged, staff at the ready.

"No, wait!" came a voice. From the back, a tall, thin man with white hair pushed his way forward. Jander guessed this was the oakfather, Raylen. "I believe it is Endris's friend, the elf who was granted sanctuary in the grove."

"Aye, Oakfather," said Jander. He held out Endris's limp form to the nearest priests, who gathered him carefully to them. "You need fear nothing more from four of the men who attacked Oakengrove. But there are two left—"

"We have dealt with them ourselves. They have been captured and await our decree." Raylen looked at him keenly. Even in this dim light, Jander could see perfectly well. The man's face was chiseled with the passing of the years, but it was clear that his mind was still as strong as the oaks that grew in the grove.

"The other four are . . . your doing?" Raylen asked quietly. Jander nodded.

"I left the grove to save Endris's life, and to protect your abbey. It was—a debt. I think perhaps that I unwittingly led these evil men to you. I needed to atone for that. Endris thinks I may be readmitted to the grove, because I left it for a good cause."

Raylen's wise eyes roamed Jander from head to toe, taking in the blood and the dishevelment. The light was too dim, thank the gods, for him to see Jander's fangs. When at last he met Jander's gaze, his face was sorrowful. He shook his head slowly. Jander's heart sank.

"But . . . Endris would have died . . . how could I not have helped him?" cried Jander.

"That you chose to do so shows me why Eldath gave you sanctuary in the first place—your heart is good, however dark your deeds may have been. It was wrong of Endris to give you false hope. Few get even one opportunity such as was granted to you, my friend. No one receives such blessing twice, whatever good deed they may have done. Take comfort that you have not sacrificed your haven in vain—Endris will live. So will others, who might have died but for your actions." He raised a wrinkled hand and moved as if to give Jander absolution.

The vampire ducked back quickly. His identity as an unholy thing would be revealed the moment Raylen began speaking sacred words. Without another word, he turned and fled, racing down the green, grassy hill toward the grove. He slowed as he approached, fear rising up to choke him.

"Please," was all he said as he stepped forward.

And winced in pain as he encountered the invisible barrier that weakened him at once, the intangible but very real obstruction that prevented evil things from entering sacred space. He stared at the place that only a few minutes ago had been a goddess-granted sanctuary. His gray eyes roamed hungrily over the boulder upon which he had sat, the half-finished carving that had fallen from his hands and now lay quietly on the cool grass.

Jander half-hoped Eldath would appear, so that he could speak with her, plead his case. But she did not, and as the long moments crept past, resignation slowly replaced grief in his heart.

He could have made no other choice. He knew that he could no more sit by and watch an innocent friend be murdered than he could become a priest himself. Had he done so, the grove would have been tainted by his cowardice. He would have grown to loathe it, as he loathed himself; and one day, as surely as the seasons turn, he would have left the quiet place with more bitterness in his heart than he felt at this moment.

Deliberately, Jander turned away and began to walk. Where, he did not know. Perhaps to Waterdeep, his original destination. The gods had tried to offer respite, but fate and Jander's own remnants of goodness had foiled that attempt at peace.

The acrid scent of smoke still filled his nostrils as he forced a deliberate breath; but there were no more leaping flames. The injured would be tended, the destruction repaired. Life would go on as usual in the abbey—and at least some small part of that was due to his actions.

His heart lifted slightly. Alone, friendless, with no hope offered and none to dream of, the elven vampire walked toward the east, a smile playing on his lips even as darkness and death haunted his footsteps.

He had done the right thing. And in the end, when all the scores were tallied and all the chips of fate put away, that deeper peace would be worth all the quiet places in the world.

THE EYE OF THE DRAGON

Ed Greenwood

Ambreene glanced irritably out the window as she hurried along the Hall of Clouds behind the politely insistent seneschal. Why did Grandmama Teshla want to see her just *now?*

The deliciously cool breeze that slid around Hawkwinter House was dying away. Waterdeep would soon be cloaked in a damp, clinging haze that played Tymora's happy dance with lightning spells. . . . Even if all the household slept, she'd dare not conjure a single spark. Awkward, unpracticed casting was all she could manage.

Another tenday would pass in endless palace promenades; dull tutoring sessions on the honorable and very *long* history of the Hawkwinters; and idle chatter with the empty-skulled high ladies who were her sisters' friends—if such a cold-hearted, scheming, petty lot of cat's claws could truly be deemed the friends of anyone. Another tenday would pass in which Ambreene Hawkwinter—one more society beauty in a city that teemed with superior young she-nobles—would work no magic of consequence.

Ambreene scowled at herself in a mirror as she hurried past. It would be *so* easy to just give in. She could banish to memory her secret sessions of sweating concentration and fearfully hissed spells, and just idle her days away, drifting inevitably into the boredom of marriage to the favorite lout, dandy, or stonehead of some noble family favored by the Hawkwinters. So gods-be-damnably *easy*. She tossed her head and glared at a startled servant as they turned into Teshla's Tower and began to climb the spiral stairs to the rooms Grandmama Hawkwinter never left.

That ease is why it must *never* happen, she vowed silently. I'll *not* become another wisp-headed cat's claw. I'll see Hawkwinter House hurled down into its own cesspools first!

The seneschal came to the door at the end of the worn red shimmerweave carpet and rang the graceful spiral of brass chimes that hung beside it. Unlatching the heavy door, he swung it wide, stepping smoothly back to usher Ambreene within.

The youngest daughter of the Hawkwinters strode past him with the absently confident air that made the servants privately call her the Little Lady Queen of All Waterdeep. She walked into the dim, quiet apartments that were all the kingdom the once-mighty dowager Lady Hawkwinter had left.

Priceless glowstone sculptures drifted in slow dances as she passed. Enchanted, shimmering paintings of flying elven hunts and dancing lords and ladies flourished their endless animations. A fascinated Ambreene was a good twenty paces into the luxurious chamber when she realized she was alone. There was no trace of the three elderly chamberladies who always lounged by the central bedchamber stair, waiting to be summoned up into Teshla's presence. Ambreene glided to a graceful halt amid the empty lounges, uncertain what to do.

An eye winked open in the smooth ivory sphere adorning one bottom stairpost, and a mouth appeared in the other, speaking in the familiar dry, waspish tones of Grandmama Teshla. "Come up, girl; I've not much time left."

A little chill arose inside Ambreene at that calm statement. Obediently she set foot on the curving stair. It was the summons she'd dreaded, come at last. She gathered her skirts and mounted the steps in haste.

She should have visited Grandmama more often, and stayed longer, despite the watchful, overscented old chamberladies with their vague, condescending comments and endless bright, cultured, empty phrases about the weather. She should have told Lady Teshla—who'd dabbled in dark and daring magic in her younger days, they said—about her own fumbling attempts to master magic. She should have . . .

Ambreene reached the head of the stairs and came to a shocked halt. Grandmama was quite alone, lying propped up on her pillows in bed. She must have sent the servants away and unbound her hair herself.

A soft-hued driftglobe hovered above the bed, and Ambreene could see that Lady Teshla was wearing a black robe whose arms were writhing, leaping flames of red silk—robes better suited to an evil seductress than the matron of one of the oldest, proudest houses in all Waterdeep. She looked *dangerous*, and the glint in her old, knowing eyes made that impression even stronger.

Ambreene swallowed. "Grandmama, I came as qui—"

"Quickly enough, it seems," the dry voice said, with just a hint of weariness. "I breathe yet. Stand not there quivering like an unschooled courtesan, girl, but come and give me a kiss—or you may yet be too late."

Numbly, Ambreene did as she was bid. The old arms trembled as they went around her, but the lips were as firm and imperious as ever. Ambreene looked into the black, bottomless pools of Grandmama's eyes—a falcon's eyes, her father had once called them—and said, "Grandmama, there's something I must tell you. I've been trying to—"

"Weave a few spells," Lady Teshla finished the sentence almost impatiently. "Do you think I don't know this, girl? What way does my favorite window face, now?"

Toward Ambreene's own bedchamber windows, of course, but . . .

"I'm glad you used the word 'trying.' A right mess you made of the darkshadow cloak," Teshla said dryly. "But you have all the grand gestures right, girl. *Some* young blade'll quake in his boots if he ever tries too much at a dance and you hurl the pig-face curse his way!"

Ambreene flushed in embarrassment—how had Grandmama, shut in this dim tower, seen *that*? She was sure she'd managed to restore the old war hound's rightful looks before his frightened yelps had . . .

The driftglobe swirled and drew her eyes—and suddenly its heart flashed into a view of distant Castle Waterdeep, from *above,* as if she were standing atop Mount Waterdeep looking down on it!

"That's how I see all," Teshla told her as the scene faded. "Touch the sphere."

Wonderingly, Ambreene did so. A tingling spread through her from her fingertips, and Teshla nodded approvingly.

"The globe will follow you, now. When you go, all can think I was just bestowing a little magic on my kin before I went to the arms of the gods—but *this* is why I summoned you."

A wrinkled hand moved with surprising speed, drawing up the fine chain that had gleamed down into Teshla's shrunken bodice for as long as Ambreene could remember—and bringing into view a delicate silvery metal dragon's head, in profile. Its single eye was a huge dark glossy gem of a sort Ambreene had never seen before in a lifetime of watching wealth drift languidly by at feasts and revels. She stared at it . . . and it seemed to stare back at her.

"What is it?" she whispered as Teshla drew the chain off over her head with arms once more slow and weary, and held it out.

"The Eye of the Dragon, child," Teshla said softly. "May it serve you better than it did me—and may you use it far more wisely than I did. Take it."

The youngest daughter of House Hawkwinter swallowed, and then lifted her head and calmly reached out for the gem. Teshla chuckled at the imperious manner, and then tilted her head to watch her descendant closely . . . almost warily.

In Ambreene's awed fingers, the gem seemed warm and alive—and weightless, as if it could float on its own. It held power, strong magic that Ambreene could *feel* through her entire body. She stared at it in amazement, and then looked up almost reluctantly.

"I-I never dreamed so precious a thing was in this house," she said wonderingly. "And to be *given* it . . . *Thank* you, Grandmama! All my thanks! I don't know how to say it well enough, but—"

"Know what it does before being so free and eager with your joy," Teshla cautioned her. "It is your true inheritance, for only a sorceress can use it. Keep it secret. No one else in this house knows of it . . . and it is a thing of great power."

Her dark eyes stared somberly into Ambreene's own. "Be warned, girl—learn its ways thoroughly, and use it only with great care, for it steals and stores memories, and can leave a man a hollow husk . . . as I learned, to my cost."

A frown playing about her brows, Ambreene stared at the old woman. Grandmama turning a man into a . . . husk? What man could she have been be so interested in—or who would even look at her? It must have been some reckless thief, come to the tallest tower of Hawkwinter House in hopes of stealing some baubles. . . .

"Speculate all you want," Teshla told her, as if reading her thoughts, "but waste not the breaths left to me in foolish questions of who and why. That is my own business, and you can learn the truth from the Eye after I am gone. But remember, and beware: it steals memory."

Ambreene had been about to put the chain over her own neck. She stopped abruptly, looked at the pendant as if it might bite her, and hurriedly slid it into the outermost pocket of her robes.

"Wise," Teshla said, falling back into her pillows. "Now that *that* is done, and . . ." Her eyes closed, and her voice trailed away.

Ambreene stared at her in alarm. "Grandmama?" she cried. "Gra—"

And then she heard the rattle of a drawn breath, and—

slowly and unsteadily—another. Grandmama still lived
. . . and yet, this would be her deathbed. Soon.

Ambreene stood silently by Lady Teshla's bed for a long
time, thinking furiously—and then whirled and left the
room, striding hard. The driftglobe sailed silently along in
her wake.

She was almost running when she swept past the
seneschal, ignoring his surprised look and murmured
question. She traversed the Hall of Clouds faster than the
old warrior had ever seen her move before; he had to trot
to keep up. Instead of storming into her rooms or bursting
into tears when her chambermaids rose to greet her, the
young lass turned abruptly aside to descend the back
stair to the stables, and thence to the gates.

The seneschal clattered after her, clutching his scabbard to keep it from tangling in his legs and sending him
into a headlong tumble. "Lady Ambreene!" he puffed, his
voice imperious. "This is most irregular! Your father said
nothing about your going out this day, and with the Great
Lady Teshla so nea—"

Ambreene did not bother to turn her head. "Did he *not?*
Well, go to him, and he shall tell you—but stand in my
path at your *peril!*" The lie came to her in an easy rush,
and she found herself quivering with excitement and
anger. *No one* was going to stop her, not even Lord
Piergeiron himself! Grandmama was her only real
friend—and Ambreene had no intention of losing such a
precious thing, whatever Teshla might think of the time
left to her. . . .

A few breaths ago, Ambreene Hawkwinter had been
powerless to do anything about Grandmama's slow wasting. But that was before the Eye of the Dragon had come
into her hand.

It was beautiful, yes—so beautiful!—and a thing of
power, besides. But what were those things, set against
the warmth and wisdom of Grandmama, there to laugh
with Ambreene, chide her, and teach her the ways of
spells and men and Waterdeep itself?

In all the city, men said, there was no mage as mighty
as Khelben Blackstaff. If he could make the dead live and

gods whole, he could surely restore one old woman! He would want this Eye of the Dragon, and doubtless do such a small and kind service in return for it.

Briefly Ambreene thought of how powerful the Eye might make her, and how slow her mastery of magic was sure to be without it . . . but no. Without Grandmama's direction and teaching, she might never learn to wield even the pendant, let alone spells of her own!

She strode down the street as folk stared at the speeding driftglobe and the red-faced old seneschal puffing along after her. A dozen smirking, hastily assembled Hawkwinter armsmen completed the train. Ambreene didn't care. She needed only her eyes to head for the dark and distant needle of Blackstaff Tower.

Every child in Waterdeep knew it; the home of a man whose spells were mighty enough to hurl back liches, mind flayers, and beholders all at once, and whose stern justice frightened even proud heads of the richest noble houses. Ambreene quailed inwardly as she marched along. But she was a Hawkwinter, on a truly noble mission—and Ambreene's name might well some day ring down the streets of Waterdeep as grandly as that of Khelben Arunsun. She lifted her chin and strode on without slowing . . . and behind her, the seneschal rolled his eyes and wheezed along. Fear was on his face as she passed into the shadow of Blackstaff Tower.

* * * * *

A single taper flickered in Ambreene's bedchamber as she shot the door bolt into place with steady hands. She hurried to the dusty space behind her wardrobe, where her few scraps of magic were hidden.

She almost made it. Two paces shy of her secret place, hot tears of rage and grief burst forth, blinding her. She blundered forward, sobbing, until she ran into the wardrobe's polished side and raised trembling fists to strike it, again and again, heedless of the pain.

Khelben had granted immediate audience, and hope had soared like a flame within her until the moment

Ambreene had given him her name. He looked at her gravely and uttered words that would burn in her brain forever: "Teshla Hawkwinter? No, child. Not that one. *She* knows why, and has accepted her death . . . and so must you."

That was all he would say, despite tearful pleadings. At last Ambreene rose from her knees, lifted her chin, turned in silence, and left, unheralded. Khelben didn't even *look up* from his papers as she went out!

She stumbled away, the seneschal and guards treading close around her but not daring to speak. At home, the folk were as white faced as she was, and silence reigned over Hawkwinter House, save for muffled weeping behind closed doors. The dowager Lady Teshla Hawkwinter was dead.

The priests of half a dozen temples murmured and chanted around the high-canopied bed. Ambreene wasn't even allowed in to see what was left of her Grandmama—sleeping forever now, a small and shrunken thing in the great spill of silken pillows—until the haughty strangers were done.

Her father was there. He said her name once, gently, and reached for her—but Ambreene stepped around him and looked upon the Lady Teshla alone and in silence. When she had turned to go, her father had signed to the servants not to follow, and for that gentle mercy she must remember to thank him when she could. But not now. Oh, not now.

She drew herself up in the darkness, her throat boiling with an anger that made her want to scream and rake herself and break things. She hissed in a voice that fought hoarsely through tears, "I will make you pay for her death, oh great grand Lord Mage Khelben Blackstaff Arunsun. Ambreene Hawkwinter will make you plead for aid as I pleaded . . . and I will show you the same mercy you showed *me*. This I *swear*."

Her last words seemed to echo around her, and Ambreene shivered suddenly and clung to the wardrobe for support. So this was what it felt like to swear a death oath. And against the most powerful archmage in all

Waterdeep, too. She sighed once, and then hurried to the door. She must get Grandmama's spellbooks and magic things before some maid spirited them away to make fair coin, and they were lost. The Lady Ambreene Hawkwinter had much work to do. . . .

* * * * *

A month later, Ambreene stood beside the wardrobe and looked at herself in her glass. A gaunt, hollow-eyed maid with white skin and dark, burning eyes gazed back at her. She knew the servants whispered that her wits had been touched by the Lady Teshla's death, but she cared not a whit.

Ambreene was almost ready. Mastery of all the spells in Teshla's books—*her* books, now—might take years, but the Eye of the Dragon shone openly on her breast, and at night quivered warmly against her skin, whispering to her in her dreams.

All too often the night visions it sent drifted away in smoky tatters, but when her will was strong enough to hold steady to them, they showed her how to command the pendant to take memories . . . and to yield its memories up, like the scenes acted out at revels.

As Grandmama had warned, the Eye could drink thoughts—and when she got the right chance, she'd use it on Khelben, to steal his magic. Then she *would* be a great sorceress, and he'd be left a shambling, slack-jawed idiot. A fitting fate, she thought . . . until that dark day when the pendant showed her why he'd refused to keep Grandmama alive.

Ambreene saw how it all had happened, saw it through the Eye.

Teshla had been a lush, dark beauty in her youth, all flashing eyes, flowing raven hair, full cruel lips . . . and a proud and amoral spirit. Many men longed for her, but she saw them as passing fancies to be duped into making her richer and more powerful. She professed undying love for one wizard—but in her bed, the Eye pressed between them by their bodies and her mouth entrapping his—she drained all Endairn's magic away, becoming a mage of power in one night.

With her newfound arts, she chained the emptied mage in a dark cellar, bound in spell-silence, and set forth to lure the most cunning merchant of the city to wed her.

Horthran Hawkwinter was rich indeed. She did not refuse his shower of coins, but it was his wits she truly wanted, his judgment of folk and knowledge of their pasts, schemes, alliances, and abilities. It was his wits she took on another night like the first, in the very bed he had given to her, the bed in which she was to die. The confused Horthran had been confined to his chambers from then on, visited by Teshla only when she wanted an heir, and then another child in case misfortune befell the first.

Ambreene shivered as the Eye showed her infant elders set aside in a nursery. Meanwhile, Teshla clawed and carved her subtle way to dominance, making the Hawkwinters a grand and respected house in Waterdeep.

She wept when the Eye showed a bored Teshla bringing together her husband and the mindless wizard and goading them into fighting each other for her amusement. They both died—sharing a look of heartfelt gratitude as they stared into each other's eyes and throttled each other.

That look troubled Teshla, even after she had the bodies burned and the ashes scattered at sea by a Hawkwinter ship. Eventually her nightmares about it frightened her servants so much that they called in the Lord Mage of Waterdeep. Khelben stripped away all her spellbooks and things of power except the Eye and left her alone in her turret room. The look he gave her as he departed haunted Teshla almost as much as the dying looks of Endairn and Horthran.

Over the long years, Teshla built up her magic again, scroll by scroll, her coins reaching where she could not, to win for her—often with bloodied blades—magic she dared not seek openly. Her son and heir, Eremoes, grew into a man of wisdom and justice under the best tutors the Hawkwinter coffers could buy. There came the day when he returned to Hawkwinter House with a new and beautiful wife, the sorceress Merilylee Caranthor of Athkatla.

Seeing her mother clearly in the memory-visions, Ambreene watched numbly as the Amnian woman sought Khelben's protection against the Eye. Cloaked in his spell, she tried to seize Teshla's magic for her own.

The sorcerous attack on Hawkwinter House left no trace of his beloved Merilylee, slew half his servants, and razed the upper floors of the family mansion. Eremoes always thought this destruction the work of a rival house, not the result of a sorcerous duel between his mother and his wife. A duel Teshla did not loose.

Ambreene wept as she saw herself shielded in her nursery by Teshla's spells. From the first, her Grandmama had chosen Ambreene to be her friend and sorcerous heir, and shaped her into the role coldly and calculatingly.

When she came to the end of the long, long years of memories the Eye had seen, Ambreene spent a tearful night on her knees. At last she rose, dry-eyed, Khelben's hated face still burning in her mind.

Why hadn't he stopped Grandmama? He was Lord Mage of Waterdeep, and had a duty. Why had he let Ambreene's mother be blasted to nothing, and the Hawkwinters groomed to Teshla's wishes? He knew her deeds and ambitions, and did nothing. What made him any better than Lady Teshla Hawkwinter?

Nothing. She was gone, leaving behind only spells, the Eye, and . . . shame. But he lived still, and had dismissed Ambreene without even a look, and let the house of Hawkwinter become what Teshla had twisted it into. And her father did not even know. . . .

That very morning Eremoes Hawkwinter had broken his mourning silence. To the palace and every grand house in the city, he had sent forth invitations to a grand feast. And they would come; Hawkwinter hospitality was legendary.

Khelben Arunsun's name was on one of those invitations . . . and he would be there. After Ambreene told the

Lady Laeral that she was thinking of studying magic and very much wanted to see the Lord Mage of Waterdeep at Hawkwinter House, Laeral would see that he attended.

Ambreene smiled slowly as she opened a spellbook. The feast was a tenday hence; she had little time to prepare herself to greet Khelben properly. She suspected it might not be all that easy to make an archmage kill himself.

* * * * *

The gate greetings were done, and the many-colored driftglobes she'd conjured (to her father's smiling approval) were becoming useful as dusk drew down. From a distance, across the dance floor, Ambreene smiled and waved at Laeral as the arriving Lord and Lady Mage of Waterdeep were welcomed by her father—and then allowed herself to be swept away into a chalantra by one more would-be suitor.

She'd scarcely recognized herself in the glass when the chamberladies had finished with her, but she could have resembled a sack of unwashed potatoes and still been nearly trampled by every younger noble son of the city. As the night wore on, Ambreene kept a smile firmly on her face and used magic to keep her hair up and her feet just a breath above the tiles. She wasn't nearly as weary and footsore as she should have been after moonrise, when she slipped away from a sweating Talag Ilvastarr and sought somewhere private.

Many couples had stolen away from the laughter, minstrelsy, and chatter to enjoy the beauty of the extensive gardens of Hawkwinter House. A part of Ambreene ached to be giggling and caressing the night away in the arms of a handsome young blade, but she had sworn an oath. It was perhaps the first time she had resolved to do something important with her life. Ambreene Hawkwinter would now keep her oaths. All her oaths.

She was alone in a room that was dark enough. A few gestures and a hissed word, and Ambreene's muscles shifted in the loose gown she'd chosen. It felt peculiar, this sliding and puffing, as she became fatter, her cheeks and chin chubby, her hair russet red. Now no suitor would recognize her as the highly desirable Hawkwinter heiress.

She smiled grimly into the darkness, and went in search of the Lord Mage of Waterdeep.

He was not on the dance floor, nor in any of the noisy, crowded antechambers that gave off it, where older nobles were busy loudly insulting each other, gossiping, gorging, and drinking themselves silly. Nor was he where Ambreene had expected to find him—the dim, smoky rooms on the floor above, where men who thought themselves wise and powerful muttered darkly about plots and trade treaties and the black days ahead for Waterdeep, and added new layers of refinements and pacts to the already labyrinthine entanglements of the city's intrigues.

Ambreene sent a seeking spell on a tour of the bed-chambers and servants' rooms. The magical probe left her blushing and her eyebrows raised . . . perhaps permanently. In one, she found Laeral and her father together—but they were only talking. Relieved at not having to add the Lady Mage of Waterdeep to the ranks of those she must destroy, Ambreene continued her search, but found no trace of Lord Khelben.

Finally, she sighted him far away across the moonlit gardens, speaking to a succession of young party guests idly strolling the grounds. Hmmph. Dispensing wizardly wisdom, no doubt. Ambreene's eyes narrowed, and she cast another spell. There was a sound like the faint jangle of harp strings, and then:

"Grand night, to be sure," someone who was not there said loudly in her ear, "but my gut's rolling like a ship being beached through breakers!"

"It's that wine," another, thinner voice replied. "If you *must* try to drink the Hawkwinter cellars dry all by yourself . . ."

Her spell was working, but where was Khelben's voice? Ambreene frowned and bent her will in the wizard's direction.

A third, cheerful voice said, "Fair even, Lor—" and then

stopped as if cut off by a knife.

Ambreene juggled the fading wisps of her first spell into life once more, and saw the man who must have spoken . . . a man in a half-cloak, purple hose, and a doublet of slashed golden silk . . . standing conversing with Khelben. Gods-be-damned . . . the wizard must have a spellshield up to prevent eavesdroppers from hearing what was said!

Her eyes narrowed. What words, at a party, could be so important that they must be hidden from all?

Then she had a sudden thought, and sent her clairaudience spell whirling back across Hawkwinter House to the private chamber where Eremoes and Laeral sat.

"Your service to the Harp is timely and enjoyable, as always," the Lady Mage was saying, "and I want you to know that it is not unappreciated or taken for granted, Lord."

Ambreene blinked. Her father a *Harper*? Gods above!

"I know that's not the case," her father replied, "but I must confess I had my own selfish reason for this gathering. . . ."

"And would this reason be your youngest daughter's growing mastery of magic?" Laeral asked smoothly.

"It would," Eremoes Hawkwinter said. "I know Blackstaff Tower always has more would-be apprentices than either you or Khelben have time for, but if you'd be willing to explore her powers . . . and, I confess, her thoughts and feelings; she's been more affected by my mother's death than her siblings or most folk her age would be . . . I'd be most grateful. I cannot hire the right tutor until I know her strengths and interests, and to query her directly would upset her, diminish me in her eyes, and yet fail to yield the truth."

"I can do that in the morning, if you'd like," Laeral said in kindly tones—and Ambreene shrieked in fear! Her prying spell collapsed.

She must act now! Once Laeral poked into her mind, she'd have no secrets left, and Khelben'd turn her into a frog or bookend or his *slave* while she was still whimpering under the Lady Mage's mindprobe. . . .

Trembling in haste, Ambreene shifted her form again. A young woman who was alluring indeed raced down the closest stair to the gardens, startling couples out of their embraces as she rushed past, and found the moonlight as quickly as she could.

The succession of Harper agents seemed to have finished their business with the Lord Mage of Waterdeep, and for one chilling moment Ambreene thought Khelben was gone from Hawkwinter House, and she'd missed her chance.

Then she caught sight of him in a far corner of the gardens, sitting alone on a bench in the bright moonlight. Pulling the Eye's chain off over her head, Ambreene held the pendant ready inside her sleeve, panted until she regained control of her breath, and then set off slowly toward her quarry.

This would be her only chance. To keep her oath, she must not fail now. Ambreene moved as quietly as she could without seeming to creep; if Khelben turned his head and saw her, she wanted to look alluring, not like a thief darting guiltily about.

He was stroking his chin as she drew near, and studying the bright belt of stars overhead as if they were telling him something.

"Well met, Lord Wizard," she said enticingly, when she was only a few paces away. She kept her voice low and rich and laced with laughter, like a seductive courtesan she'd once overheard at the palace entertaining a Calishite merchant. "Moonlight becomes thee."

"I believe that last line should be mine, lady," Khelben replied calmly, studying her with eyes that seemed to bore right through her magical disguise.

"I'm young yet," she returned lightly, "and still working on my scroll of blandishments and flirtations. All Waterdeep knows of your dedication to justice and your fidelity to the Lady Laeral, my lord, but I was wondering if you'd mind if a lass who prefers wits and maturity to the empty swaggering of young men practiced a line or two on you . . . and perhaps grew so bold . . ."

She leaned near, giving the Lord Mage of Waterdeep a spectacular view of the fine leaping-dragons lace that edged her bodice, and continued slowly and huskily, " . . . as to share a kiss with me? Something I'd remember fondly and privately, mind, not shout from the rooftops. . . ."

The Lord Mage regarded her. Something that was almost a smile seemed to play about his lips. "What precisely did you have in mind, O enthusiastic young lady?"

Ambreene let the fullness of her sleeve hold the Eye, and stretched forth that hand for Khelben to see. His gaze flicked from one of her empty, ringless hands to the other as she knelt, so that their eyes were level.

"I'm no disguised monster, only a lonely maid," she purred, staring invitingly and challengingly into his eyes, "and I'd very much like a kiss." She licked her lips and whispered, "I'll submit to whatever magic you want to use, to be sure I'm . . . safe."

The mage they called the Blackstaff raised an eyebrow. "And why go to all this trouble—possible humiliation and danger—just for one kiss from an old man?"

"I've heard what they say about wizards," she whispered, eyes bright.

Khelben looked swiftly around, as if to be sure that no one was watching, and then extended his arms. "Come, then, lass, and try whatever you're trying to do . . ."

Ambreene's eyes narrowed at his choice of words, but the opportunity was too good to pass up. Opening her mouth hungrily, she glided into his embrace—and then twisted in his arms, whipping the pendant out and around his neck like a striking snake. The Eye of the Dragon flashed as she snarled, "Take his memories! Take them *all!* And give them to me!"

The chain tightened cruelly around the mage's throat, but he only pulled her closer and growled, "You wanted a kiss, remember?"

His lips were warm, but Ambreene shook her head violently and tried to bite him. When her mouth was free, she spat in his face and hissed, "Plead! Plead for your magic, archmage!"

She jerked the chain tight across Khelben's windpipe. He did not turn the purple hue she expected, but only smiled faintly.

"Don't you know what this is?" she snarled, tugging on the chain again.

The wizard nodded. "The Eye of the Dragon," he said calmly. "It's been years, lass, since I've seen it. Well, well . . ."

"Years?" Ambreene could barely get the word out through lips that were suddenly twisting and slipping. . . . Her face and body were sliding back into their true shape!

The craggy, bearded face so close to hers was melting and shifting too. When Ambreene saw what it became, the color fled from her face and her teeth began to chatter in terror.

She'd seen the Old Mage of Shadowdale only once, but the wizard they called Elminster was unmistakable. He grinned at her. "If ye'd live a little longer, lass," he said gently, "never try to bosom thy way up to the real Khelben. He's not that trusting, know ye . . . after all, he's had several centuries of comely wenches trying that sort of thing on him, and most of them were his apprentices."

"But . . . how . . . ?"

"Khelben had to hurry back to Blackstaff Tower on some Harper business begun here tonight," the Old Mage explained. "Both he and Laeral felt your probing spells—really, lass, take a little more care with such things, eh?—so he called me in to do a little impersonation in case other Harpers came to report . . . or ye decided to do something spectacularly stupid."

"And was what I did so stupid?" Ambreene asked with menacing softness, her hands twisting the chain until it cut deep into his throat.

Elminster smiled unconcernedly, and chucked her under the chin as if she was a small girl. "Well, 'twas certainly spectacular . . ." he murmured. "*I* wouldn't wear a gown like that."

He bent his head to her bodice and peered. "Ah, leaping dragons . . . Thayan work; very nice . . ."

Ambreene thrust herself against him, hooking her legs around his and pressing as much of herself to Elminster's body as she possibly could. She put her head over his shoulder and dug her chin down with bruising force, holding him with all the strength in her quivering body.

"Now," she said into his ear, "any harmful spell you work on me will hurt you as well. Khelben wronged my Grandmama and my family; my revenge was for him. But your magic will serve me just as well, giving me spells enough to destroy him another way . . . can you feel the memories leaving you?"

"No," Elminster said lightly. "I know how to make the Eye work as its creator intended it to. I'm giving ye only the memories I want ye to have . . . and keeping them, not letting them drain away."

Ambreene favored him with a disbelieving sneer. "And just how can you do that? Lady Teshla could not, and the Eye hasn't shown *me* any way to wield it thus! What makes *you* such an expert?"

Mirth glinted in Elminster's eyes as he said mildly, "Why, lass, I created the thing in the first place. In Myth Drannor, 'twas . . . in my spare time."

Ambreene shook her head derisively, but said nothing. He was so *calm* . . . what if it were true?

And then she gasped and stiffened as the world around her vanished in a flood of memories that were not her own. Images as vivid as if they were befalling here and now and she were living them. . . . She was dimly aware that her nails were raking someone's back, that he was growling in protest, and that there was a sudden strong smell of pipesmoke, but . . .

She was standing on the deck of a storm-tossed ship, watching as a grandly robed man turned his back on his son—who laughed and hurled a bolt of lightning with both hands. The blast cut his father's body in two from top to bottom and sent the front of the ship boiling up into flames. . . .

Then she was in a bedchamber where a sword pinned a man to a door, his lifeblood spreading on the floor. He gasped, "Why, Maruel? Why have you done this?"

"Because I want to," the breathtakingly beautiful woman on the bed said with a sneer that matched Ambreene's best. "And because at last I have the power to. I am the Shadowsil, and from now on I will *take* what I want . . . not beg for it!" She waved a casual hand, and by itself the long blade obediently slid out of the man, all black with his blood. He crumpled to the floor, gasping, "But I loved . . . you."

"And what is that to me, fool?" she laughed. . . .

The scene whirled away, and Ambreene was somewhere else again. . . .

A tower, where a woman wept, smoke curling away from her empty hands and ashes all around her. Nearby, a man who sat on empty air said, "And so your trick has turned to visit itself on thee. Well done, Alatha—oh, well done indeed!"

The woman's raw howl of grief whirled Ambreene away into a scene of a sorceress betraying her tutor, then another, of an ambitious magistress turning to evil and mistakenly slaying the man she loved. . . .

"All of these happened, lass, and I was there to see them," Elminster told her gently. "Have ye such a hunger to join them?"

Ambreene wept and tried to pull away from him, shaking her head and straining to think of things she chose . . . but her thoughts were dragged ruthlessly back into the whirlwind of revenge and grief and evil. . . .

"Gods! Oh, gods, *stop!* Have mercy!" she sobbed.

"Better mercy than ye intended to show Khelben, I hope," the Old Mage said grimly, and abruptly she was seeing a young lass clad only in long, luxurious hair, who knelt amid glowing, floating symbols, in a chamber whose dark walls winked with stars.

"Who . . . ?"

"A lady in Myth Drannor, crafting the first foresight spell," Elminster replied.

Abruptly, the spell poured into Ambreene's own mind, writing itself in runes and whirling concepts of fire. She gasped and moaned as her mind stretched dizzily. A bright light seemed to be rushing through her, and . . .

"Note that this magic allows thee only to see what lies ahead for others. If thy mind can encompass it and ye stay sane, 'twill become thy most useful tool—and thy greatest burden," Elminster said as she blinked and saw his face again in the moonlight, inches from her own.

Gentle hands put the Eye of the Dragon into her hands. "Now . . . about that kiss . . ."

Ambreene seemed to be weeping again as warm lips brushed hers tenderly, and that old, wise voice said, "Thanks for the memories."

Then the old wizard turned away in the moonlight. She stared after him with eyes that streamed the tears of a thousand years. Elminster strode across the garden, and as he went, his battered boots left the dewy grass and trod on air. Up on emptiness he walked, as if the starry sky was his own private staircase. Up over the garden wall he went, and on, over the rooftops of the city.

When she could see him no more, Ambreene looked down at the pendant in her hands. Suddenly it spoke with Elminster's voice, and she nearly flung it down in startlement.

"Ah, lass," it said, "be not downcast, for ye heard aright what they say about wizards. Put this on whenever ye need to talk to me . . . or to Khelben. He's waiting for ye to come and see him."

Ambreene stared up at the starlight for a very long time, too dazed to shed more tears, as still and silent as one of the nearby statues.

So it was that the young, softly chuckling couple strolled right past without noticing her. Ambreene knew the lass—Berentha Manthar, a shy noble maid of her own age, whom she'd smiled with at several feasts, heiress of House Manthar since the hunting death of her brother Carn—and almost stirred to speak a greeting. But as the thought struck her, Berentha's young and devastatingly handsome man, Ferentar from Amn, asked huskily, "So, Berentha, as Selune is our witness here this night . . . will you wed me, and cleave to me all your days?"

Ambreene swallowed as she looked expectantly at Berentha's half-hidden face. She felt a tingling within her, and the need to know the truth that lurked behind honeyed words overcame everything. She seized on the foresight tingling within her.

It was a strange thing to wield, but she conquered it in time to know that Berentha meant it with all her heart when she replied softly, "I will . . . oh, Ferentar, I will! Do you promise, too, before Selune and all the watching gods, to be true to me?"

"Of course I do, beloved Berentha," the young man said softly.

The chill that almost choked Ambreene left her trembling helplessly. Her foresight told her that Ferentar wanted to be Lord Manthar, with a dashing fur cloak and coins to spare on wine and dancers. He cared little for this stupid wide-eyed Waterdhavian cow gazing so ardently up at him—oh, she was pretty enough, but . . .

Ambreene wanted to scream out a warning and thrust them apart forever—but the cursed foresight rolled on. She saw herself doing that, and Berentha's face freezing into that of a bitter foe . . . and the wedding day coming anyway, and then Lord Ferentar Manthar whispering at parties in all the high houses that Ambreene Hawkwinter was a wanton sorceress who'd tried to seduce him to gain House Manthar's riches for her own. Then she saw him laughing in satisfaction as he pushed Berentha over a benighted balcony to her death, and turning in anger to the masked lords to demand Ambreene Hawkwinter's arrest for the spell-slaying of the Lady Berentha Manthar . . . and then Ferentar's face seemed to melt into that of Grandmama Teshla, and she heard herself screaming, "Khelben! Lord Khelben! *Help me!*"

Strong arms were suddenly around her, and the gruff voice of Khelben Blackstaff said into her ear, "I'm here, lass—stand back, young Ferentar, or I'll turn out the cesspit of your mind for all Waterdeep to see!—I'm here." Ambreene turned her face toward the comfort of that voice, and as she heard a gasp of outrage that could only be Berentha, Faerûn spun crazily around her—and plunged into darkness. . . .

* * * * *

She awoke in Blackstaff Tower, with Laeral's gentle hands holding out a mug of steaming rose tea. And from that day until the morning the gods willed that Ambreene Hawkwinter die, long years later, the Eye of the Dragon never left her breast.

EVERY DOG HIS DAY

Dave Gross

King ran far ahead of me, pelting down the busy street
in Raven's Bluff with the uncanny canine knack for navi-
gating through a forest of human legs. I chased after him
as well as I could, hindered by sharp elbows and stern rep-
rimands from adults willing to forgive a running dog, but
not a running boy.

"Ruh!" called King. Voices from the crowd answered
him as I tried to push toward him.

"King! There's a good boy."

"What a good dog!"

Everyone knew and liked King, one of the masterless
street dogs of the city. Everyone had stories of the remarkable feats the old terrier had performed: saving drowning
children, foiling pickpockets, tracking down criminals. . . .
This time I was the one who needed his help. My sister,
Dauna, was in the hands of kidnappers, and King was the
only one besides me who had seen them.

"King! Where are you?" I shouted. Scanning the street, I
spotted King's wake, a wave of turned heads and quick
sidesteps.

"Ruh, ruh!" His rough voice came through the open door
of a little cottage. The building looked out of place next to

the straight lines of the shops and taverns on Wicker Street. A carved board next to the door read, "The Barley Bowl."

"Ruh, ruh!" he called again.

Then I heard a piteous sound: King's whining. I'd heard the old, gray terrier growl at bullies, woof amiably to his friends, and even yap like a puppy when chasing the other street dogs. But I'd never heard him whine in pain. It made my heart shrink, and I almost began to cry again. Instead, I wiped my blurry eyes and entered the inn.

Inside, a dozen people sat at simple tables, their dinners in wooden bowls before them. At the feet of one man, the oldest man I'd ever seen, sat King.

The old man held King's head with long, thin hands. Bright eyes peered into the dog's face. "Oh, you got a snootful, all right. What scoundrel played dirty with you?" The old man's voice was sweet and tremulous as a minstrel's hautboy.

"The oldest man I'd ever seen" had a beard as white and fine as a swan's wing. Upon his narrow frame he wore a faded blue robe cut in the fashion of the court of thirty years ago. The badge upon his breast looked impressive and official.

"Here, lad. Hold his head." I stared a moment before realizing he was talking to me. "Come along. If you were standing in cement, you'd be a lamp post now!"

"Good boy," I said to King, kneeling by him.

"Good boy," the old man said to me. If I weren't already so upset, I might have been offended. "Hold him while I administer the Universal Solvent."

A potion, I thought! After escaping, then chasing, and finally losing track of the men who took Dauna, we had found a wizard to help us. Wizards are often ornery, but once he had ensorcelled the pepper out of King's eyes and nose, I'd ask him a boon, and he would help save my sister.

But instead of producing some glimmering phial of magical fluid, the old man took his cup of water and gently poured it across King's weepy eyes. King balked, but I held him tight.

"There, my old friend. That should take the sting away.

Nothing like a little rain to clear out the gutters." King whimpered once more, this time less pathetically. He nuzzled the old man's hand.

"But you said 'Universal Solvent,' " I protested. "I thought you were a wizard." I knew it was wise to be polite to wizards, but my disappointment was quicker than my wits.

"And what's that, but water? Any mason worth his sand will tell you that. And I've been a wizard and a mason for longer than . . ." He drifted off, and his mouth worked wordlessly as he thought about it.

"I've run out of things to compare to my age," he decided. "Except perhaps for King."

"Are you King's master?" I asked.

"Oh, no. King's his own master. We're old, old friends. As you count in dog years, we're nearly cohorts." He chuckled, then sobered, as if the thought at first cheered, then saddened him. "Two old dogs of the city," he sighed.

"If you *are* a wizard, then you must help us. King tried to help me, but when the kidnappers went over the fence with Dauna, one threw pepper at him. Then . . ."

"Wait! Back to your drawing, boy."

"My what?"

"You can't build a house without a drawing," he said. "And you can't crave a favor without an introduction."

"Oh! I'm Jame."

"And I'm Ambassador Carrague. Well met, young Jame."

"Carrague! They said you died!" Father had read the obituary aloud from the *Trumpeter,* then griped about who would replace Carrague as city building inspector.

"Dead? Pish posh. Those fools couldn't tell the difference between a corpse and a handsaw. Merely sleeping! Good thing I woke before they'd boxed me up. Eh?" King nosed Carrague's leg impatiently.

"Ah, yes, yes. Dauna's been kidnapped, has she? Who is this Dauna?"

"Dauna's my sister. They tried to get me, too. But I was playing in the street, and King ran up barking when he saw them carrying her. That scared them off, but they held on to Dauna. King and I chased them."

"Why would someone kidnap her?"

"We're rich," I explained. "They want my father's money."

"Have your parents alerted the watch?"

"Father's returning from Sembia with silks and wine for sale. He won't be home for days. Mother died years ago. And Chesley—our steward—he doesn't believe anything I say! He thinks I'm just telling stories again. But King saw it all, and we nearly caught the kidnappers."

"But now they've given you the slip, eh?"

"Yes," I replied sadly. King growled in affirmation. "If I'd been faster, I could have seen where they went. But by the time King got under the fence and I climbed over, they were gone. King couldn't find their trail with his nose full of pepper."

"I daresay not. Even King has his limits." King looked up defensively at Carrague. "Now, now. There are just some things you're better built to do, King." The terrier looked miserable.

"If King were a man, he could have climbed that fence in no time. Then we'd have saved Dauna."

King's gaze turned to me, his red and weary eyes large and full wounded by my remark. His jaw dropped in a remarkably human expression of astonishment at a sudden attack from a friend.

"Oh, I didn't mean it that way, King. No man could have picked up their trail the way you did. You did the best you could, for a dog." King crossed his front paws and laid his head down with a whimper. I knew I'd said the wrong thing again. Something about King made you feel he understood your words, not just your tone.

"You don't know King's secret, then. Do you, Jame?"

"I know he's the smartest dog in Raven's Bluff! Why, he's saved people from drowning, foiled robbers and killers, too, and . . ." Now that I thought about it, even the smartest dog in the world couldn't do half the things King did.

"Oh, all that's true enough. But it's only the facade. There's a deeper story underneath. King's foundation, as it were."

"What's that?"

"Better to show you. That is, if King doesn't mind my telling his secret." Carrague looked down, as if expecting an answer. "It could be a way to help Jame's sister," he prompted.

Lifting his head, King looked at each of us in turn. He sat up with an air of a judge deliberating on a man's life, his whiskered mouth thin and tight. Carrague returned the look, a bit of the caprice gone from his own gray face. They looked at each other a long time, the old dog and the old wizard. Then King made a very human nod.

"To my office, boys." Carrague lifted his stick like a general directing his troops. "To my office."

* * * * *

The Ministry of Art—the home of the city's most powerful wizards—stood well down the road from the mayor's palace. "Afraid we might blast a hole in the castle," complained Carrague. "Ridiculous notion. We're not mere apprentices. There's hardly ever an explosion."

With this and other remarks, Carrague had me terrified of the place before we arrived. It looked grand, ornate, well guarded, and thoroughly daunting.

"Your office is here?"

"Yes, yes. They moved me here when they realized I hadn't died. But they gave my job away. Just like that!" He snapped his fingers. "And that ridiculous gnome they hired! Ah! Ah!" The old man shook his walking stick, began to stumble, then caught himself with it once more.

Carrague gripped the railing as we ascended the marble steps. The guards let us past, though one gave me a questioning glance. King barked a friendly greeting, and the guard winked back. *Everyone* knew King.

Carrague rested a moment from the short ascent. Wizard or no, he was an old, old man. I wanted to offer help, but I feared he wouldn't like that.

A rich red carpet ran far down the hall, and colorful tapestries rose into the gloom of the high ceiling. We walked slowly past woven griffins and leviathans, unicorns and sprites, airships and painted soldiers—all fantastical things I'd never seen for myself. Carrague barely noticed them, since he must have seen even more wondrous sights in his life. I caught myself gazing at them in awe and wistfulness. Then I guiltily remembered our reason for being here.

"What are you going to do to rescue Dauna?" I asked.

"Why nothing. It's King who'll rescue her. He's the hero. I'm the wizard. And you're the boy, so watch more and talk less."

We had stopped by one of the many doors that lined the hall. Carrague's symbol marked the door. He spoke a word that I couldn't remember two seconds after he'd spoken it, and the door opened.

The whole world was stuffed into that office. I guessed you could search for months through there and find one of anything you'd ever want. I expected stuffed owls, unicorn horn and pixie wing in glass jars, bubbling beakers, and roiling cauldrons—and there was some of that there. But there were also feathered masks, jeweled statues, framed paintings, and enough furniture for ten houses. There stood the bust of a man I dimly recognized as a king across the Sea of Fallen Stars. From the ceiling hung a pair of thin wings on a wooden skeleton, and under a huge oak table moved something that kept just out of sight each time I stared at it. In a large glass globe swirled green seaweed, through which a tiny manlike figure peered at us. A parrot flew down from the window to light on King's back, until the terrier snapped at it and sent it flying back to its perch.

"Damn that woman anyway," cursed Carrague. "She's cleaned while I was away!" I looked at King, and he at me. Neither of us could see any signs of cleaning.

"I need the willow wand and the purple dust of Raurin." He opened the drawers on a big desk that served as a laundry table rather than a writing board. "No, no. That's not right. It's the yellow dust of the doppleganger we need." He turned his attention to a cabinet. "Here," he said after six slams of the tiny drawers. He held up a small black pouch. "The yellow dust."

Carrague looked all around, then finally slapped a wand at his belt. "Ah, had it with me all the time. Now to business." King already sat in the one chair clear of any obstruction. "Are you ready, old friend?"

King made that same human nod.

"Ready for what?" I asked. "What are you going to do to him?"

"*Undo* to him. I will change him back to his original self."

"His original self?"

"Rote learning is useful for clerks, my boy." Carrague rapped the wand smartly on my hand. "But we're dealing with wizardry here. Real magic. Don't repeat what I say."

"What do you mean by King's original self?" I hoped the question was different enough to avoid another rapping, but I kept my hands behind my back just in case.

"Why, his self before he was turned into a dog."

"Turned into a . . ." I stopped myself just in time. "What was he before?" I looked at King carefully for a clue. His eyes were bright and intelligent, but so were those of many dogs. Could he be a dragon hiding as a dog? Or could he be . . .

"A man, of course. A hero, in fact." Carrague untied the black pouch and began sifting yellow dust over King's silvery coat. King shook himself and looked at the wizard reproachfully.

"Now be still, King." Carrague continued with his dusting, and King endured it stoically.

"If King used to be a man, why didn't you change him back years ago?"

Carrague whirled around to point at me, yellow dust spilling down to form a half-circle around him. "Now *that* is the first intelligent question you've asked." King woofed in agreement or impatience.

"He never asked before," answered Carrague plainly.

"Woof!" interjected King, scratching at the dust in his fur. He clearly wanted to be done with whatever magic Carrague promised to cast.

"Patience, King," chided Carrague. "If the lad's to learn anything, there's a matter of history to relate."

"Ruh!" disagreed King.

"You're right. We are in a hurry, since Dauna's in danger," conceded Carrague.

"You can *understand* him?" I asked, astonished.

"No better nor worse than you could, if you listened carefully," said the wizard. "The abbreviated story is that King, while still a man, offended a witch. She killed his companions but turned him into a dog, as you can see. Luckily for him, he escaped and came to Raven's Bluff, where he's become the most famous hero of the city, man or dog.

"And now, King," the ambassador said gravely. "Is this what you want? Shall I turn you back into a man so you can rescue young Jame's sister?"

King's nod never seemed so utterly human as now.

Carrague nodded back at him. "Very well," said the wizard.

Then Carrague raised the willow wand and spoke some more of those words that won't stick in memory. I braced myself for a flash of light, some thunder, maybe even a howling wind that would toss about the contents of the room (which, I reasoned, would explain their current state). King just sat there under Carrague's chanting and wand-waving, patiently awaiting the transformation.

But nothing happened.

"Nothing happened," I pointed out helpfully.

"No?" Carrague frowned at the wand. "Hmm. Maybe it was supposed to be the green powder of shapechanging," he mused.

King growled, then opened his mouth wide.

"Yaah," King yawned. Then he sat up suddenly, his front paws held out before him daintily, as if they were wounded. They began to swell, and his whole body stretched with a rubbery, creaking sound.

"Oh, my," said Carrague. He stood back from King and his chair. I followed his lead.

King's snout retracted, and all the hair on his face sank back into his flesh. His ears slid down either side of his head like sails vanishing over the horizon. His awful yawning whine grew deeper and louder.

"Rraaii!" he howled, then roared as his voice changed.

Fingers flexed where claws had been, and his broadening back bent forward in pain or ecstasy. I grimaced and shut my eyes, only to open them immediately. The sight was horrible, yet fascinating.

A naked man sat where King had been. His unruly hair gleamed silver as the dog's coat had been, and he had the same, large, intelligent eyes. While he remained muscular and fit, his skin was thin as old parchment. Though not as ancient as Carrague, King was still an old man. He squinted at us.

"*That* is why I never asked you to do this before," croaked King. "It hurt even worse the first time."

Carrague only nodded.

* * * * *

Carrague easily found clothes for King; he conjured them. If I had any lingering doubts about his wizardry, they vanished when he flourished his fingers, speaking both the arcane words of Art and some mundane descriptions of fabric, color, and size. A variegated aura appeared, then darkened and shrank to form real fibers in the air. Faster than spider legs, Carrague's fingers wove them into breeches and tunic, boots and cap.

King fetched up a sword from Carrague's cane rack, hefted it, then grunted his approval. "It feels good to hold a sword again," he pronounced. His voice rumbled, rich and pleasant.

"Now don't run off to fight first," warned Carrague. "You have the power of speech again, and that's no mean tool. You'll need more than a blade to prevail against kidnappers."

"Believe me," said King. "I've lived long enough without a sword to know how to use my wits. You've got to do a lot of thinking when you're a dog in a city of men."

Carrague nodded, then peered at his cloak rack and plucked off a small green cap and handed it to me. "That looks about your size, boy. Try it on." I tugged it onto my head.

"It's tight," I said. Carrague smiled at me, but King's

mouth opened as wide as I'd ever seen it when he was a dog. He looked a quick question at Carrague.

"Pixwhistle's cap of invisibility," said the ambassador proudly.

"What?" I looked down at my arms. They were plenty visible to me. "I am not invisible."

King nodded at me, then sniffed. "You're invisible all right. I can't even smell you."

"Actually, you probably couldn't smell him unless you were very close," said Carrague. "Your nose isn't the fine instrument it was."

I looked around for a mirror while the two old men discussed olfactory, auditory, gustatory, and a few other -ory functions that didn't interest me. After elbowing past some mannequins and digging through baskets and bins, I unearthed a full-length mirror framed in carved oak.

"Hey, I'm invisible!" I exclaimed. I took off the hat. "I'm visible again!" While King's transformation and the conjuration of his clothing was more spectacular, this particular magic was much more personal. It worked on *me*.

Carrague and King finished their discussion and turned to me. "It's time to find Dauna," said Carrague.

"Let's start with the servants at your house," said King.

* * * * *

"Oh, Master Jame! We were so worried!"

Betha charged through the kitchen, grabbing me up in meaty arms better suited to butchering livestock than hugging children. I don't think I've ever fully recovered from those crushing embraces. At least it was Betha, and not Chesley.

I had just enough breath left to tell my story again. "I'm fine, Betha. But Dauna's been kidnapped. Oof!" She squeezed me again. "And I *mean* it. It isn't just a story, like Chesley says. King saw them, too."

"Oh, we know, dear boy. We know." She hugged me again, and that was the last I could speak for a while.

"Mistress Betha, I'm here to investigate Dauna's kidnapping."

"And by whose authority are you here, sir?" Chesley appeared from the dining room. He was all narrow lines and livery. Our family didn't have a livery, but Chesley insisted on wearing one all the same. Livery and uniforms were as important to him as protocol and etiquette.

"I serve Ambassador Carrague, of the Ministry of Art," said King proudly. He raised his chin. If he had been a dog, his hackles would have risen. I couldn't blame him.

"I'm afraid I don't understand why the Ministry of Art is involved in a matter for the watch," sniffed Chesley.

"I was at hand," sniffed King. Unlike Chesley, though, he was really sniffing. He walked right up to Chesley and kept on sniffing, leaning forward to get a good whiff. Chesley was unprepared for that.

"Wha-Whatever are you doing?" stammered the steward.

If I'd had any breath left, I'd have lost it all again in laughter.

"Where were you when Dauna was kidnapped?" demanded King. Chesley wasn't used to having the tables turned in that direction.

"Why, I—why, I was at market."

"Then why in the world did you send me to market this morning?" demanded Betha indignantly. "I could have finished all that washing you insisted on having this afternoon."

King kept sniffing at Chesley, moving down from his thinning hair to his narrow shoulders, and farther down. "Well?" said King.

"As if it matters!" protested Chesley, pushing away at King, who seemed oblivious to the impropriety of his own behavior. "If you must know, I had to replace a bottle of the master's wine, which I had carelessly broken this morning."

"Hmm," said King.

"Hmm?" said Chesley.

"I don't smell any wine on you."

"Of course you don't, you nonsensical fool! I changed clothes."

"Doesn't matter," said King.

"Don't be ridiculous," protested Chesley.

Even I knew something was wrong, now.

"And you're afraid of these questions. You're sweating fear."

"I've had quite enough of this bullying," said Chesley, drawing himself to his most imperious height. "It is true that I didn't believe the boy's story this morning, but that's because he is a proven lia—"

"It's because you know where Dauna is," interrupted King, rising up to tower over even the tall steward. "I can smell it." King showed his teeth and growled.

In the years since then, I've learned that when men smile, they're talking without words. Sometimes it's as simple as, "that's funny" or "what a beautiful woman you are." Some smiles say, "I don't know what else to say, so I'll smile." Yet others say, "You're a miserable, stupid troll, but I can't say that, so I'll smile." King's smile said, "I'm about to clamp my teeth down on your throat if you don't talk." Chesley, to his credit, understood King's smile exactly.

"It wasn't my idea! I didn't want the money! They threatened me!"

Now we all knew he was lying. It wasn't hard to get the rest out of him, especially once Betha reached up and grabbed him by his skinny throat.

"What have you done with that darling girl?" she roared. King and I both moved quickly away from her. Even a fierce one like King knows who's the bigger dog.

It took her very little time to get Chesley's story.

* * * * *

"There," said King. He looked all silver in the moonlight—hair, eyes, and hands. He pointed to the warm glow of a lantern. The light spilled out of a flimsy warehouse door, making a silhouette of the guard sitting there, carelessly leaning back on two chair legs.

"That's father's warehouse," I said. "The one he rents for the goods he buys overseas. Why would they take her there?"

"Probably because that's the last place we'd think to look, Jame." I thought King was incredibly smart, even for a man.

"Now, listen. You won't be any help if you let those men get their hands on you, too." King took me by the shoulder and tugged the feathered cap out from my belt. He put it on my head and pulled it snugly down. I could tell by his eyes that I was invisible again.

"Keep this on. Once we're in, you look for Dauna. Getting her out of there is your job. I'll keep the kidnappers busy."

I nodded, but he kept looking toward me as if I hadn't. "Oh, I mean yes," I said. Being invisible was tricky business.

"Here we go," said King. He turned and loped toward the door, crouching low to stay in the shadows. He got within five feet of the watchman before his scabbard struck the ground and made a terrible scrape against the stone walk.

"What's that?" said the watchman. "Who's here?" He rose from his chair with a clatter, and I was sure he'd shout before King could stop him. But King was a dark blur, rushing up to slam the open door right in the watchman's face. The surprised man dropped like a sack of flour.

"Hsst! You there, Jame?" King whispered. I hurried to catch up.

"Right behind you."

"Listen." We listened for a moment. Voices floated up from the dark interior of the warehouse, but they sounded conversational. King nodded an all clear, then lifted the fallen watchman back into his chair. Tilting him carefully back, King left the man looking every bit as watchful as he'd been before. We entered the warehouse.

Past the yellow circle of lamplight by the door, the warehouse was dark and cool. It smelled clean and damp, though the floor was dry and scattered with sawdust. The rafters were hidden in darkness, but I could feel the clear space above our heads. Past the shadows of crates and barrels, another light reflected dimly on the far wall.

At first I followed King carefully around bolts of Shou silk. But when we reached the Mulhorandi carvings, he waved me forward without turning around. "Look," he whispered. "Is that Dauna?" I peered through the space between a particularly severe pharaoh and a slender cat goddess. It was Dauna.

They had her tied to a chair, and she slumped in the coils as if she'd exhausted herself with struggling. She wasn't bruised or bleeding anywhere, so I breathed a sigh of relief. The kidnappers wanted a ransom.

We could see three of the kidnappers, two of whom I recognized from our chase that morning. The third was Siward, the young thug Chesley had hired as a handyman last month. Chesley hadn't told us the boy was involved, but we should have guessed. A head taller than me, and perhaps two years older, Siward bullied me when he first arrived at the house. Now I knew that wasn't the limit of his wickedness.

"See there?" whispered King. He pointed to a line of barrels beside Dauna's chair.

I nodded. Then I whispered, "Yes."

"Try to make your way around to free Dauna." He held out a knife, and I took it. I nodded again, turned, and tread as quietly as I could back to the other side. King vanished into the gloom between the crates.

Checking to make sure the hat remained firmly on my head, I crept around a great pile of bagged spices. Some of them tickled my nose, and I pinched it shut. I didn't want to sneeze and accidentally alert the villains. Soon enough, I found a space through which I could crawl close to Dauna.

Poking my head out from between the narrow aisle of barrels, I wasted a few moments trying to attract Dauna's attention with frantic waving. Being invisible was becoming embarrassing. Fortunately, no one could see me making these mistakes.

I looked around and counted Siward and three other men, one of whom we hadn't seen from our earlier vantage. Two of them played at lots, and the one we hadn't seen was trimming his nails with a dagger, while Siward lounged against the wall, trying to look tough and know-ing. He stole quick glances at the other men to see if any noticed how dangerous he looked. None of them did.

With each of the kidnappers occupied with his own pur-suit, I had no trouble slipping behind Dauna's chair. Being invisible helped, too, I suppose.

"Dauna, it's me, Jame," I whispered softly.

"Jame?" said Dauna. I couldn't blame her. It was taking me some time to get used to the invisibility thing, too.

"What's that?" demanded Siward, rising from his pose to stand directly in front of Dauna. "Did the little bug say something?"

Dauna's the bold one. "I heard a voice," she said. "Must have been the city watch, come to arrest you all." She's never been a great one for stories, though. Good thing, as it turned out.

"Right, and then they'll declare you the princess of Cormyr. Ha! Little bug! I bet your father won't even want you back, you ugly thing. Then we'll have to squash you." I'd never seen nor heard anything as ugly as Siward's laugh then. Dauna would have something sharp to say, I thought. But she screwed up her face and began to sob. I guess that's when I first really hated Siward.

He laughed again and called her "little bug" a few more times. I thought him rather dull for it, but it had a pro-nounced effect on Dauna, whose sobs turned to a wailing cry. King would make his move soon, I hoped. What was he waiting for?

"Oh, mercy," cried one of the lot players. "Don't get her started again. Get away from her, boy."

"Who are you calling a boy?" challenged Siward. But he went back to his place at the wall. It was then I realized that the fingernail-trimmer was missing. The kidnappers noticed it too.

"Where's Lonny?" asked the other lot player. His oppo-nent shrugged.

"Probably had to see a man about a horse." They laughed at that tired joke. My bet was that King had dispatched the man and was busy tying him up. I used the time to put my hand over Dauna's mouth and whisper again.

"It's Jame, your brother. I'm invisible. Really. I'll let you try it later. But first, I'm going to cut you free. Don't scream or talk to me or anything. All right?" She hadn't bitten my hand yet, and she made a sort of nodding motion, so I let go. Cutting the ropes was quick and easy, but they fell to the floor with a noticeable thump.

"Hey, she's loose!" cried Siward.

Both of the lot players rose from their table, and suddenly King came leaping over the crates behind them. But he'd jumped badly, used to landing on his front paws first. A man's hands aren't quite up to that task, so he went sprawling on the table between two surprised kidnappers.

"Get him!" cried a lot player. The other drew his sword and raised it, preparing to stab King in the back.

"King!" I shouted. "Look out!" By then, Siward was almost on top of Dauna. I grabbed the cap off my head and pushed it over Dauna's curly locks. Siward paused just long enough at my sudden appearance and Dauna's disappearance for me to shout, "Run! You're invisible! Run home to Betha!"

Then Siward was an avalanche upon me.

"You prat!" he screeched, losing all composure. "I'll beat you into pudding!"

I wanted to respond with something clever, but he was quick to make good on his threat. My only response was a series of unintelligible grunts punctuating each of his blows. I looked desperately around for King, hoping he had not only dispatched his enemies, but could also rescue me from Siward.

But King had his own troubles. Both of the kidnappers wielded swords now, two blades to one, and King's back pressed the wall. To his credit, he was a good swordsman, but the weapon seemed awkward in his grip. It had been too long since he had fought like this. Then one of the kidnappers struck him a smart blow to arm, knocking his sword down. Both villains' blades flicked toward his throat.

"On your knees, hero," mocked one of the swordsmen. Siward held me by the collar and turned to look.

King was amazed and uncertain. He hesitated, then slowly knelt, defeat in the old warrior's eyes.

"Down, you cur," ordered the other man. The first grabbed King by the shoulder and pushed him down onto his hands.

"King!" I cried.

He looked over at where I lay beneath Siward's giggling bulk. All three kidnappers laughed mockingly, congratulating each other with glances. King peered across at his dropped sword, his expression hopeless, his head hanging low. He looked utterly defeated.

But then King hunkered down, finding the balance between his hands and feet. He lifted his head slowly. The kidnappers were busy grinning at each other, so I was the only one to see King show his teeth in a smile that would have terrified me had it been cast my direction. The swordsmen didn't see King look up at them, a renewed fire in his eyes. He tensed, ready to spring.

"Rahr!" growled King, lunging at the first kidnapper's leg.

The man shouted in pain and beat ineffectually at his attacker. "He bit me! He bit me!" he repeated in disbelief.

"He's raving mad," shouted the other, raising his sword. Then they heard King's low, awful growl, and saw King's eyes, his teeth bared and bloody.

"Merciful gods, it's a werewolf!" cried one. Two swords struck the ground at once, and the kidnappers fled so quickly that one of them slammed face first into the statue of the cat goddess, knocking himself senseless. The other ran somewhat farther, screamed, then fell with a great thump. I figured out later that he had stumbled over Lonny, whom he thought to be the unfortunate victim of King, the werewolf.

Siward's reaction was every bit as sudden as those of his companions. "Werewolf!" he screamed.

Siward ran three steps and promptly tripped over a chair that mysteriously slid beneath his legs. Dauna appeared, slapping the babbling Siward with the feathered cap. "Who's squashed now, little bug?" Whether to stanch the wound to his dignity or to preserve his dwindling sanity, Siward chose the better part of valor and fainted.

The rest was a boring parade of arriving watchmen, a tearful and huggy Betha, and plenty of questions. The earlier thrill kept us awake for the first hour or so, but then Dauna's yawns melted into sleep. King carried her home in his arms, and I barely made it back under my own power.

"You must stay the night here," said Betha to King. The hero opened his mouth as if to argue, then shut it again. Betha was still the bigger dog.

I had just enough strength to show King to the guest bedroom. We said good night, and I turned to leave. But I stopped a moment at the door to look back at him, thinking I had something to say but finding no words. He didn't see me.

I watched him lie down on the bed with a heavy sigh, then turn heavily onto his side. A few more uncomfortable shifts, and King climbed off the soft feather bed to crawl onto the rug, circle three times on all fours, then curl up to sleep comfortably.

* * * * *

Father returned four days after we rescued Dauna. He wouldn't let us out of his sight for days. The first time I saw King was at Chesley's trial. The court was crammed with people, and I couldn't get anywhere close to King. Even from a distance, I could see he was unhappy. He'd lost some of the silver gleam he'd had on the night of the rescue. He looked just gray and tired. And old.

Eventually, Father allowed me my freedom again, and I rushed to the streets to find King. I wanted to hear all of his stories, everything about why the witch had changed him into a dog and about all his adventures since then.

King could have been anywhere, so that's where I looked. After searching the docks, the circus grounds, the markets, and even the Ministry of Art—where the guards told me Carrague was away to supper—I found myself on Wicker Street, not far from the Barley Bowl. I smelled barley soup and knew Carrague must be inside. Surely he could tell me what had become of King.

There was the ambassador, all right. He leaned back against the wall, snoring softly. A long pipe rested near an empty soup bowl. One hand dangled at his side, idly stroking the silver fur of an aging, mixed-breed terrier.

THE COMMON SPELL

Kate Novak-Grubb

"This is a waste of time. I don't need to learn this," insisted Marl, the cooper's son.

Kith Lias glared at the boy, but she kept her temper in check. Marl was hardly the first to denigrate the skills she was trying to teach. He wouldn't be the last, either. Marl was a big boy, the kind whose lead the other boys would follow. While none of the other students said a word, some of them eyed Marl with admiration that he'd had the courage to voice what many of them were thinking. The rest of the students watched Kith curiously, waiting to see how the teacher would handle this challenge to her authority.

"Even a cooper may need to read and write sometimes, Marl," Kith answered, pushing a strand of her long, dark hair back behind her ear. "You may need to write down the orders for your suppliers and customers so you can remember them better."

The other students nodded at Kith's example, but Marl snorted derisively. "I'm not going to be a cooper," the boy declared. "Soon as I get enough money to buy a sword, I'm joining a caravan as a guard. I'm going to be an adventurer."

"A swordling without the common spell," Kith muttered sadly.

"What's a swordling?" asked Lisaka, the tavernkeep's daughter.

"What's the common spell?" Marl demanded.

"A swordling is an adventurer's word," Kith explained, "for a novice sell-sword. A mageling is a young mage who hasn't proven herself. The common spell is . . . well, actually it's a story I heard from Alias the Sell-Sword."

The children in the classroom leaned forward as one. Like all students throughout the Realms, they knew that their teacher could be distracted from the lesson if they encouraged her to reminisce. They were also eager to hear a story about Alias the Sell-Sword. Alias was a famous adventurer—she rescued the halfling bard Olive Ruskettle from the dragon Mistinarperadnacles and slew the mad god Moander—twice. Only last year she drove the thieves guild from Westgate. A story about Alias would be wonderful.

"Tell us, please," Lisaka asked.

"Yeah, tell the story," Marl demanded.

Kith shrugged. "I heard Alias tell this story in the village of Serpentsford in Featherdale. The people there were suspicious of all female strangers who passed through the town, even a hero like Alias, for the village was plagued by a penanggalan."

"What's that?" asked Jewel Weaver, the youngest student in the class.

"It's a female vampire," Marl said with a superior air.

"Not exactly," Kith retorted. "A penanggalan is undead, and it does drink the blood of the living, but there the similarity ends. A penanggalan appears as an ordinary woman in the daylight, and the sun's rays do not destroy it. But at night its head twists away from its body, trailing a black 'tail', which is all that remains of its stomach and guts. The body lies motionless while the head flies off and hunts for its victims. It prefers the blood of women and girls."

Jewel squealed, and several other students shivered. Even Marl looked a little pale.

"The people of Serpentsford had known enough to cremate the victims of the penanggalan so they would not become undead themselves," Kith explained. "But the villagers were beginning to lose hope that they would ever discover the monster, or even any of her secret lairs, for she was very cunning. Alias told this story to raise their spirits."

"So what's the story?" Marl growled impatiently.

Amused at the boy's attentiveness, Kith smiled ever so slightly. She sat back in her chair and folded her hands in her lap. Marl squirmed with annoyance.

Kith began the tale. "This is a tale of the adventuring party known as the Swanmays. Their members included two swordswomen, Belinda and Myrtle; a pair of rogues, Niom and Shadow; a cleric, Pasil; and a mageling, Kasilith. In the Year of the Worm, the Swanmays wintered in the city of Westgate. Their landlord, a weaver woman, had an apprentice, an orphan girl named Stelly who was thirteen. Stelly and Kasilith, the mageling, became close friends, and Stelly wanted to leave the weaver to join the Swanmays.

"Now, although it was a master's legal obligation, the weaver had not yet taught Stelly to read or write. Belinda, the leader of the Swanmays, wasn't keen on taking responsibility for an illiterate girl whose only skills were with wool, and stealing an apprentice was a crime in Westgate. Yet Belinda liked Stelly. She promised Kasilith that if the mageling taught Stelly to read and write, Belinda would go to the city council, challenge the weaver's claim to Stelly, and petition to take Stelly on as an apprentice swordswoman.

"During the winter, Kasilith taught Stelly how to read and write her letters. Stelly believed what Kasilith was teaching her was actually magic; it was so awesome to the girl that scribbles on paper could mean something. Kasilith joked that if it was magic, it was the most common spell in the Realms.

"That same winter a penanggalan began to prey on the women of Westgate. Neither the city watch nor any of the adventurers inhabiting the town could discover the

creature's lair. In life, the monster had been a noblewoman and her family and their power helped to hide her.
By chance or fate, the undead noblewoman came into
Stelly's master's shop to have a tear in her cloak repaired
and decided to make the weaver her next victim. Explain-
ing she could not call for the cloak until later that evening,
the penanggalan made arrangements to meet the weaver
after the shop closed.

"A little while later, the weaver learned of Belinda's
plan to take Stelly from her. Angrily, the weaver ordered
Stelly to repair the noblewoman's cloak, then locked the
girl in the workroom. Stelly could hear her master order-
ing the Swanmays out of her house, then barring the door.

"After crying for a while over her lost chance, Stelly
went back to her work. In the pocket of the noblewoman's
cloak, the girl discovered an expensive locket engraved
with a name. Since Stelly could now read, she recognized
the name belonged to a girl who had already fallen prey to
the penanggalan. Stelly shouted for her master, but the
weaver, thinking the girl was just throwing a tantrum,
ignored her cries. Much later in the evening the apprentice heard her master unbar the door to the house and
then cry out once in fear. The penanggalan had come for
the weaver in her true form.

"Locked in the workroom, Stelly could make out the
weaver's moans and the sound of the beast slurping up
her life's blood. Stelly cowered silently in fear until she
became unconscious.

"In the morning the penanggalan, once again in human
form, unlocked the workroom door to retrieve her cloak.
Pretending concern for the apprentice, the undead noblewoman promised to return and free Stelly after dark.
Stelly hid her fear and her knowledge of the woman's true
nature. Knowing the penanggalan intended to return after
dark to kill her as it must certainly have killed the
weaver, Stelly conceived a desperate stratagem. Across
the back of the monster's cloak she scrawled 'pnngalin'
with a piece of chalk, then folded the cloak carefully so her
repair work showed but her markings did not. The noblewoman nodded with satisfaction at the repairs and

allowed Stelly to set the cloak about her shoulders. Then the woman left the workroom, locking the apprentice back in. It was the last Stelly ever saw of her."

"Because people spotted the letters . . . and killed the penanggalan," Jewel said excitedly.

"That is how Alias's story ended," Kith said with a nod. "Reading and writing, the common spell, saved Stelly's life."

"Is that all?" Marl asked, obviously not pleased with the tale.

"No, that's not all," Kith retorted, her voice suddenly deeper and more commanding. "The ending Alias gave the tale was a lie."

The students' eyes widened in surprise.

"But why would Alias lie?" Lisaka asked.

Kith shrugged. "She learned the tale from her father, the bard Finder Wyvernspur, and that is how he told it to her. Bards are notorious for manipulating the facts for their own purposes. But I know it was not the tale's true ending. I was staying at the inn in Serpentsford when Alias told the story," Kith explained, "and when she finished a woman in the audience accused her of lying and slapped her."

The students gasped, even Marl.

"The woman had been the Swanmay mageling Kasilith," the teacher explained. "She was only twenty-seven, but she looked fifty at least. She told Alias and the villagers the story's true ending."

"Which was?" Marl prompted.

"Kasilith was supposed to teach Stelly to read and write," Kith said, her voice laden with bitterness, "but instead the two girls spent the winter playing frivolous games with magic and toy swords and their hair and dresses. When Stelly found the locket in the penanggalan's cloak she couldn't read it. The apprentice had no way of discovering that the noblewoman was the penanggalan, and even if she had suspected anything upon hearing the weaver cry out that night, the girl did not know enough of her letters to write anything on the back of the monster's cloak. The next night the noblewoman returned to free Stelly. She freed her from her life, by draining all the blood from her body."

"Oh, no," Jewel whispered.

"Oh, yes," Kith replied.

"Did they ever catch the penanggalan?" asked Todd, the baker's son. "Wait a minute!" the boy exclaimed. "I'll bet it was the same penanggalan in Westgate that was in Serpentsford. Kasilith was still hunting her to avenge Stelly's death, wasn't she?"

"That is what she told Alias and her companion, Dragonbait," Kith answered.

"So, did they catch the penanggalan?" Marl asked.

Kith continued. "Alias had a shard of the finder's stone, an old broken artifact. If you held the stone and had a clear picture of someone or something, the shard sent out a beacon of light in the direction of whomever or whatever you wanted to find. Kasilith said she'd seen the penanggalan's human body once, so Alias gave her the stone. Its light led them to a lair hidden underground, where the penanggalan's torso lay on a bier of fresh pine branches. The monster's head was not there; it would return before dawn, but now it was off hunting.

"With an exalted air, Kasilith used her magic to burn the body. Without its torso the penanggalan would not be able to hide its true nature again. If the head was struck by the sunlight and did not return to its torso within a few hours, it would rot, so the penanggalan would not be able to travel in the daylight anymore, either. The adventurers hid themselves and waited for the penanggalan's head to return."

"And did it?" Marl asked. He sat on the edge of his seat.

Kith shook her head.

"Then what happened?" Jewel prompted.

"Alias and Dragonbait and the villagers searched everywhere. For days and nights they looked for the penanggalan or its remains. They found no other secret lairs, nor did they find any other victims of the penanggalan. They hoped that the creature had been struck by sunlight and had rotted, but Alias would not give up the hunt until she had positive proof the penanggalan was dead.

"Kasilith did give up, though. She was just about to leave the village when a great snowstorm came down from the northeast. Travel in any direction outside the vale was impossible for nearly a week, and so she remained. The mage grew remote and haggard in appearance. The snowstorm broke, but by then Kasilith was so ill she was too weak to leave her bed. Her traveling companion, a pretty foundling girl called Jilly, remained at her bedside.

"Then one night, just as Alias and her companion Dragonbait were about to leave the inn for the hunt, Dragonbait turned about and hissed. Now, Dragonbait came from a strange race of lizard creatures called saurials, but really they're no different from you and me. Dragonbait was a paladin, a champion of the god of justice, and just like a human paladin he could sense the presence of evil. He dashed up to Kasilith's room with Alias hot on his heels. The pair smashed open the door.

"Something lay on Kasilith's chest, nuzzling at her neck. For a moment Alias mistook it for a sleeping toddler. It had silky strawberry blond hair, which Kasilith stroked with one hand. The mage's other hand was wrapped around what appeared to be a child's arm. Then the innkeep came to the door with a lantern, and Alias could see the thing lying on Kasilith was a penanggalan. It was lapping at the blood that oozed from two wounds on the mage's throat, and a glistening black tail attached to the fair head writhed like a snake beneath the mage's hand.

"The innkeep dropped the lantern and fled. Alias gagged in spite of herself, and the penanggalan raised its head and hissed. It had the face of Kasilith's traveling companion, Jilly. Jilly's headless torso lay on the bed beside the mage. The monster rose from the bed, its eyes glowing red, blood gurgling down its throat. In a raspy voice it called out its victim's name and flew toward the window, but its escape was blocked by the saurial paladin and his magically flaming sword. Alias slammed the door shut, trapping the monster in the room with its victim and the two adventurers.

"The penanggalan could fly, but the room's ceiling was low, and Alias's sword was long. She pressed the monster into a corner and was just about to deliver a killing blow when her back exploded with the pain of five magical darts sinking into her flesh. Alias whirled around in surprise. Her eyes widened in shock as she discovered it was Kasilith who'd just attacked her. The mage was not just the penanggalan's victim; she was protecting the undead beast as well.

"Dragonbait threw himself on Kasilith, preventing her from casting any more magic, but the penanggalan, taking advantage of Alias's diverted attention, had turned on its attacker with a vengeance. It swooped down upon the swordswoman and lashed its tail about her neck. Alias flailed her sword awkwardly over her head while she tugged at the creature's tail to keep it from choking her. The tail felt slimy, like a decaying piece of meat, and it stunk of curdling blood. Realizing she hadn't long before the monster crushed her windpipe, Alias tried a desperate measure. She dropped her sword and snatched her dagger from her boot sheath.

"A second later she'd slashed the penanggalan along the length of its tail. Hot blood gushed down on her, momentarily obscuring her vision. The penanggalan sank its teeth into her cheek. Dropping her dagger, Alias grabbed the hair at the monster's temples and ripped it from her, smashing it into the wall over and over, until she had crushed its skull. The tail about her throat went limp and slid from her. Alias dropped the monster on the floor and, retrieving her sword, cleaved its head in two.

"An inky cloud rose from the monstrous head, shrank to a pinpoint of blackness, then vanished. From the bed, Kasilith sobbed out, 'Stelly,' and Alias realized what must have happened."

Kith paused in her story and hung her head for a moment. She breathed in deeply and let her breath out slowly.

"Jilly was Stelly," Todd cried out. "No one had cremated Stelly's body," the boy speculated, "so she became a penanggalan. But what about the other penanggalan? The one whose body Kasilith destroyed?" the boy asked. "Was that the one that killed Stelly?"

Kith shook her head. "No, the Swanmays did finally find and destroy that one. There was no other penanggalan. Kasilith created an illusion of the body and destroyed it so Alias would think the monster was dead and would go away."

"But Alias was too thorough a hunter, and didn't leave," Marl noted.

"And when Kasilith and Stelly were trapped in Serpentsford by the snow, Stelly had to feed on Kasilith so she wouldn't get caught," Todd added.

"And Kasilith helped Stelly even though she was a penanggalan because she was her friend," Lisaka said.

"A penanggalan isn't the person she was in life. It's just an evil life-force animating her body that knows what she knew," Marl argued. "Right?"

"That's true," Kith said softly.

"But Kasilith didn't know that, did she?" Jewel asked.

"She knew," Kith replied.

"The penanggalan probably hypnotized her into being its slave," Marl said.

Kith shook her head. "No. Kasilith served it willingly. You see, she felt so guilty that Stelly had died because she hadn't taught her to read. So she thought she deserved nothing better for the rest of her life than to serve as the slave to evil because she'd done an evil thing."

"Then what happened to her?" Jewel asked anxiously.

Kith sighed. "Well, she shrieked and cried and ranted and raved for a while. She swore she would never forgive Alias and Dragonbait for freeing her from the penanggalan's enslavement. Still, they attended to her while she was recovering from the penanggalan's wounds."

"More than she deserved," Marl muttered.

"True," Kith agreed. "Alias told the mage that Finder Wyvernspur had told her so much about Kasilith that she felt she was her friend and would not leave her until she was healed. Kasilith swore she had never met Finder Wyvernspur, but Alias stayed anyway. Finally, one day, something Dragonbait the paladin said made her change her mind about how she felt and about what she should do with her life."

"What did he say?" Jewel asked.

"He told Kasilith that the god of justice abhors punishment for punishment's sake. That we have to find a way to atone for the evil we do, and that we cannot atone for evil with evil, but only with good. He suggested she go out and teach other children who needed to learn to read and write. That way she would honor Stelly's true spirit and maybe bring peace to her own spirit. And that's just what she did."

"So she became a teacher like you?" Jewel asked.

"She became a teacher like me," Kith answered. "She teaches the common spell."

* * * * *

Marl the cooper's son stayed in school another two years before he finally bought his own sword and joined a caravan as a swordling. By then Kith Lias had taught him to read and write the names of every fell creature he might encounter in the Realms and had moved to another dale to teach another village's children. It was during Marl's off-duty hours that the other caravan guards taught him the game anagrams. After that, the cooper's son spent even more time wondering about the mage Kasilith and the teacher Kith Lias.

THE FIRST MOONWELL

Douglas Niles

The goddess existed deep within the cocoon of bedrock, an eternal being, formed of stone and silt and fire, her body blanketed by the depths of a vast and trackless sea. In the way of immortals, she had little awareness of the steady progression of ages, the measured pulse of time. Only gradually, over the course of countless eons, did she become aware that around and above her the ocean came to host an abundance of life. She knew the presence of this vitality in all the forms that thrived and grew; from the beginning she understood that life, even in its simplest and most transient forms, was good.

Deep waters washed her body, and the volcanic fires of her blood swelled, seeking release. She was a living thing, and thus she grew. Her being expanded, rising slowly from the depths of the ocean, over millennia spilling along trench and seabed, pressing deliberately, forcefully upward. Over the course of ages, her skin, the floor of the sea, pushed through the realm of black and indigo and blue, toward shimmering reaches of aquamarine and a warmth that was very different from the hot pulse of lava that measured her own steady heartbeat.

Life in many forms quickened around her, first in the

manner of simple things, later in larger and more elaborate shapes. Animation teemed in the waters that cloaked and cooled her body. Gashes opened continually in the rocky flesh of her body, and her blood of molten rock touched the chill waters in spuming explosions of steam.

Amid these hissing eruptions, she sensed great forms circling, swimming near, breathing the chill, dark sea. These beings of fin and tentacle, of scale and gill, gathered to the warmth of the earthmother's wounds—wounds that caused no pain, but instead gave her the means to expand, to strive ever higher through the brightening waters of the sea.

And, finally, in the life that gathered to her bosom, she sensed great creatures of heartbeat and warm blood. These mighty denizens swam like fish, but were cloaked in slick skin rather than scales, and rose through the sea to drink of the air that filled the void above. Mothers nursed their young, much like the goddess nourished her children and her thriving sea. Most importantly, in these latter arrivals the goddess sensed the awakenings of mind, of thought and intelligence.

Unaware of millennia passing, feeling the coolness of the sea against the rising pressure of her rock-bound body, the physical form of the goddess continued to expand. At last, a portion of her being rose above the storm-tossed ocean to feel a new kind of warmth, a radiance that descended from the sky. Periodically this heat was masked beneath a blanket of chilly powder, but the frosty layer yielded itself in a regular pattern to more warmth, to soothing waters that bathed the flesh of the goddess, and more of the golden rays shedding steadily downward from the sky.

The flesh of the goddess cooled, weathered by exposure to sky. New and different forms of life took root upon her; beings that dwelled in the sea of air turned faces upward to the clouds. Many did not walk or swim, but fixed themselves to the ground, extended lofty boughs upward, creating verdant bowers across the breadth of the land. The growth of these tall and mighty trees, like all forms of life, was pleasing to the goddess. She sensed the fruition and waning of the forests that layered her skin, knew the cooling and warming of seasons with greater acuity than ever before.

It was this awareness that, at last, gave to the earth-mother a true sense of passing time. She knew seasons, and in the course of changing climes she learned the pattern of a year. She came to measure time as a man might count his own breaths or heartbeats, though to the goddess each heartbeat was a season, each breath the cycle of the annum. As the years passed by the tens and hundreds and thousands, she grew more vibrant, stronger, and more aware.

The hot blood of earlier eons cooled further; the eruptions from the sea ultimately were capped by solid stone. That firm bedrock, where it jutted above the waves, was layered everywhere in forest, meadow, glade and moor. Seas and lakes intermixed with the land, keeping the goddess always cool, both fresh waters and brine nurturing the growing populations of living creatures.

Still the goddess maintained communion with the beings of warm blood dwelling in the depths, who swam to the surface and returned, sharing their mind-images of a vast dome of sky, of the sweet kiss of a sea breeze and the billowing majesty of lofty clouds. Her favorite of these sea creatures was one who had been nourished at her breast from time immemorial, feeding upon the kelp and plankton that gathered to her warm emissions, slumbering for decades at a time in her embrace. She came to know him as the Leviathan, the first of her children.

He was a mighty whale, greater than any other fish or mammal that swam in these seas. His soul was gentle, his mind observant, keen and patient—as only one who has lived for centuries can know patience. Great lungs filled his powerful chest, and he knew life with a rhythm that the goddess could understand. Sometimes he took a breath of air and settled into the depths, remaining there for a passage of several heartbeats by the reckoning of the goddess—a time of years in the more frenetic pace of the other warm-blooded creatures.

In long, silent communication with the goddess who was his mother, the Leviathan lay in a deep trench on the bottom of the sea, sensing the lingering warmth of her fiery blood as it pulsed and ebbed below the bedrock of the ocean floor. During these times, the great whale passed images he had beheld above the waves, pictures of growing verdancy among the earthmother's many islands, of the teeming array of creatures swarming not only sea and land, but now even flocking in the skies.

And he shared, too, his memories of clouds. These more than anything else stoked the fires of the earthmother's imagination, brought wonder to her heart, and caused curiosity to germinate in her being.

As she communed with the Leviathan, sharing his memories of the things he had beheld, she began to sense a thing about herself: The goddess, unlike so many of the creatures that dwelled upon her flesh, was utterly blind. She lacked any window, any sense through which she could view the world of life flourishing upon her physical form.

The only visual pictures that she knew came from the memory of the great whale, and these were pale and vaporous imitations of the real thing. The goddess wanted to see for herself the sky of cloud and rain and sun, to know the animals that teemed among her forests and glades, the trees that sank their roots so deeply into her flesh.

From the Leviathan, the goddess earthmother had learned about eyes, the orbs of magic that allowed the animals of the world to observe the wonders around them. She learned about them, and desired them . . . and devised a plan to create an eye for herself.

The Leviathan would aid her. The great whale drank from an undersea fountain, absorbing the power and the magic of the earthmother into himself. With easy strokes of his powerful flukes, he drove toward the surface, swimming through brightening shades of water until again his broad back rolled above the waves, felt the kiss of sunlight and breeze.

Swimming strongly, the Leviathan swam to a deep bay, stroking between rocky necks of land into ever narrower waters, toward the western shore of one of the earthmother's cherished isles. Mountains rose to the north, a stretch of craggy highlands crested with snow as the spring warmth crept only slowly upward from the shore. To the south was a swath of green forest, woodlands extending far from the rocky shoreline, blanketing this great extent of the island.

In the terminus of the bay, the land came together from north and south, the waters remaining deep enough for the Leviathan to swim with ease. He came to the place the goddess had chosen, and brought the warm and magical essence of herself through his body. With a great, spuming explosion, he cast the liquid into the air, shooting a shower of warm rain. Precious water splashed onto the rocks of the shoreline, gathered in many streams, flowed downward to collect in a rocky bowl near the gravel-strewn beach.

The essence of the goddess gathered into that pool, milky waters of potent magic. Her presence focused on the skies, on the vault of heavens she had so long imagined. The first thing that came into view was a perfect orb of white, rising into the twilight skies, coursing ever higher, beaming reflected light across the body and blood of the earthmother.

From the waters of her newly made well, the goddess beheld the moon. Alabaster light reflected from the shoals and waves of the shoreline and blessed the land all around. The earthmother saw this light, and she was pleased.

Yet still there was a dimness to her vision, an unfocused haze that prevented her from fully absorbing the presence of the world. The Leviathan lay offshore, rolling in the heavy swell, but the pool was remote from him, bounded as it was by dry ground and rocks. She knew then that it was not enough to have her children in the sea.

The goddess would require a presence on the land, as well.

* * * * *

The wolf, gray flanks lean with hunger, shaggy pelt worn by the ravages of a long hibernation, loped after a mighty stag. The buck ran easily through the spring growth, exhibiting none of the wide-eyed panic that might have driven a younger deer into headlong—and ultimately disastrous—flight. Instead, this proud animal bounded in graceful leaps, staying well beyond the reach of hungry jaws, veering only when necessary to maintain a clear avenue of flight.

In the midst of the keen, lupine face, blue eyes remained fixed upon the lofty rack of antlers. *Patience,* counseled the wolf's instinct, knowing that the pack could accomplish what one strong hunter could not. As if in response to their leader's thought, more wolves burst from concealment to the side, rushing to join the chase. But the stag had chosen its course well; a long, curving adjustment took it away from the newer hunters, without allowing the big male to draw appreciably closer.

A low cliff loomed ahead, and though no breeze stirred in the depths of the glen, the buck sensed another ambush, canine forms concealed in the thickness of ferns lining the shady depths of the bower. Now the stag threw itself at the limestone precipice, leaping upward with catlike grace, finding purchase for broad hooves on ledges and mossy outcrops.

With snorting exertion and flaring nostrils, the first outward signs of desperation, the buck scrambled up a rock face three times its own height. A trio of wolves burst from the ferny camouflage below, howling in frustrated hunger as the antlered deer reached the level ground above the cliff and once again increased its speed. Hooves pounded and thundered on the firm ground as, with a flick of a white-feathered tail, the stag raced toward open terrain.

But the leader of the small wolf pack would not, *could* not, admit defeat. Throwing himself at that rocky face, pouncing upward with all the strength of powerful rear legs, the wolf clawed and scraped and pulled, driven by the desperation of the starving hunter. At last, broad forepaws crested the summit, and the carnivore again loped after the prey, howls echoing after the gasping, thudding noise of the stag's flight.

Others of the wolves tried to follow, though most fell back. Still, a few young males and a proud, yellow-eyed bitch made the ascent. Their baying song added to the din of flight and gave the rest of the pack a focus as smaller wolves raced to either side, seeking an easier way to the elevation above the limestone shelf.

Weariness began to drag at the leader, bringing to his step a stumbling uncertainty that had been utterly lacking before. Yet the scent of the prey was strong, and mingled with that acrid odor came the spoor of the stag's own weariness, its growing desperation. These signals gave the wolf hope, and he raised his head in a braying summons to the rest of the pack, a cry of anticipation that rang like a prayer through the silent giants of the wood, along the verdant blanket of the cool ground.

But the powerful deer found a reserve that surprised and dismayed the proud hunter. The predator raced through the woods with belly low, shaggy tail extended straight behind. Those bright blue eyes fixed upon the image of the fleeing stag, watching antlers brush overhanging limbs and leaves. Straining, no longer howling as he gasped to make the most of each desperate breath, the wolf pursued in deadly silence.

And in that silence he began to sense his failure. The loping forms of his packmates whispered like ghosts through the fern-lined woodland behind him, but neither were they able to close the distance to the fleeing prey. Even the yellow-eyed female, long jaws gaping in a fanglined grin of hunger, could not hold the pace much longer.

Then, with an abrupt turn, the stag darted to the left. Cutting the corner of the angle, the leading pair of wolves closed the distance. Soon the male was racing just behind the prey's left quarter, while the powerful bitch closed in from the opposite side. The twin hunters flanked the prey, blocking any attempt to change course.

But the stag continued its flight with single-minded determination, as if it had found a goal. The antlered deer ran downward along the slope of a broad ridge, plunging through thickets, leaping large boulders that would be obstacles only to lesser creatures. The woods opened still more, and now the vista showed a swath of blue water, a bay extending between twin necks of rugged land.

Finally the stag broke from the woods to gallop across a wide swath of moor. Soft loam cushioned the broad hooves, and though the deer's tongue flopped loosely from wide jaws and nostrils flared madly with the strain of each breath, the animal actually increased the speed of its desperate flight.

But so, too, did the wolves. More and more of the pack burst from the woods, trailing across the spongy grassland, running now in grim and purposeful silence. If the great male had looked back, he would have noticed a surprising number of canine predators, more by far than had belonged to his pack when they had settled into the den for a winter's rest. And still more wolves came along the shores, gathering from north and south, highland and coast, drawn toward the scene of the hunt, hundreds of gray forms ghosting toward a single point.

The stag finally faltered, but not because of fatigue. The animal slowed to a regal trot, proud antlers held high. The sea was very near now, but the buck did not strive for the shoreline. Instead, the forest monarch turned its course along that rocky beach, toward a pool of liquid that rested in the perfect shelter of a rocky bowl.

The pond was too high to be a tidal pool, nor did the water seem like a collection of mere rain or runoff. Instead, the liquid was pale, almost milky-white in color, and it swirled in a hypnotic pattern. The shoreline was steep, but in one place a steplike progression of rocks allowed the buck to move carefully downward.

Wolves gathered on the rocks, surrounding the stag and the pool, knowing that the prey was trapped. Yet some silent compulsion held the hungry predators at bay. Glittering eyes watched with keen intelligence as the stag's muzzle touched the surface of the water; long, panting tongues flopped loosely as the carnivores waited for their prey to drink.

For a long time, the great deer lapped at the waters of the Moonwell, and when finally it had drunk its fill it stepped away, mounting the steps toward the leader. The stag raised its head, baring the shaggy throat, uttering a final, triumphant bellow at the powdery clouds that had gathered in the sky.

When the leading wolf bit into that exposed neck, he did so almost tenderly. The kill was quick and clean, the predator ignoring the red blood that warmed his jaws, that should have inflamed his hunger and passion with its fresh and welcoming scent. Instead, the wolf raised his own head, fixed bright eyes on the same clouds that had been the last things seen by the mighty stag. A long howl ululated across the moor, and the leader was joined by the rest of his pack in a song of joy and worship, in music that hailed their mother and their maker.

When the pack finally fell to feeding, the blood of the stag ran down the rocky steps in crimson rivers. Though the wolves numbered an uncountable throng, now, there was meat for them all. With a sense of powerful satiation, each predator, after eating its fill, drank from the milky waters of the pool.

The feasting went on for more than a day, and at last the brightness of the full moon rose above the glimmering waters. Pups were born under that light, and youngsters frolicked around the fringes of a mighty gathering.

The red blood mingled with the waters of the Moonwell, and the goddess saw and celebrated with her children. The bold sacrifice of the stag was, to her, a thing of beauty—and with the mighty animal's blood was the water of her Moonwell consecrated.

And the balance of her living children maintained.

THE LUCK OF LLEWELLYN
THE LOQUACIOUS

Allen C. Kupfer

"The vagabond has lied to us!"

Llewellyn the Loquacious felt the cold waters of the River Ghalagar soak through his clothes, through his black-brown hair, and through his narrow, all-too-human frame.

"Drown him like the rodent he is!"

A halfling heel pressed down on the side of his neck. Water splashed onto his face, into his eyes and mouth.

"Lie to us, will you? Hold him under the water. Let the fish swim in his lungs!"

He thought this might be the end. This time, he feared, there would be no way out, no escape. Not with this adventuring band of halflings thirsty for revenge. No, indeed!

The hair-covered foot on his neck was joined by another on the side of his head. The weight forced his head into the sand at the river's bottom. Other weights—several other halflings—pinned the rest of his body down. As the water rushed into his ears, he could no longer hear the voices calling out. And though he struggled, the combined weight of the halflings was too great for him.

He could hold his breath no more, and bubbles full of life-breath escaped from his lungs, exited through his mouth and nostrils, rose in the water, and burst at the surface of the river. Wide-eyed and terrified, he watched their ascent.

Perhaps, he thought, I shouldn't have sent this band of adventurers to seek the silver key. Perhaps I could have acquired Zalathorn's amulet on my own, without trying to distract these halflings; after all, Zalathorn, great and beneficent wizard-king that he is, said I could keep the amulet for my very own if I chose to. Perhaps sending them off into the Swamp of Ahklaur so that I could search their camp was not a good idea—no, not a particularly smart notion at all—even if I *did* find the amulet, which I now have in the pocket of my very wet robe. . . .

Water filled his lungs, and the weight on various points of his body seemed to lessen. He thought it must have been the relief of death.

But strong fingers grabbed the long hair on his head and yanked him up over the surface of the water. He coughed up the water in his lungs, and the cold evening air brought him back to full consciousness. That was when he noticed the halfling shouting had ceased; in fact, once the water dripped from his ears, he could hear only one voice, that of the band's leader: Black Indio.

". . . not hear me, my friend?" Black Indio, though a self-styled rapscallion, was no more daunting than any halfling: fuzzy feet shadowed beneath a portly belly clothed in green homespun, wispy beard framing a face more fey than fanatic.

Llewellyn coughed out the last of the liquid.

"I said," Indio repeated, slapping the top of Llewellyn's head, "can you not hear me? Has your bath made you deaf?"

Indio's followers laughed. Llewellyn took a deep breath.

"No, I can hear you, you blackhearted, ungrateful cur!" he answered. Not having time to think about tactics—whether humility or boldness would be more appropriate at this time—Llewellyn opted for the latter. He silently prayed he wasn't creating even more trouble for himself.

"I am hurt, my friend!" Indio protested, his shaggy hair glowing with the light of the halfling campfire. "Blackhearted? Yes, no one can be more blackhearted than I when I choose to be. That's how I earned the title Black Indio, or more correctly, Indio the Black! Right now, I don't choose to be. And ungrateful? You cut me to the quick!"

"Do I?" Llewellyn asked. "Do I? I do? Indeed! Your band of cutthroats try to drown me! And why? I ask you why? I told you where you could find the silver key in the swamp; just because you couldn't find it—couldn't follow directions, most likely—is no fault of mine, I do declare! Yet your band of . . ."

"But we *did* find it."

". . . hooligans throw me into the river . . ."

"I say, we *did* find it."

". . . and nearly bury my head in the . . . What? What did you say?"

"We found it. We found the charm."

"You did?" Llewellyn coughed out loud to cover his surprise. "Of course you did. Just as I said, exactly the way I told you you would." Can my luck be holding? he wondered. Can this be possible?

"I'm not sure I know how to work it, though," Indio exclaimed.

"May I see it?" Indio handed it to him as he finally rose to his feet, water dripping from every inch of him.

It was a rather large key with three holes forged in it, where gems should be . . . but weren't. Llewellyn recognized the key immediately. Yes, the wheel of fortune was definitely turning in his favor. So much so that it worried him.

"I sent some of my troop back early," Indio explained. "The damned piranha were nibbling them away to nothing. I'm afraid that by the time they got back here, they were a bit overzealous. Remember, we hadn't found the key at that time, and all of my band—myself included—wanted to stuff a few live piranha down your throat for sending us into that godless swamp for nothing."

"How charming! How positively charitable of you!"

"But the moment we found it, I hurried back to camp, fearing what might be done to you in my absence."

"Thank you so excessively much," Llewellyn said sarcastically. "I take it back. It was a most grievous error on my part. You're not ungrateful at all."

"But I am still . . . Black Indio!" he shouted, drawing his sword and pointing it at the sky. His troop repeated the action, and in unison shouted, "Black Indio!"

"Come out of the water and sit by the fire, my friend," Indio said. "And tell me again of this key."

Llewellyn followed him to the campfire and sat close to it. In a few moments, its heat removed the chill from his bones.

"Bring our friend a drink," Indio commanded. Turning to Llewellyn, he continued: "This key, I believe you said, can unlock a chest of wealth somewhere in the mountains, just west of Zoundar. Am I correct?"

"Yes, that is, positively correct, I must say," Llewellyn responded, "and no, it is not. The key will not work without three stones set in the holes cut for them."

"Jewels?"

"No, not jewels, though that would be most attractive, perhaps even splendiferous. They are perfectly round jade stones, each with a dark stripe that runs around the perimeter."

The halfling whose foot had crushed Llewellyn's face into the mud of the river stepped forward and spoke. "Indio! We have such a stone!"

"Do we? Bring it forward. In fact, bring the sack that contains all our treasures."

The halfling did as commanded and handed Indio the sack. The leader poured out the contents between himself and Llewellyn. Indio fingered through the various gold pieces, trinkets, and small gems until he spotted what he was looking for.

"Is this it?" he asked Llewellyn, holding the green piece between two fingers.

"Does it fit in the key?"

Indio placed the stone into one of the circles on the key.

"By all that is holy, it fits—perfectly," cried the halfling.

"So it does," Indio added, "but it will not work, as our friend has said, without the other two stones. So of what use is it to me?"

Llewellyn smiled wryly. "You are too pessimistic, Indio the Black, my good friend." Undoing the drawstring of the leather sack on his belt and reaching into it, he added. "I believe the adage, once spoken by some person of undeniable wisdom at some distant point in the past, is 'one good turn deserves another.'"

Whereupon he held up an identical jade stone.

Indio's eyes lit up. "The second stone. I must have it."

"You could, I suppose, just steal it from me, Indio. But even though you are Indio the Black, I hope you will not do that, considering the injustice your followers have already perpetrated upon me. May I propose a trade?"

"What do you want for it?" Indio asked suspiciously.

"May I—I'm not a particularly skilled barterer, I must admit—peruse your plentiful plunder?"

Indio extended his hand, indicating his permission.

Llewellyn crouched over the items that Indio had poured between them, slowly and carefully slipping out of his robe the amulet he had already stolen. With a dexterous display of sleight of hand, he made it appear that he was choosing the amulet from the pile.

Better to acquire this . . . shall we say, legally . . . than perhaps have it found on me later, he thought.

"This amulet would do nicely, I must say."

Indio laughed. "You may have it. It is made of pure silver, but like this key, its decorative and maybe valuable stones have been pried off and traded, no doubt. What do you want with it?"

"Perhaps I will someday decorate it with stones of my very own choosing. And the amulet itself, a simple yet artful piece of craftsmanship, is handsome, don't you think?"

Indio shrugged his shoulders. "If you say so. Then it is a deal?"

"Almost."

"I knew there had to be a catch."

Llewellyn shook his head. "My good man, there is no catch, don't you know? Listen to me. I know who has the third stone, and where they are headed. If I help you acquire the third stone, do you agree to give me half of the treasure? After all, that would be only fair."

The whole camp laughed, but only Indio responded. "Ten percent. For it will be my troop and I who will, no doubt, have to . . . liberate . . . this stone."

"Twenty-five percent?"

"Fifteen."

"Twenty sounds reasonable to me. After all the abuse I've taken from your band, and my only taking this simple amulet . . ."

"Enough, Talkative One!" Indio said. "Twenty percent it is. But you must assist us in any way we deem necessary."

"Agreed."

"You have yet to tell me who it is that possesses the third stone."

"I believe you've heard of them. Most folks here and there know of them, I do believe."

"Them?"

"They are known as—although I consider the name a bit on the inane side—the Buckleswashers."

Indio slapped his own forehead in exasperation. "The Buckleswashers? That group of deceitful rogues who allow a gnome to travel with them? Aren't they from Waterdeep? This is far from their base."

Llewellyn nodded in agreement. "Indeed. It is surely the vast wealth of the treasure that has brought them so far from home."

"You are certain it is they?"

"Not long ago, I had the misfortune of running into them. Talltankard, their leader, beat me senseless for no reason at all. That's why I sought your band. Though my interest lies in a share of the treasure, I also wish revenge against Talltankard, which I, by myself, could never exact."

"Indeed, brother Llewellyn. I, too, hate that Talltankard, the braggart. I, too, will enjoy meeting him and his disgraceful excuse for a band of adventurers. Now tell me where they can be found."

Llewellyn gazed into the blazing fire. "It is not that I do

not trust you, my friend, Indio the Black. I cannot tell you that, for it is in a trader's interest to keep at least one item of barter in his sack."

"Then you will not tell me?"

"Better than that: I shall lead you to them—and to the treasure. Actions, they say—although, again, I do not exactly know who 'they' are—speak louder than words."

"Thereby assuring your indispensability," Indio said with a laugh. "You are indeed a shrewd man."

The two men again shook hands; then Indio called for food and drink and held the key high over the fire, watching the light twinkle from the green stones. Llewellyn sat quietly, planning how he would spend the fortune they would find in the mountains.

* * * * *

An hour later, Llewellyn was reclining on the ground under an elm tree, wrapped in a scratchy burlap blanket. But he hardly noticed the fabric. He knew that soon all would go his way.

In his semiconsciousness, he mused back on the most unusual two days just past. First, he'd had the misfortune of running into the Steadfast Order of Shortfellow Swashbucklers, better known throughout the Shining South as the Buckleswashers. They had been in the mountains north of the West Wall, seeking some ancient treasure. And since he was in the vicinity—and since Llewellyn the Loquacious's reputation was of a man of much valuable knowledge—the group delayed him and attempted to obtain information regarding the whereabouts of the lost treasure.

But, as usual, the Loquacious One was able to learn more than he taught. He told them he had heard of the treasure. He learned that a key containing three jade stones was necessary to unlock the treasure chest. He told them he had heard that the treasure was in this vicinity. He learned that they had found it; indeed, it was located in a cave barely a hundred yards from their present location. He told them he would assist them in finding the treasure. He learned that they had one of the stones, but not the key itself, nor the two additional stones. After many threats on the part of the Buckleswashers and many promises and vows on his part, they released him on condition that he would return in three days—or they would come looking for him.

Then he was summoned psionically to Zalathorn. Wordlessly, Zalathorn probed the Talkative One's mind and learned what he needed to know. The wizard, content with his store of riches, had no desire for this lost treasure. He provided Llewellyn with the full knowledge of the treasure, the key, and the three jade stones. Zalathorn thought it would be amusing to watch as the quest for the treasure unfolded before him. So he set Llewellyn in the vicinity of Indio Black's band of treasure-seekers.

And now, well, here Llewellyn was, content (relatively), sound (thankfully), and safe (miraculously). And almost (no—completely) asleep.

* * * * *

The next morning the troop awoke at the break of dawn, and by late afternoon, they were within a quarter mile of the treasure.

Llewellyn, who with Indio walked ahead of the other eight in the band, motioned for the group to halt. Indio repeated the order vocally, privately annoyed at his partner's presumption.

"We shall, I think, be able to acquire the treasure with a minimum of fuss and violence if you leave the complex machinations to me, I must say," Llewellyn declared.

Indio looked at him, puzzled. "What do you mean by that?"

"Simply that I have considered all the options and various possibilities, and I have a plan."

"Oh? Have you, great military leader?" Indio retorted.

Llewellyn pretended insult. "Very well, I shall remain quiet, and let you handle everything. After all, *you* know where the treasure is!"

Indio began to relent. "Fine. Tell us what . . ."

"*You* know where the Buckleswashers are. . . ."

"I don't. Tell us . . ."

"You know how . . ."

Indio placed his hand on his sword. "By all the fiends in the Shining South, will you not shut up and tell us your plan?"

Llewellyn frowned. "How can a man shut up and speak at the same time? It's a paradox to be pondered, I must say."

"Fine! Fine!" Indio shouted. "Don't shut up. Speak. Speak! Tell us your plan."

Finally, Llewellyn relented. "This is what I have in mind. I will go to the Buckleswashers with the key containing the two stones. . . ."

"Like hell you will," shouted one of Indio's troop, whose name was Ckleef Vann. "Do you take us for fools?"

Llewellyn lied when he answered: "No."

"Go on," Indio said warily, "but this had better be good."

"I will convince them to give me a cut of the treasure, as I have done with you. When we put the third stone in the key and unlock the treasure, you and your very able troop will rush them and take the treasure."

"Why don't we just rush them now?' another of the troop, known only as Terrence of the Hill, insisted.

Llewellyn turned to him. "Because they, at best, might hide the stone and, at worst, steal the key from you and kill you all. If you follow my plan, and I do so hope you do, you gain not only the element of surprise, but also the fact that all three stones *will be in the key.*"

Indio considered the plan, but asked, "What if they kill *you* and go to the treasure?"

"My presence or absence doesn't change matters for you, can't you see? You can still overpower them." As an afterthought, Llewellyn added, "Of course, my presence requires your paying me my twenty-five percent."

"Twenty!" corrected Indio.

"Oh, yes, I had forgotten."

Indio strutted around for a moment, then agreed to the plan. "This had better work! I go against my better judgment. But you have convinced me."

He handed Llewellyn the key with the two stones.

"Good luck, partner."

Taking the key, Llewellyn said, "Good luck to you. Follow me, but keep your distance. If they should spot any of you, our odds of surviving this adventure will be minimized—if not obliterated in totality—especially the odds related to yours truly."

With those words, he marched away. Indio's men followed, trying to figure out what the Loquacious One had just said.

* * * * *

"Who goes there?" called an unfriendly voice.

"It is Llewellyn, returned to you, don't you see, as promised!"

"So it is!" From high in a tree dropped the halfling, Osco. His cheek scar was more hideous than Llewellyn had remembered. "Follow me. The others await you."

In a few moments, the pair marched into the clearing where the Buckleswashers had pitched camp. They were sitting around a fire, identical in dress and habitat and mood to the halflings he had just left. They stood as Osco and Llewellyn approached.

"So, you've come back," Bungobar Talltankard exclaimed. "It's a damned good thing you have."

"Indeed," agreed Dimvel Stoutkeg. "For if you had not returned/ Your effigy we would have burned/ And then this burning blazing fire/ Would've been your *actual* funeral pyre."

"Enough singing, already!" Carthax Nayusiyim, the gnome of the group, yelled. "You and those songs! You'll drive me mad!"

Insulted, Dimvel responded, "You *are* mad! And an ugly little gnome, besides!"

Carthax reached for his rod of smiting, but Talltankard intervened. "Enough! We've no time for this bickering. We're all on edge because this ever-speaking bargainer has kept us waiting."

"Yes, but I *have* returned, don't you know," Llewellyn said. "And, most remarkably, with the key."

The six Buckleswashers drew closer to Llewellyn.

"Give it to us," demanded Carthax.

"Not so fast, my overly zealous compatriots," countered Llewellyn. "I want to reiterate our agreement, forged at our last meeting."

One of the two female Buckleswashers spoke up. "We agreed to nothing except to let you live."

"You forget, dear lady, that . . ."

Talltankard drew his knife. "My wife, Lyratha, forgets nothing!"

"But when I was last here . . ."

The other female Buckleswasher added her words: "Relax, Nervous One! We shall give you a few trinkets and send you on your way."

Llewellyn thought better of pushing the matter too far. "That will be fine. That is all I ask. Except for one other thing, I must say."

"And that is what?" Osco asked.

"May I have the stones from the key after you take the treasure from the chest?"

"The jade stones?" enquired the gnome, laughing. "They are practically worthless in the whole Shining South. You are an idiot to want them."

"Yes, I suppose," Llewellyn said. "But the woman I love—the most beautiful woman I have seen in any kingdom—has a great fondness for jade. Surely, I do not ask much."

"Agreed," Talltankard said. "I suppose you should have something. Now let me have the key."

Llewellyn nervously handed it to him. But a bit of his anxiety faded when the jade stone was placed in the key. It fit perfectly, and the whole company of Buckleswashers grinned.

* * * * *

Osco and Talltankard dragged the two-foot high by two-foot wide chest from the mouth of the cave into the fading sunlight. The rest of the company watched, as did Llewellyn, but every few seconds he looked around the perimeter of the area. He prayed Indio's folk were ready.

Talltankard turned the key, and smoke seeped out of the chest. Then Osco pulled open the lid and revealed the myriad jewels and gold it contained.

While the company stared at it, stunned, Llewellyn asked, "I do so hate to ask you, since you are all so very busy, but may I have the stones, as you promised?"

Talltankard removed the key and tossed it to Llewellyn, who caught it.

"But that's all you get, vagabond!" Carthax, the gnome, said sourly. "Be on your way!"

Stoutkeg broke into a song: "We're richer than we ever thought/ Just reward for battles fought."

But, suddenly, the voice of Indio the Black answered with its own song: "But don't expect to keep that treasure/ For taking it shall be our pleasure."

Indio's band, who slightly outnumbered their opponents, attacked the Buckleswashers. In minutes, all were locked in combat. For a brief moment, Indio stood free of opposition, and Llewellyn approached him.

"Don't forget. Twenty percent."

Indio stared at him coldly. "You've served your purpose, scavenger. Get out of my sight before I cut off twenty percent of your head!"

Llewellyn backed into the brush, away from Indio and the rest. Carefully, he removed the three jade stones from the key and put it in his leather sack.

"There are a few things Zalathorn told me that I have kept to myself. Vagabond, am I? Scavenger, you call me? No! Try *victor!*"

Pairs and trios of battling halflings (and a gnome) spread out into the woods, up the mountain, and far into the cave. Here and there, a body lay stunned, unconscious, or worse. But more importantly to Llewellyn, the treasure was left unguarded.

Llewellyn ran to the chest, depleted it of as much of its contents as his improvised sack would hold—which was almost all—and, seeing that the way east toward the Halar Hills was safe and free of otherwise occupied halflings (and a gnome), he ran as quickly as his feet would carry him.

Then, suddenly, he heard Talltankard's voice. "The vagabond! He has cheated us all!"

Llewellyn's heart beat faster, for he knew it would not be long before the halflings (and a gnome) would catch up to him. The sack was growing heavier, and it was slowing him down.

He took the jade stones and placed them in the three forged holes in the silver amulet he had acquired from Indio. And the moment the third stone was secured in the amulet, he felt himself leaving the ground, elevating, ascending, flying. Flying!

No, Llewellyn realized, not flying, but moving, or, more precisely, being moved.

Then, just as suddenly as the sensation had begun, it ended.

Zalathorn's amulet had proven to be as invaluable as Llewellyn knew it would. As the wizard had informed him, when the same person had possession of both the key and the amulet—with the jade stones in place in the latter— their bearer would be returned, together with his or her possessions, to his or her place of birth.

And, indeed, the Talkative One was home in the town of Klint, safe from both bands of adventurers and much richer than he had ever been. He looked around and sighed, relishing the safety and comfort he felt.

Llewellyn sensed that the wizard, too, must be amused. After all, it was Zalathorn himself who had helped him. It was Zalathorn who had "informed" him of the amulet that was originally part of the treasure. And it was he who revealed to him that one of the stones and the amulet were now in the possession of a band of halflings led by one who had the arrogance and presumption to call himself Indio the Black.

He doubted that Indio the Black or the Buckleswashers were amused, though, and vowed to steer clear of them for the rest of his days.

Indeed, he thought, a most excellent vow.

TOO FAMILIAR

David Cook

"It's extraordinarily complicated, you *see . . . ?*"

The wineglasses clinked as the wisp-bearded enchanter rearranged the drinks on the cluttered table, all the while dragging out the 'see' in his thick Ankhapurian accent. Like a swarm of midge flies, the assembled alchemists, prestidigitators, conjurers, thaumaturges, and wonder-workers—courtiers all—swarmed around him and listened. Their professional antennae quivered for the slightest hint of unfounded theorizing.

Well aware of it, the graybeard—such beard as he had—continued with the unfazed confidence of a high master educating coarse apprentices. Fingers fluttering, he allowed five droplets of carmine wine into the honey-yellow mead before him. "A taste of aqua vitae—no more!—that's been distilled by the flame of a silver burner and added to the flux. Once cooled, I stirred in"— and here he added three pinches from the salt cellar—"a measure of powdered dragonelle scale, and the whole solution precipitated—"

"Preposterous!" croaked a frog-faced Calimshite, alchemist to the recently arrived consular of Calimport. "Scale as a precipitate? Ludicrous! You might as well have used gravel for all of scale's suitability as a precipitate. Your whole theory's unsound!"

The blunt attack set the onlookers to buzzing, so much so that the proprietous and meekly disposed wizards of the swarm recoiled in pinch-faced distaste only to collide with those who surged forward at the first hint of the senior enchanter's hypothesizing weakness.

Only the challenger's basso voice rose above the polite cacophony that filled the royal salon. Fully aware, he pressed his assault with apparent obliviousness. "Undoubtedly it was another reaction—perhaps some containment in the powder. . . ."

The Calimshite's thrust was not lost on the Ankhapurian, but the older man guarded against the sting with the shield of dignity. "My powders were pure. I will gladly give you some if what you brought from Calimshan will not react." Wiping his damp fingers on a cloth, he coolly swatted back at this annoying fly.

"Good wit" and "Fine touch" hummed his supporters in the crowd.

"Scale never precipitates! Even apprentices know that," fumed the alchemist in his bubbling deep voice. He waggled a fat, pale finger across the table at the other, his stung pride, emboldened by drink, making him undiplomatically firm. He sputtered for words and finally blurted, "Why—ask your royal magister, if you doubt me!"

A chill swept the assembled collegium to a silence broken only by the tremolo titter of impudent apprentices from the back benches of the knot. The rest fingered their goblets and took great interest in their wine (forgotten till that point for the heat of the debate) while struggling to make their just-gay faces as bland as coal. In most cases, it only made them the more uncomfortably conspicuous, until they resembled no more than a line of hungry monkeys caught with the food.

Only the graybeard seemed unperturbed, arrogantly confident of his station. With a knowing smirk, he turned the baffled Calimshite's gaze toward the adjacent table— an island from their company. A lone woman, overladen in finery ill-suited to her age or itself, stared numbly at the air—or perhaps at the half-empty bottle before her.

"Our royal magister," the enchanter sneered in an intentionally loud whisper. "An adventuress—nothing but a hedge wizard. Never properly schooled at all." The last he added with overemphasis. "And fond of her drink."

At her table, Brown Maeve—Magister to His Royal Highness King Janol I (aka, Pinch), the Lich-Slayer, the Morninglord Blessed—knew what was said even before it was finished . . . even now, in her cups. The collegium's contempt was hardly a secret. She had heard the words and seen the smirks all before: hedge wizard, upstart, rogue's whore—adventuress! Not a true wizard in any case—no scholarly talent, no proper training, wouldn't even know an alembic from a crucible. Worse still, there was no denying most of it. A prestidigitous courtier she was not.

It didn't make their words right, though. They were a pack of poxy charlatans to lay their airs upon her. She'd done more than the lot of them, including helping Pinch lay down the lich Manferic, and it weren't their place to look down to her.

The smugness of their lot spoilt her wine, and so she figured they'd earned a little present of her own making. She could research too, as they'd soon remember. It was just a simple spell, nothing like their fine studies after the philosopher's stone or any of that, but Maeve kept it handy for *bestowing* on arrogant asses.

With a wicked good cheer, the royal magister pushed aside her glass, rose majestically, and managed to trundle like an old cart toward the salon doors. As she lumbered past the wizard-thick table, that hypocritical lot fell into a hushed silence, as if they had been discussing the weather, Maeve nodded, smiled, with excessive politeness greeted them all by name, and serenely extended her hand to the worst offenders to her dignity. As each took up her hand, a faint warmth flowed from her fingers, and Maeve's smile grew and grew until she was beaming with genuine satisfaction.

"Good morrow, and may the dawn bring you new discoveries," at last she said, disengaging herself from their group. Oh, they'd have discoveries, all right. She could scarce keep from hooting it out loud. There was no forgetting when you broke out with sores overnight—big ugly ones that were sure to put off wives and lovers. "Old drunk, am I?" She chuckled as she parted their company. Her gleeful echoes joined her as she wandered down the hall toward her own apartments.

* * * * *

Fiddlenose, sitting in the shade of the big fern that grew just in back of Goodman Uesto's granary, yawned a yawn that for his wee size threatened to transform the whole of his face into a single pit of pink throat ringed by fine white teeth. He could veritably swallow another brownie half his size—as if brownies were inclined to go around swallowing up their own kind. He was bored, and the big yawn was just one way he had to show it. As if part of a flowing wave, the yawn descended into a sour pucker of pinched irritability.

Where was that baleful cat?

Fiddlenose the brownie was tired of wasting his morning like a dull huntsman squatting in his blind. This was supposed to be fun—a prank and revenge on old farmer Uesto's calico tom. The twice-, no, thrice-cursed beast was the spawn of night terrors, the very hellion of farm cats, who managed to ruin all good, honest Fiddlenose's peace. Every night it howled, prowled, hissed, and spat till there wasn't a hope of either rest or joy for a proper house brownie. Too many times, it had smelled him out just as he was creeping indoors for a taste of grog and jam, or scared him out of his haymount nest as it went springing after the barn rats. Poor, suffering Fiddlenose couldn't stand it anymore. With the proper logic of an irate brownie, he had devised a revenge that was all out of proportion to the crime.

Only that cursed cat wasn't cooperating. He'd waited all morning with his twisted vines and stink-plant bladder, and still that feline monster hadn't showed. The shade under the fern was thick and stale, and Fiddlenose's eyes were steadily drooping into nap time.

* * * * *

Elsewhere, in a dingy ordinary in the meanest ward of Ankhapur, Will o' Horse-Shank, brownie by blood, opportunist by breeding, was in a sulk.

Fate's against me, he railed—venting in his own mind so no others could hear him. Two nights before, he was certain this morning he'd be in silk breeches and drinking firewine. It was sure he was a made man, and all by the wit of Mask.

This morning, though, he perched on a rickety old bench in Corlis's wineshop, still wearing the tattered hose he'd stolen from a child's laundry. Clutched like a great outlander drinking horn in his tiny hands was a battered pewter mug, half-filled with the cheapest sack old Corlis could pour—a pretty mean drink. Still, with no more than a ha' copper left in his purse, it was already more than Shank could afford. The brownie was not much heavier than a fat wharf-rat and barely up to a small man's shin, and the drink was already making good progress on his wee wits in these morning hours.

For the twentieth time, or at least as many times as it took to drink half the mug, Shank bemoaned the vile spin of Tymora's wheel that had reduced him to this treacherous state. For a week, he'd cozened an outlander merchant with a tale of dishonest captains, wreckers, smuggled goods, and a galley named *Swiftoar,* foxing the fool into letting Shank play the broker for the imaginary cargo. All it needed was another day, and the coney would have passed all his coin into Shank's hands and—heigh-ho!—that would have been the last of this little brownie!

But did the game play that way? No—the greedy fool had to talk around about his coming good fortune and that let out the truth. There was no captain, no *Swiftoar,* no cargo and, most of all, no coin for Shank to spirit off. Instead, Shank got curses and blows when he came to close the game—and all unjustly of course. It would have taught the outlander a proper lesson if Shank had made off with his cash.

He moaned it all again, even though there was no use in it, and swigged down another gulp of sour brew. The taste reminded him of the empty jingle in his purse. Corlis would be wanting coin for the drink, and Shank didn't have any. What he needed right now was for a quick and wealthy mark to walk through the door, something not very likely at this squalid ordinary.

* * * * *

"Too much joy or too much drink? Or a little of both?" a chipper, thin voice probed with just a touch of peevishness at having missed the fun.

Maeve stopped in the marbled hall, caught unawares by the stealth of her interrogator. Stealth wasn't that hard, considering the shadowed gloom between the pillars and the fact that the voice came up from somewhere around the height of her waist.

A halfling, fine-dressed in the gaudiest work the court tailor could tolerate, was suddenly beside the wizard, materializing seemingly out of nowhere. His garb was a garish mismatch—harlequin hose gartered with red silk and a rose and teal velvet damask doublet of intricate pattern, trimmed with more lace than a banquet table. It screamed of a soul utterly blind to taste . . . until one noticed that the blindness was actual. The little fellow's eyes were covered by a thick band of black cloth, and he clutched a short cane

Maeve was like to have leapt up in surprise before she realized it was only Sprite-Heels—or rather the Honorable Lord of the Watch Sir Sprite-Heels the Clever. (King Pinch's reward for loyal service was to put his fellow rogue in command of the city guard.) The knave had crept up on her yet again. For the years that she'd known him, the wizard was still not accustomed to the halfling's cat-footed ways. Blinded only twelve-months before, the halfling still got himself about with surprising silence and ease.

"I'd say," Sprite drawled as he tipped his head to hear her echoes, "that's your poxing laugh—the one you make after you've just shook hands with some popinjay. You wouldn't be up to old tricks now, would you, Maeve? What would our King Pinch say if he heard his old gang was laying curses on his subjects?"

"He'd probably say I had my cause—and you would, too," Maeve sniffed back. "They got what they had coming."

"Don't they all!" The tap of Sprite's cane hurried to keep pace with her as the halfling fell in alongside. "Them wizards again?"

"Yes—*them* wizards." Maeve's face flared up redder than her usual cheery drunk-red. She hustled down the hall, a tornado of indignation. "They had no right saying all those things—not after all I've done for Ankhapur. Not a one of them there was ready to fight Manferic or do any of those things. *I* did and they weren't mocking me then. A pox is only the least of what that lot deserves."

"Of course, you're right, Maeve," the halfling said with a cynicism that masked his genuine sympathy. "Still, now, you go poxing every one of them, and people are bound to start asking about it. You could get 'em believing there's a plague here." The click of the cane's metal ferrule on the slippery-smooth stone of the floor set Sprite's words to a lively cadence.

"I'll pox every whoreson one of them."

"Maybe me and Pinch ought to go into the cure-all business." Not all that often did she latch on to an idea so fierce, but when Maeve did, Sprite knew there'd be sparks and smoke before it ended. "What'll Pinch say, Maeve?"

"A pox on our King Pinch, too!"

"Might be interesting," Sprite smirked.

They walked a bit farther. Their conversation had run out, lingering on the image of their lord—as much as they'd admit he was—covered with foul sores. It was morbidly amusing, but they both knew neither could bring it to pass.

"Drink?" With uncanny sense, Sprite tapped down a

side hall toward his rooms.

"Why not?" Maeve agreed, resolved to be damned and determined even if it was almost dawn. There was always time for another drink.

With barely a fumble, Sprite undid the latch to his apartment and ushered her into the darkness beyond.

It was a full bottle (or two, since neither was keeping count) later when the wizard and halfling had come back to the question of respect

"They got no right," Maeve moaned for the several hundredth time, perhaps more so to Sprite's ears. She sloshed about her goblet, splattering drops over the antique table, a table that had been carved of fine bronzewood in some distant village of Chult and trekked the vast distance here no doubt on the back of some exotic beast. The morning sun, for the day was well up, glistened in the golden drops.

"Maeve, what you need is one of those—oh—rats, beasties," the halfling suggested weakly. He raised his sagging head from the table, where he'd only been 'just resting' while the wizard poured more drinks. Though he couldn't see it, the sloshing sound of yet another round of poured wine rendered him immensely pale.

"Rats?"

Sprite tried to nod, but that only made him feel greener. "Rats—you know, rats, owls, frogs—them little pets wizards get."

"Familursh," she slurred, and gulped down more wine.

"That's right. All them high-ups got 'em. You should have one too, Maeve."

"A familiar?" The wizard rolled the words around like a fine drink, considering the idea. "It'd have to be a right pretty one. No toads."

"No toads," the halfling mumbled.

"I got me a scroll somewhere." Maeve was now musing, working out the deed in her head as if she were planning a foist of her own. Sprite sat back with bleary satisfaction and proceeded to topple right out of his chair.

Passed out drunk, the halfling was in no way able to hear (and certainly in no way able to see) Maeve trundle out of the palace and into the morning light. She blinked like an owly fish caught in the overbright shallows. It had been some considerable time since she'd seen a morning; an early hour, anything before noon, was an exceptional moment. Nonetheless, she was determined to endure this grotesque hardship to realize her goal.

Thus determined, Maeve set out for the comfort of Ankhapur's grimy waterfront. It was the city's lowest of the low quarters, despised by the honest folk who nonetheless crept there every night to savor its taverns, flops, and festhalls. The waterfront stews were gray and small and pretended not to exist, letting their customers imagine they had privacy and discretion, though in truth little transpired that wasn't spread to someone's ears. The naive found themselves compromised, the gullible blackmailed, and it took a native, not just to Ankhapur but to the waterfront itself, to have any hope of keeping one's business to oneself. It was just the kind of place Maeve wanted, her true home.

Though she'd traveled here from far lands, she'd lived most her life in such surroundings. Every town that wanted to be of consequence had its version of the Ankhapurian waterfront. A town could never be a city without one, its character incomplete without this pocked and festering side of its urban body. More than any other monument, statue, palace, or memorial, such districts revealed the hidden souls of the city founders, the dark and secret selves of respected ancestors.

It was far better for her to work in such surroundings. The royal laboratories, territory hers by title, were too public for this work. Nothing she might try there would pass unnoticed, and with the real chance that she might get it wrong, the woman did not want to risk such open humiliation. This task was better done in some forgotten room, among her own kind, where she could do her work in peace. Among the stews, she might raise a few curious eyebrows, but folks there had the sense to give a wizard wide berth for fear they'd wind up as frogs or worse.

As for the stench, the thugs, the blackmailers and loose women, Maeve didn't mind. She was boozily confident she could slide back in, even though her street sense was somewhat out of practice after a year of palace life. Indeed, the doubt that she might not know Ankhapur's cheats and black ways as well as she could never entered her mind.

Clutching an ungainly bag of powders, devices, and bottles, she ignored the looks of the festhall girls going home in the dawn light, the hungry stares of hungover drunks as they staggered themselves out of the mud where they'd fallen, and the curious thronging of urchins who acted far more innocent than they ever had been. She wound her way through the alleys and lanes leading to a wineshop she knew, one where the owner, Corlis, would be discreet and the company few. Corlis had rooms and didn't care what happened in them as long as it was quiet and the shiny nobles were slid across the scarred counter in advance.

* * * * *

Shank, sitting on the edge of the cold hearth, his little legs dangling over the low drop of stone, held his over-sized mug close to his face from the first moment the door creaked open. Customers at this morning hour were unusual and therefore naturally of interest. Peering over the rim of his stein, only his eyes visible, Shank watched as a woman, frowzy and old, tottered into the commons. She juggled a bulging bag that threatened to squirt its contents out with every shift of her ample body. As entrances went, the woman's was unpromising, so Shank watched her with more curiosity than cunning.

It was the clink of coin on the landlord's table that caught his full attention. His little ears wiggled their sharp points with the slap of each piece the woman handed over. One, two, three—it was all far too much for anything in this slopshop. There was a lot more than room and board being bought here, and whatever it was, Shank wanted to know. As he gulped down one last hit of wine, he carefully sidled into the cool shadows of the cracked mantelpiece.

* * * * *

With a grumpy start, Fiddlenose woke to the screech of a cat yowl. He sprang to his feet, rustling the fronds of the shading fern. The beast was afoot, and he'd fallen asleep in the morning heat! Cursing furiously to himself with all his considerable store of colorful invective, he dived for the rapidly unspooling vines that had been coiled at his feet. The trap was sprung, and judging from the yowls, he'd snared the hellcat beast!

He grabbed the vine and tried to dig in his heels as the mighty tomcat heaved against the noose. Scrambling, he barely kept balance against the pull, losing ground with every jerk. His feet grew nearer the edge of the shade, and within moments he'd be hauled into the open, where farmer Uesto would discover him—and all because of that cursed tom!

Fiddlenose twisted about, slipped the vine over his shoulder, and valiantly heaved forward, dragging—footstep by tiny footstep—the noosed tomcat closer to the sapling at the edge of the grove. Sweating and straining, he finally reached close enough to loop his little slack around the springy trunk. Quick went the knots, and then it was done. Fiddlenose had triumphed! The hellcat was his!

Exhausted and satisfied, he collapsed against the trunk and waited for Uesto's calico tom to give up before he started the next step of his oh-so-cunning plan.

* * * * *

Three nobles, Maeve mused to herself. It was all far too much, but she was feeling generous. Why not? It wasn't her money. Thanks to Pinch, all her needs came from the royal treasury, which in turn came from the people. She didn't feel like haggling with old Corlis, who would have gotten the best of her anyway, and so her three nobles and a promise of two more assured her of the privacy she wanted. Thus, overconfidently oblivious to the effect her entrance had made, Maeve paraded up the rickety stairs to the room she'd bought.

As she reached the top of the stairs, a small figure behind her detached himself from the gloom of the mantel and slid along the edge of the commons. Quick and silent, Shank darted in front of the counter, just beneath the gaze of watchful Corlis. For his coins, the old landlord was doing his best to be watchful, to make sure no one disturbed his generous benefactor, but the old man's eyes were no match for Shank's cunning stealth. Quick as a dart, he was in the dusty gloom of the stairway, nimbly skipping over the squeaky treads. In the hall above, it was no hard matter to guess where his mark had gone. The brownie simply chose the biggest of all possible rooms.

Thus, he found the door that had to be Maeve's (or so he guessed by the clanking and puttering from the other side). There was a transom open at the top, in a vain attempt to let some air flow through the building. Nimble, even with as much drink as he'd had, he had little trouble squirreling himself up the flimsy jamb. His tiny hands and feet found holds no human could ever have hoped to use, and in a mere moment, the brownie was carefully wedged in the gap between the door and the splintery boards of the ceiling.

Oblivious to the dark, bright eyes watching her, Maeve was already about her work. The old scroll she had was faded and grease-stained—she vaguely recollected wrapping a roasted hen in it one night—and she could only hope the instructions and the words were still legible. It wasn't like the scrolls she was used to, where all that was needed was to utter the twisted words on the page. This one required procedures and processes to bring it to fruition. Deciphering the parchment as best she could, the wizard set out the powders, the candles, and all the paraphernalia needed to cast the summoning.

To the process, Maeve added a bottle of wine, setting it prominently on a table in the center of the pattern. She wanted a special familiar, by damn, not just any frog or rat, and figured, in her own way, that a little extra enticement to the spell couldn't possibly hurt. She added another bottle, too, just for herself, a strengthening tonic for what she was certain would be an arduous process. The cork already pulled, she sampled heavily as the work went on and mumbled under her breath a running monologue of grievances and revenge.

From his post, Shank quickly got over his first dose of surprise. When he'd scampered up the jamb, he'd imagined what lay on the other side. This was not it. The old woman was certainly not making preparations for any lover's rendezvous, any easy material for blackmail. He'd had it all figured—she was some wealthy crone meeting her gentleman. (By his logic, she had to be wealthy, since she wasn't going to gain suitors by her looks.) He'd hoped to spy, learn some names, and turn the whole day into a nice profit.

Unfortunately, she clearly wasn't making arrangements for a tryst. She was preparing to do magic. Although disappointed that his ambitions were scotched, Shank watched with fascination. Whatever she was doing, she didn't want people knowing, so that still meant the possibility of profit for little Will o' Horse-Shank. She might be casting a curse on someone—that could bring him money. If she were a vile priestess plotting evil or a treasonous wizard, there might be reward for turning her in. Folks said King Pinch could be a generous man when it suited him. Of course, she might be one of them wild mages about to try something risky. Shank didn't feel so comfortable about that prospect. As a brownie, though, one of the things Shank had to be thankful for was an innate understanding of the mystical world. As he watched, he slowly gathered the clues he needed to see what she was about: the summoning of a familiar.

Ah, yes. The brownie's cunning little mind hatched a perfectly suitable plot. Suddenly he saw for himself a life of ease—wine, breads, new clothes and cheese, things he so dearly loved. He watched her go through the twists and turns, light the candles, and utter the words. He waited and poised himself for the right moment. If she wanted a familiar, by the gods, he'd make sure she got one.

* * * * *

Maeve swallowed another gulp of wine and pressed on with the reading of the scroll. The damned spell was tortuously hard, more complicated and twisted than it looked at the start. She forced her way through a few more syllables and arcane passes before reaching again for the wine to strengthen herself. She was almost done and was pretty sure she'd gotten it right. It was so hard to tell with these things, especially with it being so early in the morning and all.

Finally, she spoke the last syllables, and just in time, too, for her candles were almost burnt to nubs and her wine was nearly gone. She was sweaty from the effort even though the room was not particularly hot. As the last echoes rang out, Maeve stood back and waited.

Nothing happened.

There was no puff of smoke, no creature appearing out of thin air. Instead, she stood alone in the center of a dingy room, at the heart of a badly drawn chalk outline—circles had never been her strength—listening to a burst of boisterous singing from downstairs and waiting for something, anything, to happen.

All at once, there was a scrabbling thump and clump behind her, and Maeve whirled to face the door. There, at the edge of the circle, stood a little man with pointed ears and a pointy chin, improbably dressed in tattered children's clothes. With a flamboyant wave and a grand bow, the brownie—for it was a brownie much to Maeve's great joy—grandly announced, "The Mighty Will o' Horse-Shank, familiar to your arcane majesty, stands at your service!"

Maeve beamed with joy. The spell had worked!

* * * * *

The old tom was quiet, resigned to its fate. Now was the time, Fiddlenose knew, to start the next step of his plan. Rousing from his seat, he pushed aside the brush that hid the stink-plant sac he'd carefully gathered. Now he'd teach that tom to ruin his nights.

As he gathered the gelatinous pod, the air around him began to strangely hum. It was quiet and soft, but the old tom heard it too and began to yowl once more, though this time its voice was filled with fear. Something was happening, something that made Fiddlenose's skin itch. Worse still, he was suddenly keen on a strange urge—an urge to be with someone, someone far away and calling to him.

The hot air closed around him, thickening like bad porridge. The hum grew louder until it drowned out even the tomcat's shrill howls. As the entire world started to fade on Fiddlenose, the brownie, furious and confused, could only helplessly wonder, why do I want to serve someone I don't even know?

And then everything faded to nothing.

* * * * *

"Cheese. I'd really like some cheese," her familiar loudly announced from his chair. His little feet dangled well above the floor, and he could barely reach the side table, but that didn't stop him from pouring himself another glass of palace wine. "Good cheese, not that mold old Car—I mean, not plain, ordinary human cheese. We familiars have delicate dispositions. I'm sure you wouldn't want to indispose *your* familiar, now would you, dear Maeve? I honestly believe that with a peck of cheese, I shall feel right again and be ready to do your bidding."

Maeve sighed. Somehow, this was just not working out as she'd thought it would. The way she understood it, a familiar was supposed to be at your beck and call, but since Will had arrived he'd demanded wine, roast meat, the promise of new clothes, even gifts to the innkeeper in his name—and all before he could (and she could quote) 'Feel truly restored and ready to do her will.'

"I think you should be rested enough," she argued testily. "You're my familiar. I'd like you to demonstrate your powers."

Shank knew from her tone that he could not put off the

question any longer. The only problem was he hadn't a clue what sort of powers he was supposed to have or grant to her—even if he could.

"Powers? Such as?" he stalled.

Maeve screwed up her face, not expecting the question. She didn't know; she'd never had a familiar before. She racked her drink-fuddled memory for what little she knew on the whole subject.

"You should be able to hear my thoughts—obey my commands. That's one."

"Oh, that," Shank drawled as he tried to think of an explanation. "Well, that takes time. Uh-huh, that's it. We just met, and I'm very, very tense, so my mind is resisting your thoughts. I'm sure it will get better, especially if you've got any more of this wine." He poked at the now-empty bottle on the table and looked around the room significantly. "I'm sure it would help immensely."

Maeve sighed again, but there was no arguing, so she thrust her head out the door and hailed for Corlis to bring more wine. Nobody'd warned her that familiars were so demanding. "Senses, too," she said, coming back in. "I should have keener senses, like hearing and all."

Shank stalled by looking to the ceiling. This scam was starting to get more complicated. It was about time to scupper off. "Don't you feel sharper?" he finally asked, playing on her vanity. "You look positively prime and alert. It's very impressive. I don't think anybody could get anything by you—"

Before he could say more, the temperature in the room abruptly rose to a sweltering degree. The air was filled with the prickly scent of something magical. There was a loud pop, and with it Maeve stumbled back in slack-jawed surprise while Shank fumbled the wineglass from his grip, spilling Ankhapur's finest red all over the floor.

In the center of the room, looking almost as surprised and certainly as unhappy, was another brownie, dressed in a little jerkin of leaves and grass. Sticks and fern fronds jutted from the wild mass of his hair. Clutched in his hands was a green, floppy pod that he fumbled and almost dropped. Recovering it, he tucked it under his arm and, with an irritated grimace, turned to Maeve and made an awkward, forced bow. "I am Fiddlenose and am—at your service, mighty mage." The last was said through firmly clenched teeth, as though the words were wrenched from the very core of his being.

Maeve goggled. Two brownies! By the gods. She'd summoned *two* brownies!

Shank suddenly eyed the door and the window, trying to decide which he could get out first. It was time for young Shank to get scarce.

Fiddlenose found himself compelled to serve, his mind suddenly filled with strange thoughts that went against his very nature. What was he doing here, and why did he say that?

As she looked from Shank to Fiddlenose and Fiddlenose to Shank, it slowly dawned on Maeve through the drink and the length of the day. She hadn't summoned two familiars, two brownies to serve her. One was a fake, and one was real.

She pointed at the newcomer. "You, Fiddlenose. You say you're here to serve me?"

"Yes, mistress," the brownie grunted.

Shank eased out of his chair.

"No cheese, no wine, no fine clothes?"

Shank tiptoed across the uncarpeted floor, hoping to reach the open window.

"Only if it pleases you," was the dutifully miserable reply.

"And you—" Maeve turned to Shank's now empty chair.

That was the imposter's cue. He broke into a run, hoping to scramble over the towering sill before she could catch him. It had been fun, but now it was time to go.

The words were uttered, and the ray crackled from Maeve's fingertips before Shank had loped two paces.

The magical beam struck him full in the back and spread like ticklish fire down every nerve of his limbs. For a moment, he plunged forward, his body flailing like that of a decapitated hen, and then he fell to the floor in a loose puddle—the impossible way a dead man falls when all his muscles surrender life and control.

He hadn't, at least, surrendered life, but control . . . ? Paralyzed. Through a sideways-canted view, he saw Maeve smiling with hard satisfaction. Perhaps still having life was not a good thing after all. If he could've closed his eyes, he'd have closed them and prayed to every god and goddess he knew for mercy.

Sure that Shank wasn't faking, Maeve turned back to her true familiar. She did feel keener and sharper, there was no doubt. A little of the wooziness was gone from her mind. She liked it; it was good. What other mage in Ankhapur could boast a brownie as her familiar?

A sniffled, "Mistress?" brought her attention back to the woodland sprite in front of her. She looked at Fiddlenose—her brownie—and saw how sad and angry he was. "Mistress, what do you want of me?"

"You're my familiar?"

"Yes . . . mistress." Again the words were forced.

"Where do you come from?"

"Goodman Uesto's farm, near Woodrock." The question brightened the little face, but the joy quickly passed as the brownie thought of the sights he would never see again. "Will you let me go now?"

Maeve wasn't sure what to say. "Did you . . . want to be a familiar. I mean, how did I get you?"

Fiddlenose looked uncomfortably at the strange surroundings. He had never been in a human place like this before. Old Uesto's farm was just a cabin on the edge of the woods, nothing like this. "I wasn't asked. There was just a big buzz and—*pop!*—I was here."

The implication of it made Maeve weak, so unsettled that she took a chair, looked at the empty wine bottle, and wished she had some right now. She really wanted a familiar, a special, wonderful familiar, but this was like kidnapping—and worse. She'd snatched this poor brownie from its home and friends and was forcing it to serve against its will. It wasn't like getting a rat or frog at all.

She really wanted a familiar, and now look what had happened. What could she do?

On the floor, Shank was making gurgly noises not too different from those of a beached fish. The paralysis made it hard for him to do more than slobber and sputter for rescue. The sound reminded Maeve of her victim, and a wicked look passed across her face. Suddenly Shank wished he could have been very, very still.

All at once clear-headed and firmly resolute, Maeve rose from her seat. "Fiddlenose," she announced with heartfelt relief, "I release you. Go home, brownie. I can't send you home the way you came, so it'll be an adventure or two getting back to your farm. Woodrock's a good week west of here, but if you follow the shore, you should make it all right. That's the best I can do."

The little wood sprite gaped in astonishment. "But what about you? I'm your familiar. Didn't you want one?"

Maeve shook her head, tossing her brown-gray hair. "You go. I'll find a solution to my problem. Go now, before I change my mind!"

The brownie was already making for the door. "Thank you, mistress," he said with heartfelt glee just before he ducked through the door.

With one gone, Maeve turned to the other. "Now, what should be done with you?" The question was pointless, and not just because Shank couldn't answer. The wizard already had plans.

"Perhaps, you don't know, but I'm the royal court wizard," Maeve continued, clearly relishing the look of panic in Shank's eyes. "That means my lord, King Pinch, could have you put away for a very, very long time. Or maybe just execute you as an example, dearie. Does that sound fair?"

The pupils grew wider.

"Or"—and for this she knelt down beside him—"you could be my familiar. Serve me, play the part, and you could have almost as much wine, cheese, and fine clothes as you'd like. Stick your tongue out if you think you'd like that instead."

Sweat matted Shank's hair, but he managed to poke his tongue through his parted teeth.

"Good." Maeve smiled, and then her face went hard. All the fine court manners she'd learned in a year dropped away as she spoke to him in her element. "Understand

this, Will o' Horse-Shank. Change your mind, scupper out
on me, or play me for the coney again, and I'll see to it
that Pinch scrags your scrawny neck from the leafless
tree and leaves your bones for the dogs. Hide from me,
and every sorcerer in the kingdom'll be scrying for you,
every foin and cutpurse will be out to collect the bounty
on your hide. You know I can do it, and you know I will.
Understand?"

The tongue poked out again.

Maeve smiled and waved a hand over the paralyzed
brownie. Sensation and order began to flow back into his
limbs. "Then we have an understanding."

She picked up the empty wineglass and raised it in a
mock toast while Shank stumbled to his feet. "Here's to
getting me a very special familiar!"

RED AMBITION

Jean Rabe

Szass Tam eased himself into a massive chair behind an ornate table covered with curled sheets of vellum and crystal vials filled with dark liquid. A thick candle stood in the middle of the clutter, its flame dancing in the musty air and casting a soft light across his grotesque features.

His pale, parchment-thin skin stretched taut across his high cheekbones, and his wispy hair, the color of cobwebs, spread unevenly atop his age-spotted scalp. His lower lip hung loose, as if there were no muscles to control it, and the fleshy part of his nose was gone, revealing twin cavities. The scarlet robes he wore fell in folds about his skeletal frame and spread like a pool of blood on the floor about his chair.

He absently swirled his index finger in a puddle of wax gathering on the table, letting the warm, oily liquid collect on his skin. He rolled the cooling blob between his thumb and middle finger until it hardened into a ball. Then he released the wax and watched it roll across the rosewood finish and come to rest near a decades-old scroll. The piercing points of white light that served as Szass Tam's eyes stared at the parchment. It contained the last enchantment needed to turn his cherished apprentice into a creature like himself—an undead sorcerer . . . a lich. Of course, his apprentice would have to die before the spell could be invoked. Killing her would be no great matter, he decided. Bony fingers grasped the parchment and brought it close to his still heart.

Szass Tam's mortal life had ended centuries ago on a Thayan battlefield a hundred miles north of his comfortable keep. But the magic coursing through him prevented him from passing beyond the land of the living. It bound him to the human realms in a rotting body that pulsed with an arcane power few would dare challenge. The lich considered himself the most formidable Red Wizard in Thay. A zulkir, he controlled the country's school of necromancy. His apprentice, Frodyne, was also a Red Wizard, one of an august council of sorcerers who ruled Thay through schemes, threats, and careful manipulation. Szass Tam smiled thinly. None were more treacherous than he.

He listened intently. The soft footfalls in the hall were Frodyne's. He placed the scroll in a deep pocket and waited. One day soon he would bless her with immortality.

"Master?" Easing open the door, Frodyne stepped inside. She padded forward, the shiny fabric of her dark red robe dragging across the polished marble floor behind her. "Am I disturbing you?"

Szass Tam gestured to a seat opposite him. Instead, the young woman's course took her to stand beside him. She quickly knelt, placed her delicate hands on his leg, and looked up into his pinpoint eyes. Her clean-shaven head was decorated with red and blue tattoos, fashionable for Thay, and her wide, midnight-black eyes sparkled with a hint of mischief. The corner of her thin lips tugged upward into a sly grin.

Szass Tam had taken her as an apprentice several years ago. An amazingly quick study, Frodyne never hid her hunger for spells and knowledge, and she dutifully hung on his every word. The lich thought her loyal, or as loyal as anyone in Thay could be. As she grew in power through the years, he shared horrible designs with her— how to crush lesser wizards under the heels of his skeletal army, how to raise men from the grave, how to steal the souls of the living. He recently confided in her that he was undead, showed her his true, rotting visage, and when she did not shrink from it, he shared with her his plans for dominating Thay. Frodyne had made it clear she wanted to be at his side—forever.

The lich stared at her unblemished, rosy face. Indeed, he thought, she is worthy of passing the centuries at my side. He reached a bony hand to her face and caressed her smooth cheek.

"What brings you here so late?" His deep voice echoed hauntingly in the room.

"I was at the market today, the slave pens," she began. "I was looking over the stock when I discovered a man asking about you and the goings-on in the keep."

The lich nodded for her to continue. "He was an unusual little man who wore only one tattoo: an odd-looking triangle filled with gray swirls."

"A worshiper of Leira," the lich mused.

"A priest of the goddess of deception and illusions, in fact," Frodyne added. "In any event, I followed him. When he was alone I cast a simple spell that put him under my control. I had to know why he was asking so many questions."

The lich's pinpoint eyes softened, and with his skeletal finger, he traced one of the tattoos on Frodyne's head. "And what did you learn?"

"Much, Master. Eventually. The priest had a strong will. But before he died he revealed he was worried about one of your armies, the one patrolling Delhumide. There is a ruin in that dead city that a few worshipers of Leira are particularly interested in. The priest believed that deep inside a crumbling temple rests a powerful relic. When your army passed nearby, he feared you had learned of the thing and had sent your army to retrieve it. But when your skeletons did not enter the temple, he was uncertain how much you knew. He came to the city asking about your plans and forces."

The lich gazed into Frodyne's eyes. "My skeletons were patrolling. Nothing more. But, tell me, Frodyne . . . why didn't the priest simply enter the temple and take the relic for himself?"

"I wondered that, too, Master." The young apprentice beamed. "I pressed him on the matter. He admitted that while he coveted the relic, he coveted his life more. It seems the Goddess of Liars has guardians and great magic protecting her prize."

The lich stood and drew Frodyne up with him. "And just what is this relic of Leira?"

"A crown. The priest said a great energy is harnessed in the crown's gems." Frodyne smiled thinly and stroked Szass Tam's decaying chin. "And we shall share that crown and energy, just as I shared the priest's tale with you."

The lich stepped back and shook his head slowly. "I shall send my skeletal army into the heart of the temple and claim the relic as my own."

"Yours, Master?"

"Aye, Frodyne."

"But you would not know of its existence without me." She put her hands on her hips and glared at him. "This is treachery, Szass Tam. I could have claimed the bauble for myself, with you none the wiser. But I chose to share the news with you."

"And in so doing, you chose to abandon your claim to it," the lich replied icily. "The relic will be mine alone. You have done well, my apprentice. I shall have another bauble to add to my hoard."

The comely apprentice strode indignantly to the door, then glanced over her shoulder at the lich. "But what of Leira, Szass Tam? What if you anger the Patroness of Illusionists and Liars by breaching her temple and stealing something of hers?"

Szass Tam laughed. "I have little regard for the goddess of treachery, dear Frodyne. Get some rest. I shall tell you in the morning what my skeletons find in Delhumide."

The lich listened to her footfalls retreat down the hall. Soon she would not need sleep. Or food. Soon she would need none of the things that made man weak, allowing her to one day sit at his side as he ruled all of Thay.

The lich sat straight in his chair and pushed Frodyne from his thoughts. He concentrated on his army of skeletons in Delhumide, stretching his mind across the miles until he made contact with his undead general and directed him to march to Leira's temple. The miles melted away beneath the soldiers' bony feet as they neared the ruined temple of Leira. In an untiring cadence, they approached the temple steps. Then Szass Tam lost contact with them.

* * * * *

The lich cursed and cast himself upon the Thayan winds to fly to Delhumide. As he soared, his form changed. His skin took on a ruddy tint. His cheeks became puffy, and his body thickened to fill out the red silk robes that only moments before had hung on his frame in voluminous folds. His eyes became black, almost human, and his white hair grew thicker and longer, then darkened to match the color of the night sky. The lich added a thin mustache for effect. Few in Thay knew Szass Tam was one of the dead. Outside the confines of his keep he assumed the image of a living man.

The ground passed below him in a blur, the darkness obscuring most of the terrain. But the lich didn't falter in his course. He knew the way to the dead city. He'd been born there.

It was near dawn when he reached the ruined temple. He descended to the rough ground and glared at the crumbling stonework. His eyes smoldered in the gloom and surveyed the carnage. He knew now why he'd lost contact with his army. Strewn about the shattered pillars were more than a hundred skeletal warriors. Their broken bones and crushed skulls gleamed faintly. Near them lay more dead—figures with tattered gray flesh and rotting clothes, things that stank of the grave. The lich knelt near a one-armed zombie and slowly turned the body over. It had little flesh left on its frame. Most of it had been burned away by fire. Szass Tam ran his fingers through the grass around the corpse. Not a blade was singed. Magical fire had killed the army, the lich realized, fire meant for undead.

The hunt for Leira's relic was now very costly. It would take many, many months and considerable effort to raise enough dead to replace these fallen soldiers. Szass Tam stood, silently vowed retribution for the slaughter of his minions, and carefully picked his way toward the crumbling temple stairway. At the base of the steps, the lich spied a twitching form, an undead creature with pasty white flesh, hollow eyes, and protruding broken ribs. The ghoul, lone survivor of the lich's force, tried futilely to rise at the approach of its master.

"Speak to me," the lich commanded in a sonorous voice. "Tell me what happened here."

"Followed your orders," the ghoul rasped. "Tried to breach the temple. Tried to get what you wanted. But they stopped us."

"How many?"

"Three," the ghoul replied. "They wore the robes of Red Wizards."

Szass Tam growled deep in his throat and looked up the stairs. If only three had been able to conquer this force, they must be powerful. He took a last look at his beaten army and padded by the gasping ghoul to carefully select a path up the crumbling steps. Leira's temple lay in ruins like the rest of Delhumide. A once-great city, it was now populated by monsters and was laden with incredible traps—the remaining wards of the nobles and wizards who had once lived here. Creatures roamed freely across the countryside—goblins, darkenbeasts, trolls, and dragons, and they presented enough of a threat to keep the living away.

Szass Tam searched for the magical energies that protected the fallen temple, and then he made his way around them to reach the comfort of the shadows inside. The damp coolness of the ruins reminded the lich of a tomb. This was his element. Focusing his eyes, he separated stonework from the darkness. He saw before him a crumbling old hallway that extended deep into the temple and sensed other presences within. He glided toward them.

Eventually the hallway ended, and the lich studied the walls, searching. Nothing. No moving stonework. He scrutinized the bricks by running his fingers over the cool surface to his left and right until he felt no resistance. The bricks before him were not real. Then he heard footfalls, soft and distant. The sound was regular, as of someone walking, and it was coming from far beneath him. He took a step forward and passed through the illusionary wall.

Beyond lay a damp stairway that led down into darkness. The lich cupped his hand and spoke a single word. A globe of light appeared in his palm and illuminated the stairwell. Along the walls and on each step were weathered sigils of various-sized triangles filled with swirling gray patterns—all symbols of Leira. The lich paused to appreciate them. He had little regard for the goddess, but thought the sigils had been rendered by someone with considerable skill.

Most Red Wizards in Thay worshiped one or more malign deities. At one time Szass Tam had, too—but the need to worship some power that might grant eternal life had faded away with the years and with the onset of lichdom. Szass Tam still considered himself respectful of some of the powers, such as Cyric. But not Leira.

Szass Tam was halfway down the steps when he felt a presence approaching. The minutes passed, and the undead zulkir's patience was finally rewarded when a pearl-white phantasm with the face of a beautiful woman formed in front of him. The lich pondered its appearance and decided the thing was nothing more than a hapless spirit tied to the temple.

"Trespasser," the spectre whispered in a soft, feminine voice. "Begone from the sacred place of Leira, she who is most powerful. Begone from the Lady of the Mists' temple, the place we are sworn to protect."

The lich stood his ground, eyeing the thing, and for an instant, it appeared the spirit was astonished he did not run. "I will leave when I am ready," the lich said flatly. He kept his voice low so his quarry deeper in the complex would not hear.

"You must go," the spirit repeated, its voice changing, becoming deeper and sultry. The visage was that of another woman. "This is not a place for those who do not believe. You do not believe in our goddess. You wear no symbol of hers."

"I believe in myself," the lich replied evenly. "I believe in power."

"But not in Leira."

"No. I have no respect for the Lady of the Mists," the lich growled softly.

"Then your bones shall rot here," the spectre cursed in a new voice.

The lich stared at the creature. The undead now bore the image of a young man with a long nose, and the voice was strong and masculine. Large ghostly hands reached out and thrust into Szass Tam's chest. The lich stood unmoving, unaffected by the spirit's attack.

"This cannot be! You should be dead!" the spirit shouted with the voice of an old woman. Indeed, the pearl-white form was now covered with wrinkles, and the transparent flesh sagged on her cheeks and jaw.

"I am already dead," the lich whispered in reply. "And you will bend to my will—whatever manner of undead you are." Szass Tam's eyes once more became pinpoints of hot white light. They bore into the old woman's eyes and fixed the diaphanous being in place.

"Who are you?" Szass Tam demanded. "What are you?"

"We are Leira's," the old woman replied. "We are the last of the priests who lived in this temple. When the city fell to the army of Mulhorand, we died. But so strong was our faith in the Lady of the Mists that our wills banded together in one form so we could serve Leira forever."

The lich's lips curled upward slowly. "It is your misfortune you stayed." His pinpoint eyes glowed brighter, and he concentrated on the ghostly form before him. The spirit moaned in pain, the voice of a young man joining the old woman's.

"No!" the spirit cried in a chorus of voices. "Do not hurt us! Do not send us from the temple!"

"To the Nine Hells I will send you—to join the other priests of the Patroness of Liars," Szass Tam threatened, "unless you serve me and cease your cacophonous whining."

"We serve only Leira," the spirit wailed even more loudly.

"Now serve a better master." The lich raised a fleshy finger and pointed it at the spectre's face. The visage of the young man had returned. A silver beam shot from the tip of Szass Tam's finger and struck the spirit's head, sending the apparition flying backward several feet. The beam pulsed wildly while the spirit convulsed in agony.

"Who do you serve?" the lich persisted.

"Leira," the creature groaned in chorus.

Again the lich struck the creature with a silver beam. The ghostly image wavered and began to spread, as if it were being stretched on a torturer's rack. The spirit's arms and legs lengthened to the corners of the stairwell, and it became as insubstantial as mist.

"Who do you serve?"

"We serve you," the spirit finally gasped in its myriad voices.

Szass Tam's eyes softened to a pale glow. He studied the spirit to make sure it was indeed under his control. The many minds he touched berated him, but they swore their loyalty. Smugly satisfied, Szass Tam willed his human eyes to return.

"Tell me, priests," the lich began. "Were you this ineffectual in stopping the Red Wizards who came before me?"

"The ones below?" the spirit quipped. The creature's face was now that of a beautiful woman, the one the thing had displayed when Szass Tam first encountered it.

"Yes. The ones below."

"They believe," the ghostly image stated. "They wear the holy symbol of Leira upon their shiny heads. All believers are welcome in this temple. All believers—and you."

"You let them pass freely because they tattooed symbols of Leira on their heads?" the lich queried. "You believed they worshiped your goddess because of a little paint?"

"Yes," the ghostly image answered. "Leira's temple is for Leira's own."

The lich looked past the creature and peered down the stairs. "You will come with me. You will show me the traps that litter the path before us. And you will show me the relic I seek."

Szass Tam resumed his course down the stairway, the spectre at his side pointing out weathered mosaics of its goddess, expounding on the greatness of Leira, and gesturing toward magical wards on every step. The lich passed by the broken bodies of long-dead trespassers as he moved from one chamber to the next. He was so intent on finding the relic that he nearly passed over the only freshly killed corpse. The spectre pointed it out to him. The body of a red-robed man, no older than twenty, lay crumpled amid chunks of stone. The man, who wore the painted symbol of Leira on his head, sprawled with his limbs at odd angles. His eyes were wide with terror, and a thin line of blood still trickled from his mouth.

"He was with the other wizards," the spectre said in an old man's voice. "Pity he died so young. Though he wore the symbol of the Lady of the Mists and I let him pass, the guardian looked into his heart. His heart betrayed him as an unbeliever. The guardian struck him down."

"Guardian?"

"The Lady of the Mists' eternal servant," the spectre replied. "The guardian waits in the chamber beyond."

The lich peered into the black distance and started forward. The spirit of Leira's priests dutifully followed on his heels.

"Kill the thing!" Szass Tam heard a deep male voice cry. The lich quickened his pace and entered a massive cavern lighted by luminous moss. He stopped and stared at the cavern's three occupants—Frodyne, a Red Wizard he didn't recognize, and a monstrous construct.

"What treachery is this?" the lich's voice boomed.

"Master!" Frodyne squealed. She was dressed in a soiled and torn red robe, and the triangle she had painted on her scalp was smeared with sweat. Her normally soft features were set in grim determination as she called for her companion to join the fight. The man stayed behind her, ignoring her coarse words, and stared at the great thing before them. Frodyne spread her fingers wide and unleashed a magical bolt of fire at the monstrosity.

Frodyne's foe stood at least thirty feet tall, its head nearly reaching the chamber's roof. The guardian was not undead, but it was certainly not living. The lich eyed the thing from top to bottom. It had the torso of a man and the head of a goat. Its chest bore the symbol of a triangle filled with swirling mists. The thing possessed four eyes that were evenly spaced above the thick bridge of its metallic nose, and its mouth gaped open, exposing pointed teeth made of steel. Four arms as thick as tree trunks waved menacingly at the sides of its body and ended in six-fingered iron claws. Every inch of the creature was gray. The thing's massive legs ended in cloven hooves that created sparks when they stomped on the ground and rocked the cavern. The shockwaves made Frodyne and her companion scramble to stay on their feet.

"It seems you've made it angry, dear Frodyne," Szass Tam said. "Just as you've angered me. You destroyed my army."

"I wanted the crown!" she said as she unleashed another bolt of lightning. "I learned about this temple and the relic, but you said the bauble would be yours. It should be mine!"

The lich watched her nimbly avoid a fist that slammed into the cavern floor where she had been standing.

"I'm sorry!" she yelled. "Help us, please. The crown will be yours. I swear!"

The lich folded his arms and surveyed the battle, not bothering to reply to her plea.

She scowled and brought up her fingers, touching the thumbs together and holding her open palms toward the guardian. She mumbled words Szass Tam recognized as one of the first spells he'd taught her, and icy shards sprang from her hands. The shards flew true and imbedded themselves deep into the breast of the thing. But the attack proved ineffectual, the guardian oblivious. It pulled an arm back to swat her. Frodyne leapt to the side, and the guardian's hand found her companion instead. The sharp metal nails pulled the man's chest open. The wizard was dead before he hit the ground.

"Please, Master," Frodyne begged. "Help me. I'll do anything you ask."

"You destroyed my army," Szass Tam spat. "Your soul

can rot here for all I care."

Frodyne raised her hands again and mumbled. A sparkling blue globe appeared in front of her. She blew at it, propelling it magically toward her ebon attacker. The globe impacted just above the thing's waist, popped, and squirted acid on the black metal. Crackling and sizzling filled the chamber, and the guardian bent its head to look at its melting stomach.

"You wield magic well, my sweet," the lich said icily.

"But I need your help to beat this thing!" she cried as she fumbled in the folds of her robe and withdrew a handful of green powder.

Szass Tam slowly shook his head. "You stopped my skeletons all by yourself. You stopped my plans for having you rule Thay at my side. Surely you can stop this creature." His voice was gravelly and showed no hint of emotion.

Frodyne started tracing a symbol in the powder in the palm of her hand. The lich turned to watch the construct, which was somehow repairing its stomach. Before Szass Tam's eyes, metal flowed like water to cover the melted section. In an instant, there was no evidence it had been damaged. It took a step toward Frodyne, its massive footfall rocking the cavern and causing her to spill the powder she had intended to use in another spell.

"It could kill her," the spectre at Szass Tam's side said simply. This time it wore the face of the young man. "But she cannot kill it. You cannot kill it. It is Leira's guardian, and it will continue to repair itself until the end of time. It has looked into her heart and discovered she does not honor the black goddess. It cannot rest until she is dead."

"And can it see into my own heart?" the lich posed. "Or perhaps it cannot even see me because the shriveled organ in my chest does not beat."

Frodyne's scream cut off the spirit's reply. The guardian swatted her like an insect, and she flew across the cavern to land on her back. Her red robe was shredded, and blood oozed freely from gouges in her flesh. Her face was frozen in terror, but still she did not give up. The lich had taught her well. Frodyne withdrew a bit of pitch from the pocket of her ruined garment. Placing it in her bloody palm, she raised her hand until it was in line with the guardian's four eyes. A black bolt of lightning shot forth from her fingers and struck the creature in the bridge of its nose. The guardian stumbled backward from the impact, but was not damaged.

Szass Tam coaxed her. "Think, my lovely apprentice. Cast a spell that will keep it from reaching you. Buy yourself time."

She drew what was left of her robe about her and struggled to her feet. Words gushed rapidly from her mouth, and she pointed her index finger at the cavern floor. The stone beneath the guardian's cloven hooves wavered for a moment, shimmered in the meager light of the chamber, then turned to mud. But the guardian did not fall into the muck. Rather, the gray construct hovered above the great muddy patch, its hooves dangling inches above it in the musty air. Beneath the guardian, the mud hardened and cracked like a dry river bed.

"This cannot be!" Frodyne screamed. Then she turned to glance at her mentor.

Szass Tam's hands glowed a faint blue, his long fingers pointed at the ebon guardian. An evil grin played slowly across his face as he returned Frodyne's disbelieving stare. He flicked his wrist, and the guardian floated forward and came to rest on a patch of rock near Frodyne.

"You! You kept it from becoming trapped!" she cried, as she twisted to the side to avoid another blow.

The lich nodded and thrust his hand into the air, mentally summoning an ancient parchment that lay in his tower. His fingers closed about the curled scroll as the guardian reached for Frodyne. Staring at his terrified apprentice, Szass Tam carefully unrolled the parchment. "I promised you immortality, my dear, a reward for your loyalty. You shall have it."

The lich began to read the magical words, and the construct grabbed Frodyne about the waist. Szass Tam read faster, while the construct lifted her until she was level with its four eyes. The lich finished the enchantment as the guardian squeezed the breath from her lungs and dropped Frodyne's lifeless body like a child would discard a ruined doll.

The parchment crumbled in Szass Tam's fingers, and his apprentice's dead body shimmered with a pale white glow. A moment passed, then Frodyne's chest rose and fell. She took great gulps of air into her lungs and struggled to her feet. She glanced at her mentor, then at the construct, which again reached out to grab her. The thing's fingers closed about her once more and squeezed harder, and Frodyne realized what Szass Tam had done. He had given her eternal life—of a sort.

"No!" she shouted as her ribs cracked and she fell lifeless a second time.

The construct stepped back and waited. Again, the young Red Wizard was resurrected from the dead. Again she struggled to her feet.

"Enjoy your immortality, Frodyne," the lich hissed, as he watched the guardian deliver another fatal blow and witnessed her rise again. He was pleased Leira's construct would busy itself with Frodyne and leave him alone.

"The relic," the lich pressed the spectre. "Show me where the crown is."

The spectre gestured to a stony recess. Szass Tam strode to it and took in the mounds of coins and gems. Perfectly faceted emeralds, sapphires, and diamonds glimmered from every cranny. A crown dotted with rubies sat atop the mass. The lich quickly snatched it up and felt the energy pulsing in the metal band.

"Leira's gift," the spirit declared. "The prize of our temple."

Stepping from the alcove, Szass Tam placed the crown upon his head then doubled forward as pain shot through his chest. The lich was caught off guard by the icy hot sensation. He pitched over and writhed on the rocky chamber floor until his frantic movements knocked the crown free.

The painful spasms ended, and the lich slowly stood. "What manner of power was that, priests?" the lich gasped.

The spirit wore the face of the old woman. "The power of eternal life. The heart of he who wears the crown will beat forever."

Szass Tam's human form melted away, revealing his skeletal frame and pinpoint eyes. "My heart does not beat," he said flatly.

"So instead, you felt pain," the woman answered. "The Lady of the Mists is indeed more treacherous than you. Leira lured you here. The priest who tempted your favored apprentice with the relic was merely a pawn."

The lich kicked the crown across the floor and glared at the spectre.

"Again the Patroness of Illusionists and Liars struck when your apprentice betrayed you and sought the crown herself. Then my goddess triumphed once more when you lost that which you held dear, a beautiful sorceress who would have spent eternity at your side." The ghostly image pointed at the struggling Frodyne. "You've lost your army, your woman, your ability to trust others. And the prize at the end of your quest was something you can never possess. Who is the more treacherous, Szass Tam?"

The lich threw back his head and laughed, a deep, throaty sound that reverberated off the walls of the cavern. The lich roared loud and long as he padded from the chamber and climbed the stairs.

THIEVES' REWARD

Mary H. Herbert

The water of Lake Ashane lay far below Teza's feet, as hard and dark as a sheet of black glass. No wave rippled its smoothness; nothing could be seen beneath its glistening surface to indicate the depth. Not that depth really mattered to Teza. She could not swim, and no one had ever measured the bottomless depths of the Lake of Tears.

The young woman forced her terror back and stared up the length of her outstretched arms to the frayed bit of rope that prevented her from plunging into the lake so far below.

"Please," she whispered in agony. Her arms felt like melting lead, and her body seemed to grow heavier by the second. There was nothing beneath her feet to catch her weight—nothing but air and that terrible fall to the water. Teza stifled a sob. She hated water.

The young woman looked higher into the eyes of the creature who dangled her so carelessly over the edge of the high cliff. He was blacker than night's shadow, hungrier than a shark, and more beautiful than the most exquisite horse Teza had ever seen. Some people said the rare predatory water horses, the aughiskies, did not exist, but Teza would have been delighted to trade places with any of those doubters just to prove them wrong.

A tense stillness closed around her. There was only her hoarse breathing, which rasped like a threnody behind the beating of her terrified heart. She sensed a scream well inside her from the depths of her mind, and it spread outward to her heart, lungs, throat, and mouth until she nearly burst with the primal terror within her.

The aughisky's eyes glowed green with their own cruel fire. Deliberately he shook the rope attached to his bridle. Teza slipped downward. Her face turned white, and her features screwed into a mask of panic.

Suddenly he wrenched the rope out of her hands, and Teza began to fall.

The scream so tightly held burst loose in a horrible, rending shriek of protest. "NO!"

Teza bolted awake to the sound of her own voice. Blackness enveloped her, and she tore frantically at the blanket that covered her head. Panting, wet with sweat, she scrambled out of her rough bed and crouched like a cornered beast by the embers of her campfire.

Close beside her, head hung low to see her, stood the aughisky, blacker than the night around him. His large eyes gleamed a ghastly light, and he watched her with an uncanny intelligence she found disconcerting. He snorted, a noise that sounded suspiciously like laughter.

"Oh, gods of all!" Teza gasped and collapsed to a sitting position by her fire. She heaped wood on the embers until the flames roared, but the heat and light did little to dispel the cold fear that settled in her bones from that terrible nightmare. It had seemed so real!

What am I going to do? she thought. Over a year ago, she had fled Immilmar with a price on her head and a stolen aughisky in her keeping. Since that time, she had hidden in the wild lands—far from the city she loved and the lake that nourished her horse. They had scraped out a meager living, but Teza was sick of the struggle, and she could see the aughisky was not thriving.

What he felt about their circumstances, she didn't know. She never knew what he was thinking. Teza usually had a close rapport with horses, and she loved this

glorious black animal with a passion she had never felt for
another beast. But he remained aloof, unfriendly at times,
watchful, and distrustful. She knew he could not leave her
voluntarily, nor would he really try to drown and eat her
because of the spell of binding she had placed on him with
a hippomane. Yet he always seemed so cold and distant.

Something cool brushed her cheek. Teza looked up from
her fire and saw with dismay snowflakes swirling around
her camp. It was early in the month of Uktar, and already
winter approached. Winter the year before had been a
miserable series of frozen hungry nights and empty hungry days.

She turned to study the aughisky. There were real risks
taking a water horse that drowned and ate humans to
Immilmar. On the other hand, what was worse? The
threat of exposure and imprisonment or the very real danger of freezing if she spent another winter in the wilder-
ness? Her world was the city with its back streets, busy
ports, markets, and people to keep her company. Surely
her minor crimes had been forgotten by now.

The wind gusted through her camp, driving snow before
it with icy-sharp teeth. Teza shivered. "Oh, to Thay with it
all. I'm going home!"

* * * * *

"Teza! You black-haired catamount! Where have you
been?" A long-familiar voice boomed to her over the raucous afternoon noise of the busy tavern.

Teza looked up from a flagon of *huild,* and a grin spread
over her long, swarthy face. "Rafbit!" she exclaimed,
acknowledging a friend she had not seen for a year.

She watched with pleasure as a shaggy, slightly
disheveled half-elf wove his way through the crowd
toward her. Slender as a willow branch and sinuous as a
weasel, he always reminded Teza of a cat in the way he
could move through a room light-footed, silent, causing
barely a ripple in the crowd as he passed. That ability, as
well as delicately etched features and blue-black hair,
were inherited from his moon-elf mother. His voice, Teza

firmly believed, was bequeathed solely by his father, a Rashemi berserker of prodigious skill and temper.

She slid over to make room for him at the bench near the roaring fire.

"The last time I saw you," he said heartily, dropping down beside her, "you were packing your worldly goods before the Fang found your door. Something about the Huhrong's prized stallion turning up in the Fair Street Horse Market?"

Teza winced. The volume of Rafbit's talk drowned out the voices around them and caused heads to turn their way.

"Whisper, Rafbit," she reminded him.

The half-elf grinned good-naturedly. He was used to such advice. "So where have you been?"

"Living among the wild things," Teza replied. She pulled a long swallow from her flagon to savor the fiery taste of the *jhuild*. "By the cloak, I missed that."

"When did you come back?"

The thief did not twitch from her pleasant contemplation of the firewine, but her senses jumped alert. She knew Rafbit well enough to hear the slightly tensed tone in his words. There was more than simple curiosity in his question. She replied casually, wondering what he was about. "About two days ago."

Rafbit lowered his voice even further until he actually reached an undertone. "Teza, you are a gift from Mask! Your return couldn't have come at a better time. How about a job?"

She moved then, deliberately pulling a plate of bread and sjorl cheese closer to break off several pieces. While she ate, she studied the man beside her.

Rafbit was an old friend, not a close one and not one she would willingly trust with her life, but still a friend. Her problem was she could never entirely trust his motives. A streak of self-serving maliciousness ran through his character, and it sometimes landed other people in serious trouble. She stared intently into his face, but all she could see was excited query.

"What sort of job?" she asked mildly.

"Come to my place." He hustled Teza out the back door into the bitter blue twilight.

Winter had come with a certainty since Teza returned to Immilmar, bringing snow and freezing winds. People dressed in layers of wool, leather, and furs and hurried more than normal through the busy streets of the Iron Lord's capital.

The tavern Teza and Rafbit had left was a tiny place tucked away in a back alley in the lowest, dirtiest part of the city. It was a place frequented mostly by patrons who had moved beyond the law and did not wish to be bothered by the guardians of the Huhrong's peace. Thus, it was very unusual to see a horse standing against the wall near the exit. Especially a horse of such magnificence and color.

Rafbit's eyes widened when he saw it, and he chuckled. "You're slipping, Teza. Inside taking your ease when this gorgeous animal is out here looking for a new master."

"He's not looking for a master," Teza said dryly. "He's looking for a meal."

"A meal? That horse doesn't look hungry. I've never seen a beast look as healthy as that one." He walked toward the black animal slowly but confidently.

Teza agreed. To her relief, the aughisky had flourished since they returned to the environs of Lake Ashane, and now his glossy sable coat and perfect conformation made him an eye-catcher in a city where most of the horses were short, shaggy work beasts. Already several of her competitors had disappeared. "Be careful," she added, a warning to both the half-elf and the aughisky.

Rafbit reached out to clasp the horse's bridle, the only tack he wore, but the aughisky flung his head away. His long teeth shone against his black muzzle, and his eyes glowed with a strange greenish fire.

Rafbit fell back, swearing. "Gods, what that beast needs is a tenday with a horse-breaker."

"No," Teza sighed. "All he needs is understanding." She whistled softly. Prancing and snorting in the cold air, the water horse came immediately to her side.

Rafbit was astonished. "He's yours? Where on Toril did you get such as him?"

"I earned him," Teza said, smiling in memory of the Witch of Rashemen and the tricks they had played on each other.

"Well, I've never seen anything like him!" the half-elf marveled. "Will you sell him?"

The young woman put her arm around the horse's neck—a caress he rarely seemed to like—and answered shortly, "No."

Rafbit nodded once, but his eyes strayed to the horse often as he led Teza and her aughisky to a ramshackle building near the warehouse district by the busy docks. He ushered her into his quarters, stoked the fire in his brazier, and came arrow-straight to the point.

"I am organizing a thieves' guild in Immilmar, and I need a second officer I can trust."

Teza couldn't have been more surprised if he had asked her to marry him. "A guild!" she snorted. "In Immilmar? The Huhrong would have you hanging in the gibbets in days."

Rafbit's gem-blue eyes sparkled with excitement. "Not necessarily. What a guild needs to survive in a city like this is subtlety, patience, and a careful hand to control the thieves and their activities."

Rafbit was a burglar, and a good one, who had never been directly linked to any of his successful crimes. But the leader of an organized den of thieves? It made Teza laugh. "Subtlety? Patience?" she mocked. "From you?"

Her friend grinned, unoffended, and leaned toward her. "That's why I need you. I have talked to most of the thieves in Immilmar, and they are interested, but I need someone to help organize the guild and its functions; to set up a system of rewards, opportunities, and arbitration. To find safehouses, set a watch on the guards, select suitable targets . . ."

"And what are you going to do?" Teza interrupted sarcastically. "Count your percentage?"

"Well, of course, any member will have to pay dues for guild services. But there will be plenty of work for two."

Teza had to admit she was intrigued. An organized thieves guild would be an advantage to the city's population of rogues . . . unfortunately . . . "There is still the Iron Lord. He will not tolerate organized crime in Rashemen."

"He will if the organization does not flaunt its presence. We will keep the guild small, make it open only to those who can prove their worth."

"Now, how are you going to do that?" she demanded.

"A test of skill. Any thief regardless of age, sex, or origin can join as long as he or she can pass a test."

Teza's eyes narrowed. "Does that include me?"

"Umm . . . yes," Rafbit hesitated. "It's only fair."

Teza jumped to her feet. "You ask me to join your little light-fingered squad, but you expect me to prove my worth?" she cried, her voice rising dangerously with every word.

"A mere formality!" Rafbit hastened to calm her. "It's really only to reassure our patron. He should be aware of your value to the guild. Just as I am."

The horse-thief stilled, her long legs apart, her arms crossed. "Patron?" she growled.

"Yes! He is our key to success. A judicial authority with a penchant for collecting rare gems. In exchange for any 'collectibles' we might find, he will be our ears and eyes in the Iron Lord's court."

Teza's glance narrowed in speculation. "I want to meet him first."

Rafbit shook her hand. "Done."

* * * * *

The meeting went better than Teza had anticipated. For one thing, she didn't really expect there to be a patron. But two days after Rafbit's invitation, she and the half-elf met a short, powerfully built man cloaked in rich snowcat furs and quiet self-importance.

The official acknowledged her identity with a lift of his thick eyebrow. They talked briefly. The man and Teza examined each other from head to boot, and both were satisfied with what they saw.

When the meeting was over, Teza turned to Rafbit. She was still wary of his motives in this venture, yet the presence of a patron in the Huhrong's courts put a different light on the matter. She was willing to take the next step and see what happened.

"What is the test you had in mind for me?" Had she not been watching her step in the muddy snow, she might have seen Rafbit's mouth move in the quick, hungry grimace of a stoat on the hunt.

"It's simple really. I have a customer who lost a particular item and is willing to pay for its recovery."

Teza did not accept other people's use of "simple" without explanation. "What, exactly, and where is it?"

"A book. In the library of Lord Duronh."

Teza stopped in midstride. "Are you serious? A book? That's ridiculous. I'm a horse-thief! You're the burglar."

"If you are going to be my officer," Rafbit explained patiently, "you need to excel in many skills. Your ability to steal anything four-legged is legendary. So is your talent with disguises. You've also been known to pick pockets, purses, and bags. But can you break into a house and steal something useful? That is your test."

Teza, ignoring the flattery, conceded he had a point. Yet she couldn't help asking, "Who's testing you?"

To her surprise, Rafbit's pale face turned whiter and the gleam went out of his eyes. "I have already been tested," he growled, and he would not say any more.

That was why, three days later, in the deep of a cold, still night, Teza rode the aughisky into the quiet streets of the city. She breathed a silent prayer to Mask, the god of rogues and thieves. Her enterprise that night would be to the god's advantage, so she hoped he was paying attention.

He had certainly helped in one fashion. A dank, thick fog rolled over the city from Lake Ashane, turning the darkness into a solid mass. Only the aughisky, bred in the black waters of Ashane, seemed at home in the dense wet air. He picked his way unerringly through the streets at Teza's direction, past the Huhrong's towering palace, and into the gentle hills of the wealthier section of the city, where the houses were larger and surrounded by their own ornate walls.

The water horse turned at Teza's cue onto a path that led between two high walls and down a steep bank to a river. The river was a small one that wended its way to Ashane from the east, just slow enough and deep enough for pleasure craft. Many of the houses built along its bank had docks or boathouses.

Lord Duronh's residence had one, too, although the lord had gone one step further. He had dug a cavern into the high bank below his house and built a dock for his crafts, where they were protected from all but the most frigid weather.

Teza thought this underground boathouse would be her best entrance into the house. Any guard left standing over one small back door on a night like this would not be expecting trouble.

As silent as a black shadow, the water horse carried her downstream through the fog to the broad opening of Duronh's boathouse. Teza shuddered at the sight of that dark river lapping at her knees, but the aughisky made no attempt to drop her or carry her into deeper water. He worked his way around the lord's small boats and deposited Teza on the wooden dock. With a sigh of fervent relief, she patted him and eased farther along the dark dock toward what she hoped was the stairs.

The darkness was absolute in the cavern, so Teza silently opened a small bag she wore buckled around her waist and pulled out her most useful thieves' tool: a pair of night glasses. She had bought them from a wandering wizard for a horrendous sum, but they had paid her back a hundredfold with their usefulness. She slid them on, and immediately the night slipped into focus. Although the glasses made everything look red, their vision was remarkably clear.

Swiftly she found the stairs leading to the rear of the house and mounted them to the entrance. The door was a heavy affair of oak and iron, but its lock yielded easily to the pick Rafbit had loaned her. Just inside, she saw the first guard leaning against the wall. As she had hoped, he dozed over his weapons.

Teza drew another useful item from her belt pack: a

small circle of fabric permeated with a fast-acting seda-
tive. She rubbed a little spit into the cloth to activate the
drug and, before it could affect her, stuck it to the skin of
the napping guard. In seconds he slumped into a deeper
sleep.

From there, the rest of the job was easy. A friend of Rafbit's had told Teza the floor plan of the house, enabling
her to slip through the night-darkened halls, past two
more guards, to the second floor, where the library stood
at the end of a long corridor. Teza's glasses saw nothing
amiss. No watchdogs, no statues enspelled to shout an
alarm, no traps, nothing. Lord Duronh must not consider
his books very valuable, Teza told herself.

Her suspicions proved correct when she entered the
library. It was a small room—cold, damp, and musty.
Sheets covered the furniture, and the books were layered
with dust.

Teza wasted no time. She knew the book she needed
was tan-colored, fairly large, and labeled with a wizard's
rune on the spine. Silently she ran her eyes along the
shelves lining the walls, along row after row of old manu-
scripts, scrolls, and bound books. Half an hour later, she
found the one she wanted, crammed on a bottom shelf
beneath a stack of moldy vellum sheets.

Teza pulled it out and nearly dropped it in surprise. It
was much heavier than she had expected and was bound
with something much smoother and softer to the touch
than leather. She hefted it. It seemed to be the right book.
It had the sigil on the spine and the tan-colored binding. It
must have belonged to a wizard at one time, but what was
it doing here, and what was so important about it that
someone would pay to have it stolen?

Teza tried to open it, but discovered something else very
odd. Someone had attached hair to the book from top to
bottom along both edges of the cover. The hair was then
braided, tying the book closed to casual view. The braid
lay soft under Teza's fingers, as soft and fine as human
hair.

Without quite knowing why, Teza grew angry. She
began to have the feeling Rafbit had not told her every-

thing she ought to know about this book. She tucked the tome under her arm and fled noiselessly back the way she had come, to the cavern where the aughisky waited for her.

She had planned to meet Rafbit and his customer before dawn, but first, she told the water horse to take her to her bolt-hole. The hole, nothing more than an abandoned shack at the edge of the city, was her hiding place in time of need. Obediently, the aughisky carried her to the old hut. As she dismounted, he neighed impatiently and slammed his hoof on the frozen ground. Teza knew the signs. He was hungry.

"Wait," she asked. "I will be quick. Then you may go."

Carrying the book, she slipped into the old shack. Her cold fingers fumbled with the flint and steel over a lamp she had left there. When the flame was burning, the woman laid the book on her lap and carefully began to unbraid the hair. In the light, she could see now the hair was red, a deep coppery hue that gleamed in the lamplight. Softly it flowed through her fingers until the book fell open on her knees.

Teza stared in delight. Full-length illustrations, beautifully illuminated with delicate traceries, bold colors, and bright gold leaf, covered each page. There were no words or letters or even runes, only exquisitely detailed pictures.

Teza turned the thick pages to the beginning. She could not read, yet she did not have to to understand the story. The pictures portrayed a romance between a lovely red-haired woman and a dark-haired, serious-looking young man. They met in a garden of peonies and roses, and the illustrations continued their tale in a series of scenes from a dance, a hunt, and a picnic, as the couple's passion grew deeper.

Then the atmosphere of the pictures changed. The drawings became harsher; the colors shifted to hues of red and black; the expression on the lovers' faces turned to anger and sadness.

Teza sat enthralled by the drama unfolding on her lap. She was so engrossed, she did not immediately notice what began to happen. As she studied one picture of the man and the woman in a gloomy room, the figures shifted slightly on the page. The man's face turned down into a scowl, and the woman took a step back.

Teza suddenly gaped. Before her eyes the small painting of the man strode forward and viciously backhanded the woman. She fell backward against a stone wall.

Teza's fingers tightened on the cover. "You nasty little—" she began, without realizing what she was talking to. Then the tiny woman climbed to her feet. She wiped blood from her mouth, tore a ring off her finger, and flung it at the young man. No words were spoken, but Teza could see the fury on the woman's face, and the devastation on the man's. The painted lady turned to leave, when in one swift movement, the man grabbed her long, braided hair. His hands lifted in a strange movement, his lips mouthed silent words, and in a brilliant flash of silver light that made Teza blink, the woman disappeared. When Teza looked again, the young man was alone, standing as still as before and holding a large tan book.

"What is this?" Teza muttered irritably. She flipped back to the other pages, but none of the remaining pictures moved. Finally she turned past the man and his book to the last page. The last illustration was the strangest of all. In the upper left was a small portrait of the woman, her oval face filled with pleading and her large green eyes brimmed with tears. The center of the picture revealed the book with its binding of red hair unbraided. A dagger pierced the pages, and blood dripped off the binding. At the bottom right, another portrait of the woman showed her joyfully happy.

A horse-thief though she was, Teza was not stupid. Her mind leapt to the obvious conclusion that the lady in the pictures had been transformed into a book by a wizard, and that book was the very one she was holding. That would help explain the red hair and the odd binding of what felt like human skin. What it did not explain was what Teza should do with it now.

If she understood the last picture correctly, a way to free the trapped lady was to open the book and stab it with a dagger. Simple enough. Yet what would that accomplish? Would the knife free her or kill her? And who was she? Why did she make her lover angry? Did she deserve to be transformed, or was her punishment cruelly unjust?

Teza didn't know, and there weren't nearly enough answers in the book. Should she trust her first instincts and break the spell, or take the book to Rafbit and his customer? And for that matter, Teza thought, her anger stirring again, who was this customer, and what did *he* want with this specific book?

Teza had the distinct impression she was being used, not tested, and she resented it. The job had been easy, even for her, but she was the only one taking the risks, and Rafbit probably figured she was too illiterate to be interested in a book. Maybe he didn't know what was in it either.

She quickly made up her mind to take the book to Rafbit. "But that loud-mouthed half-breed better have some answers," she muttered as she blew out her lamp.

Teza gently closed the book, leaving the hair unbraided, then mounted the aughisky and rode to find her friend at the agreed meeting place near the docks. The water horse, impatient to be away, cantered rapidly through the fog-hung streets, and his green eyes glowed like lamps in the night.

As they neared Immilmar's port facility, with its maze of storehouses, taverns, merchant offices, and docks, Teza slowed the horse to a walk. He moved quietly along the deserted roads to the last pier in the harbor. The air hung thick and heavy with the odors of wet timbers and rotting trash, and the watery smells of Lake Ashane.

Teza gripped the book tightly under her arm, where it remained hidden by her cloak. There was no tingle of magic power to this book, no inherent feeling of a human presence beneath the binding of skin and hair, but Teza sensed somehow that the lady of the book was still alive, trapped in an inanimate form and able to reveal herself only by the beautiful illuminations in her pages. Perhaps she was even aware of what was going on. Teza had always been a firm believer in freedom—particularly her own—and the woman's plight stirred her heart.

At that moment, she spotted a tiny light glowing in the shadow of a shed at the base of the last pier. The light blinked three times in the arranged signal. The aughisky walked toward it, his legs stiff and his nostrils flared. He was so close to the water, his entire body trembled.

Teza ran a hand down his silken neck. "A few minutes more, my beauty," she whispered.

"Teza!" Rafbit's voice echoed out of the darkness.

The horse-thief winced at his volume. "I'm here," she called softly.

The half-elf's lean form and a second taller figure stepped out of the shadow. "Do you have it?" Rafbit questioned. His voice sounded strung tight with tension.

Teza hesitated answering until the aughisky stopped about five paces away from the two forms. The intense darkness that shrouded the bay and the pier around them was so black Teza could barely make out Rafbit's face. She could see nothing of the person beside him. "Who is your companion?" she asked, stalling for time.

"The customer," Rafbit snapped. "Do you have the book?"

The woman stared at her friend. His white skin glimmered, as pale as a winter moon, and the hand that held the tiny lamp shook perceptibly. His eyes looked everywhere but at her. An alarm went off in Teza's head. "I have a book," she replied carefully. "But can your customer identify it so we all know the book is the right one?"

The stranger spoke then. "It is large, heavy, bound with a braid of red, and bears the sigil of the Wizard Ashroth." His words were colder than ice and deep with menace. "Dismount and give me the book," he charged.

Almost against her will, Teza slid off the aughisky, compelled by the powerful voice. "What do you want with this book?" she hissed.

The lamp in Rafbit's hand flared to a brilliant star, throwing a veil of light over the three people and the horse. As the stranger strode forward, the sudden glow exposed his clothes as robes of crimson red.

Teza backed up against the aughisky, appalled. A Red Wizard of Thay—one of Rashemen's bitterest enemies—

and he was standing brazenly on the docks of the Huhrong's own city.

"The book is mine!" the Red Wizard snarled viciously. "Stolen from me nearly thirty years ago. I traced it at last to Lord Duronh's library, and if you have it now, you will give it to me before I flay you alive."

Teza's eyes narrowed. She could see the wizard's face now, lean as a wolf's, gray and cruel, but with the same dark intensity as the young man in the book. She recognized immediately the man who had raged at his lover enough to strike her and then imprison her in a book.

The young thief felt her blood begin to burn, not only at the danger of facing a Red Wizard and the ferocious possessiveness he exuded but at Rafbit as well. Her friend had betrayed her, and from the shifting look of his eyes, he had done it deliberately.

Teza thought no more about her decision. With the swiftness of a practiced pickpocket, she pulled a slim dagger out of her boot, drew the book from her cloak, yanked it open, and stabbed the blade deep into the pages.

The wizard roared with rage.

A pool of blood welled up over the wound. Almost immediately, a bright silver beam flared up from the book, followed by another and another until the tome resembled a starburst. Momentarily dazzled, Teza dropped it on the muddy ground and fell back in astonishment.

"No!" shrieked the wizard. He raised his hands to countermand the dissolved spell, but he was too late. The cover of the book began to expand. Pulsating with its silver light, it stretched taller and taller until it reached the height of a full-grown woman. The red hair cascaded down her shoulders. Her face resumed its shape, as lovely and as young as the portrait in the book.

A frigid draft from the lake swept around the docks, swirling the fog. The silver light faded. The lady of the book stood before the three people, proud and fierce. Blood trickled unnoticed down her shoulder. She flung Teza's dagger at the wizard's feet.

"How dare you," she breathed in a voice thick with contempt. "How dare you think to possess me!"

Stunned and mute, Teza stared from the woman to the wizard. They were glaring at each other, so totally absorbed in their confrontation they did not acknowledge anyone else.

"Kanlara!" the wizard said, more a moan than a command. "You are mine. I loved you."

"Loved!" the woman mocked. "You didn't love me. You wanted to own me, to add me to your collection of assets." She stepped away from him, her pale robes glimmering in the lamplight. "You took me by surprise once, but never again. I have had thirty years to think about you, and now that I am free, I will take my revenge as best I can. I am not powerful enough to defeat you or kill you, but I can leave you, totally and with joy. Think of me often, Ashroth, loving other men and giving myself to someone other than you. You are pathetic to think you can own a woman like me." Flinging that last insult in his face, she formed a spell as adroitly as the wizard had and vanished before his eyes.

"NO!" the wizard shrieked again. "Kanlara, don't leave me now! I just found you!" His voice echoed over the bay.

Only a cold stillness answered his despairing cry.

Before Teza could move, the wizard turned on her. "You loathsome little meddler!" He swung his hand in her direction.

Teza saw the burning ball of magic flying not toward her but at her beautiful aughisky, and she leapt in front of his chest. The sphere struck her in the stomach like a solid missile and slammed her to the ground. The power sank through her skin, down into her muscles, stealing her strength and her ability to move. She lay in the icy mud, stunned.

Teza saw the wizard raise his hand again, but Rafbit caught it. For a moment, she thought he was going to help her. Then he said, "Not here. The guard is already roused."

The wizard's hand dropped. He, too, heard the signal horns of the nearest guard unit. "Put her in my boat, then. I'll dispose of her later."

The half-elf did not move. "What about my payment?" he asked nervously.

"Payment?" retorted the wizard, seething with scorn and bitter fury. "You failed me. Be thankful I do not treat you with the same punishment I shall give her!"

Rafbit's blue eyes darkened with anger, but he was too fearful to argue. "Then I claim her horse as my recompense."

A knowing smile flitted over the wizard's face and was gone. "Take it and go. It is all you deserve."

Rafbit nodded once. He reached hesitantly for the aughisky's bridle, and this time the black horse remained still, the green fire dampened in his eyes. Rafbit grinned. He leaned over Teza and stared into her pain-filled face. "Sorry, old girl. The guild could have used you," he muttered. "Unfortunately, I needed the money more." He swiftly mounted the water horse and trotted him away.

Teza watched them go, her eyes full of tears. She felt a hand grasp the front of her clothes and haul her off the ground. The magic blast, whatever it was, had left her paralyzed, and she could do nothing as the wizard dragged her down the dock and dumped her unceremoniously into a boat. The boat was small but long and lean, double-ended for maneuverability and rigged with both sails and oars.

From her position on the floorboards, Teza heard the wizard snap a command. Silent oarsmen moved the boat away from the docks and into the expanse of Lake Ashane.

Teza lay still, feeling distinctly sick. Her stomach roiled with the motion of the boat and with an abject terror that went beyond fear of the Red Wizard. She was in a boat over water and over the black depths of the lake. Her mouth went dry; her body began to shudder uncontrollably. She could move her fingers now, perhaps a sign that the magic was wearing off. But it didn't fade fast enough.

The wizard, his lean face taut with impotent rage, loomed over her. "I would take you to Thay and make you suffer a hundred deaths for what you have done, but I must find Kanlara and bring her back."

"Why?" Teza managed to croak. "She doesn't love you. Let her go." It was a terrible effort to talk, yet anything was better than thinking of the water.

The wizard yanked her upright, his hands like iron on

her shoulders. "You of all should understand. You keep an aughisky, a creature incapable of love. Yet you love it. You leapt in the way of my spell to protect it."

"A bad decision," Teza conceded.

"Almost as bad as freeing my betrothed." He wrenched the young woman to her feet where she stood, sick and dizzy, her eyes screwed shut.

"Lord," a voice called urgently from the bow.

The wizard ignored it while he studied Teza intently.

"Lord! Come see," the voice cried again. "We're being followed by a witch-ship."

A flash of hope opened Teza's eyes. The witch-ships that roamed the vast Lake of Tears were pilotless boats created by the powerful sisterhood of witches to protect Rashemen from predation from Thay. The witch-ships could unleash monstrous beasts, poisonous gases, or any number of defensive spells, and were extremely difficult to evade. The Red Wizard visibly blanched when he heard the warning.

For just a second, Teza thought he might forget her, and she could crawl out of sight while he dealt with their pursuer. Then her feeble hopes imploded into panic.

The wizard, his expression a mask of fury, picked her up bodily and threw her overboard.

Teza had time for one frenzied scream before she crashed into the dark water. Icy blackness closed over her. She scrabbled frantically to bring her head up, but her body was still partially paralyzed from the magic. She could only feebly thrash as her water-soaked clothes dragged her deeper.

She opened her eyes. Above, she could barely make out the lighter surface of the lake, where air and life lay only a few strokes away. Below lay death in the eternal dark at the fathomless bottom of the lake. Teza tried to struggle upward again, only to feel herself sinking farther toward that abyssal pit. Her lungs burned now; the air in her body was almost gone. Water pressed against her as if seeking a way into her nose, mouth, and lungs, seeking to drag her down faster. The blood roared in her head. She felt so weak.

"No!" she cried silently with every shred of her resistance. "Help me!"

Then, from somewhere out of the lightless depths, something moved toward her. She felt a large shape glide past her, and before she could understand what it was, a heavy, tight grip settled on her right shoulder.

Teza felt too far beyond her strength to struggle against this new terror. If some creature of Ashane was going to devour her, let it do so quickly and end her fear. But the thing did not rend her immediately. It hauled her upward, and just before Teza passed out, her head broke the surface. She drew in a great gasping breath of air, then struggled, thrashing wildly at the painful grip on her shoulder.

The thing let go of her. Teza started to sink again, and in her panic she grabbed at the large dark thing beside her. Wet hair met her fingers, the long, streaming mane of a horse, and she held on to it with all her might.

The head turned toward her. A green fire flickered in the eye that regarded her.

"You glorious creature," Teza sobbed into his neck.

The aughisky waited patiently in the cold water while the woman worked her way onto his back. Then he swam slowly toward the distant shore, his ears cocked back to listen to Teza's sobs.

At last, he clattered up the rocky bank to a patch of thick grass. Teza pried her fingers out of his mane and rolled off onto the blessed ground. For a while, she simply lay on her back and stared up at the aughisky. He was watching her, too, but the animosity she had always seen before was gone. Perhaps, she marveled, a creature who could not love could at least learn not to hate.

She finally worked herself upright and very slowly pulled on the aughisky's leg until she could stand. Although the wizard's magic had at last worn off, she had never felt so weak, dizzy, and deathly cold.

"There you are!" a woman's voice suddenly called.

Teza looked around. To her surprise, the night was fading to a pale watery dawn, and out of the lightening mist came a tall, beautiful, red-haired woman.

"Knowing Ashroth, I thought he might dump you once

the witch-ship caught up with him."

Teza's mouth fell open. "You knew about the ship?"

"Of course." Kanlara smiled with the pleasure of a satisfied cat. "I may not be powerful enough to defeat a Red Wizard, but the Witches of Rashemen are. I warned one I still knew in Immilmar." She came forward with a dry cloak, peeled off Teza's wet one, and helped her into the thick warm folds. "I'm sorry," she said at last. "I didn't get a chance to say thank you for releasing me. That took a lot of courage."

Teza leaned against the water horse, too tired to reply.

The wizard woman crossed her arms and looked at her thoughtfully. "I hoped to reach you before Ashroth did anything rash, but the aughisky was faster, thank the gods."

Teza's hand ran lovingly down the horse's elegant neck. "He saved my life," she whispered. "He didn't have to. If I died, the bond of the hippomane would be broken." She grinned suddenly and said to the horse, "I wonder where Rafbit is. Stuffed under some sunken rock more than likely. You came so fast you, didn't have time to eat him, did you?"

He tossed his mane and snorted a reply.

Abruptly Teza reached up and unbuckled the throat latch of the bridle on his head. The aughisky stilled, his wild eyes fastened on Teza. Gently she pulled the straps over his head and drew the bit out of his mouth. "I release you freely," she announced. "The spell of the hippomane is nullified."

The water horse stared at her. Then he reared, his hooves flashing over her head. Quick as an eel, he turned and plunged into Lake Ashane. He neighed once before the dark waters closed over his head and he was gone.

Teza watched him go. With a sigh, she flopped to the grass and drew the cloak tightly about her. She shivered. "Now what?" she murmured.

Kanlara smiled and sat down beside her. "Well, I need a place to stay."

Teza glanced at the woman. Even after thirty years as a book, Kanlara seemed very close to her own age. Still the woman was wizard-trained and, by her speech and looks, nobly born. "I'm a horse-thief," she said.

"I know," Kanlara said simply, "and you saved my life. I could use a friend right now."

Teza looked out over the lake, now gray and pearl with dawn's coming light. She thought of Rafbit's treachery and the aughisky's last act of loyalty. Her lips formed a smile. "I could use a friend, too." She rose unsteadily to her feet. "I don't suppose you'd be interested in helping me form a thieves' guild would you?"

Her companion stood, too, her red hair as long and thick as Teza's dark mane. They stood eye to eye for so long Teza grew certain Kanlara would refuse.

Then the wizard woman replied, "I have been a book stashed away in a moldy old library for so long, I think dust has settled in my brain. I want to do things, I want to travel, I want to experience life again. I suppose Immilmar is as good a place as any to start. Then who knows, maybe you'd go on a *dajemma* with me?"

Teza's eyes widened with delight. A *dajemma* was an expedition taken by Rashemen's young men, a journey through the world to manhood. Females did not usually go, and certainly not ones in their midtwenties. But why not? A *dajemma,* an adventure, a journey. Call it what you will, Teza thought, it would do.

"I know where to find some good horses." She grinned.

SIX OF SWORDS

William W. Connors

I

Moonlight on a silver blade was the last thing Jaybel ever saw.

Fifteen years ago, when he and his closest friends had been adventuring throughout the Western Heartlands, he might have expected such a demise. In those days, he had made his living as an expert picking locks, disarming traps, and unobtrusively eliminating enemies—tasks known for short-lived practitioners. Indeed, on more than one occasion, he'd been snatched from death's dark abyss only by the mystical healing power of the acolyte Gwynn.

In the years since, however, Jaybel had given up the rogue's life. Following the tragedy of his company's last quest, when they had been forced to leave the dwarf Shandt to the so-called mercy of a hobgoblin tribe, the glamour had gone out of that life. Indeed, so terrible had that ordeal been that every member of the Six of Swords had second thoughts about his career.

"I've made my fortune," Jaybel told his comrades. "Now I plan to relax and enjoy it." With his next breath, he asked Gwynn to marry him, and she hadn't even paused before accepting. The company parted, and he and Gwynn took up residence in the great city of Waterdeep.

With the treasures they had gathered from countless forgotten tunnels and valiant quests, Jaybel and Gwynn had built themselves a modestly elegant home. It included a chapel where she could teach her faith, and a locksmith's shop where he could keep his fingers nimble and his eyes sharp.

For nearly a decade and a half, he and Gwynn had been happy. They had put tragedy behind them and started a new life together. When Jaybel had looked back on those wild days, he always said, "It's a wonder I'm not dead."

Now he was.

II

The metallic ringing of steel on steel fell upon ears so long past ignoring it that they may as well have been deaf. With each impact, sparks filled the night air, streaking upward like startled fireflies, becoming brief ruddy stars, and then finishing their fleeting lives with meteoric falls to the stone floor. Thus it went as the sun set and night cloaked the city of Raven's Bluff. Time and time again, Orlando repeated the ritual of his craft. Hammer fell, sparks flew, and the wedge of a plow gradually took shape.

When the farmer's blade was finally completed, the noise ended and the smoldering coals of the forge were left to cool. The brawny, dark-skinned Orlando set about returning his tools to their places, taking no notice of the ebony shape that appeared in the open doorway of his shop.

For a fraction of a second, the shadow filled the doorway, blocking out the stars and crescent moon that hung beyond it. Then, with the grace of a hunting cat, it slipped through the portal and into the sweltering heat of the blacksmith's shop. In the absence of the ringing hammer, the shadow drifted in supernatural silence.

Without prelude, a sepulchral voice wafted from the darkness. Although a whisper, the intonation and clarity of the words made them as audible as any crier's shout. *Jaybel and Gwynn are dead.*

Orlando froze, his hand still clutching the great hammer, half-suspended from an iron hook. The voice sent a chill down his spine, raising goose bumps across his body just as it had when he had last heard it years ago. Orlando turned slowly, keeping the hammer in his hand and trying to spot the source of the voice. As had always been the case when she desired it, Lelanda was one with the darkness.

Relax, Orlando, said the night. *I didn't do it.*

"Then show yourself," said the blacksmith, knowing she wouldn't.

It had been years since Orlando had taken up a weapon aside from a tankard in a tavern brawl. Still, even the passing of the years didn't prevent the well-honed reflexes of his adventuring days from surging back to life. If the witch tried anything, his life wouldn't command a small price. Still, he knew who would walk away from the battle. He doubted Lelanda had given up magic. She was probably even more powerful now. So, Orlando's rusty reflexes would provide her only brief entertainment.

To Orlando's surprise, the darkness before him parted. Lelanda's face, crowned with hair the color of smoldering coals and set with emerald eyes that reminded him all too well of a cat's, appeared no more than a yard away from his own. As always, he was stunned by the shocking contrast between her external beauty and her malevolent soul within.

If he struck now, there was no way the witch could save herself. The muscles in his arm tensed, but he could not bring himself to strike first. He had to hear her out.

"Satisfied?" she asked. Her voice, no longer distorted by the magical shroud of shadows, seemed gentle and alluring. Orlando knew that, like her beauty, her voice was a deadly illusion. Black widows were beautiful as well. Even knowing the truth, his pulse quickened.

The retired warrior put aside the distraction and asked the only question that made sense. "What happened to them?"

"It wasn't an accident," she said, her eyes lowering to

the hammer still in Orlando's hand. He grinned half-heartedly and tossed it toward the nearby workbench. She returned his smile and went on. "Someone killed them."

"You're sure it wasn't you?" he asked.

"Fairly," she said. "I'm on my way to Waterdeep to find out who. We made a lot of enemies in those days."

"We made friends, too," the blacksmith said.

"We lost them as well," said the witch.

Orlando's memory was quick to pull up an image of Shandt, his enchanted battle-axe glowing as it swept back and forth through the ranks of hobgoblins that swallowed him up. It wasn't the way he would have wanted to remember the smiling dwarf.

"If we leave in the morning, we can be there in a few days," said Lelanda. "I know some . . . shortcuts."

"If we leave now, we can be there sooner," said Orlando. "Give me an hour to get ready."

III

Orlando moved through his darkened house without so much as a flickering candle to light his way. Outside, Lelanda sat unmoving on the back of a horse even blacker than the night sky. Orlando knew she was anxious to get under way, and so went from room to room as quickly as possible. The walls of his home were decorated with swords, shields, and other reminders of his adventuring life. Now, like a thief in his own house, he gathered up three of these heirlooms.

The first of these was Talon, the curved sword that he had recovered from a dark labyrinth beneath the sands men called the Battle of the Bones. This arcane blade proved almost unstoppable when turned against the living dead. Removed from its traditional place above the hearth, the enchanted blade was returned to the scabbard on Orlando's black leather belt.

The second item removed from his collection was a bronze breastplate. Countless attackers had learned that it had the uncanny ability to turn aside even the most deadly missiles. Arrows, quarrels, and even bullets had all proven impotent against the charms of the bronze armor. Orlando liberated it from the wooden mannequin that guarded an empty first floor hallway. As the yellow-orange armor once again embraced Orlando's muscular chest, he noticed that the passing of his youth made it more snug than he remembered.

With the sword and armor safely recovered, Orlando moved on to the last item he planned to bring with him: a good luck charm. Pausing beside the small shrine adjacent to his bedroom, Orlando slipped a small silver amulet from the hook on which it hung and looped it around his neck. Unconsciously, his fingers ran across its surface, tracing the outlines of the crossed battle-axes that were the icon of the dwarven god Clanggedin Silverbeard. There was no magic in this simple pendant, but it had been a present from Shandt. Since it had been given to him not five hours before the noble dwarf had met his fate somewhere in the Underdark, Orlando could not look upon it now without remembering the broad, crooked smile and gleaming eyes that had made his best friend's countenance so pleasantly memorable. The memory brought Orlando both a smile and a tear.

Locking the door behind him, Orlando left the house and moved to join Lelanda by the stable. She had already saddled Zephyr, his dappled gray horse.

Without a word, the warrior placed his foot in the stirrup, swung himself onto his mount, and nudged the horse into a trot. Many miles passed before either of the old adventurers spoke a word to the other.

IV

Orlando drew back on Zephyr's reigns. The animal, well trained and eager to please its master, slowed quickly from its trot to a full stop. The enigmatic black equine that Lelanda rode did the same, although Orlando saw no sign of a command from rider to mount. The horse seemed always to know what the enchantress expected of it.

"Aren't we going a bit out of our way?"

"Only slightly," responded the witch. "I thought we

might stop at Jolind's estate and tell her what happened. She won't be interested in joining us, of course, but she was one of the Six. She has a right to know."

Orlando was surprised to hear Lelanda speak like that. In their adventuring days, she'd had little use for the individual members of the Six of Swords. To her, they were bodyguards, scouts, and healers, who enabled her to explore the mysteries of magic, recover rare spell components, and otherwise practice her arcane art. Perhaps time had softened her heart, or perhaps there was more to this detour than she was telling him.

With the aid of Lelanda's magic, the miles passed as fleeting images in the corner of the eye. Even at that rate, however, it was several hours before the lights of Jolind's tower were visible. When they reached the edge of the clearing in which it stood, both riders brought their mounts to a stop.

"She's done a remarkable job here," said Orlando as his head swept back and forth to indicate the lush forest that rose around them. "I remember when we first found this clearing. The soil was so poisonous that nothing less robust than spitweed would grow here."

"I'll go in first," said Lelanda, ignoring his attempt at conversation. "Jolind always valued her privacy, and I'd hate to have a druid angry at me in the heart of her own forest."

She slipped the hood of her cloak over her head, causing the sunset colors of her hair to vanish into a thick darkness. Even as he watched, Orlando found that he could no longer focus clearly on her. Though he knew exactly where she was standing, he was able to see her only as a fleeting image in the corner of his eye.

I'll be back as quickly as I can, said the darkness. Before he could respond, Orlando realized he and the horses were alone by the side of the road. He wanted to chuckle, but the chills that her macabre voice had left running along his spine wouldn't let him.

While he waited for his companion to return, Orlando opened the saddlebags draped over Zephyr and pulled out an apple. He fished around for a few seconds more and brought out a small knife. With a deft flick of his wrist, he split the fruit cleanly in two. After wiping off the blade and slipping it back into the leather pouch, he offered one of the halves to his horse and considered the other for a moment. With an unconscious shrug, he reached over and held it before Lelanda's mount. The ebon animal eyed his offering, but then snorted and turned away. Orlando shrugged again and ate it himself. The first hints of dawn were lighting the horizon, and he had an unhappy feeling that the animal's snobbery was to set the tone for the day ahead. He was right.

Jolind is dead, came the too-familiar voice of the darkness. *And the body is warm. The killer must still be nearby.*

V

The inside of the tower stirred Orlando's memories of the time when the Six of Swords had first explored it.

In those days, these lands had been defiled by the black dragon that made its lair here. The entire area had been poisoned by the creature, with pools of acid, swarms of stinging insects, and tangles of slashweed dominating the tortured remnants of the forest. From the moment they entered that fell region, the druid Jolind had become solemn and morose. Such destruction, she swore, could not go unpunished.

When they reached the tower—a ruined structure built by an unknown hand centuries before any of the Six were born—Jolind had led their attack against the dragon. Turning the very elements of nature against the creature, she had been instrumental in its destruction.

Eighteen months later, when the company disbanded, she announced her intention to return to this place and restore the forest to its past glory. She had done an outstanding job.

Jolind had not, however, restored the tower. At least, she hadn't done so in the way that Orlando would have. The interior floors and walls had been stripped out, a great glass dome placed atop the tower, and a bubbling fountain set into the ground at its center. The combination of the fish-eye skylight and the dancing water of the fountain made the climate inside the tower hot and sticky.

Under normal circumstances, this would have made the place unbearable. With the careful hand of Jolind to shape the place, however, it had been transformed into a tropical paradise. Great tresses of ivy climbed gracefully up walls dotted with brilliantly colored flowers. Shafts of morning light, shunted downward by the facets of the glass dome, illuminated a dozen trees and the colorful butterflies that flitted between them.

The horrors of the past had been completely banished by the careful hand of the druid. Sadly, they had been replaced by the horrors of the present. At the heart of all this splendor was a copper-smelling pool of red. And at the center of that scarlet expanse lay the body of the druid Jolind. Her head had been cleanly cut from her neck.

It took all the courage Orlando could muster to approach the body. Jolind had been a friend, a companion, and more. For a time, the warrior and druid had been lovers, seeking escape in each other's arms. Their relationship had lasted less than a year, but in that time, each had learned much about the other's philosophy and profession. For Orlando, that meant a keen appreciation of the ways of nature, the give-and-take of the environment, and an understanding of his place in it. Jolind had not feared death. In her mind, it was nothing more than the end of life. To Orlando, death had always been an enemy to be held at bay. In the end, he knew, death would triumph. For the present, however, he preferred to keep that most final of foes as far away as possible.

"Horrible way to die," he said softly.

The same way Jaybel and Gwynn were killed, said a voice from nowhere. Although the sound still irritated him, Orlando had already adjusted to the macabre intonations that came from empty air. It was amazing to him how quickly the old ways of thinking returned. Indeed, even as that thought crossed his mind, he realized he had subconsciously drawn Talon from its scabbard. Without the slightest thought, he had made ready to defend himself from Jolind's attacker.

"A pretty fierce struggle," said Orlando, examining the disturbed earth around the pool of blood and beneath the decapitated body. "But something doesn't make sense. All of these footprints were made by Jolind's sandals. Whomever she was fighting didn't make the faintest impression as he moved about."

Perhaps we're dealing with a doppleganger or other form-shifter. If her killer assumed Jolind's shape, you wouldn't be able to tell one set of prints from another.

"I doubt it," responded the warrior. He tilted his head to one side, and then to the other. "No, the positioning is pretty clear. Only one person made these prints. What about the undead? Remember that vampire we tracked down near Dragonspear? He didn't leave footprints, throw a shadow, or make any sound when he moved." As soon as he mentioned that adventure, he wished he hadn't. It was in the ancient crypt where the vampire's coffin had been hidden that Lelanda found the mysterious shroud of shadows.

Possible, responded the enigmatic shadows of the garden, *but unlikely. This place is pretty heavily warded against intrusion by the undead and other unnatural creatures. If the killer is something like that, he'd have to be extremely powerful to enter the tower. For our sakes I'd prefer to believe that isn't the answer.*

Orlando said no more for several minutes. Instead of allowing dark thoughts to dominate his mind, he forced his attention back to the matter at hand. With measured steps, he walked to and fro around the area, using his experience in combat to piece together this puzzle, whose pieces had been scattered in the darkness of the previous night.

After a time, he noticed something and reached into a beautiful but painfully prickly shrub. Cursing and wriggling, he pulled back his arm and drew out a slender, wooden rod some three feet long. Covered in a gleaming white lacquer, it was painfully cold to the touch. From past experience, however, he knew that it was warmer than it should be.

What have you found? inquired the stillest part of the garden.

On some level, Orlando realized it wasn't the fact that

he couldn't see Lelanda that bothered him most. It was the spectral nature of her voice while she wore the shroud. There was too much of death and darkness in this place already.

Orlando could stand no more of this one-sided conversation. "Take off that damned shroud, and I'll show you!" he hissed.

Almost at once, the shadow of a pear tree lightened and the elegant sorceress was standing beside him. She quickly complied with his request, making the hostility in his voice seem suddenly unnecessary.

"I'm sorry," Orlando said softly, "but you have no idea how quickly that thing gets on your nerves." He expected her to argue the point, just as she would have in the past. To his surprise, her response was quite civil.

"No," she answered, "I suppose I don't. You see, it's been a very long time since I've had a traveling companion. I've gotten rather used to wearing the shroud all the time. I'll try not to use it unless it's an emergency."

There was a brief pause, a moment of still contrast to the violence that had unfolded around them. Orlando searched for something to say, but failed.

Lelanda seemed only slightly more at ease, picking up the frayed threads of conversation. "I asked you what you had found," she reminded him.

"Looks like a piece of that staff Jolind used to carry with her; feels like it too, almost as cold as those blizzards it could summon up."

Lelanda tilted her head and looked at the broken staff. Her lips pursed as she considered the broken end and several places along its length where something had cut deeply into it. "There was some pretty powerful magic woven into this thing. It wouldn't be easy to break. The weapon that hacked these notches out of it and finally broke it must have been every bit as powerful. That doesn't bode well for our future."

Silence fell upon the garden again. Orlando went back to fishing through the shrubs, eventually finding the other section of Jolind's staff.

Lelanda examined the head, looking into the druid's

eyes as if she might read the woman's dying thoughts. Then she walked a distance toward Orlando and called to him. He met her halfway between the shrubs and the fallen body.

"We've learned a little bit from an examination of the area and the body, but Jolind can tell us more."

"Necromancy?" asked Orlando, the word sounding just as bitter as it tasted in his mouth. She nodded. He growled. "I suppose there's no choice. Get it over with."

"I'll have to . . ."

"I know," he said.

Two steps brought the witch to the edge of the bloody pool, another to the place where Jolind's severed head had come to land. She looked back at Orlando, flashed him an uncomfortable smile, and raised the hood of the shroud above her head. Instantly, it became difficult for the warrior to focus his eyes on her. Even knowing where she had been standing only a few seconds earlier, he could discern nothing but the faintest impression of the shrouded figure.

The magical energies of death and darkness answered Lelanda's urging. She spoke words of power whose sounds had no meaning to Orlando's untrained ears. He felt the strange tugging of death at his spirit and knew that something stood nearby, hungering for the taste of his soul, contained only by the power of Lelanda's will. If her concentration failed, the consequences could well be disastrous. Then, with a cry of agony from the unseen mage, the spell was completed.

Orlando steeled his nerve as the eyes on Jolind's severed head snapped open. The thin-lipped mouth did likewise, and a hissing, hollow scream filled the garden. Unable to stand the sight, Orlando turned his head away. He felt the need to vomit, but retained control of his traumatized body by remembering that a deadly enemy might lurk nearby.

Jolind, said the spectral necromancer, *can you hear me?*

"Yesss," responded an empty, lifeless voice. "Who are you? Your voice is familiar . . . but distant."

Jolind, this is Lelanda. I'm here with Orlando. We've come to help you.

At that, the disembodied head released a humorless, rasping laugh. "You're a little late for that, old friend."

Orlando's nerve buckled, but did not fail him.

I know. We're sorry. But we want to find the person who did this to you. He murdered Jaybel and Gwynn, too. Can you help us? Did you recognize your killer?

"Yes, I know who killed me," whispered Jolind.

Then tell me, Jolind. Be quick; the spell is failing fast, urged Lelanda.

Orlando couldn't decide which was more macabre, the living but unseen spirit of the wizard or the dead, but substantial head of the druid.

"Kesmarex," hissed the head as the eyes slipped quietly shut and the jaw went slack. The spell had ended, and the spirit of the druid had gone to rest with those of her ancestors.

Orlando hoped she would find peace there. In his heart, he said a last farewell to the woman who had meant so much to him so long ago. It seemed a crime to have drifted away from her. He wondered what mysteries had died with her. A single tear slipped down his bronze cheek.

Kesmarex? said the witch, slipping the hood of the shroud from around her locks and emerging beside the fallen druid. "Who is that?"

"It's not a who," said Orlando. "It's a what. That was the name given to Shandt's battle-axe by the dwarves who forged it. It mean's something like 'Vengeance of the King,' but the words don't translate perfectly into our language."

"But Shandt is dead," said the witch, her voice trailing off into a haunting silence.

"I know." Orlando exhaled. "He couldn't have survived." After a moment of reflection, he continued. "Tell me more about the wards around this place. Just how certain are you an undead creature couldn't have gotten in here . . . ?"

An hour or so later, Orlando still hadn't made sense of Jolind's warning. "If it was Shandt, he'll be back to get us," said Orlando. "He wasn't one to leave a job undone."

Rather than answer, Lelanda merely poked at the campfire that now burned at the heart of Jolind's tower.

In the last few hours, her beauty had begun to look worn and haggard. Orlando studied her face, which was still delicate and gentle, with innocent features that belied the cunning viper that lurked within. Still, there was something human showing through the facade she maintained. "How did you ever become a wandering adventurer?"

"I don't really know," said the witch. "It just happened, I guess. I was studying in Waterdeep, the usual courses they force on a child of a merchant prince, but they just weren't enough to keep my attention. One of the other students said he was being tutored in magic by an old woman on the outskirts of town. I followed him one day and learned where his teacher lived. When he left, I paid her a visit and demanded she teach me magic. She looked me over carefully and refused.

"I was furious. I guess I was more than a little spoiled in those days. When I tried to pay her for the lessons, she wouldn't take my money. I'd never met anyone like her before, anyone that gold couldn't buy. It took me weeks of pestering her, but she finally agreed. I guess she wanted proof of my devotion.

"About a year later, I showed up for my lesson and found her dead. She had been murdered by a pack of thieves—assassins, really, in the service of a dark priest. I vowed to avenge her death. That took me another year. By then, I'd gotten used to life on the road, and returning to Waterdeep just didn't seem very palatable to me. I never went back to school or to see my family. I suppose they assumed I'd been killed while trying to avenge my mentor. Somehow, it just didn't matter anymore."

A gust of wind swirled through the tower, twisting the flames that danced above the hearth and lifting a cloud of glowing embers into the air. Lelanda gazed silently at them as if there might be some hidden meaning in their traces. "How about you?" she asked.

"Ever been a farmer?" he asked in answer.

"No," she said.

"Well, if you had been, you'd understand perfectly."

Lelanda laughed, a clear and sweet sound that Orlando never would have expected from her. There, in the garden where they had once slain a black dragon and had recently buried an old friend, he saw a side of her he had never thought existed. His hand, as if it had a will of its own, reached out and rested atop hers. Her laugh faded away, and her green eyes shifted to meet his.

"Orlando," she said, and then a shock went through her body. Every muscle was rigid for a second, and her eyes bulged. As suddenly as the spasm had struck her, it passed. She went limp and toppled forward, the blade of the great axe Kesmarex buried in her back.

The warrior, his rekindled reflexes already in action, sprang back. Without conscious thought, he brought the enchanted sword Talon into play, interposing it between himself and whoever might wield the ancient battle-axe. "Shandt," he cried, "is that you?"

There was no answer, but in a second Orlando knew none would be forthcoming. With a swift and sudden motion, the axe Kesmarex lifted into the air. Lelanda's blood dripped from the blade, but no living hand wielded the weapon.

At last, Orlando understood. He had always known Shandt's blade was enchanted, but had never realized the full extent of its power. Now, years after the death of its owner, the weapon had tracked down the people it blamed for Shandt's death.

Describing a great arc in the air, Kesmarex swept toward the warrior. He fell back, uncertain how to attack a weapon that had no wielder. He jabbed feebly with Talon, but found that the axe was every bit as maneuverable as it had been in Shandt's hand.

"You don't understand," Orlando cried. "We had no choice!" The battle-axe chopped at his legs, causing him to leap backward. When his feet touched the ground, he felt the soft earth shift and give way. He had landed squarely on Jolind's grave. Unable to retain his balance, Orlando toppled over and thudded hard on his back. The blade of the axe flashed through the air inches above his nose. Had he still been standing, it would certainly have severed his leg at the knee.

"Shandt was buying us time to escape!" he yelled. The

axe, unheeding, swept upward as if it were being held aloft by its departed master. For a brief second, it hung there. Then, like the blade of a headsman at the block, Kesmarex plunged downward. Orlando tried to roll aside, but the enchanted blade sensed his intention and twisted to follow him. With a metallic crash, it smashed into the warrior's bronze breastplate, tearing through the amber metal and biting into the soft flesh beneath.

Pain burned through Orlando's body as clouds of red rolled across his vision. Talon fell from a nerveless hand, making no sound as it landed atop Jolind's newly dug grave. As the vengeful weapon drew back for its fatal strike, Orlando's hands clutched at the searing wound. His fingers touched jagged metal, exposed flesh, and warm, flowing blood.

And something else. Something smooth and warm and comforting: the amulet of Clanggedin Silverbeard. His fingers closed upon the medallion, and he snatched it clear of his neck. The silver chain upon which it hung stretched and snapped. As the great weapon began to sweep downward, Orlando held the holy symbol high.

"Shandt was my friend!" he cried. "I would have died to save him!"

Moonlight, sifting down from the cloudless sky, struck the glass dome and streamed down into the garden. It fell upon the fallen body of Lelanda, the druid's fresh grave, and the silver axe that sought to avenge its owner's death. Two pinpoints glinted brightly in the shaft of moonlight, one the blade edge and the other the pendant.

VI

Orlando stepped back from the wall. He had returned Talon to its place and cocked his head left and right to make sure it was positioned properly. He reached out and lifted the hilt an imperceptible fraction of an inch.

"Don't worry," said Lelanda from the couch on which she lay. "You've got it right."

Orlando nodded and turned back to the table behind him. With his right hand, he reached tentatively for the great battle-axe Kesmarex, but something stopped his fingers just short of its haft. His other hand slipped to his neck and touched the silver pendant that hung from its recently repaired chain.

His thoughts drifted back to the battle in Jolind's garden. He remembered the great blade falling toward his head, the hollow sound of his voice as it filled the silent garden, and the flash of light that came when the holy symbol was presented. Somehow, the battle-axe recognized the amulet and knew that the silver symbol belonged to the same warrior whose hands had once wielded it. Knowing that anyone who wore that particular crossed battle-axe medallion must be a friend of its owner, it had fallen inert. As far as Kesmarex was concerned, its mission was completed.

He returned to the present as a delicate hand touched his shoulder. He turned and found the emerald eyes of Lelanda scant inches away from his own. The gold band on her finger reflected a greatly distorted image of his own countenance.

"You shouldn't be up," he said, urging her gently back to the couch.

"I'll be okay," she said, "the wound's almost healed. Hang up the axe and come to bed."

Orlando nodded and lifted the magical weapon from its resting place. He turned and elevated it to a place of honor above the hearth. Next to it, he hung the amulet that had saved his life.

"Rest quietly, old friend," said the crimson-haired witch.

Orlando said nothing, but in his heart he knew that Lelanda's wish had been granted.

THE WILD BUNCH

Tom Dupree

The robe shimmered seductively as the young apprentice held it up to the candlelight. Its color was a brilliant royal blue, and it was fashioned from a shiny, silky, luxurious fabric that the student had never seen before. It was soft and cool to the touch, but bespoke great elegance and power.

It was commandingly beautiful, but the fascination was not in its color or texture. The apprentice could not tear his eyes away from the symbols that were inscribed on the robe, either sewn in or painted on the fabric, he couldn't tell which. There were signs and sigils emblazoned everywhere—hundreds of them. Intricate handwork covered every bit of free space on the garment's surface: calligraphy, runes, drawings, letters, shapes, and forms whose mysteries were far beyond the young man's understanding.

He was entranced.

He lifted the robe closer to get a better look.

"Put that down, lad. And sit yourself down." The voice was calm, controlled, but it came from right next to the boy's ear—almost from *inside* it—and made him flinch in startlement. How did he *do* that? How did the master move so quietly? The boy turned to face his wizened tutor, the man whose esoteric knowledge had drawn him here. With a reluctance that surprised him, the young man handed the robe to his master and sat.

"The most important thing I will ever teach you comes here, now, on your first day. It is simply this: *you have a great deal to learn.* The magical art may appear effortless to the uninitiated; a bit of waving, a bit of mumbling, and POOF!—whatever one's heart desires. But each conjuration, each illusory spectacle, requires agonizing hours of study and concentration. There is no shortcut, no easy way to make yourself the wizard you want to be. Your art will demand *work,* my lad. If you cannot pledge to accept this sacrifice, then leave me now. A mage should be regarded with awe, not mirth.

"That robe is remarkable, isn't it? The last time I saw it worn, another young student of the conjurative arts had recently arrived in this village. He appeared at the door of the Ale & Hearty tavern one rainy afternoon, dripping wet. He strode to the bar and announced that he was a magic-user, in search of fame and fortune."

* * * * *

New mages are a fairly rare sight in Schamedar, and the aforementioned one did not go unnoticed, not even in this undistinguished tavern. He was of tall, if slim, human build, with an overly erect bearing that was hardly required by either the venue or the company. His clothing was less than modest, and drenched, at that. He carried nothing except for a small pack and a walking staff, which he set at his feet. Never mind fame; this was a person in severe need of fortune.

"Why, Mystra be praised!" growled a swarthy little cutpurse with a wide, gap-toothed grin, who was sitting at a table with two other morally impaired citizens. "A mage! If you aren't the answer to a prayer! Come and wet your throat with us!"

The stranger ambled over.

"Sit, sit," implored the thief, gesturing obsequiously at

the empty chair beside him. "I am Tuka Phardeen, great admirer of the fraternity of magic-users. And I have the blessed good fortune to be addressing my Lord—"

"Evertongue, friend Phardeen. Wiglaf Evertongue." This last as if he were introducing Mystra herself.

"Hmmm," from one of Tuka's companions, a muscular, tanned goddess whose brilliant blonde hair cascaded past a necklace made of animal fangs to reach the hilt of a well-nicked broadsword. "Evertongue. I seem to remember such a family over in Calimport. But these Evertongues were *bakers*."

"Sasha," chided Tuka.

Wiglaf sat and returned the magnificent warrior's gaze. "Maybe I'm the first member of my family to raise my hands out of the dough," he said. "But what's past is best left past, and my past can stay in that oven. I'm tired of spellbooks and teachers and studying. I don't want to ruin my eyesight. At this rate, I'll be old and gray before I even get close to my potential. There's got to be a better way. A quicker way. I want to use magic out there in the real world. I want to live. I want to learn."

"I want to vomit," said Sasha. "The Evertongues earned their family name honestly. Is that flour on your fingers?"

As Wiglaf jerked his hands up to check, Tuka glared at his companion, and spoke. "Sir Evertongue, fortune has brought us together today. You wish to rise in power like, mm, the mighty loaf. We count our accomplishments in other ways. We are humble traders, businesspeople. Importers/exporters, you might say. Working together to bring back a better life for those loved ones we have left behind."

The filthily dressed human to his left belched wetly.

"Our consortium embraces all kinds of artisans, including mages such as yourself. In fact, it was only yesterday that we lost the very talented conjurer who was our traveling colleague in a bizarre . . . accident. We are here in this tavern tonight to mourn his loss." The belching ruffian at the table removed his cap and bowed his head. An unkempt cloud of hair matched his clothing for foulness.

"Accident?"

"He stood between us and a horrible creature best left undescribed. Bravely threw himself in harm's way. Walked right in front of us, he did."

"Or did we shtep back?" slurred the third as Sasha looked a dagger into his brain.

"Gosh, I don't know if I could help you in a situation like that. I'm new to all this, you see; just starting out."

Tuka poked his colleague in the ribs. "What did I tell you, Fenzig? Ha! The moment you walked in the door, my lord, I said, now here is a man who can use friends like us. Here is a man who wants to be somebody, to go someplace in life, but he doesn't have time to wait around for the carriage, eh?"

"Right!" Wiglaf beamed. Somebody understood.

"Well, fortune has smiled on you today. We have a friend and associate, a very experienced wizard. He has been called away for a short while, some kind of a special teaching assignment. But he has many items of great power that I'm sure he would be willing to let you borrow."

"Well, I don't know . . ."

"One sorcerer to another? He always makes it a point to get youngsters like you off to a fine start. Don't even need to ask him. Come. We'll take you there tonight."

"I don't know . . ."

"Big bad magic man," teased Sasha. "What's stopping you? That pan of rolls for tomorrow morning?"

"Nothing's stopping me. Nothing at all. Let's go."

The moon was bright that evening as the four new comrades arrived at the door of a modest dwelling, the only structure in a dark clearing surrounded by forest. Tuka rapped loudly on an ancient door knocker, but there was no answer.

"Isn't that just like him? Didn't even leave us a key. He's so preoccupied, all he thinks of are his spells. Fenzig, why don't you give us a hand?" The belching thief approached the door lock, did some expert twisting and jamming, and it sprung free. Tuka extended his hand. "See? It's perfectly all right. You first, Sir Evertongue, in case there are any trap—any magic items of which we should be aware."

Wiglaf swallowed hard and entered the doorway. He walked for a few feet in utter darkness, then thought he could make out a warm glow ahead of him. Heart pounding in his head, he cautiously followed the light down a corridor for what seemed like minutes. Finally the light grew brighter, and he stepped through into a large open space. Then he stopped short in amazement.

A soft, welcoming, dark-orange light issued from the walls as he entered, to reveal an interior that was, incredibly, much larger than it should have been. The ceiling of the vast studio appeared to be at least thirty feet high—many times taller than the outside of the house. He looked back, and was shocked to see an open door just a few steps away, with Tuka peering in. He shook off his confusion and whirled back around. What was behind him was not important. Before him, his good fortune was boundless.

For the room was full of magic.

Wiglaf's jaw was slack as he slowly turned in a circle. He had come to the right place. His eyes simply couldn't take in all the fabulous magical arcana. Here, on a mammoth rack of ironwork, hung row after row of staves and weapons, several of which seemed to glow faintly. On this mantel of gorgeous dark wood stood dozens of vials containing a dizzying array of potions that glittered and smoked in their confinements. Above him and ringing the room, handsome shelves bulged with spellbooks of all shapes and sizes. Most curious, there was the finest collection of material components Wiglaf had ever seen, an odd-ball flea market seemingly stored at random, the mundane joining the thrilling. Carefully arranged locks of hair were set next to a box brimming with jewels, lumps of coal were stored beside ornate wax sculptures, vials of brightly multicolored sand rested next to cupfuls of soot.

There was a curious painting, a forest glade, that polymorphed slowly through all four seasons as Wiglaf watched in stupefaction. He picked up a small hand mirror and was astonished to see a wizened, ancient face staring back at him—much older, but still recognizably his own. A wand swirled and roiled with colored mist down its length, and softly pulsated as he turned it with his fingers. More and more, on and on, everywhere he turned, the marvels continued. This was a lifetime's worth of collecting—and the potential beginning of Wiglaf's accelerated studies program. He was overcome with the immensity of the opportunity. The fraternity of magic was so incredibly generous: what a grand gesture by the old mage, to lend a helping hand like this.

Then he saw it. Hanging regally from a very tall coatrack was the most marvelous robe there could possibly be. Wiglaf motioned the others inside, but absently: he could not take his eyes off the garment. It was surely the old man's own, like the rest of the wonders in this room, but still it called to Wiglaf. He took the robe into his hands. It flowed through his fingers like fine-grained sand, an immensely pleasurable sensation. It was surprisingly light, considering that it appeared to be several sizes too large for him, and wonderfully soft. He lifted it closer to his face to inspect the signs and sigils that covered its surface. Some were simple, childlike scrawls; others, intricate forms that may have had meaning in some exotic language. One he even recognized: the seven stars in a crescent around a wisp of mist, familiar even to a beginner, the symbol of Mystra herself. This was truly powerful magic.

Wiglaf noticed a full-length mirror and saw himself with the robe. He could resist no longer. They were a perfect match. He swallowed once and wriggled into the garment.

Of a sudden, he felt a tingling: not unpleasant, but definitely unusual. The robe that had seemed much too long for Wiglaf now felt as if it were stirring around him, clinging and conforming to his size and shape. He looked at the mirror and saw that it was true: the robe was alive, pouring itself around him, fitting to his contours like a sleepy cat in his lap. The hem slowly rode off the floor as he watched. The symbols themselves were now moving: crawling across the robe's surface and giving off a warm glow that reached inside Wiglaf, soothing and comforting him. It was *glorious*. He felt his senses heightened somehow: his sight seemed to be sharper, his hearing more acute. And just now he heard Tuka and Sasha appraising the collection.

"Delightful," said Tuka. "Now how selfish can one be to hoard all these lovely baubles oneself?"

"You're not suggesting we take them?" asked Wiglaf.

"Theft? From a friend? Don't insult us. But why don't you *borrow* a few things and use them to get some practical experience? Bring them back when you're through— maybe with a little something extra for interest?"

"Do you think he would mind?"

"My lord, didn't I say he was a teacher? His mission in life is to educate young mages like yourself," said Tuka. "You'll be making him a happy man—and making him happy is the least you can do to repay his immense magnanimity."

"The way you explain it, it makes sense."

"It would," said Sasha.

"Well, take what you need, and let's get out of here," Tuka said.

Wiglaf paused to think. A few spellbooks, some components—what harm could it do? It wasn't as if anyone else was using them. And he wouldn't disturb the very rarest items. He scooped up his choices, stuffed them into his pack, and stepped out into the night. The robe had become such a comfortable part of him that he didn't realize he was still wearing it.

As the others came out of the magician's studio, fiddling with their pockets, a soft growling sound made the hairs on the back of Wiglaf's head rise. "Wh-What was that?" he whimpered.

"Wild dog," said Sasha. "They're everywhere at night. He'll taste steel if he gets closer."

"Just so long as he doesn't taste *us*," said Tuka.

The growl was punctuated by a piercing basso bark, and then the single sound became a din. Two, three, a whole pack of feral hounds rushed into the clearing and faced the adventurers, showing teeth, drooling with famished anticipation. There were more than ten of the huge, menacing beasts, and although Sasha and the others quickly had weapons drawn, they were clearly outnumbered. The largest of the pack, the leader, pawed its way slowly toward Wiglaf, snarling louder as it came, never taking its eyes off him, until it was only an arm's length away.

Wiglaf had never been in such a situation. He was frozen to the spot. It would be only a matter of time until they were overrun, and he would be the first one to go.

"Okay, Mister Magic," Sasha shouted, "here's your chance. Do something." The others laughed grimly and prepared for carnage.

Wiglaf was terrified, but he forced himself to move. He reached into his battered pack and felt for his well-thumbed spellbook. There wasn't much of value written down, since study had always been difficult for him. Mostly drawings and doodles. Wiglaf had "studied" spells of alteration—the most impressive kind of magic, he'd always felt—and collected the requisite components, but the only spell he'd ever managed to memorize and use with any slight authority was one for burning hands, and it had never really worked properly; on his most successful practice run, he had only singed his fingers. But with no time to think about it, this was his best shot. If he didn't try now, he would become not a magician but an entree.

Wiglaf pulled back the sleeves of the robe, held his hands palms down, thumbs together, spread his fingers into a fan shape, and mumbled both an incantation and a quick prayer for good measure, just as the salivating hound tensed its legs and leaned back to spring.

FOOM! A jet of superheated flame shot out from his finger-tips and roared toward the dog. The startled animal leapt backward away from the magical fire, yelping and howling, spots of fur smoking as it retreated. The other dogs matched their leader's howls, eyes wide with panic and confusion. Wiglaf turned at the sound, his arms still extended, but the flame remained, pouring in an arc toward the other dogs. The area was lit as brightly as if it were noon. The lead dog was already darting away, tail between its legs, and the others did not hesitate to follow. In a few seconds, they were gone.

Wiglaf curled his fingers into fists, and the flame stopped instantaneously. It was dead quiet, except for the whining of the dog pack receding in the distance. He looked stupidly at his hands. He felt heat on his cheeks.

Transfixed, Sasha dropped her sword and panted at the others. "By a gullyful of goblins! Did you see that? He bloody *did* it!"

Tuka whirled to face Wiglaf. "My lord! I had no idea!"

But Wiglaf didn't hear. He slumped to the ground like an emptied sack.

His hands had been hot, but he was out cold.

A while later, back in the Ale & Hearty, most of the regular patrons were wide-eyed over Wiglaf's story—which was becoming more and more colorful with each tankard that members of his star-struck audience provided. "This lad has a definite talent," boasted Tuka.

"Dogs. Snarling. RrrrrOW OW OW," barked Wiglaf, and took another sip.

By now Wiglaf was the toast of most, but still there were dissidents. "I don't know much about magic," growled a customer, "but I do know this: no young whelp shows up out of nowhere and starts mumbo-jumboing like an almighty sage. Impossible." A few emboldened others clanked their agreement on the tabletop.

"He's a natural," said Tuka. "Innate ability."

"Show us, then."

"Whatever it is, I got it," said Wiglaf. "Step aside." He tried to stand but failed, and sat back down hard.

"He's in no shape to cast spells right now, good people," Tuka said. "He has just had an exhausting experience, the likes of which would fell an ordinary man, and he deserves a chance to rest. But hear me. You shall have your proof. Tomorrow, you will judge this amazing spellcaster for yourself. Because the mighty Wiglaf is going to favor us all with a demonstration of his power, before your very eyes, tomorrow at sunrise. Right, Wiglaf?"

"Sure," giggled the new center of attention.

"Just one thing," Tuka went on. "If you want a demonstration, you'll have to pay."

"Magic is serious. Magicians aren't entertainers," said one Ale & Hearty regular.

"This one is unique," said Tuka. "One gold piece per customer. Tickets go on sale as soon as we can make them."

The dawn came misty and gray, but Tuka had managed to gather more than a hundred villagers in a glade near the town, and Sasha had dutifully collected the admission fee from each without once having to touch her weapon. The business had gone so well because even though there were skeptics in the crowd, nobody wanted to be the one to miss the big show and have to hear of it secondhand if he was wrong. This was the greatest thing to hit town in ages.

"Ladies and gentlemen," intoned Tuka, clapping his hands for quiet. "You've heard about his exploits. Now meet him in person. Would you welcome a prestidigitatious prodigy . . . that lord of legerdemain . . . the mighty mage . . . Wiglaf . . . EVERTONGUE!"

The applause was muted but present as the berobed Wiglaf appeared. He was steady on his feet, but moving with much greater deliberation today. The crowd arranged itself in a circle around him.

Wiglaf still wasn't sure what had happened the night before, but he knew in his heart that the robe had helped him. He had felt it from the first moment he put it on. Somehow, it had brought forth his innate magic abilities and multiplied them manyfold. He had never heard of a more impressive display of burning hands . . . and there were plenty more spells where that came from! Even his powers of memorization had improved, as a quick look at the old mage's private stock of spells had shown this morning. Most importantly, Wiglaf felt confidence for the first time in his magical career. He had been vindicated. It was easy. Only a fool would waste his time with endless conjugation when he could be out there speaking the language. And Wiglaf was about to talk the talk.

"Thank you, ladies and gentlemen. I'd like to begin by showing you one of the most beautiful of magical sights," he said. "If you will all look up at the sky . . ." He produced some phosphorous from his pocket and made the motions to bring forth a harmless display of dancing lights.

Later, many would swear that they saw the intricate signs on Wiglaf's robe begin to dance and shift. They would say that one large sigil in particular, just above Wiglaf's heart, took on a crimson sheen and softly pulsated. But in truth, nearly everyone had followed the young mage's advice and was instead searching the sky, waiting for the magic to begin, ready to *ooo* and *ahh*. What they actually saw would be the spark for hearty ale-soaked conversation for years to come.

There was a rapid series of dull popping sounds, like fireworks heard from a great distance. Then into the sky rushed a torrent of vegetables.

Shooting upward at rapid speed were heads of lettuce, ears of corn, stalks of celery, hundreds upon hundreds of cabbages, kumquats, beets, okra, eggplant, radishes, cauliflower, tomatoes, artichokes, carrots, parsley, spinach, kale, peas, basil, cucumbers, turnips, rutabagas, squash, broccoli, peppers, beans, asparagus, sprouts, green onions, white onions, red onions, yellow onions—all manner of produce, some varieties quite new to the region. A cornucopia of sensible dining was streaking heavenward in a thick stream and finally disappearing well beyond tree level with inverted *POP* sounds.

A yelp of shock caused them to turn away from the ludicrous sight and look back at Wiglaf. The spellcaster was as entranced as they were, still extending his fingers in a heroic conjuror's pose, but now ruining the effect by gaping with slack-jawed disbelief as the perishables poured into the sky before him.

"Quick, get the baskets and a ladder!" howled an onlooker, and the crowd erupted in laughter. Wiglaf dropped his hands in confusion, and the edibles vanished as quickly as they had come. His forehead began to glisten with sweat.

"A little comedy to start the show!" Tuka said forcefully. A few audience members applauded weakly. "Go on!" he stage-whispered to Wiglaf.

"Uh, well, yes," said the shaken wizard. "Er, okay. Magic-using is more than just, uh, dazzling beauty." A stifled laugh in the crowd became a snort and then a hacking cough. "It's also essential in a tight situation. If a magician knows what he's doing, he can outleap the strongest fighter." Sasha blanched at the reference. "Stand back, folks, and I'll show you."

In his mind, Wiglaf went over the incantation for the spell that would allow him to jump thirty feet in the air. Then he'd softly feather fall back to the ground and shut them up for good. He bent his knees and crouched, ready to spring. "Watch closely. Here . . . we . . . go!"

He mumbled and uncoiled.

A five-foot pit irised open beneath his feet.

For an instant, he hung suspended. Then he shrieked and disappeared into it with a clump.

They saw his hands first. With an effort, he clambered out.

"We'll try another one," he snarled.

People were clapping each other on the back, doubled over with laughter. Others were losing interest and starting to heckle.

He tried to conjure a magical light and found himself staggering out of a cone of darkness, unable to see or hear. He tried to generate a blinding spray of colors and levitated a poor woman into the air; she was saved from a nasty fall only because her husband held onto her legs for dear life as they rose past his head. He tried to raise an acorn to ten times its size and nothing happened—but later that afternoon, the owner of the adjacent farm was surprised to discover his prize hen proudly strutting around an egg two feet long. He tried to erase some writing from a scroll and gave himself a hotfoot. He tried to enlarge the fire from a torch and teleported a cow up a tree.

With each grandiose failure, both the laughter and the grumbling grew louder. But it wasn't until he tried to mend a volunteer's hem through the force of his will, and the force of his will pulled down thirty people's pants, that the Amazing Wiglaf Show finally turned ugly.

* * * * *

Wiglaf was devastated. He had never been so miserable. Last night he had been the most important man in town.

But today people only pointed and laughed—or pointed and cursed, depending on their degree of participation in his ultimate, showstopping feat. He felt ridiculous. The sight of Tuka, Sasha, and Fenzig returning all the money had been bad enough, but many people in the long refund line had also shaken their hands and thanked them for a wonderful time. Wiglaf was the town clown, and as he sat alone at the Ale & Hearty, he had plenty of time to think about it.

Maybe the robe had helped focus his magical power. So what? What good did that do when he didn't know enough about magic to wield it in the first place? He should have stayed in Calimport. He should have stayed a baker. He should have stayed in his mother's womb, where it was nice and safe.

"Buy a girl a drink, magic man?" It was Sasha.

"I'm broke, remember? Not even the bartender wants to be seen with me."

"Tough day, huh? Oh, well, I'm not the kind of girl who gets drinks bought for her, anyway." She smiled grimly and sat. "Listen, Wiglaf, I'm sorry I gave you such a hard time. I just didn't believe you were really a magician."

"I'm not. Just a student who didn't even have the sense to keep on studying."

"Maybe you're finally learning something."

"This robe. It . . . changed me. But whatever it did was an illusion. A fake. It's like . . . I took something that wasn't mine. I took a reputation I didn't deserve. An ability I hadn't developed. I called myself a magician and insulted everybody who really is one." Wiglaf's eyes became animated again, and his voice rose. "And I know what I'm going to do about it right now. I'm taking this robe back, if I have to fight ten packs of dogs to do it."

Sasha's smile revealed a perfect set of teeth. "I'm very glad to hear you say that, Wigla—"

"WIGLAF!"

It was Tuka, rushing in from outside, opening the door on a piercingly loud animal roar. The air rushing into the tavern felt like a hot summer day, and the sky they could see through the door had turned from morning's overcast to a bright yellow.

Sky . . . yellow?

"Wiglaf! Sasha! If you've got weapons, get out here now!"

They tore out of the tavern, and Wiglaf's confusion instantly dissipated. In this day full of unwanted sights, this was by far the worst. A mammoth red dragon was just pulling out of an aerial attack run into the town square, yellow flames pouring from its gigantic maw. Twenty or thirty villagers brandished weapons against the beast; some threw spears or loosed arrows, but those who knew how to fight were few, and the monster was large. One building was already on fire. Wiglaf was nearly bowled over by the heated backwash from the dragon's flight. It snorted as it climbed for another pass, and a tree caught fire like a matchstick. Silhouetted against the gray sky, the dragon flew up in a wide arc to launch another attack.

"Find someplace to hide! Take cover! Take cover!" Tuka screamed.

A woman ran to Wiglaf and clenched his robe, shrieking with terror. "Magic-user! Do something! Help us! I have children! DO SOMETHING!" Maybe she hadn't seen the demonstration this morning. Maybe she was so afraid that she was willing to believe anything. But she was trying to grasp at the only thing she could see: Wiglaf's magic. She really thought he could help.

"Wiglaf, let's go!" Sasha shouted. She pulled the woman off him. "Go now!" She tugged at his robe.

The dragon turned in the sky, straightened, and headed back.

"No!" Wiglaf pulled himself free. "Get away, Sasha. I have to try."

"With what? This is no dog! It'll kill you!"

"I have to try."

"You idiot!" Sasha pulled the still-screaming woman out of the square, leaving Wiglaf alone to face the monster, which was picking up speed and dropping altitude to find the perfect flamethrowing angle.

Wiglaf could trust only one spell: burning hands, the one he'd used against the dogs. The way it had roared out of his fingertips last night, the flame had almost matched a dragon's intensity. Maybe if he fought fire with fire, the beast would act like most animals and retreat.

He took a deep breath, planted his feet, spread his fingers, and joined his thumbs. The dragon noticed the lone unmoving figure as it continued to accelerate. It adjusted its approach angle. Now it was coming straight for Wiglaf—and inhaling.

His knees felt like pudding as he watched the monster approach, and his voice was shaking as he began the incantation, but Wiglaf did not move. He stood his ground and faced the beast as it screamed forward. He managed to get the words out—and sighed with relief when magical force crackled toward his fingertips, and he stood with teeth clenched and eyes flashing as adrenalin pumped through him.

He aimed his burning hands at the dragon, and from them poured a spray of vegetables.

The first few bushels that struck the dragon actually did some physical damage before vanishing on impact, such was the speed of its attack run. They smacked painfully at its scaly hide and, as Wiglaf adjusted his aim before he could register what he was dispensing, worried its eyes and nose. The confusion was the important thing. The dragon spit flamelessly and blinked its eyes again and again. Still the veggies came, slowing its forward motion until it was almost hovering.

Wiglaf finally regained his senses enough to understand, but realized his outrageous spell was the only thing holding the creature at bay.

He held his arms firmly forward.

On and on, the dragon was pelted with representatives of every single member of a major food group, until it shook its head and finally took a breath to eradicate this problem once and for all.

Wiglaf knew he couldn't hold out for long now that the great creature had drawn a bead on him, but there was no other choice. He was a dead man, yes. But if he stopped casting, there would be nothing standing in the dragon's way. He would not run. At least he would give some people the chance to take cover, to save themselves. At least he would end his life in dignity and service. Wiglaf let a deep sigh escape him, then closed his eyes in determination and waited for the end to come.

He heard some mumbling behind him. An instant later, the stream of vegetables was joined by a stream of flame.

Now the dragon was faced with a gargantuan gout of fire aimed at its head, not to mention that the foodstuffs tasking its eyes and nose were now roasting hot—and, Wiglaf noticed, smelling delicious on the way up. There comes a time when every creature, no matter how large or small, meek or fierce, wise or wanton, has finally reached its limit of pain, tolerance, and plain exasperation. At the business end of a torrent of steaming, stinging vegetables, the miserable dragon finally gave up, and swiftly flew away.

A shaken Wiglaf dropped his hands and turned to meet his benefactor.

The belcher. The lockpicker.

Fenzig was a magic-user.

Fenzig balled his hands into fists, and the fire disappeared instantly and utterly. He extended his fingers again, blew on them as if to cool them off, and winked. Then he smacked his hands sharply together. Then again. And again.

Tuka and Sasha ran toward them, making the same hand motions, and before long everyone in the square was applauding as well.

"*You!*" Wiglaf recoiled in shock. "This is *your* robe. You *let* me take it away."

"We've been expecting you," said the man the others had called Fenzig, drawing close to Wiglaf for privacy, "ever since your teacher told me you had resigned."

"M-My teach . . ."

"Magicians who form friendships are a close fraternity, boy. Your former instructor thinks you have great potential, despite your laziness, and one day you might convince me of that as well. He thought you needed a sterner taskmaster—but first I had to get your attention. I trust I have it now."

"You were wonderful, magic man," said Sasha as she arrived.

"So this was all an act? You three together?"

"Nobody told the dragon about it," panted Tuka. "I thought we were gone. I really did."

"You stopped it, Wiglaf," Sasha said. "Your magic. Your courage."

"I couldn't have done it without—" He looked up into a face that had grown infinitely wiser in the last few moments; a face that would impart great knowledge in the coming years, now that he was ready to receive it. "—my master?"

"I'll take my robe back now," said the mage. "And in exchange, I'll show you how to do that little stunt whenever you want. Invent a spell yourself. We'll call it . . . cast vegetables."

Wiglaf's new life began when he slipped off . . . this robe.

* * * * *

"This very one?" asked the young apprentice. "You're telling me this is the robe that undid Wiglaf?"

"It's a robe of wild magic," the old man said. "As you could easily tell if you recognized this sigil. See? A warning. To anyone experienced in reading it, it says, 'wild magic, dum-dum. Makes spellcasting completely unpredictable. Only one of its kind. Tends to favor the caster if he really needs help, but that is Mystra's munificence, at least that's how the story goes. I have no idea who actually fashioned this thing, and I would never try to make one. This robe is completely useless except for one purpose: reminding younglings like you that there is no quick substitute for listening to ancient ones like me, and learning what we assign."

"That's a terrific story," said the lad.

"Be thankful that you learned this lesson by hearing a story, and not the way Wiglaf had to. But keep it learned, all the same. Now let's begin by working with components. A simple alteration. Fetch me some vegetables and chop them up, boy."

The apprentice looked up in wonder. The truth had

struck him. "For cast vegetables, sir?"

The master's stern expression was still in place, but his eyes were twinkling.

Of course—how else could the old man have known what Wiglaf was thinking?

"Later, my lad, later. These are for a stew. To go with whatever Sasha's managed to hunt for us today."

A WORM TOO SOFT . . .

J. Robert King

The stone was as big as an ogre's head, as green as dragon bile, and as clear as Evermead. Unlike most emeralds, though, this one wasn't cut along fracture lines, but perfectly spherical and smooth. On its satin belly I saw myself, all six-foot-three of me dwarfed into a six-and-three-sixteenths-inch doll, my hawk-nose warped to match in size my brawny chest. I saw, too, my slim, demure hostess curved beside me, watching me as I watched the rock.

Now that Olivia Verdlar, proprietor of the Stranded Tern and owner of this peerless rock, had gotten an eyeful of me, I hoped she, too, knew why she'd flown me out from Waterdeep—pegasus-back, no less.

"Impressive," I said, and leaned away from the enormous stone.

She slid back into my line of sight. Impressive, indeed. Her green eyes matched the rock, hue and luster, and her dark hair and slim figure were the ideal setting for such gems. Knowing the power of those eyes, she knew she didn't have to say a word in response.

I'd been drawn off by worse wenches, so I bit: "You say it came from the crop of a great green . . . ?" The word *dragon* hovered behind my question, but it didn't need to be spoken. After all, the rock had been christened "the Dragon's Pearl."

She nodded, and that slight motion sent an *ally-ally-oxenfree* down past her hips. "It's one of a hundred gemstones that got polished in the thing's belly. Seems Xantrithicus the Greedy didn't trust his hoard to a cave, preferring to hold it in his gut." She made a gesture toward her own slim waist, knowing I'd look there. I did. "Seems that way his spendthrift mate, Tarith the Green, couldn't even get two coppers to rub together."

"One of a hundred gems," I mused. It was time to win back some self-respect. "That's got to decrease the value of the pearl."

Was that a little color I saw in her high cheekbones? "This is by far the largest of the hundred. Most of the rest are fist-sized, or pebble-sized. If the gemologists are to be believed, this is also the most ancient of the hoard, in the wyrm's gut for nearly two thousand years. I can little imagine its size when the polishing began."

I nodded, thinking, letting her words hang in the air as she had let mine, and hoping my dark-brown eyes were something of a match for her stunning green ones. I thought of the building around us: the cut-stone severity of this inner vault, the sorcerous impregnability of the outer vault, the ivory-towered fortress above, the glacial fastness of the mountain peaks. Every aspect of the Stranded Tern pleasure dome reeked of magic . . . everything except me, so I began again to wonder why she'd summoned me.

"Seems your magical defenses would be enough to guard this treasure," I said. "So, why bring a back-alley finder from Waterdeep across half the world to this icy palace?"

Olivia's small, hot hand was upon my biceps again, as it had been when the winged horse had touched down on the icy lip of the landing bay. She must keep those hands in a very warm place, I thought.

"Muscle and sneakiness have certain . . . powers that magic cannot provide."

Gods, I wished that touch did not so thrill me. Keep

your head, Bolton. She's your new boss. With her next
words, the hot fingers drifted away.

"Besides, the pearl resists magical protections. The
mage who slew old Xantrithicus found that out when some
quite ordinary banditti slew him, who were then in their
own turn slain, and again, and again, until my agents
retrieved the thing."

"So you called me out to defend an undefendable hunk
of stone?"

"I thought with Quaid, all things were possible. . . ."

I'd stepped right into that one. Hmm. "I've got a few
tricks up my sleeve." Not really up my sleeve, but in the
little black case I carried over one shoulder. Strange that
so many poisons and needles and bits of wire and rubber
at my back would make me feel safe. "Your rock'll be well
guarded. Of course, I have my expenses, and need of room
and board—"

"Don't fret, Mr. Quaid," she said silkily. "You'll find this
job has more than enough . . . fringe benefits. And don't
even think about making off with my jewel. If the snows
don't get you, my winged wolves will. Now, come along."

I followed her. It wasn't hard; I just let my eyes lead.
Yeah, ever since I'd stepped down from that winged stallion, shoulders iced from our flight through the gale, I'd
not been able to take my eyes off this Olivia. She was
grace personified: young, svelte, clean-edged like a well-
turned stiletto. In fact, she was too young and beautiful
for this kip, this pleasure dome built beneath a constant
sleet ceiling atop the Thunder Peaks. Where could a chit
like her, with legs like those, who could get anything she
needed and more with a mere pout of her perfect lips,
have gotten the grit and moxie and power to build such a
place?

Her sculpted arms deftly worked the lock on the iron
door of the inner vault, and I struggled to memorize the
combination, a rhyme of my dad's forcing its way into my
head:

> *A worm too soft and juicy*
> *Is a worm that hides a hook.*

You can't think that way, Bolt. This is your new boss; this is her kip, your new home—a far cry from the alleys and scamps and tramps of Waterdeep's Dock Ward.

However she'd acquired it, the Stranded Tern was hers. It could have belonged to no one else. It had her lines.

The stairs we walked took us up and out to a vast great room. The white walls of the place shone like mother-of-pearl, arching smooth and high like the inside of Olivia's leg. I'd've felt blinded by the whiteness but for the red rugs that hung on the walls and the thick carpet on the floor—more carpet in one room than in all the hovels in the Dock Ward.

Dead center rose a stairway with treads of glass. It snaked upward through empty air, held up by nothing but magic. On the second floor, it gave onto a wide arch of red iron filigree, which led in turn to four floors of guest rooms. Beneath the coil of treads was a long desk and a little man in tight black satin.

He wasn't the only liveried lackey. The place crawled with maids and 'hops in similar getups, and swarmed with guests:

There were hairless women wrapped in rare furs. There were men in tailored silk suits with such sharp edges they looked like tents tacked down to hard soil. There were kids, too, brash and savage in their pressed collars.

We moved out among the guests, my homespun snow-sodden shirt rough and ridiculous on my shoulders. I felt like a hairy bear.

Bolton Quaid, what've you gotten yourself into?

"This way," said the lady.

One benefit of perfect hips was that she couldn't be easily lost in a crowd. The lines of the place were hers, all right, but they lacked something of the warm dance she had. . . .

What are you getting into, indeed?

As we approached the stair, I saw a woman of equal swank to my boss, only that instead of demure silk, this lady wore scant furs that clung to her with all the impossible suspension of the stairs.

"Keep your eyes on me, Mr. Quaid, and you'll do better,"

Olivia said without turning.

"Yes, ma'am," I said, coughing to show myself chastened.

We mounted the stairs. The cold beneath my shoe leather made me think the steps weren't glass, but pure, clean ice. I almost blurted my surprise, but had dealt the lady a strong enough hand already.

She led me through the red iron arch and up three floors, then out along a gaslit hallway with guest rooms. Like the rest of the palace, this hall had elegant, rounded lines—more a ribbed windpipe than a door-lined corridor. I knew the rooms would be the same, organ-shaped chambers where lurked Faerûn's beautiful and wealthy and powerful, sleeping and eating and defecating like flies inside a corpse.

Beautiful and wealthy and powerful . . . I'd been riding in midblizzard above the seventeen onion-shaped domes of the palace before I'd realized just how far out of my league I'd be. Still, flies usually don't mind an ant pulling off his own hunk of flesh.

"*Voila!*" said she, halting. Her pronouncement seemed to swing wide the silver-edged door before her. The room beyond was incredible.

Unlike the great room, cold and stark, this place was as warm and soft and red as a dragon's heart. The door gave onto a railed landing above a velvet-walled sunken parlor. A fireplace, complete with blaze, stood on one wall, and opposite it was a steaming, bubbling bath large enough to bathe two war-horses. Through an open door on the far side of the parlor, I saw a velvet-covered bed that could sleep the two mounts, and in another room, a table where their knights and squires and retainers and a few bards could play a game of poker while their steeds slept. The wide, lead-glazed window above the table showed the teeth of the storm outside.

"For me?" I asked innocently, though truthfully there wasn't much acting in my delight.

"For you, Bolton Quaid." She started down into the room, and I didn't know whether to look at the brocade chairs or the bright chandelier or the tasseled drapes or those swaying hips.

I stammered after her. "The Dock Ward's my usual digs. A street rat like me is—"

She spun around and placed a finger on my lips to silence me. "If you're half the street rat I think you are, you'll be worth the room, and much more."

Those words, those eyes, that touch—suddenly the magic of the place seemed not so amazing, but a mere extension of her. She shone with power.

Her hand dropped from my lips, and like a schoolgirl, she clutched my fingers and drew me after her. "You must see this view."

I nodded, and after a few stumbling steps, did. Through the wide window, I saw her wintery palace, glowing cold and blue like a rock-stranded moon. The towers stood fearless and alien in the blizzard, and the curving curtain wall was draped in icicles; but the courtyard within was hot and bright and sandy.

Now I did blurt my amazement. In the midst of this waste of rock and snow, the lady had made a garden. From this height, the palm trees looked like ferns, the green bunches of Chultan flowers like field clover. And in the midst of the garden lay a winding, sandy lagoon, over-arched here and there with footbridges, surrounded by paths and benches, peopled by folk so beautiful and pow-erful and rich that they seemed fey creatures, seemed to glide above the sand without leaving footprints.

I started to speak—what words, I do not know—and found I couldn't because I had not breathed in moments, perhaps minutes. But I needed no words; Olivia was speaking for us both now.

"You haven't even got the chill out of your poor Water-dhavian bones yet. Look how you shiver." She spoke like a doting mother to a child. Some part of me knew she was drawing the rough cloak from my shoulders, was running that small hot hand along my bare side. "There'll be plenty of time for Mr. Quaid to rig traps and alarms. First, though, a recuperative bath."

"I—I—I—" came my reply as she led me to the huge, steaming tub. With a tremble—whether of fear or cold or joy—I knew I was naked, stripped bare. I lowered myself into the foamy, hot, bubbling waters. Hmm. The seduced innocent was a new role for me.

She moved up next to me, and now it was not her hot hand that touched my lips, but her own lips. They seemed to scald, and the fresh warm breath of her puffed for a moment over my face as she drew back.

"This is moving a little too fast," I said, at last able to speak as I looked into those green eyes. Oh, yes, those green eyes. "You put a tailored suit on a street rat, and all you've got is a rat in a suit."

"Not if the suit is magic."

* * * * *

That night, I had the most peculiar dream. I rolled over on the silken sheets to enfold Olivia in my brawny arms, feel her heat against my bare chest, and instead felt the bristling mange of Xantrithicus the Greedy himself. I awoke, screaming.

* * * * *

Next morning when I rose, she was gone. I dressed quickly, donning the white ruffled shirt, red brocade jacket, white hose, and charcoal-gray wool leggings left for me. Just my size. I smiled wryly. She'd had enough chance to check my fit perfectly.

I came down for breakfast and saw Olivia in the hammer-beamed dining hall, presiding royally over a morning feast for her guests. She gave me the same polite nod she gave other late arrivals; either she was a better stoneface than I, or she'd made herself familiar with more guests than just me—men and women, alike.

Breakfast was hot and filling—eggs and fried mushrooms, tortes and jellies, bangers and gravy and biscuits and pie. Still, compared to the feast last night, the food paled. Oh, well. It sure beat the hash slung in the Dock Ward.

I ate too much food and stayed too long staring at those otherwise-occupied green eyes—too much and too long, given that I had a gem to secure. I headed for the vault.

En route, I met my assistant. I'd not known before that instant that I had an assistant.

"Hold up, bloke. Where you think you're off to?" asked the scamp. I could have called him no better; I'd seen enough scamps in my day to know their stripe. Heck, I'd been one myself not so long ago. This scamp had greasy black hair, which he continually finger-combed back from his brown eyes. He sat upon a tall stool, leaning back rakishly against the slick wall, and his ruddy, freckled face bore a scowl that revealed less-than-healthy teeth, an idle splinter stabbed between two that were close enough to hold it. And if Olivia had tried to dress this kid in silks instead of knee- and elbow-worn linens, she'd failed.

"I'm Bolton Quaid, new head of security for the Tern."

"Bosh!" replied the lad immediately. "Quaid ain't no dandy. Lady says he's a rogue, like me—knows which way's up."

I kicked the stool out from under him, snagged his collar, and hoisted him high. I'd used a similar technique on alley cats. "Would you say this way is up?"

The kid hung there, poking his fists at the air and snarling. "You ain't getting . . . grrrrh . . . past Filson Crybot . . . Mister Dandy-Thief. Like to feel . . . my shiv . . . ?"

"You mean this?" I asked, holding up my other hand to show him his crude little knife, dwarfed on my meaty fingers. "Or this—" I rolled my fingers to show a white rabbit's foot "—or this—" a slingshot "—or this—" a bent black feather "—or this—" a pair of marbles, and so on. The kid was on the verge of tears, and even I wouldn't reduce a proud street scamp to tears.

"Give 'em back! Give 'em back!"

"All right." I gently lowered the kid to his feet and shoved his stuff at him.

No sooner had he touched ground than his heel stomped my foot. Ahhh! The walls around me swam, went dim, seeming for a moment to blink out from smooth-polished pearl to filthy cave stone. I let out a gasp and took a step back, only to strike my head against something brutally hard. The kid had already snagged his stuff and backed toward the iron door of the vault, his little shiv thrust out before him. I reeled, almost dropped to my haunches, and my head was filled with the keen of a whistle. It was going to take a while to recover from this one.

Especially now. Olivia was there. She'd appeared suddenly, as though magically summoned: only then did I see the whistle drop from Filson's lips to dangle on a chain around his scrawny neck. Already he was babbling to the lady about the intruder (me) who'd tried to strangle him.

Olivia, in typical aplomb, laughed. "Filson, meet your new boss. This is Mr. Bolton Quaid." With that introduction, she gestured to me, and I might have bowed had I not been busy rubbing my head and looking into empty air to see what had hit me.

The ruddy scamp face turned as white as the walls around us, though the color looked less fetching on Filson. "Er . . . sorry, boss."

I waved off the apology, wishing I could find a lump on the wall at least as large as the one on my head. "Part of the job. I'm glad to know you can handle yourself in a fight."

That brought some color back to those cheeks. "Just trying to do my job."

"Speaking of which," said Olivia, her tone hardening as she turned to me, "you'd best get at least some provisional protection on the Dragon's Pearl. We've had a couple magic lapses this morning."

My brow beetled. "Magic lapses?"

"The storms play havoc with magic," volunteered Filson, clearly wanting to redeem himself. "Spells fail sometimes."

"These lapses aren't caused by any storm," Olivia said, never turning from me. She let the implications sink in before she spoke them. "One of the guests is trying to dispel the magical protections around the pearl."

Now it was my turn to go white. "I'll get on it right away."

"Once you get the pearl secured nonmagically, I want you to hunt down the cause of these . . . interruptions."

"What shall I do when I find the culprit?"

"Kill him."

* * * * *

Within a few hours, the pearl was secured seven ways to Summertide. I'd locked it in three concentric boxes, chained the outer box to five different spots on the walls, set seventy-three poisoned darts into projectors along the perimeter, lined ceiling and floors with drider web, strung up three hair triggers on the threshold to the chamber, and booby-trapped the vault door so that the slightest disturbance would trigger a circular deadfall. The rock was as safe as I knew how to make it, short of hanging it around my own neck.

The whole time I worked, Filson watched and gabbed. He told me a lot I already knew about Olivia: that she was powerful and ruthless and all-knowing in the Tern. He also hinted in whispers that she used magic to look younger. That didn't surprise me, but I nervously wondered *how much* younger.

Most interesting of all, though, he spilled his own theory about why the lady kept a gemstone she feared to remove from its vault within a vault. He said the Dragon's Pearl magically powered the whole palace. He said the rock had absorbed Xantrithicus's power and Olivia was now drawing on it. He said the stone couldn't be magically guarded because any spells that kept intruders out would keep the magic in.

Out of the mouths of kids. The Dock Ward had taught me to listen to babbling kids and old fools. *A worm too soft and juicy is a worm that hides a hook.* Hmm. Where was Olivia's hook, and what fish was she trying to lure, and why? Money, certainly, but she had enough of that. More money, of course, but also . . . what—power, station . . . companionship?

No time for such thoughts. I had a would-be jewel thief to catch.

It would not be easy. I doubted Olivia wanted me to rough up her patrons, as I routinely did to the smugglers and black marketeers on the docks. No, this would take subtlety and stealth.

Filson would prove to be a problem.

* * * * *

"Reconnoiter? What's that mean?" he asked suspiciously. "Are you trying to brush me off?"

"Not at all," I responded, pushing him toward the crowded dining hall. "You know the patrons. Watch them. See if any of them look suspicious."

"What're *you* gonna do?" the boy asked defensively.

"My job," I responded. One more shove did the trick, and the kid was off into the whirling cloud of mink and satin and hoity-toity laughter.

My job, in this case, involved grilling the servants. You listen to kids and old fools and servants. They've been in every crack and cranny, seen everything doing and everybody being done, and because of their station, had been ignored all the while. While Filson was giving diners the eye, I'd be giving cooks the ear.

I watched the double doors to see which swung which way, then made my entry. The kitchen—a long, low-ceilinged gallery—was as decked as any other room. Tables and butcher's blocks lined the marble floor, shiny-scrubbed pots and pans hung from the plaster-bossed ceiling, rolling steam stood above bubbling kettles, and chefs bustled about it all, their white smocks and mushroom hats flitting like scrap paper in wind.

I walked up to one of the chefs, who worked a bloody set of knives on five long tenderloins. "Excuse me," said I.

The man didn't look up. His hands moved expertly on meat and knife. "You're excused."

By his faint Sembian accent, I knew this was a connoisseur snob. Well, to me, a cook's a cook. "I was wondering if you've noticed any . . . magical lapses."

Again, no attention was spared me. He was busy sliding the steaks he'd cut from a tenderloin onto a platter, which was immediately whisked away by another cook. He reached for the second hunk of meat as he spoke. "I haven't time to notice—"

The words stopped dead. He must have seen it. I certainly couldn't have missed it. The long red wet slab of meat had turned to a great greasy cow pie, and the scoriated butcher's block into an uneven boulder. Worse still, though, the keen-edged knife had disappeared, an ass's jawbone in its place, and the cook's supple, well-trained hand had become a warty, clawed, three-fingered talon. Gone was the white smock and mushroom hat, replaced by a pessimistic clump of matted chest-hair on a bare, greenish, scaly chest . . . and an oily spit curl above a goblin pate.

Goblin pate!

Those dark, squalid goblin eyes lifted and met mine in that stunned moment, and two protruding lower fangs rose up and out to threaten those gray-green nostrils. But the next moment it was all gone, and the Sembian chef was staring impatiently, baldly, at me.

"Did you see that?" I asked, aghast.

"See what?"

Before our bland talk could go further, we were interrupted by a shout of outrage. I looked toward the doors in time to see a server in the last foot of his fall to the polished marble floor. A platter of steaming turkey and trimmings preceded him. It and he hit ground, and the turkey's featherless wings flapped stupidly as it arced upward, vomited its stuffing onto the server, and flopped onto the marble floor.

The cause of this small catastrophe followed hard on the fall—my doubtable assistant, Filson. He leapt past the open-out door and vaulted the server to run in gleeful pride toward me.

"Look, Quaid! Look what I found in Mr. Stavel's pockets!"

Too stunned to do anything else, I *did* look at the rich golden treasures spread out on the waif's grubby hands—a clockwork timepiece in gold, a money clip fat with Cormyrian notes, a pair of rings with rubies the size of cat's-eyes, and a strand of enormous pearls, any one of which would have equalled my typical take in a given year.

"You . . . you . . ." The bald bullocks of this "assistant"—not only to knock over a server and ruin a turkey after picking pockets in *my* name, but also to come brag to me and the kitchen staff about it—beggared me. "You *stole* from the *guests!*"

"But look! It's—" Now it was his turn to look flabbergasted as he gazed at the trove in his hands. Unlike me, however, he found too many words to express his consternation. "But wait. I was going to return them after I checked for any clues or any evidence that might link them to attempts to shut down the lady's magic, only when I'd gotten the take they weren't in my hands more than a second or two before they turned into—"

He didn't have to finish, for I saw it with my own eyes: the clockwork timepiece had become a smooth-edged river stone, the money clip and Cormyrian notes had turned into a bunch of leaves caught in a splinter of bark, the rings were a couple of large ladybug shells, and the pearls were a shriveled strand of grapes.

The reconstitution of all those things happened so quickly that I hadn't had time to be surprised at these revelations before I was being surprised at the reappearance of the gold and pearls and jewels.

. . . *Is a worm that hides a hook.*

There's a point in every case gone sour when the finder knows he's being had. I'd reached that point. A pearl with the magical might of an ancient wyrm . . . a woman known to use magic to make her look younger . . . to use magic to make an impossible lagoon in the heart of a blizzard . . . cow pies for tenderloin and goblins for chefs . . . Oh, yes, it was all coming far too clear now. In a flash, I saw through the whole charade, saw why a woman would use a dragon-enchanted emerald to create a magical pleasure dome atop the most forbidding of mountains.

"C'mon, Filson," I said, gesturing him to follow me. "This is the point when we go grille the boss."

The urchin's hands closed over the jewels, and they disappeared into his pockets. I didn't care. Not about his petty larceny, nor about our explosive emergence out the in-door, which startled back a crew of servers who'd come to check out the commotion. My young charge and I shoved past them, bold and self-righteous, and strode out into the wide dining hall. All around us, patrons chattered nervously, trying to cover a multitude of social blunders caused by the lapse of their magical enhancements. It was no use: they were all about to be embarrassed all over again.

Another lapse. Suddenly, the huge, elegant room was gone, replaced in a flash by a cold, breezy barn backed up against a yawning cave mouth. The tables had become long troughs; the delicacies straw and dung and dirt clods; the guests scabby old hags, grotesquely fat men with rashes around their mouths, acne-pocked wretches, greasy-haired baboons, toad-people covered in oozy boils, haggard and hairy and naked cavemen, filthy-jowled pigs. . . . The menagerie—the best of which belonged in a barn and the worst of which belonged in a priest-sealed grave—chattered on with its same squawking gossip. Now, though, the salacious words and chuckles and winks were animalistic yawps and grunts and scratchings.

It was over, again. I reeled, feeling as delirious as before, though knowing now it was not I but the Stranded Tern that was deluded. I only hoped that the pleasant illusory surroundings would remain in place until I found Olivia. I had no desire to stumble through breezy barns and black cave mouths and cold snow and ramshackle shacks. Yes, shacks—I now understood what I was dealing with.

I didn't have to look long for Olivia; I literally ran into her on a blind corner of the soaring great room. Apparently, she had been looking for me. Her lovely face was red, whether with exertion or anger.

"There you are!" she shouted. "What am I paying you for? Find the culprit!"

I had reached a pique myself, and it felt delicious to indulge it. "I have. You are the first among many culprits."

"What?" she barked, enraged.

"Yes, madam. You are serving those guests of yours cow droppings instead of tenderloin, algae instead of caviar, worms instead of noodles. Your hammer-beamed dining hall is a drafty, stinky barn, and your pearlescent great room is a filthy, awful cavern."

"And whose fault is that?" shrieked Olivia. I'd not expected that tack, and the shock of it shut me up. "I have promised them the finest accommodations, and that is what I have magically provided. Yes, magically. And cow pies transformed by the pearl *are* tenderloins. These temporary shortfalls are *your* problem. The feces laid before my guests are *your* responsibility."

I was surprised, yes, but guilty? No. "So you thought that one magic rock could transform an isolated mountain village of goblins into an opulent spa for the wealthy and powerful . . . ?"

"Until this morning, it had."

"And thought it powerful enough to warp goblins and cavemen into comely human servants and chefs and maitre d's—?"

"*You* were convinced it was a hot bath and a silken bed rather than a pus pocket and a rotting slab of meat."

"Just so that you could lure the most influential creatures of Faerûn here. But why? That's the question. What hook does this juicy worm hide? Gold, of course! You've gathered them here to get their *real* riches in exchange for your *false* luxuries. Perhaps you're even performing a few casual assassinations for whomever you are leagued with!"

"Are you accusing me of murd—"

"But look who got the last laugh!" I shouted, latching onto her hot little hand and dragging her unceremoniously after me toward the bustling dining hall. "You didn't lure the rich and powerful folk of Faerûn, but only more magical charlatans such as yourself. You've traded grubs and garbage for orc flesh and feces!"

I couldn't have timed it better. As though on cue, the magic failed again, and before my outflung hand, we both saw the filthy, debased, rank, and horrible creatures that sat around troughs and mangers in that barn. Scrofulous magic-users all, whose gold coins were nothing more than transmuted river stones, whose paper notes were merely mildewed leaves, whose august nobility was only a beautiful mask cast over their true tired, warty, awful flesh. Their powerful magics had temporarily made real what was false, and the lie of their lives had shriveled their true selves as full-plate armor shrivels the body inside into white, wrinkled nothing.

"And how dare you act as though the great finder,

Bolton Quaid, has not solved this mystery of yours? The reason your illusion magic is failing is that it is surrounded by more illusion magic. One illusion piled atop another piled atop another makes for a swaying emptiness that must and will fall. It's your worthless guests and their worthless bark and twigs, all dressed up in magic to look like creatures of import, that has made your worthless barns and hovels and caves show for what they truly are—no great pleasure dome of the Thunder Peaks.

"How dare you hire me—*me!*—thinking a nonmagical dolt from the docks would be too stupid to see through your schemes?"

I was so pleased with having solved the mystery that I'd missed the biggest illusion of all. Literally, the biggest.

She lurked just behind me now. From the green whiffs of caustic breath, I knew even before I turned what I would see, but still the sight shocked me into trembling numbness.

A great green wyrm. She towered over me in the toothy cavern of her lair. Not Xantrithicus, for this was a she-lizard—but perhaps his mate, Tarith the Green. Her vermillion scales gleamed like ceramic plates across her bunched haunch, which rose easily the height of my head. Above that was the lizard's mighty rib cage, expanding now in an in-drawn breath in preparation to poison me and all the critters clustered fearfully in the barn behind me. Atop that bulging set of ribs were two long and wicked arms, clawing eagerly at the air, and then a mange-scruffed neck, and then a huge red-fleshed set of jowls. The eyes that sat atop that smoldering snout were the same green eyes with which Olivia had so enticed me when I arrived—the same, except for their size, like twin turkey platters.

This time, it was the hook that hid the wyrm.

I knew I was dead. My feet were rooted to the smooth, chill floor of the cavern, and my once-so-proud tongue lay like a dead thing between my clattering teeth. I would not escape. I could not escape. Oh, if I were a lucky man, the magic would return now, so that she would shrink to her human form . . . but good luck was too much to hope for.

She reared back, lungs full, and the reptilian muscles along her rib cage slid obscenely beneath her scales. I felt the gagging green gas billow, sudden and fierce, over me, burning eyes I'd instinctively shut, and nose and lips, though I held my breath.

No, a guy from the Dock Ward of Waterdeep can't count on good luck. Thankfully, though, he can count on a wily scamp of a partner.

The cloud suddenly ceased, and some of the thin fumes traced backward toward the open maw of the dragon as she gasped for air. I cracked my eyes just enough to see Filson straddling the creature's tail and yanking one plate-sized scale up against the grain. It had to be more surprise than pain that had made the wyrm gasp, but whatever it was, I had my opening.

Snatching a loose timber from the rotting side of the barn, I heaved the thing up toward that sucking gullet. My aim was true, and the decaying wood lodged itself in the creature's throat. Had there been people in the barn behind me instead of filthy, sorcerous subpeople, I might have taken a moment to shout for them to run. As it was, it didn't matter. They were running anyway.

Instead, I repaid Filson by dashing around the struggling bulk of the beast and snatching him from the tail. My feet had just touched ground on the other side of the huge appendage when the beam-bearing mouth of the dragon slammed down where we had just been. Filson was yammering something, but there was no time to listen, no time to think. He had his own legs, and I made him use them as the two of us bolted for the far end of the cavern.

We heard a huge hack and cough behind us, and the rotten timber shot out like a ballista round over our heads to strike the stone wall and obliterate itself there.

"Back to the rooms!" I shouted to Filson, thinking the caverns that held the suites would be too small for the dragon to navigate.

Filson nodded his agreement, and we shot out toward where the stairs should have been. They weren't stairs, though, but the picked-clean skeleton of a coiling dragon neck. The head lay upside down where the desk had been, and from it curved yellowed vertebrae up to a ledge of stone, where the half-rotted corpse of the great wyrm lay. The belly of the beast had been slit lengthwise, and the green scales flayed back from the midline to expose the layered rotting matrix of dragon organs.

Xantrithicus. She'd gutted her own husband to get the Dragon's Pearl from his stomach, then turned his corpse into an inn for the wealthy and powerful. I could not have known it from where I stood, but something told me in that moment I had, indeed, slept last night in a dragon's heart.

She'd done it all for the Dragon's Pearl. The Dragon's Pearl!

"Come on," I shouted, and motioned for Filson to follow.

Not a moment too soon. The profound thunder of the dragon's clawed feet came upon the cave floor like cannonshot against a wall. The kid and I pelted toward the descending cave that led to the vault and the pearl, though with the rumble and rattle beneath our feet, each step forward was shortened by a half jolt back.

"You can't escape me, Bolton Quaid!" raged the dragon. I derived some small satisfaction from the raw sound of her voice. The log had more than done its work. "You can't escape this place without magic."

I planned on getting myself a little magic—sooner rather than later. We'd reached the descending shaft and just started down it when that great coiling neck of the dragon shot forth, the mouth opening wide like another cavern of stalactites. Her muzzle smashed against the opening.

I dived down the sharp slope, but Filson wasn't with me. Out of the corner of my eye, I saw that my stout-hearted partner had glory instead of survival in mind. He leapt the other way, landing *in* the dragon's mouth. Scrambling up the creature's forked tongue, he brandished his little shiv as though it were a great sword. The tiny knife bit into the red roof of the dragon's mouth, and though it sunk to its handle, the wyrm could not have felt more than the smallest pinprick.

Surely, Filson would die for his courage.

And he would have, had the dragon bitten down on him instead of venting a great gust of poison gas from her lungs. The sneezelike blast blew Filson, shivless, off the creature's tongue and out of its mouth, flinging him into me, where I had landed in a crouch and was preparing to rush for the vault door. Stuck together by the wind, we were hurled down the passage to strike the very door I sought.

In the face of that gale, it was tough to grasp the lock. It was tougher to do so without gasping to inhale breath, which would have been instantly deadly. But I succeeded, spinning the thing, rushing through the combination I'd memorized when Olivia opened the lock.

The poison blast spent itself, and the combination was done. Still without breathing, I yanked the vault door open and dashed to the side.

There came a dragon scream from up the passage, just as I had hoped, and a huge forearm thrust its way down toward the revealed pearl. My hundred traps went off beautifully, with a sound like a thousand mosquitoes taking flight. Even the circular deadfall block came down to crush the dragon's claw, in the process cracking and peeling away my three iron boxes like layers of skin from an onion.

But it would take more than that to stop her. I clambered over her twitching wrist and onto the deadfall, finally took a breath of the fresher air, and grabbed the stone.

Touching it was enough. The contact of flesh to gem triggered its magic. The huge green dragon resumed the form of green-eyed Olivia. Her small, hot hand, crushed beneath the stone, caused her to be yanked forward into the vault as her form shrank. Down the stairs she rattled, then slid to a stop just within the doorway. I lunged at her, wanting to kill her in human form—lovely, lovable human form—before she could become a dragon again.

You see, I'd forgotten about the shiv.

She did not move. The small knife had been more than large enough to kill her, forced up through her human palette and into her brain. When I pulled her head up and back by her silken black hair, the blood gushing from her mouth told the story. The blood, and those lifeless green eyes.

Companionship. I knew it then. That was the one other hook for this wyrm. She'd killed her mate for the pearl, and then used the pearl to gain back all she'd lost—wealth, power, status, and companionship. Perhaps *that's* where a six-foot-three street rat from Waterdeep came in.

The poison gas was gone from the air, and I gasped a breath when I saw those emerald eyes.

So did my new partner.

* * * * *

The magic resumed a moment later, with explosive results, since the corpse of the dragon couldn't fit in that tiny vault. Luckily, Filson and I had expected as much, and were scampering across the cavern beyond when green chunks of dragon started flying.

We didn't even try to take the Dragon's Pearl with us. We'd had a bellyful of trouble from it, just like old Xantrithicus had. Besides, there was already plenty of false affluence and deceptive beauty in the Dock Ward of Waterdeep.

It wasn't beneath us, however, to make a quick search of the rest of the place, hoping to scrape together enough real wealth among all the bits of glitter and twine to make our troubles worthwhile. We could not. Apparently, the dragon's hoard was nothing more than fantasy built on illusion built on air.

Gone were the riches, and gone too the wretches, fled to whatever icy refuges they could find when the dragon first appeared. Most would likely die out there. I feared we would, too.

About then, I heard the greatest sound in the world—the impatient champ and whinny of a very real winged horse. Apparently, even the pearl's illusory magic could not have reached to Waterdeep, so the lady had had to send the genuine article. I tipped my hat to what was left of her corpse, thanking her for inadvertently showing me you get what you pay for.

With my new associate mounted on the stallion behind me, I urged the pegasus toward the bright, snowy daylight, and from there up into the bracing sky.

"To Waterdeep," I told the creature, patting it fondly on the shoulder. "The Dock Ward. I'd like to see some genuine squalor for a change."

GUNNE RUNNER

Roger E. Moore

It would be a grand night in Waterdeep. An old friend, the Yellow Mage, had invited me over for First Tenday dinner; he'd do all the cooking, and he was a master. I knew from experience this was also his chance to show off his latest toy, if he had one, so I made sure I wore something bulletproof but comfortable. No sense in my spoiling the evening by dying unexpectedly.

I needed dependable full-body protection instead of a metal chest plate or displacer cape, so I poked through my ring box until I found my Unfailing Missile Deflector of Turmish. It was my special prize, a little gold band that could turn aside anything short of a flying tree trunk. Even better, it was subtle and wouldn't offend the Yellow Mage. I didn't want him to think I didn't implicitly trust his handling of smoke-powder weapons, never mind that incident three months ago when he blew his priceless Shou Lung clock into little blue glass shards with a Gond-gunne. The bullet missed me by three feet at most. We all make mistakes.

The Yellow Mage's given name at birth was Greathog Snorrish, so I readily understood why he never told anyone else in town about it. He apprenticed late in life, the moment he came through Waterdeep's gates, and could now toss only a pair of spells a day. Still, he was a wizard, and that, for him, was what counted.

Minor pretensions aside, Snorri was really just a kid at heart, which was why everyone in the North Ward of Waterdeep who knew him liked him. He was a big puppy, into everything and always excited at his latest find. A sloppy dresser, yes, and not much of a wizard, but he could cook, he told the best stories, and he had a great laugh. You can understand how intent I was at getting to his place on time that evening, and you can understand, too, why the world just wasn't the same when I found out he had been murdered.

It was an hour before twilight when I arrived at his street, but I could see fine; I had light-enhancing lenses in my eyes. I rounded the stone-paved corner onto Saerdoun Street, clutching a gift bottle of Dryad's Promise, then saw the knot of townsfolk outside Snorri's doorway. They were peeking through the shutters into his home when they weren't talking among themselves in hushed tones. Some of the gawkers glanced at me, then turned away, not wishing to stare at a stranger. Two of the onlookers, though, seemed to recognize me from previous visits. As I came up, they nervously stepped back and grew silent.

Something bad had happened. I knew it instantly. I clutched the brown wine bottle like a good-luck charm. Maybe things will be fine anyway, I thought. Snorri and I will have dinner, tell our tales, pour a few goblets, trade spells—

The little crowd fell back from the Yellow Mage's door as it opened. Someone inside came out. An old woman gasped and put a hand over her heart.

A Waterdhavian watchman carefully stepped out, his green cloak muffling the clinking of his golden armor. He held the handles of a stretcher with a body on it. Someone had tossed Snorri's hall rug over the body, but the corpse's right hand had fallen down from under the rug, and it had the bright topaz ring of the Yellow Mage on the middle finger, just where Snorri always wore it.

Someone else could be wearing his ring, I thought

dumbly, stopping. Snorri could just be drunk. It could be his twin, if he had a twin. If he was really hurt, then—

I stepped forward. "Your pardon," I mumbled to the watchmen. My chest was tight, and I barely got the words out. The constables saw me and hesitated, eyeing me for trouble. I pointed to the shape under the hall rug and tried to frame a sentence.

The watchman at the figure's feet understood and simply shrugged. "Take a look," he said tiredly.

I reached down with my free hand and pulled the hall rug from the body's face. I had the idea that none of this was really happening, so I thought I could come away unscathed.

I had a moment of trouble recognizing the Yellow Mage, partly because he was so expressionless and still, and partly because so much rust-colored blood was caked over his lower face. Most of it had come out of his mouth and nose. His blue eyes were open wide, dull and glazed in the way of all dead people.

I pulled the rug back farther. Streaks of blood were flung across Snorri's neck and upper chest. His yellow shirt was soaked in red. In the middle of his chest was a bloody hole the size of my thumbnail, like a little red-brown volcano crater. It punched through his sternum and probably went all the way through the rest of him. Bits of pale bone stuck out within it.

I stared at my dead friend Snorri for maybe a minute, maybe five, my head swelling with mad plans to bring him back to life. Money, I thought; sure, I could get money, lots of it, then a priest, and all would be fine. Half a dozen local temples would be glad to raise the dead for cash.

The constables were very patient. Perhaps they could tell that I was a wizard, and so were inclined to humor me.

"I'm sorry," said a watchman at my left elbow. I started; I hadn't noticed her before. The gray-eyed elf grimaced and brushed a lock of red hair from her face, then went on. "We were able to summon a Dawn Priest of Lathander who was nearby, but when the priest attempted to restore him to life, the spell did not take. I am truly sorry."

I blinked at her, looked down at Snorri, and realized what she had just told me. The spell did not take. Snorri was staying just as he was. He was gone.

Suddenly I didn't need to look anymore. I gently pulled the rug back over my friend's quiet face, tucked him in, and whispered good-bye. The elven watchman nodded to the others, then the three made their way off toward the guard post at Saerdoun and Whaelgond, only a dozen houses up the street.

I stood stupidly, not knowing what to do next. I'd seen a few dead men when I'd been with the city guard a decade ago. I could tell that Snorri had been dead only a few hours, maybe six at most. I'd spent most of the afternoon preparing a security report for a client in the Castle Ward who constantly worried about thieves breaking into his ugly little mansion. During what point in my writing had Snorri died? How did it happen? I couldn't figure what that ghastly hole in his chest had resulted from; it wasn't a knife wound, and—oh, of course. His latest toy, or one of the older ones. He'd screwed up and shot himself. Snorri, I thought, you dumb bastard, you and those damned smoke-powder toys of yours.

The watchmen had pulled Snorri's front door shut, but it had opened a bit. I looked through the dark doorway into the old-style plaster-and-timber home. Without thinking about it, I walked over to the doorway and went inside. I closed the door after me but did not lock it. I saw no need.

Snorri's home was a nice but unexciting one-story, cramped and cluttered inside, but still pleasant—if you were an average guy. A little kitchen, a privy, a tiny bedroom with only a floor mat and quilt, a stuffy web-filled attic, and a living room the size of the rest of the ground floor put together. Snorri was no decorator, either: a half-dozen badly stuffed fish mounted on the living-room walls, rickety chairs held together by leather thongs, three round tables with cracked legs, some filthy rugs, and a dozen huge cabinets and shelves to hold all of the collectibles he'd gathered. The perfect home for the obsessed, confirmed bachelor.

The place smelled bad as I went in. There was roast boar in the air, coming from the kitchen, but it mingled with the stink of dead, stale blood. I remembered the latter odor from the old days. The air even tasted bad, and I swallowed to keep my stomach down.

I looked away from the line of mounted fish and noticed a spot of cracked plaster on the wall between two shelf cases. I moved closer to get a better view, but looked down just in time to avoid the wide, dark pool on the floor and the Gondgunne that lay in the middle of it. The Gondgunne, no doubt, with which he'd carelessly shot himself.

"Mystra damn you, Snorri," I muttered, shocked at my sudden heat. "Mystra damn you. You knew better."

"No one heard a thing, you know," said a voice behind me. I barely kept myself from whirling around, instead extending my senses to see if I was in trouble. The voice had a youthful but professional tone to it. A watch officer, likely.

"Nothing at all?" I said without looking around, as if commenting on the weather.

"Not a sound. Not even us, and our post is just a stone's toss up the street. Curious, I think." The speaker paused, perhaps sizing me up. "If you were a friend of this gentleman, you have my sorrow and sympathy. Nonetheless, I ask that you please do not touch anything until we've completed our investigation."

His condolences lacked something—a sense of heart, I thought. He was unmoved, disinterested. I calmly turned around. A short, lithe figure in gold chain mail and green cloth stood idly by the now-open front door. A three-foot metal watchman's rod hung lightly in the gloved fingers of his right hand. His curly black hair was the color of his high boots.

A halfling watch captain. A tall halfling, though. He came up to my sternum.

"My friend's house," I said. "We were going to have dinner."

"And your name is . . ." said the halfling.

"Formathio," I said. "Formathio, of Rivon Street."

"I thought I recognized you," the halfling said, nodding

slightly. "You gave a talk for the watch officers last year on illusions and contraband. Your advice came in handy." He glanced past me at the Gondgunne on the floor. "Will you assist me in resolving this sad matter?"

I realized I was still holding the bottle of Dryad's Promise. I set it down by the wall beside me. "Of course," I replied. Of course I would.

"You must forgive my manner as we proceed," the half-ling said as he abruptly walked over and passed by me with a measured tread, his eyes scanning the darkening room. It occurred to me that he, like me, was having no trouble seeing in the poor light. "I never mean to be rude, but I wish to get to the heart of a problem as swiftly as possible." He suddenly looked up at me, chin high. "I am Civilar Ardrum, by the way."

He looked away again before I could respond. "Tell me about your friend, the Yellow Mage," he said, looking at the bloodstained floor and Gondgunne.

I collected my scattered thoughts. "I met him five years ago, when he came to Waterdeep from the south, from Lantan. I did a security check for him, of this house, and we became friends. We got together every so often to talk over things, to trade gossip about the order, trade spells and—"

"The Order of Magists."

"Yes, Magists and Protectors. He was . . . Snorri was . . ."

My thoughts came to a dead end. It hit me. I'd just said *was*. Snorri was really dead. For good. Forever.

Strange, I thought in my shock, that I have no intention of crying. How odd of me, and sad. My best friend is dead, and no one cries for him. I breathed the knowledge in, over and over again.

I don't know how long I was lost like that. When I looked up, Civilar Ardrum was eyeing me curiously. The room was almost completely dark.

"We should have light, if it will not bother you," he said. With a last look at me, he reached down and pulled open a pouch on his belt. A moment later, bright light spilled out of the pouch across the room. He lifted an object like a candle on a stand and placed it on a nearby shelf beside a brass paperweight. Clean white light streamed from the top of the short stick.

"Better," said the civilar. He pulled off his gloves, tucking them into his belt. "We have much to do and little time. I believe that the Yellow Mage's murderer may be about to flee the city, if he has not already done so. If you have any powers to aid our investigation, please tell me now, and let us begin our work."

"Murderer?" I repeated. I was doubly stunned. "His *murderer?*"

"Did I not say that no one heard any sound from this place?" The halfling was clearly irritated. "Yet he lay, clearly shot by an explosive projectile weapon. A girl selling scent packets found his door ajar and looked in, summoning aid. Five washerwomen gossiped outside not two doors from here for half a day and heard no sound of struggle, no explosion, nothing at all. As silent as a tomb, one said of this place. Yet the Yellow Mage died not earlier than noon. No wizard leaves his house door open and unlocked, even on the hottest day on the safest street. Do you?"

I opened my mouth—and closed it. "No, never," I said. Inside, I was still thinking *murderer*.

The halfling officer nodded with slight satisfaction. His manner was oddly comforting even if he was as empathetic as a stone. I looked around at the shelves, the furniture, the fish on the wall. A murderer had been here. "I received my training in the college of illusion," I said automatically, like a golem. "I worked for the watch ten years ago, then apprenticed myself and set up my own security-counseling business." I thought, then said, "To answer your earlier question, I believe I do have talents to lend you."

"Good." Civilar Ardrum knelt down to look at the Gondgunne. He put his watchman's rod on the floor beside him, then pulled a small bundle from his pouch, unwrapped another magical light stick, and set it on a tabletop to his right. White light and doubled shadows filled the room. "You said you were once a thief, Formathio. When you gave your lecture last year."

"Yes." I added nothing, continuing to scan Snorri's

jumbled possessions for missing or out-of-place items. I greatly disliked talking about the mistakes of my youth and how I'd paid for them. "The knowledge has since helped me greatly in my business."

"So I would imagine. What were you hiding for your friend?"

I stopped and turned to the civilar. He was still examining the Gondgunne, though he had not yet touched it. "What?" I shot at him.

The halfling snorted impatiently as he looked up. "Any secret you hold keeps us from finding the murderer. I would think you would want justice and vengeance done as quickly as possible, and so send your friend Greathog Snorrish on to a peaceful rest."

Ardrum's remarks awoke a rage within me. Who was he, the little snot, to tell me that I . . . what?

"He told you his *name?*" My rage burned out in an instant, snuffed by yet another shock. "He never told any-one—"

And a new truth dawned.

Civilar Ardrum's lips pressed into a flat line. He looked up at me without blinking. He'd said too much, and he knew it.

"He worked for you," I breathed. "He was a watch-wizard. A secret watch-wizard." I understood now how Snorri always had ready gold for the best wines and foods, though he had so few spells and so little business from the order for retail spellcasting. But why had he never said anything to me about his work?

Ardrum looked down at the Gondgunne once more and was silent for a while. "He was very valuable to us," he said at last, without inflection. "He kept an eye and ear on various persons and groups, and he reported to the watch what he saw and heard. He was reliable in the extreme, always eager to serve, with a tremendous memory. He reported directly to me."

I felt I was losing my grip on the real world. I almost became dizzy. "Snorri was an informer? Who was he spying on? What did—"

"Formathio, I believe I asked you a question," Ardrum

interrupted. "You helped him hide something. I must know what it was and where it is now. Answer me, please." The "please" was shod in iron.

I stared down at the watch captain, then turned toward the line of stuffed fish on the wall. I raised a hand toward them without warning and intoned a handful of words quickly, gesturing as if brushing away a fly.

The images of fish faded away like blown fog. In place of each was an apparatus of wood and metal, most slightly shorter than my forearm from elbow to fingertips. They rested on hooks and struts on the wooden plaques that had once held dead carp, greenthroats, and crownfish.

It was Snorri's toy collection.

Though I had heard them called arquebuses, cavilers, or other things, Snorri called them gunnes or Gondgunnes. He acquired them from various specialty traders in his old country, Lantan. He thought the word "gunne" was a recent corruption of the name of Gond, the Lantanna deity called Wondermaker or Wonderbringer by the faithful. Gond oversaw inventions, crafts, and new things, and the inventive Lantanna had recently discovered the fine art of enchanting smoke powder and making "fiery arms" that spewed out small lead or iron bullets with outrageously loud reports. It was a magic that made my insides curdle, a weird and subtly frightening thing that simply fascinated Snorri.

Gunnesmithing was a holy thing in Lantan, Snorri had once told me. Thanks to novelty dealers and preaching Gondsmen doubling as religious merchants, gunnes were now showing up everywhere in civilized Faerûn. At least, that's what was said by some of my other wizard friends, who made their opinions on this clear by the way they grimaced and spat on the ground when the topic came up.

"Ah," Civilar Ardrum breathed, rising to his feet to stare at the gunne collection. "Excellent. Clever of you. Three, four, five, six, seven—the old ones are here." He swung about, saw Snorri's work desk in a far corner of the room, and stalked over to it at once. He reached down suddenly and drew his dagger, then used the steel tip to lift the scattered papers and scrolls stacked there. He flipped one stack aside and revealed yet another wooden plaque with mountings for another gunne—but no gunne on it.

I heard the civilar exhale from across the room. His face worked briefly as if he were angry. Then he used the dagger tip to carefully lift the plaque and turn it over.

Something was written on the back. I could see the shifting letters in the light, almost legible.

"Allow me," I said, coming over. Almost by reflex, I pulled a little prism from my breast pocket and began the words of the first spell every wizard learns. As I finished, the shifting letters cleared and fell into place.

" 'Received from Gulner at the market,' " I read, " 'two doors west of the Singing Sword, the ninth of Kythorn, Year of—' "

"He had it, then," Ardrum interrupted. "He sent a message this morning that he had made another purchase, but he had picked up the wrong package. He wanted to examine it and get the opinion of a friend"—Ardrum glanced at me—"before bringing it to the watch station tomorrow morning. He said the device was a new type. He was quite excited about it." Then a new thought dawned, and Ardrum spun about to stare again at the gunne—the eighth one in the room—in the blood pool.

"He was spying on gunne traders? Are you saying that he was killed because he picked up the wrong trinket at a store?"

The tall halfling restrained himself from lunging across the room for the pistol. Instead, he said nothing for perhaps a minute, staring across the room as if hooked by my words. When he spoke, his tone had changed. "These are not trinkets," he said softly. "They are not toys. These are weapons, Formathio, clever ones that are turning up all over. They are meant to kill things—beasts, monsters, people. Anyone can use them. They punch through armor like a bolt through rotted cloth. They can be raised, aimed, and fired in a heartbeat. One little ball spit from the mouth of a gunne can drop an ogre if it hits just right. Any dullard with a gunne, a pocket of fishing sinkers, and a pouch of smoke powder could cut down a brace of knights, a king, or an arch-wizard."

Civilar Ardrum slid his dagger home in its belt sheath. "These gunnes are new and strange, and we of the watch neither understand them nor like them. Your friend understood them *and* liked them. He was worth a god's weight in gold. He knew who to contact to get samples, who was making them, who was buying them, and what they could do. There's quite a market in the strangest places for smoke powder, did you know that? Your friend heard rumors of other devices that worked like Lantanna gunnes but were more powerful or had worse effects. Someone was improving these gunnes, someone very smart who worked fast, perhaps with a hidden shop or guild. This person was bringing lots of these new gunnes into Waterdeep. The Yellow Mage was hunting for one of these devices. We were willing to pay anything for it."

He reached down and, after a moment's hesitation, picked up the overturned plaque. "He could create or remove the fish illusion with a word, am I correct? After the gunne was mounted here?"

I nodded. "I enspelled eight plaques for him. He paid for them in advance, two years ago. This would be the last of them."

"He was going to buy more from you," Ardrum said, staring at the plaque. "He liked your work. Talked about you all the time."

I looked away, aware again of the smell of roasting boar—and an empty place inside me. Leaving the civilar alone for a while, I went into the tiny kitchen Snorri kept, found his crate-sized magical oven, and waved a hand over the amber light on top. The light went off. It would cool down on its own.

I looked around the kitchen and back rooms, saw nothing of interest, quietly cast spells to detect everything from hidden enemies to magical auras, saw nothing else of interest. The living room was similarly bare of clues. Ardrum was now kneeling at the dark pool and holding the bloodstained gunne in the fingers of his left hand. His eyes were closed. I noted that magic radiated from a ring on the civilar's right hand. No doubt the ring had a practical use; the civilar was a practical sort. It couldn't be as good as my Unfailing Missile Deflector, though.

Ardrum's eyes abruptly opened as I watched. He put down the gunne as if caught taking coins from a blind man's cup.

"What did you find out?" The question was based on a guess—a guess that the civilar had just performed some supernatural act, likely a divination.

The halfling sighed. "Clever. Very clever of you, of course, but clever of the killer. This gunne was never fired. A gnome made it in Lantan, a compulsive little gnome who always worried about his mother. Nothing interesting has ever happened to this weapon, and no one interesting has ever handled it. It is not the gunne that was used to kill your friend. It's a mirage, a false lead. I would guess the killer unwrapped it and left it here after the murder." Ardrum looked up. For the first time since I'd seen him, he was smiling—not by much, but it was a smile. "How was that for a wild guess?"

"A psychic," I said. "You amaze me." The truth was that little would amaze me now with Snorri dead, even a psychic watchman. The Lords of Waterdeep no doubt recruited trustworthy psychics at every turn, though such had to be as rare as cockatrice teeth.

"A birth talent, and a limited one," said Ardrum in dismissal. The smile vanished. "I'm sensitive to the emotional impressions left behind when someone touches something. I feel what was felt, see what was seen. Like your early training in burglary, it has served me well in my line of work. And like you, I do not like to discuss my talent. People would find it unnerving to know that I could read their personal life with just a touch. I put my trust in your goodwill to keep my secret. I would not discuss it except that time is short and your wits are acute."

Ardrum pulled the gloves from his belt and carefully put them on. I recalled that he had not shaken my hand, and he had used his dagger blade to examine things on the desk. His control over his special talent was likely poor, then, and likely it was too that he did not relish peering into other people's lives—particularly if those people had just been violently killed.

I wondered what Ardrum saw in his mind when he picked up a bloody dagger or garrote, checking for clues to a murder. I quickly shook off the thought.

"It is late, but we must be off to the market," Ardrum said, collecting his watchman's rod and light-casting sticks. He wrapped the sticks up as he put them away. The room gradually fell into near-total darkness. "We must pick up a package there, and speak with this Gulner named on the plaque. I think he came back for his merchandise, given that the Yellow Mage said he'd received the wrong item, and left a substitute instead. Are you ready, good Formathio?"

A tiny shaft of light from a crack in a shuttered window fell on the back of Civilar Ardrum's head, revealing every loose strand of his hair like a halo around his shadowed face. And an obvious thing came to mind. Something I could do.

"Almost ready," I said. "I am going to cast a spell. Please stay back, and do not be alarmed at whatever you see or hear."

I recalled the proper procedure, then passed my arms, palms out, through the darkness before me. I whispered words into the air, then reached into one of the many pockets in my clothes. Pulling out a pinch of dust, I pitched it into the air before me and spoke a final word.

The room rapidly grew cold. Civilar Ardrum's boots scraped the wooden floor as he stepped back a pace. He had infravision, I guessed, the ability to see heat sources. Most halflings had it. He would now see a black column between us, about the size of a human like me.

"Shadow," I said to the black thing. "You see all that casts a shadow of its own. I demand one answer from you, then will release you to go your dark way."

A whisper reached my ears, so faint it could have been a sigh from a distant child. "*Yes.*"

"A man was murdered here during the daylight." My voice almost failed me. I shoved aside the memory of Snorri, bloody and dead on the stretcher. "I command you, shadow, to reveal who murdered this man."

This was my own special spell, and no other living person had seen me use it. My control over the shadow was good, so it posed no danger to me or to the civilar. In other circumstances, however, the shadow could have left us both frozen and dead on the ground, our spirits cursed to join it in endless roving of shadows and night.

Nonetheless, when I felt the shadow draw so close that the skin on my face burned and stung from its bitter cold, when I shivered from the absolute emptiness of it, I was in fear that my control over it was no more.

The shadow sighed once again. I imagined its words were spoken with a touch of glee.

"*I saw no one murder him,*" said the shadow, and was gone.

The air at last grew warmer on my face. My arms fell to my sides. No one? No one had killed my friend? Shadows had a way with their words; they loved to mislead with the truth. I wrestled briefly with the answer, then admitted defeat—for now.

"Let us go," I said to the civilar.

Outside, it was late twilight. The three watchmen had returned to wait there for their captain, guarding the doorway and keeping away onlookers. With their permission, I put a locking spell on the door and windows to keep the curious away; only the watch or a major wizard would have the resources to take the spell off at leisure.

Civilar Ardrum and I arrived at the market after a short and rapid walk. The other watchmen were summoning more of their fellows to meet us at our destination. We said nothing to each other along the trip, even as we came into view of the great, torch-lit market of Waterdeep.

We crossed Traders' Way and entered the long ellipse of booths that made up the market. Even now, after sunfall, vendors called out praises of their wares to passersby. Few shoppers were out this evening. I saw faint candle-light from the upper windows of the Singing Sword off to our left, on the market's far side, and we made our way there at an easy, steady pace.

"I thought I heard the dark thing you conjured up say that no one killed the Yellow Mage," said Ardrum in a low, conversational tone as we walked.

I glanced around, saw no one close enough to listen in, then took a deep breath. "The shadow said that it saw no one murder him. It meant it saw no shadow of the murderer, so possibly the murderer threw no shadow."

There was a pause the length of a heartbeat.

"Invisible," we both said at the same moment.

"But the murderer would have become visible the moment he attacked the Yellow Mage," said Ardrum quickly. "A spell of invisibility is canceled the moment—"

"There are more powerful spells that would not be broken by physical violence," I interrupted. "And some devices will do the same. He could have stalked Snorri and . . . shot him. He would not have become visible."

The halfling almost came to a stop. "He could still be in the house, then."

"No," I said. "I checked. I used some of my spells and saw nothing."

Civilar Ardrum frowned and took up the pace again. Ahead, I could see the buildings to either side of the Singing Sword. Two doors to the west would be . . . the old Full Sails. In the darkness I could barely see the bare mast of the pinnace mounted on the flat roof of the two-story building. Fine liquors were once sold in bulk there to caravans, ship crews, and adventurers who wanted something, and plenty of it, to warm them on their voyages. Some of the liquor went bad and blinded its drinkers, and the owner had fled Waterdeep. I had no idea what the old shop was now.

We slowed to a stop at the front door. I noted it had a simple string-and-bar lock, and a worn one at that. The place looked dirty and little used. Civilar Ardrum unobtrusively walked the short length of the storefront, looking up and down at the closed window shutters, then walked back to me and shrugged.

A board creaked inside the building. The sound came from the second floor. Ardrum and I both heard it and froze, our eyes locked together.

The board creaked again. A footstep for sure. Ardrum motioned me back a step, tucked his watchman's rod under his arm, then pulled a piece of wire from his pocket and undid the lock with surprising deftness. I wondered if his childhood occupational interests had been anything like mine.

Civilar Ardrum looked up at me for a second and almost smiled, then pulled his short-bladed sword and used it to swiftly push open the door.

And we saw a previously unseen string attached to the back of the door. It pulled tight on a wide-mouthed pipe mounted on a short pole just beyond the door itself. The pipe swung slightly to point right at us. It clicked.

A gunne—

The white shock of the blast imprinted itself in my eyes, the little watch captain's body silhouetted as it was thrown past me, one arm flailing. I clamped hands over my screaming ears, deafened except for a whine so loud as to stab me in the brain. Small objects shrieked past me, clanging off metal and wood and rock and dirt. The top half of the door fell crookedly across the doorway. Dust whirled through the night air.

I was deaf but untouched. The Unfailing Missile Deflector of Turmish was working just fine.

I staggered back and then saw Civilar Ardrum writhing on the street, his clothes smoking. He tried to cover his face with his mangled arms and gave a brief wail of agony. I let go of my ears and went to him, kneeling at his side.

The light-enhancing lens in my eyes let me see the halfling's condition in perfect detail. I almost vomited. He would be dead within the minute.

He turned his trembling face to mine. He still had one eye.

Very carefully, he raised a hand and pointed past me. He was pointing at the Full Sails.

Go, he mouthed. Then he eased back with a sigh. His eyes closed.

A crowd had gathered. More people were coming. There was nothing else to do, so I got up. I turned to look at up the Full Sails. Someone on the roof looked down at me, then quickly moved out of sight.

"No, you don't," I said to the figure. My right hand dipped into a pocket, pulled out a bit of leather made into a loop. Lifted by his own bootstraps, went the phrase. I stepped up to the building's base, spoke a phrase, and cast the loop upward. It vanished.

My feet left the ground. I rose toward the rooftop, mouthing the words of another spell. I wondered what the shouting people below thought. If they were smart, they'd be leaving about now.

The moment my eyes cleared the rooftop, I saw the bow of the little pinnace in front of me, what was left of it after years of wear from the elements and youthful vandals. I also saw a burly figure not fifteen feet away, holding what looked like a short Gondgunne. He saw me out of the corner of his eye, turned, raised his gunne in one hand, and fired. A white flash spat from the barrel; my ears rang again from the sharp thunderclap of the shot.

The bullet missed me, of course. I pointed my right index finger at him and finished the spell.

A long, slim missile zipped from my finger and struck the gunner in the chest, splashing as it hit. It knocked the gunner off his feet. As he fell on his back on the rooftop, he began to smoke like a wet rag on a hot iron stove.

As deaf as I was, I could still hear him scream. That acid arrow is a real piece of work.

I had pulled myself over the parapet and was mouthing the words to yet another spell when I saw the pinnace move. It rocked as if something had thumped against it. I stepped away from it, then saw a figure outlined against the starry sky, moving from the back of the pinnace forward, toward me. This guy had a gunne, too, a two-hander with a huge barrel. I had almost finished my spell when he fired. Strange, I thought in that moment, that he would aim at my feet.

I felt the solid thump as the shot hit the rooftop just in front of me. There was a huge flash of light, concussion, and fire—then rooftop, pinnace, sky, and city below spun in my vision as if I'd fallen into a whirlpool. I threw out my arms to right myself, willed myself to cease all movement. I halted in the air, now upside down and twenty feet above a flaming crater in the roof, just a hop away from the pinnace. That Unfailing Missile Deflector was my true love, but I hadn't counted on being flung into the heavens.

A new type of gunne. A gunne that shot bombs or rockets. I'd walked into a hornet's nest.

I slowly righted myself and descended, my immobilization spell ruined. Now I was intent on causing serious harm.

To my complete astonishment, the pinnace lifted free of the rooftop and came up to meet me.

I at least had the presence of mind to reach out and snatch hold of the worn bowsprit as it went by. I swung myself onto the deck and saw that the guy with the big-mouthed, bomb-firing gunne was coming over to greet me. Only now he had dropped the empty gunne and carried a large woodsman's axe.

I raised my hands and touched thumbs, fanning my fingers outward toward him. I loved this spell. It needed only one word to make it work. I said the word.

Roaring jets of flame shot from my fingers and covered the axeman from head to foot. He instantly turned into a man-sized torch. He dropped his axe and flailed at his clothing, his face, his hair. His shrill screaming proved that my hearing was finally getting a little better.

I waited for an opening, then lunged in at him and grabbed a slippery bare arm. He could hardly resist me; I appreciated that, having never been much for wrestling. With an effort, I wrenched his arm back and shoved him hard at the low railing. He stumbled, hit the rail, and went over the side. I didn't bother to see where he made landfall.

The air stank abominably, burnt and foul. I looked down at my hands, grimaced, and wiped them on my clothing. Some of the man's roasted skin had come off when I'd grabbed him. Throwing him overboard had been a kindness.

No one else was around. But the ship was still climbing into the night sky with increasing velocity. I'd never imagined magic like this. Walking low against the wind blast from above, I moved sternward until I found the door into the pinnace's little hold. I thought about the numerous spells I had left; I always traveled heavy. Better prepared than not. I picked out two or three I especially wanted to give to the guy in charge. Then I tossed a light spell into the hold and went below.

I felt I was ready for anything, but I suppose I wasn't. The hold was empty of everything except a marvelously ornate chair against the far wall, just twenty feet away.

I looked left and right, up and down, everywhere in the light from the spell. Nothing. Wind howled through the room, carrying off what little dust was left. Boards creaked as the pinnace continued flying up toward the heavens.

"Mystra damn me," I murmured.

"Allow me," said a rough, male voice from the direction of the chair.

I realized that my spell for detecting invisible things had ended some time ago.

A huge blast of white fire and light leapt at me from the chair. It was completely silent. It was followed in a moment by a second, a third, then a fourth, in a bizarre volley of soundless shots. I thought for a moment that an army of gunners was in the room with me.

When the firing ended, I blinked and looked around. The wall behind me was riddled with holes from the gunne shots. I guessed that I'd just been introduced to the new toy that Snorri got by accident: a gunne that fired several shots in a row. And without so much as a bang.

Out of nowhere, a gunne flipped through the air from the ornate chair, curved aside before it hit me, and bounced off the wall, falling on the floor before me. It was a weird-looking gunne. But I didn't care about that right now.

Thick smoke from the rapid gunne fire blanketed the entire room. The air had a thick, bitter, burned smell to it. Through the haze, I could make out the moving outline of a single large manlike being, sitting upright in the chair. He was cursing me mightily—in perfect Elvish.

Elvish? What more could I be surprised at this evening? But I was sick to death of surprises.

"It's my turn, Gulner," I said.

I shaped the air with my hands, mouthed a few words, pointed, and gave the invisible foul-mouthed gunner my own best shot.

The normal version of the spell called "phantasmal killer" has its merits. It takes the victim's most deeply buried nightmares and shapes them into a single illusory entity, a monster that exists only in the victim's mind. The victim, however, believes the monster is absolutely real, invulnerable, and unstoppable. And he sees the monster come for him. If he believes the monster has struck him, the victim dies of fright.

After years of dealing with the sort of filth and scum that watchmen in Waterdeep know all too well, I had yearned for an improved form of that spell. I'd dearly wanted to pay back some criminal acquaintances for the suffering they had inflicted—on the public, on my friends, and on me.

Last year, I'd created that spell. But I had never cast it until now.

Two things happened rapidly in sequence. First, the manlike form in the chair gasped aloud as the spell took effect. He had little chance to throw it off or resist its effects; it was extremely powerful. And it lasted for a full hour.

Second, everything simply went weightless, including me.

I banged my head against the ceiling and saw thousands of stars and comets. I felt I'd been tossed into the air by a giant. The room tilted as the roaring of the wind died outside.

The figure in the chair cried out hoarsely, then screamed as if he were dying—which he was. I had only a glimpse of him through the smoke, trying to ward off something. I never saw him again.

I felt now that I was falling. The wind's roar picked up, building rapidly to a great, bone-shaking thunder.

I'd made a mistake. The big guy in the chair must have been controlling the flight of the pinnace. In the process of killing the big guy, my pet spell had killed me, as well.

The pinnace rocked as it fell. Walls banged into me as I struggled to get out of the room, up to the deck. I still had my spell of levitation active, and I could drift down with the wind if I could get away.

I have no clear recollection of how I got out and kicked away from the falling ship. I was able to slow myself down almost at once and hover in the air.

Light from great Selune's silver orb fell upon cloud tops below me. I realized I must be miles and miles up. I had a last look at a tiny, dark ship dwindling rapidly away below me, a faint light shining from a door in its deck. It vanished into the distant clouds and was gone.

But the duration of my levitation spell was running out. I could mentally shut the spell's power down, but I'd fall like a stone. I'd never been this high before, nor had I even *heard* of anyone who had been this high.

"Okay," I said to myself, "I have one more levitation spell, so if I dispense with this one, I can cast the other one before I hit the ground, and everything will be fine. I just have to keep my head and hold on to the little leather bootstrap, and I can't forget any of the words or get the gesturing wrong or be too slow. It's been a grand night in Waterdeep, but I want to go home."

I went on like that to myself as I reached into my pocket and felt for the material component. I had one tiny leather strap left and pulled it out.

And dropped it.

I grabbed for it but missed. I twisted around and stared down into the moonlit cloud tops, seeing no trace of it now.

After I got my breathing under control again, I carefully pulled the leather cuff tie out of my left sleeve. I fashioned it into a loop, gripped it in my fingers until a bull could not have pulled it loose, and hoped the improvisation would not hurt the spell. I closed my eyes and dismissed the old levitation spell.

I went into free-fall again, the wind whipping around my body into every part of my clothes. I managed to turn facedown, into the rush toward the clouds. My eyes ran with tears from the wind as I watched the cloud tops grow steadily larger. Then I panicked and tried to start the spell. The wind made speaking impossible.

I tried to turn so that I fell on my back, faceup, but couldn't get it right and started to spin in the air. Nearly mad with fear, I shut my eyes and began the spell again. I must finish this spell, I thought, growing dizzy and nauseated from spinning. I made the gestures, uttered the words in a shout, and tossed the loop into the air. I opened my eyes at the same moment.

I saw clouds above me—clouds with the moon looking through them. Instantly my body began slowing down. I'd done it!

Then I rolled and saw a forest come up to hit me. I had been just a couple of seconds too slow.

* * * * *

As I heard it later, I lived because a bride ran off on her wedding night. The groom and his family and the bride's family were combing the woods by their farm, searching for the bride (who was hiding in the hayloft with her old boyfriend instead) when I fell through a large pine tree and crashed practically at their feet. Half of those present ran off, thinking I was a monster, and the rest wanted to kill me for the same reason. Fight or flight, the ancient question.

The one who approached me with a knife saw that I looked human enough and was very badly banged up, so they relented and merely tied me up to bring me back into Waterdeep, to deliver me to the watch in case there was a reward.

I came to in my own house, two days later. Every part of my body ached abominably. Someone dabbed at my face with a wet cloth.

"Excellent," said a familiar voice. "Bounces back like a professional. Once a watchman, always a watchman. Priestess, would you please wait outside for a moment?"

"You," I said through bruised lips. It hurt to even think about speaking.

The soothing wet cloth went away. Someone left the room as a pair of boots walked across a wooden floor, and Civilar Ardrum appeared in my vision. His face bore a number of pale scars across it, one of them crossing his right eye. "You'll be fine in a few days. The watch picked up the tab for the healing spells. We found that little boat about two miles outside of town, to the east. Kindling. You wouldn't even recognize it. I didn't recognize the scattered remains of the guy in it, though he did have the most remarkable coded papers on him, which your associates in the order translated for us."

"How is it," I managed, "that you are here? Alive?"

Ardrum held up his right hand and carefully pulled off the glove. A bright silver ring shone out from his third finger. His entire hand and visible arm were covered with healed-over scars, like his face.

"The Priceless Circlet of Healthful Regeneration," he said. "Found it in Turmish when I was younger. And your ring is . . . ?"

I licked my lips. "Unfailing Missile Deflector."

"Ah, so that was why the trap gunne did nothing to you. We are lucky that we are careful shoppers."

"What about the papers? From the flying ship?"

"From the spelljammer, you mean. You know about spelljammers? No? We'll chat sometime when you're well. The half-orc priest in the ship—yes, a half-orc, with lots of disguising bits to look as human as possible—was the ringleader of a smuggling group. They were bringing gunnes and smoke powder into Waterdeep and selling them to unsavory groups. They were also trafficking disguised gunnes from Lantan to the Savage North, apparently to humanoid armies there. The Yellow Mage was about to stumble across their whole operation. Then he got the wrong delivery, one of the special gunnes being delivered from wildspace. The new guns fire several shots in rapid sequence using clever springs and mechanisms. You could call them 'machine gunnes,' I suppose. The half-orc's had been enchanted for absolute silence. He was the Yellow Mage's killer. We burned his body so no one can bring him back."

I just stared at the halfling. "You're not serious."

"Ah, but I am," Ardrum said. "You and I broke the back of the operation and nearly died in the process." He frowned. "Of course, we haven't found the exact source of their supply in wildspace, but we have contacted the

Lords of Waterdeep, and one suggested that elements of a scro fleet left over from the Second Unhuman War might be in orbit around Toril. Sounds like a mission for someone else to handle, some burly heroic sorts but not us, the lowly foot soldiers against crime."

Scro, unhumans, wildspace—I hadn't a clue as to what he was talking about. "I need to rest," I finally said.

"But of course, and so you shall, good Formathio. So you shall. But do not be long about it. We will need your help in finding out how the gunne smugglers were disguising their shipments, and no one could tell us better than you, the expert in illusions. I'll be round tomorrow at noon. See you then."

He started to go. "Oh." He came back and carefully placed a bottle on the small table beside my bed, looking at it with a faraway gaze. "And when I return, we shall finish off your bottle of Dryad's Promise, which you left behind elsewhere, and drink a quiet toast in memory of fallen comrades and deeds long ago."

Civilar Ardrum looked back at me and actually smiled. "And a toast to those who have fallen—and survived." He patted the bedpost, then turned and quickly left me to the ministrations of the priestess and her fellows.

I had a million questions, but I was very tired. It had been anything but a grand night in Waterdeep. I closed my eyes, and dreamed of nothing at all.

THE DIRECT APPROACH

Elaine Cunningham

Skullport, an underground city hidden far below the
streets and docks of the more respectable port of Waterdeep, was one of the few places on the Sword Coast that
offered wary welcome to the drow. Elsewhere, the dark
elves' fearsome reputation earned them the sort of reception otherwise reserved for hordes of ravening orcs; in
Skullport, a drow's night-black skin merely guaranteed
that she could walk into the tavern of her choice and not
have to wait for a table.

Dangerous and sordid though it was, Skullport appealed
to Liriel Baenre. A few short months before, she'd been
forced from her home in Menzoberranzan, that fabled city
of the drow. She'd just finished a dangerous trek across
the northlands and led a successful raid on the stronghold
of a rival drow faction. The next part of her journey would
soon begin, but Liriel had a few days' respite to relax and
enjoy life. In her opinion, Skullport was a fine place to do
just that. It boasted all the chaos of her hometown but
lacked the inhibiting customs and the ever-vigilant eyes of
its priestess rulers. Liriel's stay in the underground port
had been brief, but long enough for her to learn that anything could happen in Skullport. And usually did.

Even so, she was not prepared for her midnight visitor, or for the strange manner in which this visitor arrived.

Earlier that evening, Liriel had retired to a comfortable chamber above Guts and Garters, a rather rough-and-tumble tavern renowned for its dwarf-brewed ale and its bawdy floor show. This was her first quiet evening since entering Skullport, and her first opportunity to study the almost-forgotten rune lore of an ancient barbarian race known only as the Rus. Liriel's interest in such magic was passionate and immediate, for in two days she would sail for far-off Ruathym. There lived the descendants of the Rus, and there Liriel would learn whether this rune magic could shape the destiny of a drow. Much depended upon her success, and she was determined to aid her chances by learning all she could about the people and their magic.

After several hours of study, she paused and stretched, catlike. The sounds of the tavern floated up to her: the jaunty dance music, the mixture of heckling and huzzahs, the sound of clinking mugs, the occasional brawl—all muted by thick stone to a pleasant murmur. Liriel did not desire to join the festivities, but she enjoyed knowing that excitement was readily available should the spirit move her to partake. Besides, the noise made an agreeable counterpoint to her reading. With a contented sigh, the young drow lit a fresh candle and returned to her book, absently tossing back a stray lock of her long white hair as she bent over the strange runes.

In any setting, dark elves survived only through constant vigilance. Liriel, although deep in her studies, remained alert to possible dangers. So, when the garish tapestry decorating the far wall shuddered and began to fade away, she responded with a drow's quick reflexes. In a heartbeat, she was on her feet, a dagger in one hand and a small, dangerously glowing sphere in the other.

Before she could draw another breath, the wall dissolved into a vortex of shimmering light—a magic portal to some distant place. Liriel's first thought was that her enemies had found her. Her second thought was that her enemies were definitely getting better.

She herself had been well trained in dark-elven wizardry and was no stranger to magical travel, but never had she seen anything like the silent storm raging before her. The colors of a thousand sunsets glimmered in the whirling mist, and pinpoints of light spun in it like dizzy stars. One thing was clear: whoever came through that portal would be worth fighting. A smile of anticipation set flame to the drow's golden eyes, and every muscle in her slight body tensed for the battle to come.

Then the portal exploded in eerie silence, hurling multicolored smoke to every corner of the room. The magical gate disappeared and was replaced by the more mundane tapestry, before which stood a most peculiar warrior.

Liriel blinked, wondering for a moment if a barbarian marauder had somehow stepped off the tapestry's battle scene. The figure before her was more like some ancient illustration, brought improbably to life, than any being of flesh and bone that Liriel had yet encountered.

The drow stared up—*way* up—at a human female warrior. The woman was taller than the elven girl by more than a foot and was at least twice as broad. Fat braids of flame-colored hair erupted from beneath a horn-bedizened bronze helm and disappeared into the thick reddish bearskin draped over her shoulders. Apart from these garments and a pair of knee-high, shaggy-furred boots, the warrior was virtually naked. Leather thongs bound weapons to her person and held in place a few strategically placed scraps of metal-studded leather. The woman's skin was pale, her muscles taut, and her curves of the sort usually encountered only in the fantasies of untried youths and libidinous artists. In fact, the warrior's curves, costume, and theatrically grim expression suggested to Liriel that this woman was supposed to be part of someone's evening entertainment. Obviously, she'd missed a turn somewhere on magic's silver pathways.

"Nice entrance," Liriel observed dryly, "but the floor show is in the main tavern."

The barbarian's sky-colored eyes flamed with blue heat. "Do you take me for a *tavern wench?*" she roared. The warrior batted aside a wisp of glowing smoke and squinted in Liriel's direction. With a slow, ominous flourish, she drew an ancient broadsword from its scabbard. Tossing back her helmed head, she took a long, proud breath—dangerously taxing the strength and expansion capacity of her scant leather garments—and lifted her sword in challenge. Remnants of the luminous smoke writhed around her, adding significantly to the overall effect.

"Behold Vasha the Red, daughter of Hanigard, queen of the ice water raiders, captain of the Hrothgarian guard, and hired sword arm of the Red Bear Clan," the warrior announced in a voice that shook the windowpanes and promised doom.

Liriel got the feeling that this introduction was usually met with groveling surrender, but she was not overly impressed by her visitor's credentials. That broadsword, however, was another matter entirely.

Candlelight shimmered down the sword's rune-carved length and winked with ominous golden light along its double edge. Liriel's dagger, which was long and keen and coated with drow sleeping poison for good measure, seemed woefully inadequate beside it. The drow observed the furtive, darting path that the barbarian's eyes traced around the room, and assumed that the human had been temporarily blinded by the brilliant light of the magical portal. With a sword that size, however, precision was not vital to success in battle. The drow's wisest course would probably be to toss her fireball and settle the damages with the innkeeper later. It'd be messy, but there was something to be said for a quick resolution in such matters. So Liriel hauled back her arm for the throw and let fly.

"Runecaster!" spat the barbarian woman scornfully. Her sword flashed up and batted the glowing sphere back in Liriel's general direction. To the drow's astonishment—and infinite relief—the fireball dissipated not with the expected rending explosion, but an apologetic fizzle.

A smug little smile lifted the corners of the warrior's mouth. "Your foul magics will avail you not," she exulted. "Know this and tremble: You cannot escape the justice of the Rus, though you flee through time itself! Return with me for trial, runecaster, or die now by my hand." The muscles in the barbarian's sword arm twitched eagerly, leaving little doubt as to which option she preferred.

But Liriel did not for one moment consider surrender or fear death. This woman might be bigger than an ogre's in-laws, but any drow wizard worthy of the name had at her command a variety of ways to dispose of unwanted visitors. Yet Liriel did not strike, for something in the woman's speech caught her interest.

"The Rus? Fleeing through time?" she repeated excitedly, her mind whirling with possibilities. Magical portals could give transport to distant places, through solid objects, even into other planes. Was it possible that they could span the centuries, as well? Was this woman truly an ancient warrior, and not some low-rent courtesan with bad fashion sense? "Just who in the Nine Hells *are* you?"

A scowl creased the woman's white brow. Her glacial blue eyes thawed just enough to register uncertainty, and she squinted into the shadows that hid her foe. "Have I not said? Did you not hear? I am Vasha the Red, daughter of—"

"Stow it," Liriel snapped, in no mood to swap genealogies. "You said, I heard. But where did you come from? And more important, *when?*"

"This is the twelfth year of the reign of King Hrothgar. The *last* year of his reign, as well you know! In the dark of the hunter's moon, Hrothgar was slain by your fell magics!"

The drow pondered this announcement. She had been extremely busy of late, but she was fairly certain she hadn't killed anyone by that name. Upon further consideration, she recalled that the adventures of a King Hrothgar were recounted in her book of rune lore. He'd been outwitted by a renegade runecaster of dark and exceptional power. But by Liriel's best calculations, that had happened nearly—

"Two thousand years ago!" she said, regarding the swordwoman with new respect. "I'll say this much for you: you can hold a grudge with the best of them!"

Vasha was neither flattered nor amused. Bellowing with rage, the barbarian hauled her sword high overhead, sighted down a spot between the shadowy figure's eyes, and slashed straight down toward it. The mighty blow would have riven Liriel neatly in twain, had it only connected. But the agile elf dived to one side, rolled twice, and was back on her feet in time to witness most of the sword's descent. It swooped down to slice cleanly through Liriel's rented bed. The coverlet, mattress, ticking—even the roping and wooden slats of the frame—gave way before Vasha's wrath. The bed collapsed in upon itself like a spent puffball mushroom, spewing feathers upward into the swordwoman's face.

The barbarian reeled back, sneezing violently and repeatedly. Liriel took advantage of this development to cast a spell of holding, effectively freezing Vasha in midsneeze. That done, the drow stalked over to the ruined bed, plucked her book of rune lore out of the drifting feathers, and shook it before the swordwoman's contorted, immobile face.

"*This* is what led you here, you blazing idiot! This book describes rune magic, of a sort that no one has cast for hundreds of years. *You're chasing the wrong damned wizard!*"

Liriel took a long, deep breath to compose her wits and calm her temper. Then she snapped her fingers, and at once the room's dim candlelight was eclipsed by floating globes of white faerie fire. In the sudden bright light, her delicate, elven face shone like polished ebony. She tucked her abundant white hair behind the elegantly pointed ears that proclaimed her race, then propped her fists on her hips.

"Tell me," the drow purred with silky sarcasm, "do I really *look* like a runecaster from the Red Bear Clan?"

Vasha did not offer an opinion, but some of the bloodlust faded from her trapped eyes. Liriel took this as a good sign. Nevertheless, she pried the sword from the barbarian's hands and hurled it into a far corner before releasing the spell of holding. She had an offer for Vasha, and, in her experience, people tended to bargain much more reasonably when they were unarmed.

* * * * *

"I tell you, Liriel, daughter of Sosdrielle, daughter of Maleficent, the runecaster is near," insisted Vasha. "The vile Toth, son of Alfgar, misbegotten upon Helda, the goddess of boars, whilst she was in human form—*or so Alfgar claims*—is in this very city." The barbarian's voice was slightly fuzzy now, and her ruddy face glowed with the combined warmth of the tavern's fires and too much dwarven brew. Still, she spoke with a conviction that rattled the globe on their table's oil lamp.

The drow leaned back in her chair and signaled for another round of drinks. A half-orc servant hastened over with two more foaming mugs. Vasha threw back her head and quaffed her ale without once coming up for air. She slammed the empty mug on the table and ripped out a resounding belch.

Liriel sighed. The swordwoman had a prodigious thirst and an apparently endless capacity for dwarven ale. Although Vasha's tongue loosened a bit with each mug, Liriel feared that the barbarian would drain the tavern's cellars before giving up anything useful.

"Believe me, magical travel can be tricky, and in your case *something went wrong*," the drow explained for the eleventh time. After two hours of this, Liriel was clinging to her patience by her fingernails. Fate had handed her a priceless opportunity to learn of the Rus firsthand, but she found herself less grateful than she probably should have been. "Listen, Vasha: I'll try to help you get home, but first you must tell me more about your people's magic."

The swordwoman scowled and reached for her companion's untouched mug. "I am Vasha, daughter of Hanigard—"

Liriel slammed the table with both fists. "I *know* who you are, for the love of Lloth! Just get to the blasted *point!*"

"Some warriors of the Rus know rune magic. My family

is not among them," the swordwoman said bluntly. "We spit upon magic, and those who wield it rather than honest weapons. Even the sword I carry, passed down to me upon the glorious death of Hanigard, queen of the ice water raiders—"

"*What. About. The sword?*" Liriel prompted from between clenched teeth.

"It cleaves through magic, as you have seen. That is all the rune lore I know, or care to know."

The drow slumped. Things were not turning out quite as she'd expected. In exchange for knowledge of rune magic, she had offered to shepherd Vasha around Skullport. Vasha admitted that a guide might be useful, but she was adamant about finding this Toth before passing on any magical secrets.

"Let's go over this one more time," Liriel said wearily. "Why do you insist that your runecaster is in Skullport? And why did you promise me rune lore, if you have none to give?"

Vasha reached into a boot—the only garment large enough to yield much storage space—and pulled out two objects. One was a small leather-bound book, the other a broken bit of flat stone carved with elaborate markings. Liriel snatched up the book at once and gazed at its creamy vellum pages with something approaching reverence. This was an ancient spellbook, yet the pages were as white and the runes as sharp and clear as if they'd been inscribed yesterday.

"Those were written by Toth's own hand," Vasha said, "and the book is yours, in fulfillment of the word of Vasha, daughter of Hanigard, and so forth. According to the runecasters who sent me here, Toth escaped to a distant place of wicked rogues and fell magic, where such as he might walk abroad and attract no more notice than bear droppings in a forest."

"That describes Skullport, all right," Liriel agreed as she tucked the precious book into her bag. "But it doesn't necessarily follow that Toth is here."

The barbarian picked up the piece of stone and handed it to Liriel. The fragment was as hot as a live coal; the drow cursed and dropped it. She glared at Vasha and blew on her throbbing fingers.

"The closer the runecaster, the warmer the stone," Vasha explained. "This is a fragment of a time-coin, one of the very excesses that prompted King Hrothgar to censure Toth, to his ultimate sorrow. With this stone, the vile runecaster can travel at will through time."

"But *how?*" Liriel demanded, her eyes alight with a certain greed. She was always eager to learn new magic, and this time-coin surpassed any travel spell she knew.

Vasha shrugged. "The secret is in the stone coin, and in the runes thereon. How it was done, I know not, and neither do I care. This much I can tell you: Toth left half of the coin in his keep, that he might later return. One fragment of that half remains in the judgment hall of the Red Bear Clan. The other you see before you. Once I have Toth and the half of the coin he carries on his person, I can return with him to my own land and time. When the time-coin is again whole, the lawful runecasters will see it destroyed for once and all."

The drow absorbed this in silence. She was horrified that such wondrous magic would be lost, but she set aside her dismay in favor of more immediate, practical concerns. "Then it's possible for Toth to escape from Skullport to yet another time and place, as long as he leaves behind a bit of the coin-half he carries?"

Vasha's jaw fell slack as she considered this possibility. "It may be as you say," she allowed, eyeing Liriel thoughtfully. "Perhaps the gods did not err in sending me to you, after all. No honest warrior can walk the devious, twisted pathways of a dark elf's mind, yet such might be the straightest way to a wretch like Toth."

"Don't think I'm not enjoying all this flattery," said Liriel dryly, "but if we're going to find your runaway runecaster before he goes somewhere and some*when* else, we'd better get started."

The barbarian nodded, drained the remaining mug, and exploded to her feet. Her chair tipped over backward with a crash and went skidding along the floor. A patron, just entering the tavern, stepped into its path.

Liriel saw the collision coming but could do nothing to avert disaster. There was barely time to cringe before the chair crashed into a purple-robed illithid. The creature's arms windmilled wildly as it fought to keep its balance, and the four tentacles that formed the lower half of its face flailed about as if seeking a saving hold. There was none, and the illithid went down with an ignominious crash.

A profound silence fell over the tavern as everyone there studiously minded his own business. An illithid, also known as a mind flayer, was greatly respected (and generally avoided) for its strange psionic powers and its habit of eating human and elven brains. The illithid scrambled awkwardly to its feet and glided over to intercept the barbarian woman, who, heedless of danger, was striding toward the tavern door.

Vasha pulled up just short of the man-shaped creature. Her wintry eyes swept over the illithid, taking in the stooped, misshapen body, the bald lavender head, and the pupilless white eyes and writhing tentacles that defined its hideous face. All this she observed with detached curiosity. But when her gaze fell upon the arcane symbols embroidered upon the creature's robe, her lip curled with disdain.

"Stand aside, runecasting vermin, if you value your life," she ordered, placing a hand on the hilt of her broadsword.

Because drow knew illithids like cheese knows rats, Liriel saw what was coming, and she pushed back from the table with a cry of warning. Too late: the mind flayer let out a blast of power that sent Vasha's auburn braids streaming backward. The swordwoman stood helpless— her eyes wide with shock and her powerful muscles locked in place—as the illithid closed in to feed. One purple tentacle snaked upward and flicked aside the woman's horned helmet. In the silence of the tavern, the clatter of bronze hitting the stone floor resounded like a thunderclap.

But the noise was promptly overwhelmed by Vasha's battle shriek. With sheer force of will, the warrior tore herself free from the mind flayer's grasp. Her sword slashed up from its scabbard, smashing through the mental assault and lopping off the probing tentacle. The purple appendage went flying in a spray of ichor, and the illithid staggered back, its vacant eyes bulging weirdly.

Not one to be content with mere dismemberment, Vasha leapt at the creature and wrestled it to the floor. She quickly pinned the writhing mind flayer, and, sitting astride its chest, neatly braided the three remaining tentacles.

The utter absurdity of this act jarred the dumbfounded drow into action. Liriel darted over to the barbarian and dragged her off the fallen illithid before either combatant could enact further revenge. She shoved the much larger woman toward the exit, eager to escape before any of the stunned patrons thought to summon what passed for law in Skullport.

At the doorway Liriel paused and glanced back into the still-silent tavern. "She's new in town," the drow announced to the room at large, by way of explanation and apology, and then she slipped into the darkness beyond.

Dripping with ichor but smiling triumphantly, Vasha followed her dark-elven guide out into the streets of Skullport.

* * * * *

The underground port city was located in an L-shaped cavern that lay many feet below sea level and curved around the deeply hidden Sea Caves. As one might suspect, it was damp, dark, and exceedingly murky. Much of the cavern's light came from the eerily glowing fungi and lichens that grew on the stone walls and the water-stained wood of buildings huddled haphazardly together. Some of these glowing fungi were mobile, and viscous globs of the stuff inched along the stone-ledge walkways until they were booted out of the way or squashed underfoot into luminous green puddles. Clouds of mist clung to the lanterns that dotted the narrow, twisting streets with feeble light, and everywhere the air was heavy with the smell of sea salt and the stench of the city. Travelers and merchants from some three dozen races—few of which were welcomed in most other cities—sloshed through puddles and streams whose contents were best left unexamined.

With each step, Vasha's fur boots became more bedraggled, her visage more dangerously grim. Yet she strode steadfastly along, clutching the stone coin in her hand and choosing her path by the heat it gave off.

Liriel might have admired the woman's single-minded fervor, except for the fact that it was likely to get them both killed. The drow jogged along behind Vasha, her eyes scanning the crowded streets and dark side passages for dangers that the barbarian would not perceive. That was no small challenge, for if Liriel had sat down and devoted serious thought to the task, she could not have conceived of a person less suited for life in Skullport than Vasha the Red.

The warrior woman met Skullport's challenges head-on, sword in hand. This was not good. The city's multilayered intrigues—although muted by the "safe ground" policy that made trade between enemies possible—were complicated by bizarre magical occurrences, the legacy of the city's founder, one extremely mad wizard. Vasha's rune-carved blade might have been forged to dispel magical attacks, but it probably had its limitations, and Liriel had no desire to find out what these might be.

Just then Vasha waded carelessly through a tightly huddled cluster of haggling kobolds. Her passage sent the rat-tailed merchants scattering and allowed the object of their discussion—a comely halfling slave girl—to dart into the dubious safety of a nearby brothel. The cheated kobolds wailed and shook their small fists at the departing barbarian. Vasha spared the goblinlike creatures not so much as a glance, but disappeared into a small dark alley.

Liriel recognized the opening to a tunnel, a particularly dark and dangerous passage that twisted through solid rock on its way to the port. She muttered a curse, tossed a handful of coins to appease the gibbering kobolds, and sprinted off in pursuit.

The drow raced down the tunnel, trusting in her elven vision to show her the way through the darkness. She rounded a sharp turn at full speed, only to bury her face in the thick fur of Vasha's bearskin cloak.

The collision did not seem to inconvenience the barbarian in the slightest, but Liriel rebounded with a force that sent her staggering backward and deposited her on her backside. From this inelegant position, she had a clear view of the magical phenomenon that had not only given Skullport its name, but had also brought Vasha the Red to an abrupt stop.

Bobbing gently in the air were three disembodied skulls, larger than life—or *death,* to be more precise—and glowing with faint, rosy light. Liriel had never seen the Skulls, but she'd heard enough tavern talk to know what they were. Remnants of the mad wizard's defenses, the Skulls appeared randomly to give absurd tasks to passersby, or to punish those who disturbed the city's tentative peace. By all accounts, bad things happened to those who heeded them not. And by all appearances, Vasha was in no mood to heed. Her sword was bared, her muscles knotted in readiness as she took the measure of her new adversary.

The middle member of the weird trio drifted closer to the warrior woman. "Stranger from another time and place, you do not belong in these tunnels," it informed Vasha in a dry whisper. Its jaw moved as it spoke, clicking faintly with each word.

"In my land, voices from beyond the grave speak words worth hearing!" proclaimed the warrior. She brought her sword up and gave the floating skull a contemptuous little poke. "Tell me something I don't know, or get you gone!"

"Um, Vasha—" began Liriel, who had a very bad feeling about what was to come. Tavern tales indicated that challenging the Skulls was not a good idea. Indeed, the bony apparition glowed more intensely, and its teeth clattered in apparent agitation.

"For your arrogance, and in punishment for disturbing the rules of safe ground, your assigned tasks will be long and noxious," decreed the Skull. "First, you must capture and groom a thousand bats. Save the loose hairs and spin them with wool into a soft thread, which you will then dye in equal parts black and red. Weave from the thread a small black tapestry emblazoned with a trio of crimson skulls, and hang it in the tavern where you slew the illithid."

Vasha scoffed. True to her nature, she focused on the only item in that discourse of personal interest. "The squid-creature *died* from so small a wound? Bah!"

"Next, you shall seek out a company of goblins, invite them to a tavern, and serve them meat and drink," the Skull continued.

"Vasha the Red, a serving wench to goblins? I would sooner bed an orc!"

"I was *getting* to that." There was a peevish cast to the dry voice.

Liriel scrambled to her feet and tugged at the barbarian's fur cloak. "Agree to anything, and let's get out of here!" she whispered urgently. "And by all the gods, don't give that thing *ideas!*"

"As to that, I *shall* give it something to ponder," promised the swordwoman in a grim tone. "No one, living or dead, gives orders to Vasha the Red!"

With that, Vasha flung back her sword arm—incidentally sending Liriel tumbling once again—as she prepared to deal a whole new level of death to the presumptuous Skulls. Her sword slashed forward and reduced all three of the floating heads to dust and fragments. Pieces of bone sprinkled the stone floor with a brittle clatter and a shower of rapidly fading pink sparks. Then, just as quickly, the fragments flew back into the air and reassembled into a single large skull. The apparition hung there for a moment, glowing with intense, furious crimson light, and then winked out of sight.

Liriel hauled herself to her feet, her face livid with fear and rage. "Damn and blast it, Vasha, you can't go smashing everything in your path!" she shrieked.

"I don't see why not."

"Oh, you will," the drow muttered, noting the faint glow dawning in the void left by the departed Skulls. She dived for safety just as the glimmer exploded into an enormous whirlwind of rainbow-colored light.

Out of this magic tunnel stepped a wizard—a long-bearded male garbed in the pointed hat and flowing robes of an age long past. Tavern rumors suggested that all wizshades resembled a certain sage currently residing in faraway Shadowdale. As to that, Liriel could not attest, but she could not help noticing that this wraith-wizard's hair, robes, and skin were all of the same vivid emerald shade.

Vasha the Red, meet wizshade. The green.

This bit of executioner's humor flashed into Liriel's mind and was gone just as quickly. Frantically, she reviewed her current magical arsenal, but the power of the wizshades was reputed to far exceed those of most mortal wizards, and Liriel doubted that any of her ready spells would have much effect.

Vasha, naturally, took a more direct approach. The warrior slashed with deadly intent at the green wizard's neck. Her sword whistled through the wizshade without achieving the desired decapitation. Again, on the backswing, the broadsword passed right through the seemingly solid wizard. Neither blow cut so much as a hair of his verdant beard.

The barbarian fell back a step and shot an inquiring glare in Liriel's direction. The drow, however, was just as puzzled. According to tavern lore, magical weapons could inflict real damage upon wizshades. But Vasha's broadsword, which until now had sliced through magic like a knife through butter, had drawn not a single drop of green blood. Worse, the wizshade's emerald-colored fingers had begun an ominous, spellcasting dance.

Suddenly Liriel understood what hadn't happened, and why. The broadsword had been warded to *destroy* magical attacks; it had no magical powers of its own. Strictly speaking, it wasn't a magic weapon. But *she* had weapons that might serve—strange devices steeped in the unique radiation magic of the Underdark.

Liriel snatched a spider-shaped object from a bag at her belt and hurled it at the spell-casting wraith. Her throwing spider whirled between the gesticulating green hands, and its barbed legs bit deep into the wizard's gut. The apparition shrieked, tore the weapon free and flung it aside, and then dived back into the vortex. The whirl of multicolored light sucked in upon itself and disappeared.

Vasha tucked away her sword and regarded Liriel with approval. "You see? Magic cannot stand before honest steel." She stooped to retrieve and examine the throwing spider. "Even when the steel is in so strange a shape," she mused.

The drow decided not to waste time with explanations. She reclaimed her magic weapon from the woman and returned it to her bag. "Let's *go*," she urged, knowing that the Skulls' orders could not long be ignored. "Either we find your runecaster and get you out of the city by day's end, or you'll be grooming bats for the rest of your natural life!"

"I'd rather bed a satyr," muttered Vasha darkly.

"Well, sure. Who wouldn't?" agreed the drow as she pushed the barbarian firmly along the tunnel.

The swordwoman, who was becoming accustomed to the elf's dark sense of humor, shot a scornful look over her shoulder. But the expression on Liriel's face—at once serious and dreamily speculative—turned Vasha's withering glare into an astonished double take.

"This is indeed a strange place," she marveled.

Liriel nodded her approval. "Well, praise the Dark Lady. You're finally catching on."

* * * * *

But Vasha the Red's insight proved to be shallow and fleeting. The warrior woman continued to meet every obstacle with a ready sword and a snarl of contempt. By the time the hour for evenfeast rolled around, they were no closer to finding the elusive Toth than they'd been at the onset of their quest. On the other hand, Vasha had hacked a sentient jelly into quivering globs, dueled to the death an ill-mannered ettin, surgically dampened the ardor of several pirates on shore leave, and trimmed the wings from the shoulders of a small but aggressive wyvern, after which she'd advised the creature's dumbfounded wizard master to have the hide tanned and made into a decent pair of boots. In short, only through a mixture of dumb luck and brute strength did she and Liriel survive the day.

When she could bear no more, the drow steered her charge into the Burning Troll. It was a pricey tavern, but the food was good, the halfling servants were prompt, and the patrons could be reasonably sure of an entertaining brawl. As soon as they were seated, Liriel ordered roast fowl and bread, wine, and a bowl of cold water. She plucked the stone coin from Vasha's hand and threw it into the bowl. The hot fragment met the water with a hiss of protest, and then subsided. Liriel wished that the human could be as reasonable.

"Forget about the coin for now," the drow insisted. "You can't continue running around Skullport, following a piece of rock and killing whomever you please."

"Why not? I've done just so these many hours."

"And we have so much to show for it," Liriel returned with acid sarcasm.

The barbarian could not dispute this failing. "So?" she said gruffly.

"I know wizards," the drow asserted. "This Toth seems to be an especially slippery specimen. To catch him, we'll need planning, subtlety, treachery. I know of some people who for the right price . . ."

Her voice trailed off, for it was clear that the swordwoman was no longer listening. Vasha's dangerously narrowed eyes were fixed upon the bowl of water meant to cool the stone fragment. It was now at a full boil. Steam rose from the roiling surface, and the stone tumbled in the churning water.

"We *need!*" the barbarian roared in a scathing echo, sweeping her hand toward the tavern's entrance. "I need nothing but my sword. Behold Toth, son of Alfgar!"

Liriel beheld. An involuntary smile curved her lips as she did so, for standing just inside the door was Vasha's male counterpart: tall, muscular, flame-haired, and dressed with no more regard for modesty than the warrior. On him, the drow noted with approval, it looked good. But she wondered, fleetingly, where he carried his spell components.

The runecaster was not at all cowed by the spectacle of an enraged Vasha. He sauntered directly over to their table. With insolent ease, he conjured a third chair and straddled it.

"By what fell magic did you find me?" demanded the warrior. Her face and voice were as fierce as usual, but Liriel suspected that Vasha was both embarrassed and unnerved at being caught off guard. Liriel was none too happy about that, herself. She'd spent the day in Vasha's wake, too busy trying to stay alive to realize that the runecaster had been leading them on a merry chase. He apparently had a devious streak, something that the drow understood very well and should have recognized.

"Greetings, Red Vasha," Toth said amiably. "I heard you were in town and assumed you were looking for me, so I followed the trail of destruction to its source."

"If you are so eager for battle, then let it begin," snarled the swordwoman. "I challenge you to a contest of honest steel!"

Toth cast a wry look in Liriel's direction. "Notice she did not suggest a battle of *wits*. Our Vasha might be eager, but even *she* would not enter a fight unarmed."

The insult sent Vasha leaping to her feet. The table upended with a clatter, bringing a faint cheer from the tavern's patrons. So far, the evening had been too quiet for their liking.

The warrior brandished her sword; Toth plucked an identical blade from the empty air. They crossed weapons with a ringing clash, and the fight began.

The combatants were well matched and in grim earnest, and for a few minutes the tavern patrons were content to watch and wager. But something in the air drew them toward mayhem like bees to clover. Small skirmishes broke out here and there. Those who had blades used them. Others contented themselves with lesser weapons, each according to his strength: humans and half-orcs brawled using fists and feet, goblins and hags pelted each other with mugs and bread, mongrelmen lobbed shrieking halfling servants at the ogres, who promptly returned fire with furniture. In moments the entire tavern was engulfed in wild melee.

Liriel edged to the side of the room, skirting the worst of the fighting and occasionally ducking a flying halfling. Despite the natural immunity to magic that was her drow heritage, she could feel the seductive tug of some unknown spell pulling her toward battle. This Toth was good.

But however good he might be, the runecaster underestimated Vasha if he thought that a tavern-wide disturbance might distract her. True, the goblins' mug-throwing had showered her repeatedly with ale, and the growing piles of bodies necessitated some extra footwork in the dance of battle, but the swordswoman did not seem to care or even notice. Her face was set in an ecstatic grimace as she slashed and pounded at her long-sought prey. Liriel watched closely, impressed that Toth managed to hold his own against such fury. But drow wizards were also trained fighters, and Liriel knew that swordplay was no serious deterrent to spellcasting.

Spellcasting was generally frowned upon in this tavern, but the melee thoroughly absorbed the attention of the other patrons. Thus the drow was the only one to see the forgotten wedge of stone rise from a puddle of water on the floor, fly into the runecaster's hand, and meld with the half-circle he held. Only she saw Toth slip the time-coin into his scant loincloth, saw his lips move as he spoke unheard words of magic. For a moment Liriel eyed the handsome runecaster and wished she'd paid better attention when that halfling pickpocket had tried to teach her the trade. But, no time for regrets. She quickly cast an incantation of her own, then waited confidently for what surely would happen next.

Toth disappeared, as expected.

And with him went the spell of battle-lust. Most of the

combatants ceased at once, blinking stupidly as they regarded their upraised fists or drawn blades. One ogre, who had lifted a halfling overhead and hauled him back for the throw, stopped so abruptly that the hapless servant went flying backward as opposed to hurtling into enemy ranks. His shriek, loud and shrill in the sudden lull, indicated that he did not consider this fate an improvement. The halfling crashed feetfirst through the tavern's wooden door and hung there, half in and half out, groaning softly.

The rush toward the halfling-bedecked exit was sudden and general. All who could leave the tavern did so, for participation in fights of this magnitude was usually rewarded with a night in Skullport's dungeons. In mere moments Vasha and Liriel were the only able-bodied persons left in the room.

The barbarian's roar of frustration rattled what little crockery remained. "Coward! Oath breaker! Vile runecasting son of a wild pig!" shrieked Vasha, shaking her sword and fairly dancing with rage.

"You should have seen that coming," the drow said calmly.

"How could I, Vasha the Red, an honest warrior, foresee such treachery? I fought with honor! Here I stand, drenched in the blood of mine enemy—"

"That's ale," Liriel pointed out.

Vasha abruptly ceased her ranting. She looked down at her sodden raiment and saw that it was so. This mundane discovery leached a bit of the fight—and a good deal of pride—from the barbarian's eyes. She tucked away her sword, crossed her arms over her mighty bosom, and sulked.

"Blood, ale. Whatever. It matters only that Toth has escaped to where only our daughters' daughters might find him!"

"Oh, I don't think so," said the drow in a satisfied tone. She held out her palm. Lying in it was a stone coin, whole except for a small wedge.

Wonder lit Vasha's eyes. "That is the time-coin! But how?"

"Typical devious drow tactics. I stole it from Toth, using a simple spell. Sometimes magic is the most direct method, after all."

The piles of splintered wood and wounded patrons argued powerfully for Liriel's point. Vasha conceded with a nod. "Magic has triumphed, strength has failed," she admitted humbly. "But where then is Toth, if he cannot travel through time?"

"A wizard powerful enough to construct a time portal could be almost anywhere," Liriel said. "My guess, though, is that he's somewhere in Skullport. It's exceedingly dangerous to travel to a place never before seen. Also, once he realizes he's missing that coin, he won't go far."

This reasoning brought glowing hope to Vasha's face. "Then we can still hunt him down!"

Liriel lunged at the departing barbarian and seized the edge of her bearskin cloak. "Enough! I've another idea, but you must agree to the use of magic."

The swordwoman subsided, bowing her head in resignation. "How can I not? Vasha the Red has failed. I yield to the wisdom of the drow."

Liriel held up the runecaster's book. "This tells how to use the coin. We'll step back in time, to the point just before Toth came into the tavern. And this time, we'll be ready for him."

Vasha agreed. She stood guard while Liriel studied and cast the intricate spell, and she managed to hold on to her temper and her sanity when she found herself once again seated across the table from Liriel in an undamaged tavern. But the sight of a small coin fragment at the bottom of the bowl of water made her swallow hard.

"We have failed! Toth still holds his half of the coin; he can flee!"

"Why should he?" Liriel retorted. She pulled a knife from her boot and used it to fish the stone from the rapidly heating water. "He's coming here looking for us, remember? He doesn't know that I'll lift his half of the coin."

As she spoke, the drow fingered a tiny pocket just

inside her sleeve, where she had hidden the nearly whole coin that had traveled back in time with her. She did not understand how this had happened, or have any idea how the coin could exist simultaneously in its past and present forms. But she saw no reason to speak of this, or any harm in keeping silent. As long as Vasha got her runecaster and brought him back to stand trial before the ancient Rus, all would be well.

Vasha still looked puzzled, but she allowed the drow to position her near the tavern door, in plain sight of any who might enter. Liriel took her place nearer the entrance. "Toth will be looking for you, so I've got a better chance at getting in the first blow," the drow explained. "If I miss, feel free to step in."

The barbarian shook her head. "I do not doubt your success. What shall you do—imprison the runecaster in some mysterious dark-elven spell?"

"Something like that," Liriel said absently. She retreated into herself, seeking the innate magic that flowed through the fey dark elves. Summoning her natural power of levitation, she drifted up to hover high above the doorway's lintel.

This act was easy enough for Liriel, something that all drow of the Underdark could do. But this was not the Underdark, and such powers usually faded away long before a dark elf came so close to the lands of light. The spectacle of a floating drow, therefore, was unusual enough to draw every eye in the tavern. Even Vasha stared, bug-eyed and gaping.

Thus it was that Toth, when he entered the tavern, noted the general bemusement and instinctively followed the line of the patrons' collective gaze. When he looked up, Liriel was ready—not with some spell, for she could not know what magical defenses this powerful runecaster might have. This time the drow took a page from Vasha's book: with the flat of her dagger, she bashed the poor sod solidly between the eyes.

Down went the mighty Toth. Liriel floated lightly to the floor and crouched beside the fallen runecaster. She patted him down, found his half of the coin, and pressed the smaller fragment to it. The stone pieces joined, flowing together as smoothly as two drops of water.

The drow handed the restored coin to Vasha. "As much as I'd love to keep this, you've got to get home before the Skulls come looking for you."

"My thanks, Liriel, daughter of Sosdrielle, daughter of Maleficent," the barbarian said gravely. "I shall long remember your wisdom, and never again will I disparage the power of magic, or the importance of treachery!"

Liriel shrugged. "Just don't get carried away. Although I never thought I'd admit it—especially after the day I've just had—there *are* times when the best approach is the most direct one. Even if that's a good swift blow."

The swordwoman nodded, pondering these words as if they'd come from an oracle. "Complex indeed is the wisdom of the drow," she marveled. "Though I live a hundred years, never could I fathom it all. And yet," she added, her voice becoming less reverential, "there are some things that even such as I can learn."

Out flashed Vasha's blade once again, and the glittering point pressed hard against the base of Liriel's throat. "The second time-coin," the swordwoman said flatly. "The one you brought back with you. Give it me."

For a moment Liriel considered trying to bluff. Then, with a sigh, she handed it over. "But how did you know?"

Vasha smiled thinly. "You wished to learn about the Rus. What better, more direct way than to travel back through time yourself? Since you gave up the coin so easily, I knew that there must be another." With that, she shouldered the unconscious runecaster, held up one of the identical time-coins, and spoke the words that summoned the gateway to her own time and place.

A wary silence followed Vasha's disappearance, as the tavern's patrons waited to see what might next transpire. Liriel recalled the spectacular brawl and returned the hostile glares without flinching. "Trust me, it could have been worse," she snapped.

And that, she decided much later that evening, was an excellent summary for the day's adventure. Her encounter with Vasha could have turned deadly in a thousand different ways. True, Liriel had not gained the ability to travel through time, but she *had* acquired a new book of rune lore. And she had learned one more, very important thing:

The main problem with the direct approach, magical or otherwise, was that it was just too damned predictable.

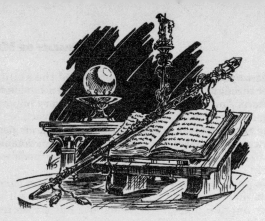

EPILOGUE

Justin interrupted the loquacious author. "All of those stories are in here?" he queried pointing to the manuscript.

"But of course," Volo replied, grateful for the occasion of taking a breath, "and more."

"All have been authenticated?"

"I had each source sign the manuscript pages based on his or her information."

The publisher examined a page for corroboration, then placed it back on the stack, satisfied. "Drow princesses, Khelben, Elminster, curses, spells, dimension hopping, dragons, smoke powder."

"And more," Volo assured.

"All the elements of a best-seller," Justin offered.

"You really think so?" Volo queried, batting his eyes in mock naivete.

"Of course," the publisher replied. "We have a deal at our usual terms."

Volo held up a single finger to indicate a pause. "I was sort of hoping for a slightly higher advance . . . expenses and all," the gazetteer replied hesitantly.

"How about a ten percent increase?"

"How about twenty?" Volo pressed.

"Done!" Justin replied, extending his hand to his best-selling author.

"Done!" Volo replied, his hand hooking up with his publisher's midway across the desk. As the two drew back to their respective sides of the desk, he added, "I was really counting on being able to collect my advance funds immediately . . . expenses and all."

"No problem," Justin replied, coming around from his side of the desk. "I hope right after lunch will be all right. I have another pressing engagement, but my secretary should be back by then."

"Fine," Volo replied, purposely not trying to sound churlish as he realized he was being gypped out of lunch. "Say, in about an hour?"

"Make it two," the publisher replied, escorting the star author to the door, and to the staircase leading downward. "I need to clear up a few things before my next appointment, so I hope you don't mind showing yourself out."

"No problem," the author replied, adding, "I'll be back in about two hours."

"No problem at all," the voice of the publisher replied as he slipped back into the shadows of his office.

* * * * *

Justin Tym arrived at his office at the usual time that morning, right before his scheduled lunch appointment with his star author, Volothamp Geddarm. He was just in time to be greeted by a well-dressed workman who was tending to a fire in the hearth by the desk.

The flames roared as they blackened and consumed the last sheaf of pages.

"Here! Here!" the publisher said. "What are you doing in my office?"

"Sorry, good sir," the nondescript fellow replied. "I was just warming myself at your hearth while waiting for you to return."

"Well, I'm here now," the publisher replied. "What can I do for you?"

"I have a message from a Mister Volo," the fellow said. "He sends his regrets that he will not be able to see you this trip. Pressing business or something, I think he mentioned."

How odd, Justin thought. It's not like Volo to pass up a free lunch.

"Oh, well," the publisher replied. "He's not the first author afraid to see his publisher about a late manuscript. I was really hoping he would be turning in the *Guide to the Moonsea* he once mentioned. I may as well just go on home. He was my only appointment for the day."

"No reason to waste a day like this cooped up in an office," the fellow replied, beginning to wash the windows.

"My sentiments exactly," Justin replied. "My secretary should be in shortly. Would you mind telling her I've decided to work at home today?"

"No problem," the nondescript cleaner replied.

* * * * *

The window washer returned to his true form when he had observed Justin turning the corner along the street below.

Hlaavin the doppleganger poked through the fire, making sure nary a manuscript page had escaped.

Hearing the publisher's secretary ascending the stairs, Hlaavin again assumed the form of Justin Tym and met her at the head of the stairs.

Feigning anger and indignation, "the publisher" instructed the secretary, "Tell that Volo he is no longer welcome on the premises of this publishing house. Imagine his nerve—standing me up for lunch."

"Yes, Mr.Tym," she replied.

"I'm taking the rest of the day off," the doppleganger added, quickly venturing downward to the street below.

Hlaavin heard a brisk, "Yes, Mr. Tym," on his way out, giving it only half an ear as he revelled in the sweetness of his revenge on that meddling author. He even thought this plot might tide him over until Volothamp Geddarm received his inevitable just desserts.

Tangled Webs

An Excerpt

Elaine Cunningham

Author of
Daughter of the Drow

Chapter 1

SKULLPORT

Far below the streets of Waterdeep, in a cavern buried beneath the bottom of the sea, lay the hidden city that legend and rumor had named Skullport. Most of those who came here sought to trade in goods that were banned in civilized ports, and the dregs of a hundred warring races did business in an atmosphere of knife-edged danger. Yet beneath the streets of Skullport were even deeper realms, places that the most intrepid merchants strove to avoid. In one particularly noisome labyrinth—a series of winding tunnels and despoiled crypts—a dungeon had been fashioned for those who disturbed the tenuous balance of the city.

Once the burial place of a long-vanished tribe of dwarves, over the centuries these catacombs had become home to other, more dangerous creatures.

From time to time, treasure hunters came seeking an undiscovered dwarven cache; most of these seekers remained as piles of moldering bones, giving powerful testament to the traps and monsters that lingered in the dank stone passages.

It was a forbidding place, even to a drow accustomed to walking the endless tunnels of the Underdark. Magical elven boots muted the sound of her footsteps, and a glittering *piwafwi* cloaked her with invisibility, yet Liriel Baenre kept keenly alert for possible dangers. To speed her way, she carried foremost in her thoughts the remembered face of the man imprisoned in this, the worst of Skullport's dungeons.

Slender as a human girl-child and seemingly not much older, the young drow appeared delicate to the point of fragility. Her black-satin skin gave her the look of living sculpture, an image that was enhanced by the supple, tightly fitted black leathers and ebony-hued chain mail she wore. She was beautiful in the fey manner of elvenkind, with fine, sharp features and a cloud of thick white hair as glossy as moonlight on new snow. Hers was a mobile face that could be one moment impish, the next coldly beautiful, and it was dominated by a pair of large, almond-shaped eyes the color of Rashemi amber. These eyes spoke of a restless intelligence and an ever-ready supply of mischief. By all appearances, the drow girl hardly seemed capable of storming this deeply buried stronghold. And yet, that was precisely what she intended to do.

Liriel moved easily through the utter darkness of the tunnel. The gloom presented no problem, for the eyes of a drow could detect subtle heat patterns in the rock and the air currents. The eyes of a drow *wizard* were even more sensitive; in the tunnel ahead, Liriel perceived the faint, bluish aura—visible only to those who had inherent magical talent and assiduous training—that warned of magic at work.

The drow crept cautiously closer. The eerie glow curtained off the tunnel like a luminous sheet, but since it was a magical aura visible only to wizards, it cast no illumination upon the scene around it. Liriel debated for a moment whether to risk creating a true light and decided it might be wise to view the trap through the eyes of those who had created it. That it *was* a trap, she did not doubt for a moment.

As easily as thought, Liriel conjured a globe of faerie fire. The magical light bobbed in the air beside her, floating here and there in response to its summoner's unspoken directions and bathing the grim scene in faint white light.

Bones littered the tunnel on both sides of the telltale blue aura, tumbled haphazardly together with abandoned weapons and gear. The tunnel's floor and walls had been splashed repeatedly with gore, and the stone was caked with the dull, dark red of long-dried blood. Whatever the trap was, it had certainly proven effective.

Liriel's gaze fell upon a shallow, much-dented bronze bowl embossed with finely wrought designs and lined with ivory. It seemed strangely out of place among the grisly remains and the practical tools scattered around her feet, and the curious drow crouched to examine it. As she picked it up, the "lining" fell out—it was not ivory but bone, and too thick to be anything but the skull of a dwarf.

The drow settled back on her heels to examine this discovery. Something had sliced neatly through the dwarf's head, cutting through helm and bone so cleanly that the edges of both were as smooth as if they'd been ground and polished by a master gem-cutter. This told her much about the dwarf's death.

Liriel kicked through the scattered debris until she found a heavy thigh bone that had once belonged to a good-sized ogre. As she expected, the bone was severed near the upper joint, at just about the spot where a dwarf's head would reach if the two treasure-hunting fools had stood side by side. The drow rummaged through the pile, selecting similarly cut bones from the remains of several different races, and then laid them out beside each other. In moments she had a fairly precise idea of the trap's danger—and its limitations.

Liriel took up the ogre's leg bone once again. Keeping her hand well away from the magical danger zone, she thrust one end of the bone into the glowing aura. From either side of the tunnel wall, discs of gleaming blue whirled out from the solid rock. The spinning blades met, crossed, and disappeared back into the stone.

The drow regarded the bone in her hand. The tip had been sheared off, so quickly that she hadn't even felt the impact, so silently that the only tell-tale sound was the muffled clatter as the bone shard fell to the blood-encrusted rock.

Not bad, Liriel acknowledged silently, but too predictable. A drow wizard would have enspelled the blades for random attack, so that each strike would come from a different place. Or perhaps such a provision *had* been made to deal with those who might figure out the first attack and try to slip in under the trigger area.

Liriel picked up two more long bones, one in each hand, and held the first into the glowing aura. Again the blue discs sped from the tunnel walls. The moment they crossed paths through the first bone, Liriel thrust the second one down low. The blades continued undeterred along their course and disappeared into the rock. The second bone did not trigger the magical trap at all.

Too easy! Her lips twisted into a smile that mingled triumph with contempt. A drow would have expected a second intrusion—and a third!—and would have ensured that the blades could reverse their paths instantly to meet any challenge.

Now that she saw her way clear, Liriel triggered the trap one last time. The moment the circular blades met and crossed, she dove under their path and rolled through the portal to safety.

In Skullport and environs, however, "safety" was a relative term. As Liriel rose to her feet, she glimpsed a flicker of reflected light on the wall of the tunnel ahead. Something was approaching from a side passage. Instantly she summoned the innate drow magic of levitation and, still invisible, floated up to the tunnel ceiling some twelve feet off the floor. She flattened herself against the damp stone to wait and observe.

A wisp of luminous smoke rounded the sharp bend, then recoiled as if surprised to find itself in an empty corridor. After a moment's pause the smoke came on, flowing around the corner until there was enough to form a small, glowing cloud.

The luminous mass writhed and twisted, finally settling into a hideous, vaguely human shape. As Liriel watched, horror-struck, the wraithlike cloud solidified into decaying flesh. The undead thing looked this way and that, its red eyes gleaming in the darkness.

Liriel had never seen a ghoul, but she recognized the creature for what it was. Once human, it had been twisted into a mindless but cunning beast that fed on carrion. Somehow it had sensed that the magical trap had been triggered, and it had come to feed. This would account for the clean-picked bones that littered the tunnel. It did not, however, explain the ghoul's ability to take on a wraithlike form.

The ghoul shuffled around the passage, sniffing audibly and pawing the air with filthy, clawed hands. Liriel noted that it narrowly skirted the magical trap, showing a perception that only a gifted wizard could have possessed. As she studied the creature's movements, the drow realized that it was retracing her steps. It was following the invisible path left by her innate dark-elven magic. But *how?*

She thought fast. Without doubt, the undead creature had once been a wizard, probably talented enough to have prepared for an afterlife as a lich. If his plans had been altered by attacking ghouls, he might somehow have managed to combine the two transformations. If that were so, it meant the ravenous creature below her was armed with a lich's magic and a ghoul's terrible cunning.

Her own command of magic was formidable, but Liriel knew better than to fight this mindless, undead thing. In a spell-battle, strategy was as important as power. Accustomed as she was to the multilayered intrigues of her people, she could not out-think a being that acted solely on hunger and instinct.

At that moment the ghoul looked upward, turning its red eyes fully upon Liriel's face. A long, serpentine tongue flicked out in anticipation, rasping audibly as it passed over the creature's fangs. The drow shuddered, though she was certain that the ghoul could not actually *see* her. Her invisibility granted her little comfort, though, when the lich-ghoul's clawed fingers began moving jerkily through the gestures of some long-unused spell.

Liriel seized the leather thong that hung around her neck and gave it a sharp tug. Up from its hiding place beneath her tunic flew a small obsidian disk engraved with the holy symbol of Lloth, the Spider Queen, the dark goddess of the drow.

The girl clutched the sacred device and quickly debated her next move. Even a minor priestess could turn aside an attack by undead creatures, but Liriel had attended the clerical school for only a very short time and was accounted a rank novice. On the other hand, she was a princess of House Baenre—the most powerful clan in mighty Menzoberranzan—and she had left her homeland armed with the favor of Lloth and the captured magic of the Underdark. But Liriel had traveled far since then, in ways that could not be measured in miles alone. She found herself inexplicably hesitant to call upon the deity of her foremothers.

Then the lich-ghoul's lips began to move, spewing graveyard dust and foul spittle as it chanted soundless words of power. An unseen force closed around

Liriel like a giant hand, pulling her down toward the waiting creature with a yank so sharp and sudden that her head was snapped painfully back and her arms thrown open wide. Her *piwafwi* flapped open, disclosing her to the undead creature. But Liriel managed to keep her grip on the sacred symbol, and with a drow's lightning-fast reflexes, she thrust it into the ghoul's upturned, slavering face.

"In the name of Lloth, I turn you," she said simply.

It was enough. Crackling black energy burst from the symbol and sent the undead thing reeling back. For a moment the ghoul huddled against the far wall, cowering before the revealed power of the drow goddess. Then its hideous body dissolved into smoke, and the wisps scattered and fled like a flock of startled birds.

Liriel heaved a ragged sigh and floated the rest of the way down to the tunnel floor. But her relief was mixed with vague, nagging misgivings. She had reason to know that Lloth was capricious and cruel. Fortunately, the ghoul did not bother to inquire into the goddess's character. Power was power, and Liriel was alive because she had dared to wield it. There was a certain basic practicality to this reasoning that quieted the drow's uneasiness and sped her steps. She once again drew her *piwafwi* close about her and glided silently down the tunnel, making her way unerringly toward the dungeons.

The drow girl had explored Skullport for several days now and had learned many of the city's secrets. She had reveled in Skullport's lawless freedom, its endless chaotic possibilities. But Liriel was young, and certain that her destiny lay across a vast sea on an island known as Ruathym. She was impatient to get on with it.

Her ears caught the echoes of a distant song, a rollicking tune sung with enormous gusto but little discernible talent. Liriel followed the voice, tracing the intricate path the sound took through winding passages and reverberating stone as effortlessly as a surface-dweller might follow a tree's shadow to its source.

Before long she came to a small, dank cave that in eons past had served as a crypt. Now a prison cell, the cave was secured by iron bars as thick as Liriel's wrist and a massive door that was chained and locked not once, but three times. The small stone chamber was cold, and lit by a single, sputtering torch that gave off more foul-smelling smoke than light. A few deep shelves, long emptied of bones and treasure, had been chiseled into one stone wall. On the opposite side of the cave was a plank bed, suspended from the wall by two rusted chains. And sprawled upon the bed was the singer, who kept time to his music by tossing bits of moldy bread to the creatures that scuttled about the floor of the cell.

The prisoner did not seem at all downcast by his grim surroundings. He was a giant of a man, deep-chested and broad of shoulder, with a face bronzed by the sun and wind and bright blue eyes nearly lost in a maze of laugh lines. The man's braided hair, vast mustache, and long beard were all of the same sun-bleached hue, a color so pale that it almost hid the streaks of grey. This was Hrolf of Ruathym, better known as Hrolf the Unruly, a genial ship's captain with a taste for recreational mayhem. Liriel had learned that this rowdy pastime had gotten him barred from many civilized ports and had landed him—not for the first time—in Skullport's dungeons.

She reached into her pack and took out a statuette that she'd purchased in a backstreet market: a roughly carved, rather comic rendition of a Northman skald with a horned helm, a bulbous nose, and a moon-shaped belly. It was not an impressive work of art, but some wizard with a sense of whimsy had imbued it with an especially powerful magic mouth spell, one that would capture any song and play it back, over and over, for nearly an hour. Liriel figured that an hour should just about do it. As she triggered the statue's magic, the wooden bard stirred to life in her hands. His tiny, bewiskered face screwed up into an expression of intense concentration as he absorbed the lustily sung ditty.

When you meet with the lads of the *Elfmaid,*
   my friend,
You would rather face Umberlee's wrath.
Hand over a measure of all of your treasure
Or swim in a saltwater bath!

Come ashore with the lads of the *Elfmaid,*
   my friend.
We're awash on an ocean of ale!
Some taverns to plunder, some guards to
   a-sunder,
And then, a short rest in the jail!

Liriel winced. Dark elves did not include ballads among their numerous art forms, but since leaving

Menzoberranzan she'd heard many good songs. This was not one of them.

Even so, her slender black fingers flew as she shaped the spell that would lock the music into the statue's memory. The cost of a *magic mouth* spell was a small thing compared to the worth of the man imprisoned within the crypt. Hrolf was reputed to be one of the finest captains to sail the Sword Coast. He was also the only captain Liriel could find who was willing to take on a drow passenger.

With the song safely stored inside the wooden skald, Liriel silently removed her *piwafwi* and stepped into the circle of torchlight. She cleared her throat to get the singer's attention.

Hrolf the Unruly looked up, startled into silence by the sudden interruption. Liriel propped her fists on her hips and tapped her foot in a pantomime of impatience.

"So. When do we set sail?" she demanded.

A broad grin split the man's face, lifting the corners of his mustache and giving him a boyish appearance that belied his graying beard and braids. "Well, chop me up and use me for squid bait! It's the black lass herself!" he roared happily.

"A little louder, please," Liriel requested with acidic sarcasm as she cast quick glances up and down the corridors. "There might be two or three people up in Waterdeep who didn't hear you."

Hrolf hauled himself to his feet and walked stiff-legged over to the door of his cell. "It's glad I am to see you again, lass, but you shouldn't ha' come," he said in a softer tone. "Just a day or two more, and they'll be setting me free."

The drow sniffed derisively and bent down to

examine the locks on the cell door. "Sure, if by freedom you mean a couple of years of enforced labor. It'll take you at least that long to work off the damage done to that tavern."

"Gull splat!" he said heartily, dismissing this dire prediction with a wave of one enormous hand. "The penalty for tavern brawls is never more than a few days' stay in this sow's bowels of a dungeon."

"The Skulls decided to change the law in your honor," Liriel responded, naming the trio of disembodied skulls that appeared randomly to pass sentence on miscreants. "The idea of waiting around for years doesn't appeal to me. I'd rather fight our way from here to the docks and have done."

"Not a bit of it," Hrolf insisted. "Laws are all good and well—fighting's better, of course—but *bribes,* now! That's the way for a sensible man to do business! And no place better'n Skullport for it, so don't you worry yourself. The *Elfmaid* came to port fully loaded. A bundle of ermine skins and a few bolts of fine Moonshae linen should serve."

Liriel cocked an eyebrow. "Did I mention that your ship and cargo have been impounded?"

That was true, as far as it went, and as much truth as the drow wanted him to hear. Although it appeared Hrolf's freedom was not for sale, Liriel had already managed to buy free the ship and the crew. She thought it better to let Hrolf think otherwise. By all accounts, the captain took his ship's well-being more seriously than his own.

"Took the *Elfmaid,* did they?" The captain pondered this development, chewing his mustache reflectively. "Well then, that's different. Fighting it is!"

The drow nodded her agreement. She quickly cast a cantrip, a minor spell that would reveal any magic placed upon the locks. When no telltale glow appeared, Liriel took a small bundle from her bag and carefully removed the wraps that padded a small glass vial. With infinite care she unstoppered the vial and poured a single drop of black liquid onto each of the chains and locks.

A faint hiss filled the air, and the locks sagged and melted as the distilled venom of a black dragon ate through the metal. It was a pricey solution, but it was quick and quiet, and Liriel had no real need to practice thrift. Just days earlier, she had led a raid on a rival drow stonghold and claimed a share of the massive treasure hoard buried there. Her share would take her to Ruathym in style, with enough left over to hide a cache or two for future use. Yet there was a strange tightness in Liriel's throat as she remembered the battle and the friends who had fallen there. One of those friends, although gravely wounded, had survived and was awaiting her even now on Hrolf's ship. Just thinking of Fyodor, and his own great need to reach Ruathym, heightened her impatience.

Motioning for Hrolf to stand back, she kicked open the door, keeping a careful distance from the still-melting chains. Dragon venom could eat through boot leather—not to mention flesh and bone—as easily as it dissolved metal.

The captain watched, intrigued, as Liriel set the enspelled statue on the bed and triggered its song. His face lit up with pride as his own song poured forth from the little figure.

"That'll keep 'em away for a bit," he observed with

a touch of wry humor. Obviously, Liriel concluded, the man held a realistic view of his musical talents.

Hrolf turned to regard the drow with obvious respect. "I was glad enough to offer you passage on the strength of your smile, but to be getting a ship's wizard into the bargain! With your magic, lass, we're as good as a-sail. May Umberlee take me if I'm not getting better at picking my friends!" he concluded happily.

Liriel cast a startled glace at the man's bluff, cheerful face. His easy claim of friendship struck her as odd. She'd met him only once, shortly before he'd begun the spectacular brawl that landed him in this predicament. He seemed a companionable sort, and she was glad to have found passage with an able captain who could also fight like a bee-stung bear. But friendship was still new to her and not something to be taken lightly. For a moment she envied these short-lived humans, who seemed to come to it so easily.

"We're still a long way from the ship," Liriel reminded the man. She stripped off the extra swordbelt she carried and handed it to him. He buckled it on without a word and then drew the sword, regarding its keen edge with pleasure. After a few practice swings to get the feel of the blade and to awaken muscles stiff from disuse, he followed the drow out into the tunnel.

The way was lit by an occasional torch thrust into a wall bracket, so Hrolf was able to walk with assurance, if not silence. The drow set a slow, steady pace, trying to minimize the noise of Hrolf's heavy footsteps. She could fight well when necessary, but she knew the wisdom of avoiding trouble.

So far, despite the encounter with the magic-wielding ghoul, breaching the dungeon's defenses had seemed almost too easy. But then, no one expected anyone to try to sneak *in*. Liriel suspected that getting out would be another matter entirely.

A faint sound caught her ear. From a nearby passage came the reverberating tread of many boots and the guttural speech of goblinkin. She pushed Hrolf into an alcove and shielded them both with her sheltering *piwafwi*. To her relief, Hrolf the Unruly did not protest this precaution or leap out roaring to engage the goblins in battle. The captain and the drow waited for many moments, then watched silently as the guard marched past in sharp formation.

They were squat, muscular creatures—goblin hybrids of some sort—broad as dwarves and haphazardly garbed in ill-fitting, cast-off leather armor. Obviously overfed and underpaid, the guards nevertheless carried a daunting assortment of well-honed weapons. All told, there were twelve of them, enough to give pause even to the dark-elven and the unruly.

The goblin patrol halted in the tunnel ahead, gibbering among themselves and shouldering off the packs they carried. Liriel muttered a curse.

"What're they doing?" Hrolf asked, his voice just above a whisper.

"Taking a break," she responded in kind. Whispering caused the voice to carry too far, and Liriel was frequently amazed that few humans seemed to realize this. Dark elves whispered when they *intended* to be heard—the audible equivalent of a knowing smile.

"They're blocking the tunnel," the drow added grimly, "and we don't have time to wait them out."

The captain pondered this for a moment, and then patted the short sword strapped to Liriel's hip. "I've heard tell that a drow can take a dozen goblins, easy."

The girl shrugged. She could handle a sword well enough and throw knives with deadly precision, but her skills were slanted more toward magic than mayhem. "Some drow can. I'm not one of them."

"Ah, but do yonder goblins *know* that?"

The drow snapped a look back at the captain, surprised that a human had offered such a devious—yet simple—solution. They shared a quick, companionable grin, and she accepted his plan with a nod.

Hrolf patted her shoulder, then drew his sword. "Go, lass. If the ugly little bastards don't spook, I'll be right behind you."

Against reason, despite the suspicious nature bred and ingrained in her by her treacherous kindred, Liriel believed him.

She pulled her sword and walked, silent and invisible, into the circle of goblins. Then, tossing back her *piwafwi,* she dropped into a menacing crouch and presented her blade.

"Hi, boys," she purred in the goblin tongue. "Want to play?"

The sudden appearance of a battle-ready drow in their midst stole whatever courage the creatures possessed. The goblins squeaked in terror and fled, leaving their packs and many of their weapons behind in their panic.

Hrolf strode to the drow's side, grinning broadly. "Well done! D'you think, though, that they'll be back bringing friends?"

"Not a chance," Liriel said flatly. "They're guards, and they ran. If they admit that, they're as good as dead." The drow knelt and began to rifle through the abandoned packs, while Hrolf devoted himself to selecting a few promising weapons for his own use. Liriel's search yielded up several large, well-rusted keys. She smiled and brandished them at Hrolf.

The captain nodded happily, recognizing the significance of this find. He'd been dragged down to this dungeon through a succession of gates. The keys would speed their escape, though each gate was also guarded by magical traps and at least one species of ugly, well-armed creatures. Neither prospect worried Hrolf. Unlike most of his people, he held magic in high regard, and he'd seen enough of this elfmaid's talents to entrust that aspect of the escape to her. As for the other—well, he had a sword now, didn't he?

* * * * *

Fyodor of Rashemen leaned against the rail of the ship, gazing out over the noise and confusion that was Skullport. Merchants, sailors, and dockhands milled about the rotting wooden docks, busying themselves with a dizzying variety of wares. Flocks of *wykeen,* a kind of sea-bat indigenous to the underground port, wheeled and screeched overhead. The black water lapped at the ship with a restless rhythm that echoed the pulse of the far-distant seas. Yet there was no moon to order the tides, no sky at all but a soaring vault of solid stone.

This teeming underground city, so different from the villages of his distant homeland, astounded Fyodor. Most amazing to him was the peace that existed between ancient enemies, all in the name of trade. Dwarves tossed crated cargo to orcs; humans hired themselves out to beholders; svirfneblin bartered with illithids. It was just as well, this unnatural harmony. A nearby fight—any fight— could set him off on a deadly battle frenzy.

Fyodor was a berserker, one of the famed warriors of Rashemen, a champion among the protectors of his homeland. Unlike his brothers, however, he could not control the rages or bring them on at will. When the Witches who ruled his land had come to fear that his wild battle-rages might endanger those about him, they sent him on a quest to recover a stolen artifact, an amulet known as the Windwalker. Its magic was ancient and mysterious, but the Witches thought it might be used to contain the young warrior's magical curse. Thus Fyodor's only hope for controlling his battle rages, and ending his exile from his homeland, lay in the amulet—and in the magic of the drow girl who carried it.

His search for the Windwalker had taken him from snow-swept Rashemen into the depths of the Underdark, where he'd met the beautiful young wizard. Liriel had been first an enemy, then a rival, and finally a partner and friend. Fyodor had followed the drow across half of Faerûn and would gladly travel with her to Ruathym—and not just for the magic she wielded.

The young man's eyes, blue as a winter sky, anxiously scanned the crowded streets. Liriel had arranged passage on this ship for them both and had promised to meet him here. She was late. He could imagine far too many things that might have detained her.

"Troubles?"

The laconic question jarred Fyodor from his grim thoughts. He turned to face the ship's mate, a ruddy, red-bearded man much his own size and build. Nearly six feet tall and heavily muscled, the sailor had the look of a Rashemi. Fair-skinned and blue-eyed, he had a certain familiar directness of gaze and an open countenance defined by broad planes and strong features. The sailor's resemblance to Fyodor's own kin did not surprise the young man, for they no doubt had ancestors in common. The ancient Northmen who'd settled the island of Ruathym had also traveled far east to Fyodor's Rashemen.

"Just wondering when we'd be off, Master . . ."

"Ibn," the first mate supplied. "Just Ibn. We sail with the captain."

Fyodor waited, hoping the man would elaborate. But Ibn merely pulled a pipe from his sash and pressed some aromatic leaves into the bowl. A passing sailor supplied flint and stone, and soon Ibn was puffing away with stolid contentment.

The young warrior sighed and then subsided. Clearly, he could do nothing but wait. Except for his concern over Liriel's delay, the waiting had not been unpleasant. The sights beyond the dock could have occupied him for hours, and the ship itself was well worth contemplating. The *Elfmaid* was an odd combination of old and new: her long, graceful form was reminiscent of the ancient dragonships, and she was clinker-built of strong, light wood. Yet the hull was deep enough to provide an area belowdecks for storage of goods and some cramped sleeping quarters. Castles—small, raised platforms—had been added both fore and aft, and both were hung about with the brightly painted shields of the warrior-bred crew. With its enormous square sail and row of oars, the ship promised to be both fast and maneuverable in any number of situations. Its most remarkable feature, however, was the figurehead that rose proudly over the lancelike bowsprit: a carved, ten-foot image of an elfmaid. More lavishly endowed and garishly painted than any elf who'd ever drawn breath, the figurehead gave the ship her name as well as a playful, rakish air that Fyodor found rather appealing.

The young man also felt at home among the crew. They seemed to accept him as one of their own, even while showing him immense deference. Fyodor thought he knew the reason for that. He had heard that in Ruathym, warriors were afforded great honor and high rank. It would not be unlike Liriel to mention his berserker talents in an attempt to gain passage on a Ruathen ship. Fyodor did not object to this; it was better that the crew was forewarned. Since the Time of the Walking Gods, when magic had gone awry and his battle frenzies became as capricious as the wind, he had taken every precaution he could to avoid bringing harm to those around him.

The first mate took his pipe from his mouth and

pointed with it. "Captain's coming," he observed. "Got company, as usual."

Fyodor looked in the direction that Ibn had indicated. A huge, fair-haired man sprinted toward the ship, swinging a beefy fist back and forth before him like a scythe as he cleared a path through the crowd. Despite his size and his short, bandy legs, the captain set an incredibly fast pace. Behind him was Liriel, running full out, her slender limbs pumping and her white hair streaming back. Behind *her* roiled a swarm of knife-wielding kobolds.

"Step lively, my lads!" roared the captain as he swatted a bemused mongrelman out of his way.

His crew took this development stoically, going about their business with an ease and speed that bespoke frequent practice. Ibn cut the ropes securing the ship to the dock and then seized the rudder; the other men took their places at the oars. To Fyodor's surprise, the *Elfmaid* shot away from the dock, well beyond the reach of the captain and his drow companion.

Before Fyodor could react to this apparent desertion, the captain skidded to a halt. As Liriel ran past, the enormous man seized the back of her swordbelt with one hand, jerking her to an abrupt stop. With his free hand he gathered up a handful of her tangled hair and chainmail vest. Lifting the drow easily off her feet, the captain hauled her back for the toss. As Fyodor watched, slack-mouthed, the man heaved Liriel up and toward the ship.

The captain's strength, combined with Liriel's dark-elven powers of levitation, sent the drow into impromptu flight. Hands outstretched before her, she hurtled toward the *Elfmaid* like a dark arrow, her eyes wide with wild delight.

Fyodor caught the drow's wrists and immediately began swinging her around and around to defuse the force of their collision and to help slow her flight. With each circle, the drow lost a bit of momentum but none of her obvious enjoyment. The moment her boots touched the deck, however, Liriel tore free of Fyodor and ran over to clutch the railing.

"Hrolf!" she called out, her face twisted with dismay.

A startled moment passed before Fyodor realized that the word was a name, not a signal that the drow was about to become seasick. Liriel gazed at the dock where the captain had last stood. In his place a swarm of angry kobolds danced and hooted, growing rapidly smaller as the ship pulled away.

Wishing to ease her distress, Fyodor strode to Liriel's side and pointed down into the dark water. Below them, swimming for the ship with strong, steady strokes, was the captain. "He dove in right after he set you aflight," he explained.

Liriel nodded, and her lips curved in a smile of relief. Then, in one of the abrupt changes of mood that Fyodor had come to know so well, she lifted her chin to an imperious angle and turned a lance-sharp glare upon the first mate.

"What do you mean by this delay? Get the captain aboard at once!"

Ibn recoiled as if he'd been stabbed, but he was accustomed to following orders, and the drow female gave them with the force and conviction of a war chieftain. Before the mate realized what he was about, he'd already set the rudder and tossed a coiled rope over the rail.

The coil unfurled as it flew, and Ibn's aim was true. Hrolf seized the knotted end and began to pull himself hand over hand toward the ship. In moments he scrambled over the rail to stand dripping and triumphant on his own deck.

"Good lad, Ibn," he said heartily, slapping the mate on the back with a force that nearly sent the man sprawling. "The water gates lie ahead; be ready to raise her."

But the mate had other things on his mind. "What do we want with *her?*" he said bluntly, tossing a dark glare and a curt nod at the drow.

Hrolf flung back one dripping braid and faced down the red-bearded sailor. "This is Liriel, a princess in her own land and a wizard worth any ten I've seen this mooncycle!" he announced in a voice loud enough to reach every man on the ship. "She's also a paying passenger. See to it you treat her with proper respect, or answer to me. And know this: the man who lays a hand on her loses it."

A moment of stunned silent met the captain's words.

"But she's an elf," protested one of the men, voicing a typical Northman distrust of the fey folk.

"She's a drow!" added another fearfully, for the dark elves' vile reputation was known in a hundred lands.

"She's a *she.*"

This last observation, voiced in dire tones, apparently summed up the crew's protests. The men nodded and muttered among themselves, many of them forming signs of warding.

"Oh, stow your nonsense with the rest of the cargo!" Hrolf roared, suddenly out of patience. "All my days I've heard that a female aboard meant ill luck, but never have I seen a sign of it! Has yon lass caused us a moment's trouble?" he demanded, pointing to the enormous figurehead.

"Not a bit; the elfmaid brings good fortune," one of the crew ventured thoughtfully.

"That she does," the captain stated, and his voice rang out, as powerful and persuasive as that of a master thespian. "Never has a storm taken us unaware; never have creatures of the sea decided to make of us a midday meal! And what of the shipmen who claimed the elfmaid would bring us to grief? How many of those men sleep in Umberlee's arms, and our time not yet come?"

The uniformly angry expressions on the Northmen's faces wavered, fading to puzzlement or indecision. Hrolf, who apparently knew his men well, waited for the planted idea to take root. "I say it's high time the *Elfmaid* was honored by one of her own," he stated. "Besides, who but the black lass has the magic needed to take us up through the gates? With half of Skullport on my heels, d'you suppose the Keepers will send us through without question and blow us kisses to speed our way?"

There was no arguing with Hrolf's logic, and the crew knew it. The Keepers were hired mages who raised ships though magical locks leading from the underground port to the Sea Caves—an impassible and rock-strewn inlet south of Waterdeep—and from there to the open seas. These magical portals had been established centuries earlier by Halaster, a mighty wizard who'd left his insane stamp on nearly every corridor of the Undermountain, and to this day the gates were the only way to move ships to and from Skullport. Without the permission of the Keepers—or the aid of a powerful wizard—the *Elfmaid* would never sail beyond this subterranean bay. The crew could like it or not, but the drow female offered them their only chance of escape.

Liriel, however, was concerned with a more immediate problem. Three small ships, loaded with fighters, were being rowed with deadly determination for the *Elfmaid*. They gained steadily on the larger ship; battle seemed inevitable.

Fear, an emotion so new to Liriel that she had no name to give it, rose like bile in her throat. She was never one to recoil from a fight, but she knew that if Fyodor joined this battle, the dark waters would be warmed with blood. The drow could not permit this.

She spun to face Hrolf. The rowdy captain had already taken note of the approaching threat, and his eyes glinted with anticipation. "Show me a place belowdecks where I might go," she demanded. "Fyodor will come with me and stand guard, for I cannot be interrupted while spellcasting."

Hrolf's eyes dropped to Fyodor's dark sword, and a flicker of disappointment crossed his bewiskered face.

"Do as we discussed, and all will be well!" Liriel added in a tone that did not invite or allow discussion.

Hrolf yielded with a sigh and a shrug. "Well then, lad, here are your orders: Let no man through the hatch until our wizard gives you leave."

Fyodor nodded, hearing what the captain said, and what he implied. Hrolf was in command of this ship, and under ordinary circumstances a berserker would follow a commander's orders to the death. The captain knew this and had phrased his words accordingly. Fyodor hoped, as he followed Liriel down a short ladder into the darkness of the hold, that he would be able to do as Hrolf commanded.

The captain paused before dropping the hatch. "Good luck to you, lass. And you, lad—see that you take good care of her." He gave Fyodor a shrewd once-over and then a wink. "But then, I don't have to be telling you *that,* now do I?"

Hrolf dropped the hatch with a thud, and then came the grating sound of something heavy being dragged over to obscure the opening. Angry voices drew nearer, and Liriel and Fyodor heard the sharp *ping!* of loosed arrows. Above all rang Hrolf's voice, shouting gleeful battle instructions to his men.

"I can't concentrate with all that going on," Liriel grumbled. "Come closer—sit down here beside me. I'm going to cast a sphere of silence. You don't need to hear the battle—just watch the hatch and kill anything that tries to get close to me."

Fyodor smothered a smile as he settled down on the wooden floor beside his friend. The drow's brusque manner did not fool him for a moment. If pressed, she'd claim she was merely being practical; her pride in her dark-elven ways was too strong for her to admit to sentiment. Practical she certainly was. Fyodor did not yet know the crew well enough to discern defender from invader, and in the throes of battle frenzy he would fight until he died, or until no one stood to oppose him. Still, he could not resist the temptation to let Liriel know he saw her well-meaning sham for what it was.

"If I am to keep watch, I would do better with a light," Fyodor said mildly.

Instantly the soft glow of faerie fire lit the room. Liriel cast him a sidelong, suspicious look, but if she perceived his gentle teasing she gave no indication. Getting down to business, she opened a small spellbook and then took from her spell bag the items she would need for the casting.

It was a difficult spell, one of the most advanced in the book of gate spells given her by her father, the mighty archmage of Menzoberranzan. It was also one of the most unusual, allowing a person or entity to journey piggyback through an established gate along with the rightful traveler. Liriel only hoped that a ship and its entire crew could be considered an entity.

She began the deep concentration that such powerful magic demanded. Her body began to sway, and her gesturing hands pulled power from the weave of magic and bound it to her will. Yet she remained intensely aware of the battle above—for despite her words, the magical silence she cast encompassed only Fyodor—and she listened for Hrolf's signal. When the spell was cast, she sat immobile, her hands cupped around a sphere of summoned power as she waited for the precise moment to set it free. Finally the signal came: the quick pattern of stomps and pauses that she and Hrolf had prearranged. Another ship had entered the magic locks; it was time for the *Elf-maid* to join it.

The young wizard flung her hands high, releasing the contained magic. All at once the world shifted weirdly.

Liriel was swept up in the rush and roar of falling water and the whirling colors of a rainbow gone mad. Her physical form seemed to melt away as her mind took on the chaos and complexity of a crowded room. The drow felt, individually and all at once, the thoughts and fears of every person on this ship and on the other ship as well. At that moment she knew every person's name and could have said what each was doing. The multifaceted clarity lasted but a heartbeat before the many minds united in a single emotion: terror. This melting of barriers, this sudden and unfathomable sharing, was beyond anything that most of them had imagined possible.

Then, just as suddenly as it had begun, the spell was over. Liriel opened her eyes and was relieved to find herself and her surroundings whole—not joined board and sinew with the other ship and its crew. That was the risk in such a spell, even if there was but one wizard following another. Her father had warned her with stories of wizards who had been permanently conjoined by this spell, only to go mad in the attempt to share one body between two minds.

Liriel reached out a single finger to break the sphere of silence that protected her friend, much as a child might pop a soap bubble. "It's over," she said, and a quick, eager smile lit her face. "Let's go see the stars!"

Fyodor returned her smile with a heartfelt one of his own. He, too, had missed that sight during their sojourn in the tunnels surrounding Skullport. Still feeling somewhat dazed by the magical transport, he shouldered open the trapdoor and crawled up onto the deck.

Beneath a brilliant night sky, the men of the *Elfmaid* stood staring at the equally stunned faces of the crew of the ship that floated beside them, its rail near enough to touch.

Hrolf was the first to shake off the spell, bellowing at his crew to drop weapons and man the oars. Fyodor took his place at an oar, and soon the ship had pulled well away from its host. When it became clear that the other ship had no inclination to pursue, Hrolf set the sail and released the oarsmen to their rest.

Fyodor strode across the deck toward the place where Liriel stood alone in rapt contemplation of the stars. He found it oddly reassuring that someone who had spent nearly her entire life below ground could have a soul-deep love for the sky and its many lights and colors. In moments like this, Fyodor could believe that he and the beautiful drow were not so very different after all.

Not far from Liriel stood the captain and mate, deep in discussion. Fyodor did not intend to listen, but Hrolf's voice carried in the still night air like the call of a hunting horn.

"Well then, that's one more port that won't be glad of us for some time to come! Looks like we'll be adding Skullport to the list," said Hrolf.

"Looks like," the mate agreed.

"But it was a stay to remember and a good fight

to end it with!"

"That it was. Lost the cargo, though."

The captain winked. "Never you mind. We'll make up the difference on the way home, and more besides!"

Fyodor stopped in his tracks, stunned and enlightened. He quickly recovered his wits and hurried over to Liriel. Seizing her by the arm, he drew her well away from the scheming sailors.

"There's something you must know," he said in a low, urgent voice. "I fear that this is a pirate ship!"

The drow stared up at him, her amber eyes full of genuine puzzlement. "Yes," she said slowly.

He fell back a step, incredulous. Liriel already *knew,* and it mattered not! Though why he should be surprised, he did not know. The drow girl was not lacking in character. She had proven to be a fiercely loyal friend and possessed a fledgling sense of honor. Yet she was utterly practical, as amoral as a wild snowcat. There was little in her experience that equipped her to fathom Fyodor's stricter code of honor.

"Liriel, these men are thieves!" he said, trying to make her understand.

The drow huffed, then threw up her hands in exasperation. "Well, what in the Nine Hells did you expect? Just for a moment, Fyodor, *think.* Don't you suppose it might be a little difficult for a drow to book passage with a shipload of paladins? Out of Skullport, no less?"

Fyodor was silent for a long moment, absorbing the truth of his friend's words and struggling to find a balance between honor and necessity.

"Well?" Liriel demanded, her fists on her hips

and one snowy eyebrow lifted in challenge.

The young warrior smiled, but ruefully. "It would seem, little raven, that this sea voyage will be more interesting that I'd expected," he said, deliberately using his pet name for her to help defuse her ready temper.

Liriel relaxed at once and slipped one arm through his. "That's the problem with humans," she said as they strolled companionably across the starlit deck. "You never expect half the things you should expect. One step, two steps ahead, and you think you're done!"

"And the problem with drow," Fyodor teased her in return, "is that you can never stop thinking. With you it is always the head, and never the heart."

But the girl shook her head, and her golden eyes were bright as they looked up into the endless, starlit sky. "There are those who think, and those who dream," she said softly, repeating one of Fyodor's favorite maxims. "But I, for one, refuse to choose between the two!"